Praise for *Pandora*

"HYPNOTICALLY READABLE."

—*Mademoiselle*

"Rice writes as vividly about the turbulent Roman Empire as she has about New Orleans, Venice, and Paris. Her prodigious research, evident in the peripheral stories that inform us about Pandora's background and character, provides a bridge to the next installment—the much anticipated tale of Armand."

—*Trenton Times*

"A marvelous book . . . Pandora in many ways fulfills the promise she first showed in *Interview*. . . . She is the most fascinating character to come from Rice's fertile imagination."

—*Grand Rapids Press*

"Pandora has long been one of her more elusive characters, so fans will relish this vivid rendering of her life and times."

—*Publishers Weekly*

"A nicely crafted, action-packed tale."

—*New York Post*

Praise for *Vittorio, the Vampire*

"A FASCINATING TALE . . . REAFFIRMS RICE'S TITLE AS THE QUEEN OF VAMPIRE LITERATURE."
—*The Denver Post*

"Rice resurrects the opulent world of the Renaissance. . . . The destruction of the trio of angels are the highlights of this installment of the New Tales of the Vampires. Rice does an excellent job of contrasting the tortured souls of the vampires and the pure beauty of the angels."
—*The Tampa Tribune*

"A taut, finely crafted plot, shot through with lush imagery and compelling history, seduces the reader into Vittorio's world as surely as Vittorio himself is seduced into the realm of the Undead . . . Rice once again makes us see the world through the eyes of the vampire. . . . *Vittorio, the Vampire* is at once a morality play, a vampiric and sensual *Romeo and Juliet*."
—Fredericksburg *Freelance Star*

"A neatly compressed little tale, with many pleasures, not the least of which is its ability to transport the reader to another time, another place, filled with angels and demons, light and darkness . . . Rice is at her best when writing of a historical period she loves, and the Renaissance is obviously dear to her heart. The political intrigues of the conflict between Florence and Milan, the renowned patronage and complex politics of the Medici, the scandalous life and divine art of Fra Lippo Lippi, the splendors of Michelozzo's Dominican Monastery of San Marco—all are described in vivid detail."
—New Orleans *Times-Picayune*

BY ANNE RICE

Interview with the Vampire
The Feast of All Saints
Cry to Heaven
The Vampire Lestat
Queen of the Damned
The Mummy
The Witching Hour
The Tale of the Body Thief
Lasher
Taltos
Memnoch the Devil
Servant of the Bones
Violin
Pandora
The Vampire Armand
Vittorio, the Vampire
Merrick
Blood and Gold
Blackwood Farm
Blood Canticle

UNDER THE NAME ANNE RAMPLING

Exit to Eden
Belinda

UNDER THE NAME A. N. ROQUELAURE

The Claiming of Sleeping Beauty
Beauty's Punishment
Beauty's Release

NEW TALES
OF THE
VAMPIRES

PANDORA

VITTORIO, THE VAMPIRE

ANNE RICE

BALLANTINE BOOKS
NEW YORK

This is a work of fiction. Names, characters, places, and incidents are the products of the author's imagination or are used fictitiously. Any resemblance to actual events, locales, or persons, living or dead, is purely coincidental.

A Ballantine Book
Published by The Random House Publishing Group

 Published in the United States by Ballantine Books, an imprint of The Random House Publishing Group, a division of Random House, Inc., New York, and simultaneously in Canada by Random House of Canada Limited, Toronto. *Pandora* was originally published by Alfred A. Knopf, a division of Random House, Inc., in 1998. *Vittorio, the Vampire* was originally published by Alfred A. Knopf, a division of Random House, Inc., in 1999.

www.ballantinebooks.com

A Library of Congress Control Number can be obtained from the publisher upon request.

ISBN 0-345-47686-7

Manufactured in the United States of America

First Trade Paperback Edition: October 2004

2 4 6 8 9 7 5 3 1

Contents

PANDORA

Dedicated
To
Stan, Christopher, and Michele Rice

To
Suzanne Scott Quiroz
and
Victoria Wilson

To the memory of
John Preston

To
the Irish of New Orleans
who, in the 1850s,
built on Constance Street
The Great Church of St. Alphonsus,
while passing on to us
through faith, architecture, and art
a splendid monument

To
"The glory that was Greece
and
the grandeur that was Rome"

Of Mrs. Moore and the echo
in the Marabar Caves:

. . . but the echo began in some indescribable way to undermine her hold on life. Coming at a moment when she chanced to be fatigued, it had managed to murmur "Pathos, piety, courage—they exist, but are identical, and so is filth. Everything exists, nothing has value."

E. M. FORSTER
A Passage to India

Thou believest that there is
one God; thou doest well: the devils
also believe, and tremble.

The General Epistle of James
2:19

How ridiculous and what a stranger he is who is surprised at anything which happens in life.

MARCUS AURELIUS
Meditations

Another part of our same belief is that many creatures will be damned; for example the angels who fell from heaven through pride, and are now fiends; and those men on earth who die apart from the Faith of Holy Church, namely, the heathen; and those, too, who are christened but live unchristian lives, and so die out of love—all these shall be condemned to hell everlastingly, as Holy Church teaches me to believe. This being so I thought it quite impossible that everything should turn out well, as our Lord was now showing me. But I had no answer to this revelation save this: "What is impossible to you is not impossible to me. I shall honour my word in every respect, and I will make everything turn out for the best." Thus was I taught by God's grace. . . .

JULIAN OF NORWICH
Revelations of Divine Love

I

NOT twenty minutes has passed since you left me here in the café, since I said No to your request, that I would never write out for you the story of my mortal life, how I became a vampire—how I came upon Marius only years after he had lost his human life.

Now here I am with your notebook open, using one of the sharp pointed eternal ink pens you left me, delighted at the sensuous press of the black ink into the expensive and flawless white paper.

Naturally, David, you would leave me something elegant, an inviting page. This notebook bound in dark varnished leather, is it not, tooled with a design of rich roses, thornless, yet leafy, a design that means only Design in the final analysis but bespeaks an authority. What is written beneath this heavy and handsome book cover will count, sayeth this cover.

The thick pages are ruled in light blue—you are practical, so thoughtful, and you probably know I almost never put pen to paper to write anything at all.

Even the sound of the pen has its allure, the sharp

scratch rather like the finest quills in ancient Rome when I would put them to parchment to write my letters to my Father, when I would write in a diary my own laments . . . ah, that sound. The only thing missing here is the smell of ink, but we have the fine plastic pen which will not run out for volumes, making as fine and deep a black mark as I choose to make.

I am thinking about your request in writing. You see you will get something from me. I find myself yielding to it, almost as one of our human victims yields to us, discovering perhaps as the rain continues to fall outside, as the café continues with its noisy chatter, to think that this might not be the agony I presumed—reaching back over the two thousand years—but almost a pleasure, like the act of drinking blood itself.

I reach now for a victim who is not easy for me to overcome: my own past. Perhaps this victim will flee from me with a speed that equals my own. Whatever, I seek now a victim that I have never faced. And there is the thrill of the hunt in it, what the modern world calls investigation.

Why else would I see those times so vividly now? You had no magic potion to give me to loosen my thoughts. There is but one potion for us and it is blood.

You said at one point as we walked towards the café, "You will remember everything."

You, who are so young amongst us yet were so old as a mortal, and such a scholar as a mortal. Perhaps it is natural that you so boldly attempt to collect our stories.

But why seek to explain here such curiosity as yours, such bravery in face of blood-drenched truth?

How could you have kindled in me this longing to go back, two thousand years, almost exactly—to tell of my mortal days on Earth in Rome, and how I joined Marius, and what little chance he had against Fate.

How could origins so deeply buried and so long denied suddenly beckon to me. A door snaps open. A light shines. Come in.

I sit back now in the café.

I write, but I pause and look around me at the people of this Paris café. I see the drab unisex fabrics of this age, the fresh American girl in her olive green military clothes, all of her possessions slung over her shoulder in a backpack; I see the old Frenchman who has come here for decades merely to look at the bare legs and arms of the young, to feed on the gestures as if he were a vampire, to wait for some exotic jewel of a moment when a woman sits back laughing, cigarette in hand, and the cloth of her synthetic blouse becomes tight over her breasts and there the nipples are visible.

Ah, old man. He is gray-haired and wears an expensive coat. He is no menace to anyone. He lives entirely in vision. Tonight he will go back to a modest but elegant apartment which he has maintained since the last Great World War, and he will watch films of the young beauty Brigitte Bardot. He lives in his eyes. He has not touched a woman in ten years.

I don't drift, David. I drop anchor here. For I will not have my story pour forth as from a drunken oracle.

I see these mortals in a more attentive light. They are so fresh, so exotic and yet so luscious to me, these mortals; they look like tropical birds must have looked when I was a child; so full of fluttering, rebellious life, I wanted to clutch them to have it, to make their wings flap in my hands, to capture flight and own it and partake of it. Ah, that terrible moment in childhood when one accidentally crushes the life from a bright-red bird.

Yet they are sinister in their darker vestments, some of these mortals: the inevitable cocaine dealer—and they are everywhere, our finest prey—who waits for his contact in the far corner, his long leather coat styled by a noted Italian designer, his hair shaved close on the side and left bushy on the top to make him look distinctive, which it does, though there is no need when one considers his huge black eyes, and the hardness of what nature intended to be a generous mouth. He makes those quick impatient gestures with his cigarette lighter on the small marble table, the mark of the addicted; he twists, he turns, he cannot be comfortable. He doesn't know that he will never be comfortable in life again. He wants to leave to snort the cocaine for which he burns and yet he must wait for the contact. His shoes are too shiny, and his long thin hands will never grow old.

I think he will die tonight, this man. I feel a slow gathering desire to kill him myself. He has fed so much poison to so many. Tracking him, wrapping him in my arms, I would not even have to wreathe him with visions. I would let him know that death has come in the form of a woman too white to be human, too smoothed by the centuries to be anything but a statue come to life. But those for whom he waits plot to kill him. And why should I intervene?

What do I look like to these people? A woman with long wavy clean brown hair that covers me much like a nun's mantle, a face so white it appears cosmetically created, and eyes, abnormally brilliant, even from behind golden glasses.

Ah, we have a lot to be grateful for in the many styles of eyeglasses in this age—for if I were to take these off, I should have to keep my head bowed, not to startle people with the mere play of yellow and brown and gold in my eyes, that have grown ever more jewel-like over the centuries, so that I seem a blind woman set with topaz for her pupils, or rather carefully formed orbs of topaz, sapphire, even aquamarine.

Look, I have filled so many pages, and all I am saying is Yes, I will tell you how it began for me.

Yes, I will tell you the story of my mortal life in ancient Rome, how I came to love Marius and how we came to be together and then to part.

What a transformation in me, this resolution.

How powerful I feel as I hold this pen, and how

eager to put us in sharp and clear perspective before I begin fulfilling your request.

This is Paris, in a time of peace. There is rain. High regal gray buildings with their double windows and iron balconies line this boulevard. Loud, tiny, dangerous automobiles race in the streets. Cafés, such as this, are overflowing with international tourists. Ancient churches are crowded here by tenements, palaces turned to museums, in whose rooms I linger for hours gazing at objects from Egypt or Sumer which are even older than me. Roman architecture is everywhere, absolute replicas of Temples of my time now serve as banks. The words of my native Latin suffuse the English language. Ovid, my beloved Ovid, the poet who predicted his poetry would outlast the Roman Empire, has been proved true.

Walk into any bookstore and you find him in neat, small paperbacks, designed to appeal to students.

Roman influence seeds itself, sprouting mighty oaks right through the modern forest of computers, digital disks, microviruses and space satellites.

It is easy here—as always—to find an embraceable evil, a despair worth tender fulfillment.

And with me there must always be some love of the victim, some mercy, some self-delusion that the death I bring does not mar the great shroud of inevitability, woven of trees and earth and stars, and human events, which hovers forever around us ready to close on all that is created, all that we know.

Last night, when you found me, how did it seem

to you? I was alone on the bridge over the Seine, walking in the last dangerous darkness before dawn.

You saw me before I knew you were there. My hood was down and I let my eyes in the dim light of the bridge have their little moment of glory. My victim stood at the railing, no more than a child, but bruised and robbed by a hundred men. She wanted to die in the water. I don't know if the Seine is deep enough for one to drown there. So near the Ile St.-Louis. So near Notre Dame. Perhaps it is, if one can resist a last struggle for life.

But I felt this victim's soul like ashes, as though her spirit had been cremated and only the body remained, a worn, disease-ridden shell. I put my arm around her, and when I saw the fear in her small black eyes, when I saw the question coming, I wreathed her with images. The soot that covered my skin was not enough to keep me from looking like the Virgin Mary, and she sank into hymns and devotion, she even saw my veils in the colors she had known in churches of childhood, as she yielded to me, and I—knowing that I needn't drink, but thirsting for her, thirsting for the anguish she could give forth in her final moment, thirsting for the tasty red blood that would fill my mouth and make me feel human for one instant in my very monstrosity—I gave in to her visions, bent her neck, ran my fingers over her sore tender skin, and then it was, when I sank my teeth into her, when I drank from her—it was then that I knew you were there. You watched.

I knew it, and I felt it, and I saw the image of us in

your eye, distractingly, as the pleasure nevertheless flushed through me, making me believe I was alive, somehow connected to fields of clover or trees with roots deeper in the earth than the branches they raise to the welkin above.

At first I hated you. You saw me as I feasted. You saw me as I gave in. You knew nothing of my months of starvation, restraint, wandering. You saw only the sudden release of my unclean desire to suck her very soul from her, to make her heart rise in the flesh inside her, to drag from her veins every precious particle of her that still wanted to survive.

And she did want to survive. Wrapped in saints, and dreaming suddenly of the breasts that nursed her, her young body fought, pumping and pumping against me, she so soft, and my own form hard as a statue, my milkless nipples enshrined in marble, no comfort. Let her see her mother, dead, gone and now waiting. Let me glimpse through her dying eyes the light through which she sped towards this certain salvation.

Then I forgot about you. I would not be robbed. I slowed the drinking, I let her sigh, I let her lungs fill with the cold river air, her mother drawing closer and closer so that death now was as safe for her as the womb. I took every drop from her that she could give.

She hung dead against me, as one I'd rescued, one I would help from the bridge, some weakened, sickened, drunken girl. I slid my hand into her body, breaking the flesh so easily even with these delicate fingers, and I closed my fingers around her heart and brought it to my lips and sucked it, my head tucked down by her face, sucked the heart like fruit, until no blood was left in any fiber or chamber, and then slowly—perhaps for your benefit—I lifted her and let her fall down into the water she had so desired.

Now there would be no struggle as her lungs filled with the river. Now there would be no last desperate thrashing. I fed from the heart one last time, to take even the color of blood out of it, and then sent it after her—crushed grapes—poor child, child of a hundred men.

Then I faced you, let you know that I knew you watched from the quay. I think I tried to frighten you. In rage I let you know how weak you were, that all the blood given to you by Lestat would make you no match should I choose to dismember you, pitch a fatal heat into you and immolate you, or only punish you with penetrating scar—simply for having spied upon me.

Actually I have never done such a thing to a younger one. I feel sorry for them when they see us, the ancient ones, and quake in terror. But I should, by all the knowledge of myself I possess, have retreated so quickly that you could not follow me in the night.

Something in your demeanor charmed me, the manner in which you approached me on the bridge, your young Anglo-Indian brown-skinned body gifted by your true mortal age with such seductive grace.

Your very posture seemed to ask of me, without humiliation:

"Pandora, may we speak?"

My mind wandered. Perhaps you knew it. I don't remember whether I shut you out of my thoughts, and I know that your telepathic abilities are not really very strong. My mind wandered suddenly, perhaps of itself, perhaps at your prodding. I thought of all the things I could tell you, which were so different from the tales of Lestat, and those of Marius through Lestat, and I wanted to warn you, warn you of the ancient vampires of the Far East who would kill you if you went into their territory, simply because you were there.

I wanted to make certain you understood what we all had to accept—the Fount of our immortal vampiric hunger did reside in two beings—Mekare and Maharet—so ancient they are now both horrible to look upon, more than beautiful. And if they destroy themselves we will all die with them.

I wanted to tell you of others who have never known us as a tribe or known our history, who survived the terrible fire brought down on her children by our Mother Akasha. I wanted to tell you that there were things walking the Earth that look like us but are not of our breed any more than they are human. And I wanted suddenly to take you under my wing.

It must have been your prodding. You stood there, the English gentleman, wearing your decorum more lightly and naturally than any man I'd ever seen. I marveled at your fine clothes, that you'd indulged yourself in a light black cloak of worsted wool, that you had even given yourself the luxury of a gleaming red silk scarf—so unlike you when you were newly made.

Understand, I was not aware the night that Lestat transformed you into a vampire. I didn't feel that moment.

All the preternatural world shimmered weeks earlier, however, with the knowledge that a mortal had jumped into the body of another mortal; we know these things, as if the stars tell us. One preternatural mind picks up the ripples of this sharp cut in the fabric of the ordinary, then another mind receives the image, and on and on it goes.

David Talbot, the name we all knew from the venerable order of psychic detectives, the Talamasca, had managed to move his entire soul and etheric body—into that of another man. That body itself was in the possession of a body thief whom you forced from it. And once anchored in the young body, you, with all your scruples and values, all your knowledge of seventy-four years, remained anchored in the young cells.

And so it was David the Reborn, David with the high-gloss India beauty, and raw well-nourished strength of British lineage, that Lestat had made into a vampire, bringing over both body and soul, compounding miracle with the Dark Trick, achieving once more a sin that should stun his contemporaries and his elders.

And this, this was done to you by your best friend!

Welcome to the darkness, David. Welcome to the domain of Shakespeare's "inconstant moon."

Bravely you came up the bridge towards me.

"Forgive me, Pandora," you said so quietly. Flawless British upper-class accent, and the usual beguiling British rhythm that is so seductive it seems to say that "we will all save the world."

You kept a polite distance between us, as if I were a virgin girl of the last century, and you didn't want to alarm me and my tender sensibilities. I smiled.

I indulged myself then. I took your full measure, this fledgling that Lestat—against Marius's injunction—had dared to make. I saw the components of you as a man: an immense human soul, fearless, yet half in love with despair, and a body which Lestat had almost injured himself to render powerful. He had given you more blood than he could easily give in your transformation. He had tried to give you his courage, his cleverness, his cunning; he had tried to transport an armory for you through the blood.

He had done well. Your strength was complex and obvious. Our Queen Mother Akasha's blood was mixed with that of Lestat. Marius, my ancient lover, had given him blood as well. Lestat, ah, now what do they say, they say that he may even have drunk the blood of the Christ.

It was this first issue I took up with you, my curiosity overwhelming me, for to scan the world for knowledge is often to rake in such tragedy that I abhor it.

"Tell me the truth of it," I said. "This story *Memnoch the Devil*. Lestat claimed he went to Heaven and to Hell. He brought back a veil from St. Veronica. The face of Christ was on it! It converted thousands to Christianity, it cured alienation and succored bitterness. It drove other Children of Darkness to throw up their arms to the deadly morning light, as if the sun were in fact the fire of God."

"Yes, it's all happened, as I described it," you said, lowering your head with a polite but unexaggerated modesty. "And you know a few . . . of *us* perished in this fervor, whilst newspapers and scientists collected our ashes for examination."

I marveled at your calm attitude. A Twentieth-Century sensibility. A mind dominated by an incalculable wealth of information, and quick of tongue with an intellect devoted to swiftness, synthesis, probabilities, and all this against the backdrop of horrid experiences, wars, massacres, the worst perhaps the world has ever seen.

"It all happened," you said. "And I did meet with Mekare and Maharet, the ancient ones, and you needn't fear for me that I don't know how fragile is the root. It was kind of you to think so protectively of me."

I was quietly charmed.

"What did you think of this Holy Veil yourself?" I asked.

"Our Lady of Fatima," you said softly. "The Shroud

of Turin, a cripple rising from the Miraculous Waters of Lourdes! What a consolation it must be to accept such a thing so easily."

"And you did not?"

You shook your head. "And neither did Lestat, really. It was the mortal girl, Dora, snatching the Veil from him, who took it out into the world. But it was a most singular and meticulously made thing, I'll tell you that, more worthy of the word 'relic' perhaps than any other I've ever seen."

You sounded dejected suddenly.

"Some immense intent went into its making," you said.

"And the vampire Armand, the delicate boylike Armand, he believed it?" I asked. "Armand looked at it and saw the face of Christ," I said, seeking your confirmation.

"Enough to die for it," you said solemnly. "Enough to open his arms to the morning sun."

You looked away, and you closed your eyes. This was a simple unadorned plea to me not to make you speak of Armand and how he had gone into the morning fire.

I gave a sigh—surprised and gently fascinated to find you so articulate, skeptical, yet so sharply and frankly connected to the others.

You said in a shaken voice, "Armand." And still looking away from me. "What a Requiem. And does he know now if Memnoch was real, if God Incarnate who tempted Lestat was in fact the Son of the God Almighty? Does anyone?"

I was taken with your earnestness, your passion. You were not jaded or cynical. There was an immediacy to your feelings for these happenings, these creatures, these questions you posed.

"They locked up the Veil, you know," you said. "It's in the Vatican. There were two weeks of frenzy on Fifth Avenue in St. Patrick's Cathedral in which people came to look into the eyes of The Lord, and then they had it, gone, taken to their vaults. I doubt there is a nation on the Earth with the power to gain even a glimpse of it now."

"And Lestat," I said. "Where is he now?"

"Paralyzed, silent," you said. "Lestat lies on the floor of a chapel in New Orleans. He doesn't move. He says nothing. His Mother has come to him. You knew her, Gabrielle, he made a vampire of her."

"Yes, I remember her."

"Even she draws no response from him. Whatever he saw, in his journey to Heaven and Hell, he doesn't know the truth of it one way or the other—he tried to tell this to Dora! And eventually, after I'd written down the whole story for him, he passed within a few nights into this state.

"His eyes are fixed and his body pliant. They made a curious Pietà, he and Gabrielle, in this abandoned convent and its chapel. His mind is closed, or worse—it's empty."

I found I liked very much your manner of speaking. In fact, I was taken off guard.

"I left Lestat because he was beyond my help and my reach," you said. "And I must know if there are old ones who want to put an end to me; I must make my pilgrimages and my progresses to know the dangers of this world to which I've been admitted."

"You're so forthright. You have no cunning."

"On the contrary. I conceal my keenest assets from you." You gave me a slow, polite smile. "Your beauty rather confuses me. Are you used to this?"

"Quite," I said. "And weary of it. Come beyond it. Let me just warn, there are old ones, ones no one knows or can explain. It's rumored you've been with Maharet and Mekare, who are now the Eldest and the Fount from which we all spring. Obviously they've drawn back from us, from all the world, into some secret place, and have no taste for authority."

"You're so very correct," you said, "and my audience with them was beautiful but brief. They don't want to rule over anyone, nor will Maharet, as long as the history of the world and her own physical descendants are in it—her own thousands of human descendants from a time so ancient there is no date for it—Maharet will never destroy herself and her sister, thereby destroying all of us."

"Yes," I said, "in that she believes, the Great Family, the generations she has traced for thousands of years. I saw her when we all gathered. She doesn't see us as evil—you, or me, or Lestat—she thinks that we're natural, rather like volcanoes or fires that rage through forests, or bolts of lightning that strike a man dead."

"Precisely," you said. "There is no Queen of the Damned now. I fear only one other immortal, and that's your lover, Marius. Because it was Marius who laid down the strict rule before he left the others that no more blood drinkers could be made. I'm baseborn in the mind of Marius. That is, were he an Englishman, those would be his words."

I shook my head. "I can't believe he would harm you. Hasn't he come to Lestat? Did he not come to see the Veil with his own eyes?"

You said No to both questions.

"Heed this advice: whenever you sense his presence, talk to him. Talk to him as you have to me. Begin a conversation which he won't have the confidence to bring to a close."

You smiled again. "That's such a clever way of putting it," you said.

"But I don't think you have to fear him. If he wanted you gone off the Earth, you'd be gone. What we have to fear is the same things humans fear—that there are others of our same species, of varying power and belief, and we are never entirely sure where they are or what they do. That's my advice to you."

"You are so kind to take your time with me," you said.

I could have wept. "On the contrary. You don't know the silence and solitude in which I wander, and pray you never know it, and here you've given me heat without death, you've given me nourishment without blood. I'm glad you've come."

I saw you look up at the sky, the habit of the young ones.

"I know, we have to part now."

You turned to me suddenly. "Meet me tomorrow night," you said imploringly. "Let this exchange continue! I'll come to you in the café where you sit every night musing. I'll find you. Let us talk to each other."

"So you've seen me there."

"Oh, often," you said. "Yes." You looked away again. I saw it was to conceal feeling. Then your dark eyes turned back to me.

"Pandora, we have the world, don't we?" you whispered.

"I don't know, David. But I'll meet you tomorrow night. Why haven't you come to me there? Where it was warm and lighted?"

"It seemed a far more outrageous intrusion, to move in on you in the sanctified privacy of a crowded café. People go to such places to be alone, don't they? This seemed somehow more proper. And I did not mean to be the voyeur. Like many fledglings, I have to feed every night. It was an accident that we saw each other at that moment."

"That is charming, David," I said. "It is a long time since anyone has charmed me. I'll meet you there . . . tomorrow night."

And then a wickedness possessed me. I came towards you and embraced you, knowing that the hardness and coldness of my ancient body would strike the deepest chord of terror in you, newborn as you were, passing so easily for mortal.

But you didn't draw back. And when I kissed your cheek, you kissed mine.

I wonder now, as I sit here in the café, writing . . . trying to give you more with these words perhaps than you ask for . . . what I would have done had you not kissed me, had you shrunk back with the fear that is so common in the young.

David, you are indeed a puzzle.

You see that I have begun to chronicle not my life here, but what has passed these two nights between you and me.

Allow this, David. Allow that I speak of you and me, and then perhaps I can retrieve my lost life.

When you came into the café tonight, I thought nothing much about the notebooks. You had two. They were thick.

The leather of the notebooks smelled good and old, and when you set them down on the table, only then did I detect a glimmer from your disciplined and restrained mind that they had to do with me.

I had chosen this table in the crowded center of the room, as though I wanted to be in the middle of the whirlpool of mortal scent and activity. You seemed pleased, unafraid, utterly at home.

You wore another stunning suit of modern cut with a full cape of worsted wool, very tasteful, yet Old World, and with your golden skin and radiant eyes, you turned the head of every woman in the place and you turned the heads of some of the men.

You smiled. I must have seemed a snail to you beneath my cloak and hood, gold glasses covering well over half my face, and a trace of commercial lipstick on my lips, a soft purple pink that had made me think of bruises. It had seemed very enticing in the mirror at the store, and I liked that my mouth was something I didn't have to hide. My lips are now almost colorless. With this lipstick I could smile.

I wore these gloves of mine, black lace, with their sheared-off tips so that my fingers can feel, and I had sooted my nails so they would not sparkle like crystal in the café. And I reached out my hand to you and you kissed it.

There was your same boldness and decorum. And then the warmest smile from you, a smile in which I think your former physiology must have dominated because you looked far too wise for one so young and strong of build. I marveled at the perfect picture you had made of yourself.

"You don't know what a joy it is to me," you said, "that you've come, that you've let me join you here at this table."

"You have made me want this," I said, raising my hands, and seeing that your eyes were dazzled by my crystalline fingernails, in spite of the soot.

I reached towards you, expecting you to pull back, but you entrusted to my cold white fingers your warm dark hand.

"You find in me a living being?" I asked you.

"Oh, yes, most definitely, most radiantly and perfectly a living being."

We ordered our coffee, as mortals expect us to do, deriving more pleasure from the heat and aroma than they could ever imagine, even stirring our little cups with our spoons. I had before me a red dessert.

The dessert is still here of course. I ordered it simply because it was red—strawberries covered in syrup—with a strong sweet smell that bees would like.

I smiled at your blandishments. I liked them.

Playfully, I mocked them. I let my hood slip down and I shook out my hair so that its fullness and dark brown color could shimmer in the light.

Of course it's no signal to mortals, as is Marius's blond hair or that of Lestat. But I love my own hair, I love the veil of it when it is down over my shoulders, and I loved what I saw in your eyes.

"Somewhere deep inside me there is a woman," I said.

To write it now—in this notebook as I sit here alone—it gives architecture to a trivial moment, and seems so dire a confession.

David, the more I write, the more the concept of narrative excites me, the more I believe in the weight of a coherence which is possible on the page though not in life.

But again, I didn't know I meant to pick up this pen of yours at all. We were talking:

"Pandora, if anyone does not know you're a woman, then he is a fool," you said.

"How angry Marius would be with me for being pleased by that," I said. "Oh, no. Rather he would seize it as a strong point in favor of his position. I left him, left him without a word, the last time we were together—that was before Lestat went on his little escapade of running around in a human body, and long before he encountered Memnoch the Devil—I left Marius, and suddenly I wish I could reach him! I wish I could talk with him as you and I are talking now."

You looked so troubled for me, and with reason. On some level, you must have known that I had not evinced this much enthusiasm over anything in many a dreary year.

"Would you write your story for me, Pandora?" you asked suddenly.

I was totally surprised.

"Write it in these notebooks?" you pressed. "Write about the time when you were alive, the time when you and Marius came together, write what you will of Marius. But it's your story that I most want."

I was stunned.

"Why in the world would you want this of me?"

You didn't answer.

"David, surely you've not returned to that order of human beings, the Talamasca, they know too much—"

You put up your hand.

"No, and I will never; and if there was ever any doubt of it, I learnt it once and for all in the archives kept by Maharet."

"She allowed you to see her archives, the books she's saved over the course of time?"

"Yes, it was remarkable, you know . . . a storehouse of tablets, scrolls, parchments—books and poems from cultures of which the world knows nothing, I think. Books lost from time. Of course she forbade me to reveal anything I found or speak in detail of our meeting. She said it was too rash tampering with things, and she confirmed your fear that I might go to the Talamasca—my old mortal psychic friends. I have not. I will not. But it is a very easy vow to keep."

"Why so?"

"Pandora, when I saw all those old writings—I knew I was no longer human. I knew that the history lying there to be collected was no longer mine! I am not one of these!" Your eyes swept the room. "Of course you must have heard this a thousand times from fledgling vampires! But you see, I had a fervent faith that philosophy and reason would make a bridge for me by which I could go and come in both worlds. Well, there is no bridge. It's gone."

Your sadness shimmered about you, flashing in your young eyes and in the softness of your new flesh.

"So you know that," I said. I didn't plan the words. But out they came. "You know." I gave a soft bitter laugh.

"Indeed I do. I knew when I held documents from your time, so many from your time, Imperial Rome, and other crumbling bits of inscribed rock I couldn't even hope to place. I knew. I didn't care about them, Pandora! I care about what we are, what we are now."

"How remarkable," I said. "You don't know how much I admire you, or how attractive is your disposition to me."

"I am happy to hear this," you said. Then you leaned forward towards me: "I don't say we do not carry our human souls with us, our history; of course we do.

"I remember once a long time ago, Armand told me that he asked Lestat, 'How will I ever understand the human race?' Lestat said, 'Read or see all the plays of Shakespeare and you will know all you ever need to know about the human race.' Armand did it. He devoured the poems, he sat through the plays, he watched the brilliant new films with Laurence Fishburne and Kenneth Branagh and Leonardo DiCaprio. And when Armand and I last spoke together, this is what he said of his education:

" 'Lestat was right. He gave me not books but a passage into understanding. This man Shakespeare writes,'—and I quote both Armand and Shakespeare now as Armand spoke it, as I will to you—as if it came from my heart:

Tomorrow, and tomorrow, and tomorrow,
Creeps in this petty pace from day to day,
To the last syllable of recorded time;
And all our yesterdays have lighted fools
The way to dusty death. Out, out brief candle.
Life's but a walking shadow; a poor player,
That struts and frets his hour upon the stage,
And then is heard no more; it is a tale
Told by an idiot, full of sound and fury,
Signifying nothing.

" 'This man writes this,' said Armand to me, 'and we all know that it is absolutely the truth and every revelation has sooner or later fallen before it, and yet we want to love the way he has said it, we want to hear it again! We want to remember it! We want to never forget a single word.' "

We were both silent for a moment. You looked down, you rested your chin on your knuckles. I knew the whole weight of Armand's going into the sun was on you, and I had so loved your recitation of the words, and the words themselves.

Finally, I said, "And this gives me pleasure. Think of it, pleasure. That you recite these words to me now."

You smiled.

"I want to know now what we can learn," you said. "I want to know what we can see! So I come to you, a Child of the Millennia, a vampire who drank from the Queen Akasha herself, one who has survived two thousand years. And I ask you, Pandora, please will you write for me, write your story, write what you will."

For a long moment I gave you no answer.

Then I said sharply that I could not. But something had stirred in me. I saw and heard arguments and tirades of centuries ago, I saw the poet's lifted light shine on eras I had known intimately out of love. Other eras I had never known, wandering, ignorant, a wraith.

Yes, there was a tale to be written. There was. But at the moment I could not admit it.

You were in misery, having thought of Armand, having remembered his walking into the morning sun. You mourned for Armand.

"Was there any bond between you?" you asked. "Forgive me my boldness, but I mean was there any bond between you and Armand when you met, because Marius had given you both the Dark Gift? I know no jealousy exists, that I can feel. I wouldn't bring up the very name Armand if I detected a hurt in you, but all else is an absence, a silence. Was there no bond?"

"The bond is only grief. He went into the sun. And grief is absolutely the easiest and safest of bonds."

You laughed under your breath.

"What can I do to make you consider my request? Have pity on me, Gracious Lady, entrust to me your song."

I smiled indulgently, but it was impossible, I thought.

"It's far too dissonant, my dear," I said. "It's far too—"

I shut my eyes.

I had wanted to say that my song was far too painful to sing.

Suddenly your eyes moved upwards. Your expression changed. It was almost as if you were deliberately trying to appear to enter a trance. Slowly you turned your head. You pointed, with your hand close to the table, then let your hand go lax.

"What is it, David?" I said. "What are you seeing?"

"Spirits, Pandora, ghosts."

You shuddered as if to clear your head.

"But that's unheard of," I said. Yet I knew that he was telling the truth. "The Dark Gift takes away that power. Even the ancient witches, Maharet and Mekare, told us this, that once Akasha's blood entered them, and they became vampires, they never heard or saw the spirits again. You've recently been with them. Did you tell them of this power?"

He nodded. Obviously some loyalty bound him not to say that they did not have it. But I knew they did not. I saw it in his mind, and I had known it myself when I had encountered the ancient twins, the twins who had struck down the Queen of the Damned.

"I can see spirits, Pandora," you said with the most troubled expression. "I can see them anywhere if I try, and in some very specific places when they choose. Lestat saw the ghost of Roger, his victim in *Memnoch the Devil*."

"But that was an exception, a surge of love in the man's soul that somehow defied death, or delayed the soul's termination—something we can't understand."

"I see spirits, but I haven't come to burden you with this or frighten you."

"You must tell me more about this," I said. "What did you see right now?"

"A weak spirit. It couldn't harm anyone. It's one of those sad sad humans who does not know he's dead. They *are* an atmosphere around the planet. The 'earthbound' is the name for them. But Pandora, I have more than that in myself to explore."

You continued:

"Apparently each century yields a new kind of vampire, or let us say that our course of growth was not set in the beginning any more than the course of human beings. Some night perhaps I will tell you everything I see—these spirits who were never clear to me when I was mortal—I'll tell you about something Armand confided to me, about the colors he saw when he took life, how the soul left body in waves of radiating color!"

"I've never heard of such a thing!"

"I too see this," you said.

I could see it hurt you almost too much to speak of Armand.

"But whatever possessed Armand to believe in the Veil?" I asked, suddenly amazed at my own passion. "Why did he go into the sun? How could such a thing kill Lestat's reason and will? Veronica. Did they know the very name means *Vera Ikon*, that there was never any such person, that she could not be found by one drawn back to ancient Jerusalem on the day Christ carried his cross; she was a concoction of Priests. Didn't they know?"

I think I had taken the two notebooks in hand, for I looked down and I saw that I did indeed hold them. In fact, I clutched both of them to my breast and examined one of the pens.

"Reason," I whispered. "Oh, precious reason! And consciousness within a void." I shook my head, smiling kindly at you. "And vampires who speak now with spirits! Humans who can travel from body to body."

I went on with a wholly unfamiliar energy.

"A lively fashionable modern cult of angels, devotion thriving everywhere. And people rising from operating tables to speak of life after death, a tunnel, an embracing love! Oh, you have been created perhaps in an auspicious time! I don't know what to make of it."

You were obviously quite impressed by these words, or rather the way that my perspective had been drawn from me. So was I.

"I've only started," you said, "and will keep company alike with brilliant Children of the Millennia and street-corner fortune tellers who deal out the cards of the Tarot. I'm eager to gaze into crystal balls and darkened mirrors. I'll search now among those whom others dismiss as mad, or among *us*—among those like you, who have looked on something that they do not believe they should share! That's it, isn't it? But I ask you to share it. I'm finished with the ordinary human soul. I am finished with science and psychology, with microscopes and perhaps even with the telescopes aimed at the stars."

I was quite enthralled. How strongly you meant it. I could feel my face so warm with feeling for you as I looked at you. I think my mouth was slack with wonder.

"I am a miracle unto myself," you said. "I am immortal, and I want to learn about us! You have a tale to tell, you are ancient, and deeply broken. I feel love for you and cherish that it is what it is and nothing more."

"What a strange thing to say!"

"Love." You shrugged your shoulders. You looked up and then back at me for emphasis. "And it rained and it rained for millions of years, and the volcanoes boiled and the oceans cooled, and then there was love?" You shrugged to make a mock of the absurdity.

I couldn't help but laugh at your little gest. Too perfect, I thought. But I was suddenly so torn.

"This is very unexpected," I said. "Because if I do have a story, a very small story—"

"Yes?"

"Well, my story—if I have one—is very much to the point. It's linked to the very points you've made."

Suddenly something came over me. I laughed again softly.

"I understand you!" I said. "Oh, not that you can see spirits, for that is a great subject unto itself.

"But I see now the source of your strength. You have lived an entire human life. Unlike Marius, unlike me, you weren't taken in your prime. You were taken near the moment of your natural death, and you will not settle for the adventures and faults of the earthbound! You are determined to forge ahead with the courage of one who has died of old age and then finds himself risen from the grave. You've kicked aside the funeral wreaths. You are ready for Mount Olympus, aren't you?"

"Or for Osiris in the depths of the darkness," you said. "Or for the shades in Hades. Certainly I am ready for the spirits, for the vampires, for those who see the future and claim to know past lives, for you who have a stunning intellect encased beautifully, to endure for so many years, an intellect which has perhaps all but destroyed your heart."

I gasped.

"Forgive me. That was not proper of me," you said.

"No, explain your meaning."

"You always take the hearts from the victims, isn't it so? You want the heart."

"Perhaps. Don't expect wisdom from me as it might come from Marius, or the ancient twins."

"You draw me to you," you said.

"Why?"

"Because you do have a story inside you; it lies articulate and waiting to be written—behind your silence and your suffering."

"You are too romantic, friend," I said.

You waited patiently. I think you could feel the tumult in me, the shivering of my soul in the face of so much new emotion.

"It's such a small story," I said. I saw images, memories, moments, the stuff that can incite souls to action and creation. I saw the very faintest possibility of faith.

I think you already knew the answer.

You knew what I would do when I did not.

You smiled discreetly, but you were eager and waiting.

I looked at you and thought of trying to write it, write it all out . . .

"You want me to leave now, don't you?" you said. You rose, collected your rain-spattered coat and bent over gracefully to kiss my hand.

My hands were clutching the notebooks.

"No," I said, "I can't do it."

You made no immediate judgment.

"Come back in two nights," I said. "I promise you I will have your two notebooks for you, even if they are completely empty or only contain a better explanation of why I can't retrieve my lost life. I won't disappoint you. But expect nothing, except that I will come and I will put these books in your hands."

"Two nights," you said, "and we meet here again."

In silence I watched you leave the café.

And now you see it has begun, David.

And now you see, David, I have made our meeting the introduction to the story you asked me to tell.

2

PANDORA'S STORY

WAS born in Rome, during the reign of Augustus Caesar, in the year that you now reckon to have been 15 B.C., or fifteen years "before Christ."

All the Roman history and Roman names I give here are accurate; I have not falsified them or made up stories or created false political events. Everything bears upon my ultimate fate and the fate of Marius. Nothing is included for love of the past.

I have omitted my family name. I did this because my family has a history, and I cannot bring myself to connect their ancient reputations, deeds, epitaphs to this tale. Also Marius, when he confided in Lestat, did not give the full name of his Roman family. And I respect this and that also is not revealed.

Augustus had been Emperor for over ten years, and it was a marvelous time to be an educated woman in Rome, women had immense freedom, and I had a rich Senator for a father, five prosperous brothers, and grew up Motherless but cherished by teams of Greek tutors and nurses who gave me everything I wanted.

Now, if I really wanted to make this difficult for you, David, I'd write it in classical Latin. But I won't. And I must tell you that, unlike you, I came by my education in English haphazardly, and certainly I never learnt it from Shakespeare's plays.

Indeed I have passed through many stages of the English language in my wanderings and in my reading, but the great majority of my true acquaintance with it has been in this century, and I am writing for you in colloquial English.

There's another reason for this, which I'm sure you'll understand if you've read the modern translation of Petronius's *Satyricon* or Juvenal's satires. Very modern English is a really true equivalent to the Latin of my time.

The formal letters of Imperial Rome won't tell you this. But the graffiti scratched on the walls of Pompeii will make it obvious. We had a sophisticated tongue, countless clever verbal shortcuts and common expressions.

I'm going to write, therefore, in the English which feels equivalent and natural to me.

Let me say here quickly—while the action is at a halt—that I was never, as Marius said, a Greek Courtesan. I was living with such a pretense when Marius gave me the Dark Gift, and perhaps out of consideration for old mortal secrets he so described me. Or maybe it was contemptuous of him to style me this way. I don't know.

But Marius knew all about my Roman family, that it was a Senatorial family, as purely aristocratic and privileged as his own mortal family, and that my people dated back to the time of Romulus and Remus, the same as Marius's mortal line. Marius did not succumb to me because I had "beautiful arms," as he indicated to Lestat. This trivialization was perhaps provocative.

I don't hold anything against either of them, Marius or Lestat. I don't know who got what wrong.

My feeling for my Father is so great to this very night, as I sit in the café, writing for you, David, that I am astonished at the power of writing—of putting words to paper and bringing back so vividly to myself my Father's loving face.

My Father was to meet a terrible end. He did not deserve what happened to him. But some of our kinsmen survived and re-established our family in later times.

My Father was rich, one of the true millionaires of that age, and his capital was invested widely. He was a soldier more often than required of him, a Senator, a thoughtful and quiet man by disposition. And after the terrors of the Civil War, he was a great supporter of Caesar Augustus and very much in the Emperor's good graces.

Of course he dreamed that the Roman Republic would come back; we all did. But Augustus had brought unity and peace to the Empire.

I met Augustus many times in my youth, and it was always at some crowded social function and of no consequence. He looked like his portraits; a lean man with a long thin nose, short hair, average face; he was rather rational and pragmatic by nature and not invested with any abnormal cruelty. He had no personal vanity.

The poor man was really blessed that he couldn't see into the future—that he had no inkling of all the horrors and madness that would begin with Tiberius, his successor, and go on for so long under other members of his family.

Only in later times did I understand the full singularity and accomplishment of Augustus's long reign. Was it forty-four years of peace throughout the cities of the Empire?

Alas, to be born during this time was to be born during a time of creativity and prosperity, when Rome was *caput mundi*, or capital of the world. And when I look back on it, I realize what a powerful combination it was to have both tradition and vast sums of money; to have old values and new power.

Our family life was conservative, strict, even a little dusty. And yet we had every luxury. My Father grew more quiet and conservative over the years. He enjoyed his grandchildren, who were born while he was still vigorous and active.

Though he had fought principally in the Northern campaigns along the Rhine, he had been stationed in Syria for a while. He had studied in Athens. He had served so much and so well that he was being allowed an early retirement in the years during which I grew up, an early withdrawal from the social life that whirled around the Imperial Palace, though I did not realize this at the time.

My five brothers came before me. So there was no "ritual Roman mourning" when I was born, as you hear tell of in Roman families when a girl comes into the world. Far from it.

Five times my Father had stood in the atrium—the main enclosed courtyard, or peristyle, of our house with its pillars and stairs and grand marblework—five times he had stood there before the assembled family and held in his hands a newborn son, inspected it and then pronounced it perfect and fit to be reared as his own, as was his prerogative. Now, you know he had the power of life and death over his sons from that moment on.

If my Father hadn't wanted these boys for any reason, he would have "exposed" them to die of starvation. It was against the law to steal such a child and make it a slave.

Having five boys already, my Father was expected by some to get rid of me immediately. Who needs a girl? But my Father never exposed or rejected any of my Mother's children.

And by the time I arrived, I'm told, he cried for joy. "Thank the gods! A little darling." I heard the story ad nauseam from my brothers, who, every time I acted up—did something unseemly, frisky and wild—said sneeringly, "Thank the gods, a little darling!" It became a charming goad.

My Mother died when I was two, and all I recall of her are gentleness and sweetness. She'd lost as many children as she had birthed, and early death was typical enough. Her Epitaph was beautifully written by my Father, and her memory honored throughout my life. My Father never took another woman into the house. He slept with a few of the female slaves, but this was nothing unusual. My brothers did the same thing. This was common in a Roman household. My Father brought no new woman from another family to rule over me.

There is no grief in me for my Mother because I was simply too young for it, and if I cried when my Mother did not come back, I don't remember it.

What I remember is having the run of a big old rectangular palatial Roman house, with many rectangular rooms built onto the main rectangle, one off another, the whole nestled in a huge garden high on the Palatine Hill. It was a house of marble floors and richly painted walls, the garden meandering and surrounding every room of it.

I was the true jewel of my Father's eye, and I remember having a marvelous time watching my brothers practice outside with their short broadswords, or listening as their tutors instructed them, and then having fine teachers of my own who taught me how to read the entire *Aeneid* of Virgil before I was five years old.

I loved words. I love to sing them and speak them and even now, I must admit, I have fallen into the joy of writing them. I couldn't have told you that nights ago, David. You've brought back something to me and I must make the admission. And I must not write too fast in this mortal café, lest human beings notice!

Ah, so we continue.

My Father thought it was hysterical that I could recite verses from Virgil at so young an age and he liked nothing better than to show me off at banquets at which he entertained his conservative and somewhat old-fashioned Senatorial friends, and sometimes Caesar Augustus himself. Caesar Augustus was an agreeable man. I don't think my Father ever really wanted him at our house, however. But now and then, I suppose, the Emperor had to be wined and dined.

I'd rush in with my nurse, give a rousing recital and then be whisked away to where I could not see the proud Senators of Rome glutting themselves on peacock brains and *garum*—surely you know what *garum* is. It's the horrible sauce the Romans put on everything, rather like today's ketchup. Definitely it defeated the purpose of having eels and squids on your plate, or ostrich brains or unborn lamb or whatever other absurd delicacies were being brought by the platterful.

The point is, as you know, the Romans seemed to have a special place in their hearts for genuine gluttony, and the banquets inevitably became a disgrace. The guests would go off to the vomitorium of the house to heave up the first five courses of the meal so that they could then swallow the others. And I would lie upstairs, giggling in my bed, listening to all this laughter and vomiting.

Then the rape of the entire catering staff of slaves would follow, whether they were boys or girls or a mixture of both.

Family meals were an entirely different affair. Then we were old Romans. Everyone sat at the table; my Father was undisputed Master of his house, and would tolerate no criticism of Caesar Augustus, who, as you know, was Julius Caesar's nephew, and did not really rule as Emperor by law.

"When the time is right, he will step down," said my Father. "He knows he can't do it now. He is more weary and wise than ever he was ambitious. Who wants another Civil War?"

The times were actually too prosperous for men of stature to make a revolt.

Augustus kept the peace. He had profound respect for the Roman Senate. He rebuilt old Temples because he thought people needed the piety they had known under the Republic.

He gave free corn from Egypt to the poor. Nobody starved in Rome. He maintained a dizzying amount of old festivals, games and spectacles—enough to sicken one actually. But often as patriotic Romans we had to be there.

Of course there was great cruelty in the arena. There were cruel executions. There was the ever present cruelty of slavery.

But what is not understood by those today is that there coexisted with all this a sense of individual freedom on the part of even the poorest man.

The courts took time over their decisions. They

consulted the past laws. They followed logic and code. People could speak their minds fairly openly.

I note this because it is key to this story: that Marius and I both were born in a time when Roman law was, as Marius would say, based on reason, as opposed to divine revelation.

We are totally unlike those blood drinkers brought to Darkness in lands of Magic and Mystery.

Not only did we trust Augustus when we were alive, we also believed in the tangible power of the Roman Senate. We believed in public virtue and character; we held to a way of life which did not involve rituals, prayers, magic, except superficially. Virtue was embedded in character. That was the inheritance of the Roman Republic, which Marius and I shared.

Of course, our house was overcrowded with slaves. There were brilliant Greeks and grunting laborers and a fleet of women to rush about polishing busts and vases, and the city itself was choked with manumitted slaves—freedmen—some of whom were very rich.

They were all our people, our slaves.

My Father and I sat up all night when my old Greek teacher was dying. We held his hands until the body was cold. Nobody was flogged on our estate in Rome unless my Father himself gave the order. Our country slaves loafed under the fruit trees. Our stewards were rich, and showed off their wealth in their clothes.

I remember a time when there were so many old Greek slaves in the garden that I could sit day after day and listen to them argue. They had nothing else to do. I learned much from this.

I grew up more than happy. If you think I exaggerate the extent of my education, consult the letters of Pliny or other actual memoirs and correspondence of the times. Highborn young girls were well educated; modern Roman women went about unhampered for the most part by male interference. We partook of life as did men.

For example, I was scarcely eight years old when I was first taken to the arena with several of my brothers' wives, to have the dubious pleasure of seeing exotic creatures, such as giraffes, tear madly around before being shot to death with arrows, this display then followed by a small group of gladiators who would hack other gladiators to death, and then after that came the flock of criminals to be fed to the hungry lions.

David, I can hear the sound of those lions as if it were now. There's nothing between me and the moment that I sat in the wooden benches, perhaps two rows up—the premium seats—and I watched these beasts devour living beings, as I was supposed to do, with a pleasure meant to demonstrate a strength of heart, a fearlessness in the face of death, rather than simple and utter monstrousness.

The audience screamed and laughed as men and women ran from the beasts. Some victims would give the crowd no such satisfaction. They merely stood there as the hungry lion attacked; those who were being devoured alive almost invariably lay in a stupor as though their souls had already taken flight, though the lion had not reached the throat.

I remember the smell of it. But more than anything, I remember the noise of the crowd.

I passed the test of character, I could look at all of it. I could watch the champion gladiator finally meet his end, lying there bloody in the sand, as the sword went through his chest.

But I can certainly remember my Father declaring under his breath that the whole affair was disgusting. In fact, everybody I knew thought it was all disgusting. My Father believed, as did others, that the common man needed all this blood. We, the highborn, had to preside over it for the common man. It had a religious quality to it, all this spectacular viciousness.

The making of these appalling spectacles was considered something of a social responsibility.

Also Roman life was a life of being outdoors, involved in things, attending ceremonies and spectacles, being seen, taking an interest, coming together with others.

You came together with all the other highborn and lowborn of the city and you joined in one mass to witness a triumphant procession, a great offering at the altar of Augustus, an ancient ceremony, a game, a chariot race.

Now in the Twentieth Century, when I watch the endless intrigue and slaughter in motion pictures and on television throughout our Western world, I wonder if people do not need it, do not need to see murder, slaughter, death in all forms. Television at times seems an unbroken series of gladiatorial fights or massacres. And look at the traffic now in video recordings of actual war.

Records of war have become art and entertainment.

The narrator speaks softly as the camera passes over the heap of bodies, or the skeletal children sobbing with their starving mothers. But it is gripping. One can wallow, shaking one's head, in all this death. Nights of television are devoted to old footage of men dying with guns in their hands.

I think we look because we are afraid. But in Rome, you had to look so that you would be hard, and that applied to women as well as men.

But the overall point is—I was not closeted away as a Greek woman might have been in some old Hellenistic household. I did not suffer under the earlier customs of the Roman Republic.

I vividly remember the absolute beauty of that time, and my Father's heartfelt avowal that Augustus was a god, and that Rome had never been more pleasing to her deities.

Now I want to give you one very important recollection. Let me set the scene. First, let's take up the question of Virgil, and the poem he wrote, the *Aeneid*, greatly amplifying and glorifying the adventures of the hero Aeneas, a Trojan fleeing the horrors of defeat by the Greeks who came out of the famous Trojan horse to massacre Helen's city of Troy.

It's a charming story. I always loved it. Aeneas

leaves dying Troy, valiantly journeys all the way to beautiful Italy and there founds our nation.

But the point is that Augustus loved and supported Virgil all of Virgil's life, and Virgil was a respected poet, a poet fine and decent to quote, an approved and patriotic poet. It was perfectly fine to like Virgil.

Virgil died before I was born. But by ten I'd read everything he'd written, and had read Horace as well, and Lucretius, much of Cicero, and all the Greek manuscripts we possessed, and there were plenty.

My Father didn't erect his library for show. It was a place where members of the family spent hours. It was also where he sat to write his letters—which he seemed endlessly to be doing—letters on behalf of the Senate, the Emperor, the courts, his friends, etc.

Back to Virgil. I had also read another Roman poet, who was alive still, and deeply and dangerously out of favor with Augustus, the god. This was the poet Ovid, the author of the *Metamorphoses*, and dozens of other earthy, hilarious and bawdy works.

Now, when I was too young to remember, Augustus turned on Ovid, whom Augustus had also loved, and Augustus banished Ovid to some horrible place on the Black Sea. Maybe it wasn't so horrible. But it was the sort of place cultured city Romans expect to be horrible—very far away from the capital and full of barbarians.

Ovid lived there a long time, and his books were banned all over Rome. You couldn't find them in the bookshops or the public libraries. Or at the book stands all over the marketplace.

You know this was a hot time for popular reading; books were everywhere—both in scroll form and in codex, that is, with bound pages—and many booksellers had teams of Greek slaves spending all day copying books for public consumption.

To continue, Ovid had fallen out of favor with Augustus, and he had been banned, but men like my Father were not about to burn their copies of the *Metamorphoses*, or any other of Ovid's work, and the only reason they didn't plead for Ovid's pardon was fear.

The whole scandal had something to do with Augustus's daughter, Julia, who was a notorious slut by anyone's standards. How Ovid became involved in Julia's love affairs I don't know. Perhaps his sensuous early poetry, the *Amores*, was considered to be a bad influence. There was also a lot of "reform" in the air during the reign of Augustus, a lot of talk of old values.

I don't think anyone knows what really happened between Caesar Augustus and Ovid, but Ovid was banished for the rest of his life from Imperial Rome.

But I had read the *Amores* and the *Metamorphoses* in well-worn copies by the time of this incident which I want to recount. And many of my Father's friends were always worried about Ovid.

Now to the specific recollection. I was ten years old, I came in from playing, covered with dust from head to foot, my hair loose, my dress torn, and breezed into my Father's large receiving room—and I plopped down at the foot of his couch to listen to what was being said, as he lounged there with all appropriate Roman dignity, chatting with several other lounging men who had come to visit.

I knew all of the men but one, and this one was fair-haired and blue-eyed, and very tall, and he turned, during the conversation—which was all whispers and nods—and winked at me.

This was Marius, with skin slightly tanned from his travels and a flashing beauty in his eyes. He had three names like everyone else. But again, I will not disclose the name of his family. But I knew it. I knew he was sort of the "bad boy" in an intellectual way, the "poet" and the "loafer." What nobody had told me was that he was beautiful.

Now, on this day, this was Marius when he was alive, about fifteen years before he was to be made a vampire. I can calculate that he was only twenty-five. But I'm not certain.

To continue, the men paid no attention to me, and it became plain to my ever curious little mind that they were giving my Father news of Ovid, that the tall blond one with the remarkable blue eyes, the one called Marius, had just returned from the Baltic Coast, and he had given my Father several presents, which were in fact good copies of Ovid's work, both past and current.

The men assured my Father that it was still far too

dangerous to go crying to Caesar Augustus over Ovid, and my Father accepted this. But if I'm not mistaken, he entrusted some money for Ovid to Marius, the blond one.

When the gentlemen were all leaving, I saw Marius in the atrium, got a measure of his full height, which was quite unusual for a Roman, and let out a girlish gasp and then a streak of laughter. He winked at me again.

Marius had his hair short then, clipped military-Roman-style with a few modest curls on his forehead; his hair was long when he was later made a vampire, and he wears it long now, but then it was the typical boring Roman military cut. But it was blond and full of sunlight in the atrium, and he seemed the brightest and most impressive man I'd ever laid eyes upon. He was full of kindness when he looked at me.

"Why are you so tall?" I asked him. My Father thought this was amusing, of course, and he did not care what anyone else thought of his dusty little daughter, hanging onto his arms and speaking to his honored company.

"My precious one," Marius said, "I'm tall because I'm a barbarian!" He laughed and was flirtatious when he laughed, with a deference to me as a little lady, which was rather rare.

Suddenly he made his hands into claws and ran at me like a bear.

I loved him instantly!

"No, truly!" I said. "You can't be a barbarian. I know your Father and all your sisters; they live just down the hill. The family is always talking about you at the table, saying only nice things, of course."

"Of that I'm sure," he said, breaking into laughter.

I knew my Father was getting anxious.

What I didn't know was that a ten-year-old girl could be betrothed.

Marius drew himself up and said in his gentle very fine voice, trained for public rhetoric as well as words of love, "I am descended through my mother from the Keltoi, little beauty, little muse. I come from the tall blond people of the North, the people of Gaul. My mother was a princess there, or so I am told. Do you know who they are?"

I said of course I knew and began to recite verbatim from Julius Caesar's account of conquering Gaul, or the land of the Keltoi: "All Gaul is made up of three parts . . ."

Marius was quite genuinely impressed. So was everybody. So I went on and on, "The Keltoi are separated from the Aquitani by the river Garonne, and the tribe of the Belgae by the rivers Marne and Seine—"

My Father, being slightly embarrassed by this time, with his daughter glorying in attention, spoke up to gently assure everyone that I was his precious joy, and I was let to run wild, and please make nothing of it.

And I said, being bold, and a born troublemaker, "Give my love to the great Ovid! Because I too wish he would come home to Rome."

I then rattled off several steamy lines of the *Amores*:

She laughed and gave her best, whole hearted kisses,
They'd shake the three pronged bolt from Jove's hand.
Torture to think that fellow got such good ones!
I wish they hadn't been of the same brand!

All laughed, except my Father, and Marius went wild with delight, clapping his hands. That was all the encouragement I needed to rush at him now like a bear, as he had rushed at me, and to continue singing out Ovid's hot words:

What's more these kisses were better than I'd taught her,
She seemed possessed of knowledge that was new.
They pleased too well—bad sign! Her tongue was in
them,
And my tongue was kissing too.

My Father grabbed me by the small of my upper arm, and said, "That's it, Lydia, wrap it up!" And the men laughed all the harder, commiserating with him, and embracing him, and then laughing again.

But I had to have one final victory over this team of adults.

"Pray, Father," I said, "let me finish with some wise and patriotic words which Ovid said:

" 'I congratulate myself on not having arrived into the world until the present time. This age suits my taste.' "

This seemed to astonish Marius more than to amuse him. But my Father gathered me close and said very clearly:

"Lydia, Ovid wouldn't say that now, and now you, for being such a . . . a scholar and philosopher in one, should assure your Father's dearest friends that you know full well Ovid was banished from Rome by Augustus for good reason and that he can never return home."

In other words, he was saying "Shut up about Ovid."

But Marius, undeterred, dropped on his knees before me, lean and handsome with mesmeric blue eyes, and he took my hand and kissed it and said, "I will give Ovid your love, little Lydia. But your Father is right. We must all agree with the Emperor's censure. After all, we are Romans." He then did the very strange thing of speaking to me purely as if I were an adult. "Augustus Caesar has given far more to Rome, I think, than anyone ever hoped. And he too is a poet. He wrote a poem called 'Ajax' and burnt it up himself because he said it wasn't good."

I was having the time of my life. I would have run off with Marius then and there!

But all I could do was dance around him as he went out of the vestibule and out the gate.

I waved to him.

He lingered. "Goodbye, little Lydia," he said. He then spoke under his breath to my Father, and I heard my Father say:

"You are out of your mind!"

My Father turned his back on Marius, who gave me a sad smile and disappeared.

"What did he mean? What happened?" I asked my Father. "What's the matter?"

"Listen, Lydia," said my Father. "Have you in all your readings come across the word 'betrothed'?"

"Yes, Father, of course."

"Well, that sort of wanderer and dreamer likes nothing better than to betroth himself to a young girl of ten because it means she is not old enough to marry and he has years of freedom, without the censure of the Emperor. They do it all the time."

"No, no, Father," I said. "I shall never forget him."

I think I forgot him the next day.

I didn't see Marius again for five years.

I remember because I was fifteen, and should have been married and didn't want to be married at all. I had wriggled out of it year after year, feigning illness, madness, total uncontrollable fits. But time was running out on me. In fact I'd been eligible for marriage since I was twelve.

At this time, we were all standing together at the foot of the Palatine Hill, watching a most sacrosanct ceremony—the Lupercalia—just one of so many festivals that were integral in Roman life.

Now the Lupercalia was very important to us, though there's no way to relate its significance to a Christian's concept of religion. It was pious to enjoy such a festival, to participate as a citizen and as a virtuous Roman.

And besides it was a great pleasure.

So I was there, not so far from the cave of the Lupercal, watching with other young women, as the two chosen men of that year were smeared with blood from a sacrifice of goats and then draped in the bleeding skins of the sacrificed animals. I couldn't see all of this very well, but I had seen it many times, and when years before two of my brothers had run in this festival, I had pushed to the front to get a good look at it.

On this occasion, I did have a fairly good view when each of the two young men took his own company and began his run around the base of the Palatine Hill. I moved forward because I was supposed to do it. The young men were hitting lightly on the arm of every young woman with a strip of goatskin, which was supposed to purify us. Render us fertile.

I stepped forward and received the ceremonial blow, and then stepped back again, wishing I was a man and could run around the hill with the other men, not an unusual thought for me at any time in my mortal life.

I had some sarcastic inner thoughts about "being purified," but by this age I behaved in public and would not on any account have humiliated my Father or my brothers.

These strips of goatskin, as you know, David, are called *Februa*, and February comes from that word. So much for language and all the magic it unwittingly carries with it. Surely the Lupercalia had something to do with Romulus and Remus; perhaps it even echoed some ancient human sacrifice. After all, the young men's heads were smeared with goat blood. It gives me shivers, because in Etruscan times, long before I was born, this might have been a far more cruel ceremony.

Perhaps this was the occasion that Marius saw my arms. Because I was exposing them to this ceremonial lash, and was already, as you can see, much of a show-off in general, laughing with the others as the company of men continued their run.

In the crowd, I saw Marius. He looked at me, then back to his book. So strange. I saw him standing against a tree trunk and writing. No one did this—stand against a tree, hold a book in one hand and write with the other. The slave stood beside him with a bottle of ink.

Marius's hair was long and most beautiful. Quite wild.

I said to my Father, "Look, there's our barbarian friend Marius, the tall one, and he's writing."

My Father smiled and said, "Marius is always writing. Marius is good for writing, if for nothing else. Turn around, Lydia. Be still."

"But he looked at me, Father. I want to talk to him."

"You will not, Lydia! You will not grace him with one small smile!"

On the way home, I asked my Father, "If you're going to marry me to someone—if there's no way short of suicide that I can avoid this disgusting development—why don't you marry me to Marius? I don't understand it. I'm rich. He's rich. I know his Mother was a wild Keltoi princess, but his Father has adopted him."

My Father said witheringly, "Where have you learned all this?" He stopped in his tracks, always an ominous sign. The crowd broke and streamed around.

"I don't know; it's common knowledge." I turned. There was Marius hovering about, glancing at me. "Father," I said, "please let me speak to him!"

My Father knelt down. Most of the crowd had gone on. "Lydia, I know this is dreadful for you. I have caved to every objection you have raised to your suitors. But believe you me, the Emperor himself would not approve of you marrying such a mad wandering historian as Marius! He has never served in the military, he cannot enter the Senate, it is quite impossible. When you marry, you will marry well."

As we walked away, I turned again, thinking only to pick Marius out from the others, but to my surprise he was stark still, looking at me. With his flowing hair, he much resembled the Vampire Lestat. He is taller than Lestat, but he has the same lithe build, the same very blue eyes and a muscular strength to him, and a squareness of face which is almost pretty.

I pulled away from my Father and ran up to him.

"Well, I wanted to marry you," I said, "but my Father has said no."

I'll never forget the expression on his face. But before he could speak, my Father had gathered me up and gone into obliterating respectable conversation: "How now, Marius, how goes it with your brother in the Army. And how is it with your history. I hear you have written thirteen volumes."

My Father backed up, virtually carrying me away.

Marius did not move or answer. Soon we were with others hurrying up the hill.

All the course of our lives was changed at that moment. But there was no conceivable way Marius or I could have known it.

Twenty years would pass before we would meet again.

I was thirty-five, then. I can say that we met in a realm of darkness in more respects than one.

For now, let me fill up the gap.

I was married twice, due to pressure from the Imperial House. Augustus wanted us all to have children. I had none. My husbands seeded plenty, however, with slave girls. So I was legally divorced and freed twice over, and determined then to retire from social life, just so the Emperor Tiberius, who had come to the Imperial throne at the age of fifty, would not meddle with me, for he was more a public puritan and domestic dictator than Augustus. If I kept to the house, if I didn't go abroad to banquets and parties and hang around with the Empress Livia, Augustus's wife and mother of Tiberius, perhaps I wouldn't be pushed into becoming a stepmother! I'd stay home. I had to care for my Father. He deserved it. Even though he was perfectly healthy, he was still old!

With all due respect for the husbands I have mentioned, whose names are more than footnotes in common Roman histories, I was a wretched wife.

I had plenty of my own money from my Father, I listened to nothing, and yielded to the act of love only on my own terms, which I always obtained, being gifted with enough beauty to make men really suffer.

I became a member of the Cult of Isis just to spite these husbands and get away from them, so that I could hang around at the Temple of Isis, where I spent an enormous amount of time with other interesting women, some far more adventurous and unconventional than I dared to be. I was attracted to whores. I saw the brilliant, loose women as having conquered a barrier which I, the loving daughter of my Father, would never conquer.

I became a regular at the Temple. I was initiated at last in a secret ceremony, and I walked in every procession of Isis in Rome.

My husbands loathed this. Maybe that's why after I came home to my Father I gave up the worship. Whatever, it was a good thing perhaps that I had. But fortune could not be so easily shaped by any decision of mine.

Now Isis was an imported goddess, from Egypt, of course, and the old Romans were as suspicious of her as they were of the terrible Cybele, the Great Mother from the Far East, who led her male devotees to castrate themselves. The whole city was filled with these "Eastern cults," and the conservative population thought them dreadful.

These cults weren't rational; they were ecstatic or euphoric. They offered a complete rebirth through understanding.

The typical conservative Roman was far too practical for that. If you didn't know by age five that the gods were made-up creatures and the myths invented stories, then you were a fool.

But Isis had a curious distinction—something that set her far apart from the cruel Cybele. Isis was a loving mother and goddess. Isis forgave her worshipers anything. Isis had come before all Creation. Isis was patient and wise.

That's why the most degraded woman could pray at the Temple. That's why none were ever turned away.

Like the Blessed Virgin Mary, who is so well known today throughout the East and West, the Queen Isis had conceived her divine child by divine means. From the dead and castrated Osiris, she had drawn the living seed by her own power. And many a time she was pictured or sculpted holding her divine son, Horus, on her knee. Her breast was bare in all innocence to feed the young god.

And Osiris ruled in the land of the dead, his phallus lost forever in the waters of the Nile, where an endless semen flowed from it, fertilizing the remarkable fields of Egypt every year when the River overflowed its banks.

The music of our Temple was divine. We used the sistrum, a small rigid metal lyre of sorts, and flutes and timbrels. We danced, and we sang together. The poetry of Isis's litanies was fine and rapturous.

Isis was the Queen of Navigation, much like the Blessed Virgin Mary would be called later, "Our Lady Star of the Sea."

When her statue was carried to the shore each year, the procession was so splendid that all Rome turned out to see the Egyptian gods with their animal heads, the huge abundance of flowers and the statue of the Queen Mother herself. The air rang with hymns. Her Priests and Priestesses walked in white linen robes. She herself, made of marble, and carried high, holding her sacred sistrum, dressed regally in a Grecian gown with Grecian hair.

That was my Isis. I fell away from her after my last divorce. My Father didn't like the worship, and I myself had enjoyed it long enough. As a free woman, I wasn't infatuated with prostitutes. I had it infinitely better. I kept my Father's house and he was just old enough, in spite of his black hair and his remarkably sharp vision, that the Emperor left me alone.

I can't say I remembered or thought of Marius. No one had mentioned Marius for years. He had disappeared out of my mind after the Lupercalia. There was no force on Earth that could come between me and my Father.

My brothers all had good luck. They married well, had children and came home from the hard wars in which they fought, keeping the boundaries of the Empire.

My youngest brother, Lucius, I did not like much,

but he was always a little anxious and given to drinking and apparently also to gambling, which very much annoyed his wife.

She I loved, as I did all my sisters-in-law and my nieces and nephews. I loved it when they descended upon the house, these flocks of children, squealing and running rampant with "Aunt Lydia's blessing," as they were never allowed to do at home.

The eldest of my brothers, Antony, was in potential a great man. Fate robbed him of greatness. But he had been most ready for it, well schooled, trained and most wise.

The only foolish thing I ever knew Antony to do was say to me very distinctly once that Livia, Augustus's wife, had poisoned him so that her son, Tiberius, would rise. My Father, the only other occupant of the room, told him sternly:

"Antony, never speak of that again! Not here, not anywhere!" My Father stood up, and without planning it, put in perspective the style of life which he and I lived. "Stay away from the Imperial Palace, stay away from the Imperial families, be in the front ranks of the games and always in the Senate, but don't get into their quarrels and their intrigues!"

Antony was very angry, but the anger had nothing to do with my Father. "I said it only to those two to whom I can say it, you and Lydia. I detest eating dinner with a woman who poisoned her husband! Augustus should have re-established the Republic. He knew when death was coming."

"Yes, and he knew that he could not restore the

Republic. It was simply impossible. The Empire had grown to Britannia in the North, beyond Parthia in the East; it covers Northern Africa. If you want to be a good Roman, Antony, then stand up and speak your conscience in the Senate. Tiberius invites this."

"Oh, Father, you are much deceived," said Antony.

My Father put an end to this argument.

But he and I did live exactly the life he had described.

Tiberius was immediately unpopular with the noisy Roman crowds. He was too old, too dry, too humorless, too puritanical and tyrannical at the same time.

But he had one saving grace. Other than his extensive love and knowledge of philosophy, he had been a very good soldier. And that was the most important characteristic the Emperor had to possess.

The troops honored him.

He strengthened the Praetorian Guard around the Palace, hired a man named Sejanus to run things for him. But he didn't bring legions into Rome, and he spoke a damned good line about personal rights and freedom, that is, if you could stay awake to listen. I thought him a brooder.

The Senate went mad with impatience when he refused to make decisions. They didn't want to make the decisions! But all this seemed relatively safe.

Then a horrible incident occurred which made me positively detest the Emperor wholeheartedly and lose all my faith in the man and his ability to govern.

This incident involved the Temple of Isis. Some

clever evil man, claiming to be the Egyptian god Anubis, had enticed a highborn devotee of Isis to the Temple and gone to bed with her, fooling her completely, though how on Earth he did it I can't imagine.

I remember her to this day as the stupidest woman in Rome. But there's probably more to it.

Anyway, it had all happened at the Temple.

And then this man, this fake Anubis, went before the highborn virtuous woman and told her in the plainest terms that he had had her! She went screaming to her husband. It was a scandal of extraordinary flair.

It had been years since I had been at the Temple, and I was glad of it.

But what followed from the Emperor was more dreadful than I ever dreamed.

The entire Temple was razed to the very ground. All the worshipers were banished from Rome, and some of them executed. And our Priests and Priestesses were crucified, their bodies hung on the tree, as the old Roman expression goes, to die slowly, and to rot, for all to see.

My Father came into my bedroom. He went to the small shrine of Isis. He took the statue and smashed it on the marble floor. Then he picked up the larger pieces and smashed each of them. He made dust of her.

I nodded.

I expected him to condemn me for my old habits. I was overcome with sadness and shock at what had happened. Other Eastern cults were being persecuted. The Emperor was moving to take away the right of Sanctuary from various Temples throughout the Empire.

"The man doesn't want to be Emperor of Rome," said my Father. "He's been bent by cruelty and losses. He's stiff, boring and completely in terror for his life! A man who would not be Emperor cannot be Emperor. Not now."

"Maybe he'll step down," I said sadly. "He has adopted the young General Germanicus Julius Caesar. This means Germanicus is to be his heir, does it not?"

"What good did it do to the earlier heirs of Augustus when they were adopted?" my Father asked.

"What do you mean?" I asked.

"Use your head," said my Father. "We cannot continue pretending we are a Republic. We must define the office of this Emperor and the limits of his power! We must outline a form of succession other than murder!"

I tried to calm him.

"Father, let's leave Rome. Let's go to our house in Tuscany. It's always beautiful there, Father."

"That's just it, we can't, Lydia," he said. "I have to remain here. I have to be loyal to my Emperor. I must do so for all my family. I must stand in the Senate."

Within months, Tiberius sent off his young and handsome nephew Germanicus Julius Caesar to the

East, just to get him away from the adulation of the Roman public. As I said, people spoke their minds.

Germanicus was supposed to be Tiberius's heir! But Tiberius was too jealous to listen to the crowds screaming praise of Germanicus for his victories in battle. He wanted the man far from Rome.

And so this rather charming and seductive young general went to the East, to Syria; he vanished from the loving eyes of the Roman people, from the core of the Empire where a city crowd could determine the fate of the world.

Sooner or later there would be another campaign in the North, we all figured. Germanicus had hit hard at the German tribes in his last campaign.

My brothers vividly described it to me over the dinner table.

They told how they had gone back to avenge the hideous massacre of General Varus and his troops in the Teutoburg Forest. They could finish the job, if called up again, and my brothers would go. They were exactly the kind of old-fashioned patricians who would go!

Meantime there were rumors that the *Delatores*, the notorious spies of the Praetorian Guard, pocketed one-third of the estate of those against whom they informed. I found it horrible. My Father shook his head, and said, "That started under Augustus."

"Yes, Father," I said, "but then treason was considered a matter of what one did, not what one said."

"Which is all the more reason to say nothing." He sat back wearily. "Lydia, sing to me. Get your lyre.

Make up one of your comic epics. It's been a long time."

"I'm too old for that," I said, thinking of the silly, bawdy satires on Homer which I used to make up so quickly and freely that everyone marveled. But I jumped at that idea. I remember that night so palpably that I cannot tear myself loose now from the writing of this story, even though I know what pain I must confess and explore.

What does it mean to write? David, you'll see this question repeated, because with each page I understand more and more—I see the patterns that have before eluded me, and driven me to dream rather than live.

That night I did make a very funny epic. My Father laughed. He fell asleep on his couch. And then, as if from a trance state, he spoke, "Lydia, don't live out your life alone on account of me. Marry for love! You must not give up!"

By the time I turned around, he was breathing deeply again.

Two weeks later, or maybe it was a month, our life came abruptly to an end.

I came home one day, found the house completely empty except for two terrified old slave men—men who actually belonged to the household of my brother Antony—who let me in and bolted the door ferociously.

I walked through the huge vestibule and then into the peristyle and into the dining room. I beheld an amazing sight.

My Father was in full battle dress, armed with sword and dagger, lacking only his shield. He even wore his red cloak. His breastplate was polished and gleaming.

He stared at the floor and with reason. It had been dug up. The old Hearth from generations ago had been dug up. This had been the first room of this house in the very ancient days of Rome, and it was around this Hearth that the family gathered, worshiped, dined.

I had never even seen it. We had our household Shrines, but this, this giant circle of burnt stones! There were actually ashes there, uncovered. How ominous and sacred it appeared.

"What in the name of the gods is going on?" I asked. "Where is everybody?"

"They are gone," he said. "I have freed the slaves, sent them packing. I've been waiting for you. You have to leave here now!"

"Not without you!"

"You will not disobey me, Lydia!" I had never seen such an imploring yet dignified expression in his face. "There's a wagon out back, ready to take you to the coast, and a Jewish merchant who is my most trusted friend who will take you by ship out of Italy! I want you to go! Your money's been loaded on board the ship. Your clothing. Everything. These are men I trust. Nevertheless take this dagger."

He picked up a dagger from the nearby table and gave it to me. "You've watched your brothers enough to know how to use it," he said, "and this." He reached for a sack. "This is gold, the currency that all the world accepts. Take it and go."

I always carried a dagger, and it was in the sling on my forearm but I could not shock him with this just now, so I put the dagger in my girdle and took the purse.

"Father, I'm not afraid to stand by you! Who's turned on us? Father, you are Senator of Rome. Accused of any crime, you are entitled to a trial before the Senate."

"Oh, my precious quick-witted daughter! You think that evil Sejanus and his *Delatores* bring charges out in the open? His *Speculatores* have already surprised your brothers and their wives and children. These are Antony's slaves. He sent them to warn me as he fought, as he died. He saw his son dashed against the wall. Lydia, go."

Of course I knew this was a Roman custom—to murder the entire family, to wipe out the spouse and offspring of the condemned. It was even the law. And in matters such as this, when word got out that the Emperor had turned his back on a man, any of his enemies could precede the assassins.

"You come with me," I said. "Why do you stay here?"

"I will die a Roman in my house," he said. "Now go if you love me, my poet, my singer, my thinker. My Lydia. Go! I will not be disobeyed. I have spent the last hour of my life arranging for your salvation! Kiss me and obey me."

I ran to him, kissed him on the lips and at once the slaves led me through the garden.

I knew my Father. I could not revolt against him in this final wish. I knew that, in old-fashioned Roman style, he would probably take his life before the *Speculatores* broke down the front door.

When I reached the gate, when I saw the Hebrew merchants and their wagon, I couldn't go.

This is what I saw.

My Father had cut both his wrists and was walking around the household hearth in a circle, letting the blood flow right down onto the floor. He had really given his wrists the slash. He was turning white as he walked. In his eyes there was an expression I would only come to understand later.

There came a loud crash. The front door was being bashed in. My Father stopped quite still. And two of the Praetorian Guard came at him, one making sneering remarks, "Why don't you finish yourself off, Maximus, and save us the trouble. Go on."

"Are you proud of yourselves!" my Father said. "Cowards. You like killing whole families? How much money do you get? Did you ever fight in a true battle. Come on, die with me!"

Turning his back on them, he whipped around with sword and dagger, and brought down both of them, as they came at him, with unanticipated thrusts. He stabbed them repeatedly.

My Father wobbled as if he would faint. He was white. The blood flowed and flowed from his wrists. His eyes rolled up into his head.

Mad schemes came to me. We must get him into the wagon. But a Roman like my Father would never have cooperated.

Suddenly the Hebrews, one young and one elderly, had me by the arms and were carrying me out of the house.

"I vowed I would save you," said the old man. "And you will not make a liar of me to my old friend."

"Let go of me!" I whispered. "I will see him through it!"

Throwing them off in their polite timidity I turned and saw from a great distance my Father's body by the hearth. He had finished himself with his own dagger.

I was thrown into the wagon, my eyes closed, my hands over my mouth. I fell among soft pillows, bolts of fabric, tumbling as the wagon began to roll very slowly down the winding road of the Palatine Hill.

Soldiers shouted at us to get the hell out of the way.

The elderly Hebrew said, "I am nearly deaf, sir, what did you say?"

It worked perfectly. They rode past us.

The Hebrew knew exactly what he was doing. As crowds rushed past us he kept to his slow pace.

The one young one came into the back of the wagon. "My name is Jacob," he said. "Here, put on all these white mantles. You look now like an Eastern woman. If questioned at the gate, hold up your veil and pretend you do not understand."

We went through the Gates of Rome with amazing ease. It was "Hail David and Jacob, has it been a good trip?"

I was helped aboard a large merchant vessel, with galley slaves and sails, nothing unusual at all, and then into a small barren wooden room.

"This is all we have for you," said Jacob. "But we are sailing now." He had long wavy brown hair and a beard. He wore striped robes to the ground.

"In the dark?" I asked. "Sailing in the dark?"

This was not usual.

But as we moved out, as the oars began to dip, and the ship found its proper distance and began to move South, I saw what we were doing.

All the beautiful Southwestern coast of Italy was well lighted by her hundreds and hundreds of palatial villas. Lighthouses stood on the rocks.

"We will never see the Republic again," said Jacob wearily, as though he were a Roman citizen, which I think in fact he was. "But your Father's last wish is fulfilled. We are safe now."

The old man stepped up to me. He told me that his name was David.

The old man apologized profusely that there were no female attendants for me. I was the only woman on board.

"Oh, please, banish any such thoughts from your mind! Why have you taken these risks?"

"For years we have done business with your Father," said David. "Years ago, when pirates sank our ships, your Father carried the debt. He trusted us again, and we repaid him fivefold. He has laid up riches for you. They are all stowed, among cargo we carried, as if they were nothing."

I went into the cabin and collapsed on the small bed. The old man, averting his eyes, brought a cover for me.

Slowly I realized something. I had fully expected them to betray me.

I had no words. I had no gestures or sentiments inside me. I turned my head to the wall. "Sleep, lady," he said.

A nightmare came to me, a dream such as I have never had in my life. I was near a river. I wanted to drink blood. I waited in high grass to catch one of the villagers, and when I had this poor man, I took him by his shoulders, and I sank two fang teeth into his neck. My mouth filled with delicious blood. It was too sweet and too potent to be described, and even in the dream I knew it. But I had to move on. The man was nearly dead. I let him fall. Others who were more dangerous were after me. And there was another terrible threat to my life.

I came to the ruins of a Temple, far from the marsh. Here it was desert—just with the snap of the fingers, from wetland to sand. I was afraid. Morning was coming. I had to hide. Besides, I was also being hunted. I digested this delicious blood, and I entered the Temple. No place to hide! I lay my whole body on the cold walls! They were graven with pictures. But there was no small room, no hiding place for me.

I had to make it to the hills before sunrise, but that wasn't possible. I was moving right towards the sun!

Suddenly, there came above the hills a great fatal light. My eyes hurt unbearably. They were on fire. "My eyes," I cried and reached to cover them. Fire covered me. I screamed. "Amon Ra, I curse you!" I cried another name. I knew it meant Isis, but it was not that name, it was another title for her that flew from my lips.

I woke up. I sat bolt upright, shivering.

The dream had been as sharply defined as a vision. It had a deep resonance in me of memory. Had I lived before?

I went out on the deck of the ship. All was well enough. We could see the coastline clearly still, and the lighthouses, and the ship moved on. I stared at the sea, and I wanted blood.

"This is not possible. This is some evil omen, some twisted grief," I said. I felt the fire. I could not shut out the taste of the blood, how natural it had seemed, how good, how perfect for my thirst. I saw the twisted body of the villager again in the marshes.

This was a horror; it was no escape from what I had just witnessed. I was incensed, and feverish.

Jacob, the tall young one, came to me. He had with him a young Roman. The young man had shaved his first beard, but otherwise he seemed a flushed and glistening child.

I wondered wearily if I were so old at thirty-five that everyone young looked beautiful to me.

He cried, "My family, too, has been betrayed. My Mother made me leave!"

"To whom do we owe this shared catastrophe?" I asked. I put my hands on his wet cheeks. He had a baby's mouth, but the shaven beard was rough. He had broad strong shoulders, and wore only a light, simple tunic. Why wasn't he cold out here on the water? Perhaps he was.

He shook his head. He was pretty still and would be handsome later. He had a nice curl to his dark hair. He didn't fear his tears, or apologize for them.

"My Mother stayed alive to tell me. She lay gasping until I came. When the *Delatores* had told my Father that he plotted against the Emperor, my Father had laughed. He had actually laughed. They had accused him of plotting with Germanicus! My Mother wouldn't die until she'd told me. She said that all my Father was accused of doing was talking with other men about how he would serve under Germanicus again if they were sent North."

I nodded wearily. "I see. My brothers probably said the same thing. And Germanicus is the Emperor's heir and *Imperium Maius* of the East. Yet this is treason, to speak of serving Rome under a pretty general."

I turned to go. To understand gave no consolation.

"We are taking you to different cities," said Jacob, "to different friends. Better that we not say."

"Don't leave me," said the boy. "Not tonight."

"All right," I said. I took him into the cabin and

closed the door, with a polite nod to Jacob, who was watching all with a guardian's conscience.

"What do you want?" I asked.

The boy stared at me. He shook his head. He flung his hands out. He turned and drew close to me and kissed me. We went into a rampage of kisses.

I took off my shift and sank into the bed with him. He was a man all right, tender face or no.

And when I came to the moment of ecstasy, which was quite easy, given his phenomenal stamina, I tasted blood. I was the blood drinker in the dream. I went limp, but it didn't matter. He had all he needed to finish the rites to his satisfaction.

He rose up. "You're a goddess," he said.

"No," I whispered. The dream was rising. I heard the wind on the sand. I smelled the river. "I am a god . . . a god who drinks blood."

We did the rites of love until we could do them no more.

"Be circumspect and very proper with our Hebrew hosts," I said. "They will never understand this sort of thing."

He nodded. "I adore you."

"Not necessary. What is your name?"

"Marcellus."

"Fine, Marcellus, go to sleep."

Marcellus and I made a night of every night after that until we finally saw the famous lighthouse of Pharos and knew we had come to Egypt.

It was perfectly obvious that Marcellus was being left in Alexandria. He explained to me that his maternal grandmother was still alive, a Greek, and indeed her whole clan.

"Don't tell me so much, just go," I said. "And be wise and safe."

He begged me to come with him. He said he had fallen in love with me. He would marry me. He didn't care if I bore no children. He didn't care that I was thirty-five. I laughed softly, mercifully.

Jacob noted all this with lowered eyes. And David looked away.

Quite a few trunks followed Marcellus into Alexandria.

"Now," I said to Jacob, "will you tell me where I'm being taken? I might have some thoughts on the matter, though I doubt I could improve on my Father's plan."

I still wondered. Would they deal honestly with me? What about now that they had seen me play the whore with the boy? They were such religious men.

"You're headed to a great city," Jacob said. "It couldn't be a better place. Your Father has Greek friends there!"

"How could it be better than Alexandria?" I said.

"Oh, it is far and away better," Jacob said. "Let me talk to my Father before I talk to you further."

We had put out to sea. The land was going away. Egypt. It was growing dark.

"Don't be afraid," Jacob said. "You look as though you are terrified."

"I'm not afraid," I said. "It's only that I have to lie in my bed and think and remember and dream." I looked at him, as he shyly looked away. "I held the boy like a Mother, against me, night after night."

This was about the biggest lie I've told in my life.

"He was a child in my arms." Some child! "And now I fear nightmares. You must tell me—what is our destination? What is our fate?"

3

NTIOCH," said Jacob, "Antioch on the Orontes. Greek friends of your Father await you. And they are friends with Germanicus. Perhaps in time . . . but they will be loyal to you. You are to be married to a Greek of breeding and means."

Married! To a Greek, a provincial Greek? A Greek in Asia! I stifled my laughter and my tears. That was not going to happen to me. Poor man! If he really was a provincial Greek, he was going to have to experience the conquest of Rome all over again.

We sailed on, from port to port. I mulled all this over.

It was nauseating trivia like this which of course protected me from my full and inevitable grief and shock over what happened. Worry about whether your dress is properly girdled. Don't see your Father lying dead with his own dagger in his chest.

As for Antioch, I had been far too embroiled in the life of Rome to know or hear much about this city. If Tiberius had stationed his "heir," Germanicus, there to get him away from Roman popularity, then I thought: Antioch must be the end of the civilized world.

Why in the name of the gods had I not run away in Alexandria, I thought? Alexandria was the greatest city in the Empire, next to Rome. It was a young city, built by Alexander, for whom it was named, but it was a marvelous port. No one would ever dare raze the Temple of Isis in Alexandria. Isis was an Egyptian goddess, wife of the powerful Osiris.

But what had that to do with things? I must have been plotting in the back of my mind already, but I didn't allow any conscious plot to surface and blemish my highborn Roman moral character.

I quietly thanked my Hebrew guardians for this intelligence, for keeping it even from the young Roman Marcellus, the other man they had rescued from the Emperor's assassins, and I asked for frank answers to my questions regarding my brothers.

"All taken by surprise," said Jacob. "The *Delatores*, those spies of the Praetorian Guard, are so swift. And your Father had so many sons. It was your eldest brother's slaves who jumped the wall at their Master's command and ran to warn your Father."

Antony. I hope you shed their blood. I know you fought with your last breath. And my niece, my little niece Flora, had she run screaming from them, or did they do it with mercy? The Praetorian Guard doing anything with mercy! Stupid to even think so.

I didn't say anything aloud. Just sighed.

After all, when they looked at me, these two

Jewish merchants beheld the body and face of a woman; naturally my protectors should think a woman was inside of me. The disparity between outward appearances and inner disposition had disturbed me all my life. Why disturb Jacob and David? On to Antioch.

But I had no intention of living in any old-fashioned Greek family, if such still existed in the Greek city of Antioch, a family in which women lived apart from the men, and wove wool all day, never going out, having no part in the life of the world whatsoever.

I'd been taught all the virtuous female arts by my nurses and I could indeed do anything with yarn or thread or loom that any other woman could do, but I knew well what the "Old Greek Ways" had been, and I remembered vaguely my Father's Mother, who had died when I was very young—a virtuous Roman matron who was always making wool. So they had said of her in her Epitaph, and in fact, they had said in my Mother's Epitaph: "She kept the House. She made wool."

And so they had said of my Mother! The very same tiresome words.

Well, no one was going to say that on mine. (How humorous to reflect on the fact now, thousands of years later, that I have no Epitaph!)

What I failed to realize in my overall dejection was that the Roman world was enormous, and the Eastern portion of it differed dramatically from the

Northern barbarian lands, where my brothers had fought.

The entire of Asia Minor, towards which we sailed, had been conquered by Alexander of Macedon hundreds of years before. As you know, Alexander had been the pupil of Aristotle. Alexander had wanted to spread Greek culture everywhere. And in Asia Minor Greek ideas and styles found not mere country towns or farmers, but ancient cultures, like the Empire of Syria, willing to receive the new ideas, the grace and beauty of the Greek enlightenment, and willing to bring in tune with it their own centuries-old literature, religion, styles of life and dress.

Antioch had been built by a general of Alexander the Great who sought to rival the beauty of other Hellenistic cities, with splendid Temples, administrative buildings and libraries of books in the Greek language, its schools where Greek philosophy was taught. A Hellenistic government was established—quite enlightened compared to ancient Eastern despotism, and yet there lay beneath all this the knowledge and customs and possibly the wisdom of the mysterious East.

The Romans had conquered Antioch early on because it was a huge trade center. It was unique in this way, as Jacob showed to me, drawing a crude map with his wet finger on the wooden table. Antioch was a port of the great Mediterranean because she was only twenty miles up the Orontes River.

Yet on the Eastern side she was open to the desert: all the old caravan routes came to Antioch, the camel merchants who brought fantastic wares from fabled lands—lands we know now to have been India and China—silk, carpet and jewels which never reached the markets of Rome.

Countless other traders came and went to Antioch. Fine roads connected it in the East with the Euphrates River and the Parthian Empire beyond, and to the South you could go to Damascus and Judea, and to the North, of course, lay all the cities made by Alexander, which had flowered under Roman rule.

Roman soldiers loved it there. It was an easy and interesting life. And Antioch loved the Romans because the Romans protected the trade routes, and the caravans, and kept peace in the port.

"You will find open places, arcades, Temples, all that you seek and such markets you would not believe. There are Romans everywhere. I hope to One Most High that you are not recognized by someone from your own background! That is one danger of which your Father had no time to plan."

I waved it away.

"Does it have teachers now, and markets of books?"

"From everywhere. You will find books which no one can read. And Greek is spoken by everyone. You have to go out in the country to find some poor farmer who does not understand Greek. Latin has now become common.

"The philosophers never stop; they speak of Plato and Pythagoras, names that don't mean much to me; they talk about Chaldean magic from Babylon. Of course there are Temples to every imaginable god."

He went on, reflecting as he spoke:

"The Hebrews? I think personally they are too worldly—they want to hang around in short tunics with the Greeks and go to the public baths. They are too interested in the Greek philosophy. It invades everything, all this thinking that Greeks did. Not good. But a Greek city is an inviting world."

He glanced up. His Father was watching over us, and we were too close together, at this table on the deck.

He hastily filled me in on other facts:

Germanicus Julius Caesar, heir to the Imperial throne, the official adopted son of Tiberius, had been granted the *Imperium Maius* in Antioch. That is, he controlled all of this territory. And Gnaeus Calpurnius Piso was the governor of Syria.

I assured him that they would know nothing of me or my old-fashioned family or our quiet, old house on the Palatine Hill, squeezed between so many other extravagant new mansions.

"It's all Roman-style," Jacob protested. "You'll see. And you come with money! And forgive me, but you are still beautiful at your age; you have fresh skin and you move your limbs like a girl."

I sighed and gave Jacob thanks. Time for him to break away unless we wanted his Father coming down upon us.

I watched the ever rolling blue waves.

I was thankful in secret that our family had withdrawn from the parties and banquets at the Imperial Palace, but then I blamed myself for such thankfulness, knowing that our reclusiveness must have paved the way for our downfall.

I'd seen Germanicus on his triumphal procession through Rome, a gorgeous young man, much as Alexander had been, and I knew from my Father and my brothers that Tiberius, fearing the popularity of his appointed heir, had sent him off to the East to get him away from the Roman crowds.

The Governor Piso? I had never laid eyes on him. The gossip was that he was sent East to devil Germanicus. Oh, such a waste of talent and thought.

Jacob returned to me.

"Well, you go nameless and unknown into this vast city," said Jacob. "And you have protectors of high character who are beloved of Germanicus. He's young and sets a tone of vitality and gaiety in the city."

"And Piso?" I asked.

"Everyone hates him. Especially the soldiers, and you know what that means in a Roman province."

You can look at the crashing, undulating sea from the railing of a deck forever, or just for so long.

That night I had my second blood dream. It was keenly similar to the first. I was thirsty for blood. And enemies were after me, enemies that knew I was a demon and must be destroyed. I was running. My own kind had forsaken me, thrust me out unprotected to the superstitions of the people. Then I saw the desert and knew I would die; I awoke, sitting up and crying out, but covering my mouth quickly so no one heard it.

What disturbed me so terribly was the thirst for blood. I could not imagine such a thing when I was awake, but in these dreams I was the monster that Romans called the Lamia. Or so it seemed. Blood was sweet, blood was all. Was the old Greek Pythagoras right? Souls do migrate from body to body? But my soul in this past life had been that of a monster.

During the day, I closed my eyes now and then and found myself dangerously on the edge of the dream, as if it were a trap in my mind, waiting to engulf my consciousness. But at night, that is when they came most strongly. *You have served me before!* What could this mean? *Come to me.*

Blood thirst. I closed my eyes, curled up in bed and prayed, "Mother Isis, Cleanse my Mind of this Blood madness."

Then I resorted to plain old ordinary eroticism. Get Jacob into bed! No such luck. Little did I know that Hebrews had been, and would be forever, the most difficult of men to seduce!

It was all made clear with great grace and tact.

I considered all the slaves. Out of the question. First off were the galley slaves, among whom no great "Ben Hur" was chained, waiting for me to rescue him. They were just the dregs of the criminal poor, fastened Roman-style, so they would drown if the ship went down, and they were dying, as all galley slaves do from the monotony and the whip. It wasn't a pleasant sight to go down into the hold of a galley ship and see those men bending their backs.

But my eyes were as cold as those of an American

watching color television pictures of the starving babies of Africa, little black skeletons with big heads screaming for water. News Break, Commercial Break, Sound Bite, CNN now switches to Palestine: rock throwing, rubber bullets. Television blood.

The rest on board were boring sailors, and two old pious merchant Hebrews who stared at me as if I were a whore, or worse, and turned their heads whenever I came out on deck in my long tunic with my long hair swinging free.

Such a disgrace I must have seemed! But what a fool I was then, really, living in numbness, and how pleasant that voyage—all because true grief and rage had not yet taken hold of me. Things had happened too fast.

I gloated over my last glimpse of my Father dispatching those soldiers of Tiberius, those cheap assassins sent by a cowardly, indecisive Emperor. And the rest—I banished it from my mind, affecting the attitude of the hardened Roman man or woman.

A modern Irish poet, Yeats, best characterizes the official Roman attitude towards failure and tragedy.

> *Cast a cold eye on life, on death.*
> *Horseman, pass by!*

There was never a Roman born who would not have agreed with that.

That was my stance—sole survivor of a great house, commanded by her Father to "live." I didn't dare to dwell on the fate of my brothers, their lovely wives, their little children. I couldn't envision the slaughter of the children—little boys being run through by broadswords, or babies bashed against the wall. Oh, Rome, you and your bloody old wisdom. Be sure to kill the offspring. Kill the whole family!

Lying alone at night, I found myself amid more horrid blood dreams. They seemed fragments of a lost life, a lost land. Deep echoing vibrant tones of music dominated the dreams, as though someone were striking a gong, and others beside him beat solemnly on deep drums with soft coverings. I saw in a haze a world of stiff and flat alien paintings on the walls. Painted eyes around me. I drank blood! I drank it from a small shuddering human being, who knelt before me as if I were Mother Isis.

I woke to take the big jug of water by my bed and drink all of it down. I drank water to defy and satisfy this dream thirst. I was almost sick from drinking water.

I racked my mind. Had I ever had such dreams as a child?

No. And now these dreams had the heat of recollection! Of initiation into the doomed Temple of Isis, when it had been still the fashion. I had been intoxicated, and drenched in the blood of a bull, and dancing wildly in circles. My head was filled with the litanies of Isis. We were promised rebirth! "Never tell, never tell, never tell . . ." How could an initiate tell anything of the rites, when you were so drunk you could hardly remember them?

Isis brought me memories now of lovely music of lyres, flutes, timbrels, of the high magical sound of the metal strings of the sistrum, which the Mother Herself held in her hand. There were only fleeting recollections of that naked blood dance, that night of rising into the stars, of seeing the scope of life in its cycles, of accepting perfectly just for a little while that the moon would always be changing, and the sun would set as it always rose. Embraces of other women. Soft cheeks and kissing and bodies rocking in unison. "Life, death, rebirth, it's no series of miracles," said the Priestess. "To understand it and accept it, that is the miracle. Make the miracle within your own breast."

Surely we had not drunk blood! And the bull—it was a sacrifice only for the initiation. We did not bring helpless animals to her flower-laden altars, no, our Blessed Mother did not ask that of us.

Now, at sea, alone, I lay awake to avoid these blood dreams.

When exhaustion won out, a dream came with sleep as if it had been waiting for my eyes to close.

I lay in a gold chamber. I was drinking blood, blood from the throat of a god, or so it seemed, and choruses were singing or chanting—it was a dull, repetitive sound not quite worthy of being called music, and when I had had my fill of blood, this god or whoever this was, this silken-skinned proud thing, lifted me and placed me on an altar.

Vividly, I could feel the cold marble beneath me. I realized I wore no clothes. I felt no modesty.

Somewhere far off, echoing through these great halls, came the weeping of a woman. I was full of blood. Those who chanted approached with little clay oil lamps. Faces around me were dark, dark enough to be from far faraway Ethiopia or India. Or Egypt. Look. Painted eyes! I looked at my hands and arms. They were dark. But I was this person who lay on the altar, and I say person now because it had come clear to me with no disturbance during the dream itself that I was a man lying there. Pain tore at me. The god said, "This is merely the passage. You will now drink from each of us, only a little blood."

Only when I woke did the brief transition in the masculine gender leave me as puzzled as everything else. I was drenched with a sense of Egyptian art, Egyptian mystery—as I'd seen it in golden statues for sale in the marketplace, or when the Egyptian dancers performed at a banquet, like walking sculptures with their black-lined eyes, and black plaited wigs, whispering in that mysterious tongue. What had they thought of our Isis in Roman dress?

A mystery taunted me; something attacked my reason. The very thing the Roman Emperors had so feared in Egyptian cults and Oriental cults swept over me: mystery and emotion which claim a superiority to reason and law.

My Isis had been a Roman goddess, really, a universal goddess, the Mother of us all, her worship spreading out in a Greek and Roman world long before it had come into Rome itself. Our Priests were

Greeks and Roman, poor men. We the congregation were all Greeks and Romans.

Something scratched at the back of my mind. It said, "Remember." It was a tiny desperate voice within my own brain that urged me to "remember" for my own sake.

But remembering only led to confused and jumbled thoughts. Suddenly a veil would fall between the reality of my cabin on the ship, and the tumbling of the sea—between that and some dim and frightening world, of Temples covered in words that made magic! Long narrow beautifully bronzed faces. A voice whispered, "Beware the Priests of Ra; they lie!"

I shivered. I closed my eyes. The Queen Mother was bound and chained to her throne! She wept! It had been her crying. Unspeakable. "But you see, she has forgotten how to rule. Do as we say."

I shook myself awake. I wanted to know and I did not want to know. The Queen wept beneath her monstrous fetters. I couldn't see her clearly. It was all in progress. It was busy. "The King is with Osiris, you see. You see how he stares; each one whose blood you drink, you give to Osiris; each one becomes Osiris."

"But why did the Queen scream?"

No, this was madness. I couldn't let this confusion overcome me. I couldn't deliberately slip from reason into these fantasies or recollections supposing they had a true root.

They had to be nonsense, twisted images of grief

and guilt, guilt that I had not rushed to the hearth and driven the dagger into my breast.

I tried to remember the calming voice of my Father, explaining once how the blood of the gladiators satisfied the thirst of the dead, the *Manes*.

"Now, some say that the Dead drink blood," spoke my Father from some long ago dinner talk. "That's why we are so fearful on all these unlucky days, when the Dead are supposed to be able to walk the Earth. I personally think this is nonsense. We should revere our ancestors . . ."

"Where are the Dead, Father?" my brother Lucius asked.

Who had piped up from the other side of the table, to quote Lucretius in a sad little female voice that nevertheless commanded silence of all these men? Lydia:

> *Of earth return to earth, but any part*
> *Sent down from heaven, must ascend again*
> *Recalled to the high temples of the sky*
> *And death does not destroy the elements*
> *Of matter, only breaks the combinations.*

"No," my Father had replied to me quite gently. "Rather quote Ovid: 'The ghosts ask for but little; they value piety more than a costly gift.' " He drank his wine. "The ghosts are in the Underworld where they can't harm us."

My eldest brother Antony had said, "The Dead are nowhere and are nothing."

My Father had raised his cup. "To Rome," he said, and it was he this time who had quoted Lucretius: " 'Too many times, religion mothers crimes and wickedness.' "

Shrugs and sighs all around. The Roman attitude. Even the Priests and Priestesses of Isis would have joined Lucretius when he wrote:

Our terrors and our darknesses of mind
Must be dispelled, then, not by sunshine's rays,
Not by those shining arrows of light,
But by insight into nature, and a scheme
Of systematic contemplation.

Drunk? Drugged? Bull's blood? Systematic? Well, it all came down to the same thing. Know! Twist the poetry as you will. And the phallus of Osiris lives forever in the Nile, and the water of the Nile inseminates the Mother Egypt eternally, death giving birth to life with the blessing of Mother Isis. Merely a particular scheme and a sort of systematic form of contemplation.

The ship sailed on.

I languished some eight more days in this torment, often lying awake in the dark, and sleeping only in the day to avoid the dreams.

Suddenly, in the early morning, Jacob pounded my door.

We were midway up the Orontes to the city.

Twenty miles now from Antioch. I did up my hair as best I could (I'd never done it without a slave) into a chignon on the back of my head, then covered my Roman gowns with a great black cloak and prepared to disembark—an Eastern woman, her face draped, protected by Hebrews.

When the city came into view—when the immense harbor greeted us and then embraced us with all its masts and racket and odors and cries, I ran to the deck of the ship and looked out at this city. It was splendid.

"You see," Jacob said.

Taken from the ship by litter I found myself carried rapidly through vast waterfront markets, and then into a great open square, crowded with people. I saw everywhere the Temples, porticoes, booksellers, even the high walls of an amphitheater—all that I could have expected in Rome. No, this was no town.

The young men were crowded about the barbershops ready to have their obligatory shave and the inevitable fancy curls on their foreheads, which Tiberius with his own hairstyle had made fashionable. There were wine shops all over. The slave markets were jammed. I glimpsed the entrances to the streets devoted to crafts—the street of the tentmakers, the street of the silversmiths.

And there in all its glory, in the very center of Antioch, stood the Temple of Isis!

My goddess, Isis, with her worshipers coming and going, undisturbed, and in huge numbers. A few very proper-looking linen-clad Priests stood at the doors! The Temple was aswarm.

I thought, I can run away from any husband in this place!

Gradually I realized a great commotion had come upon the Forum, the center of the city. I heard Jacob ordering the men to hurry out of the broad market street and into the back streets. My bearers were running. The curtains were brought shut by Jacob's hand so I couldn't see out.

News was being shouted out in Latin, in Greek, in Chaldean: Murder, Murder, Poison, Treachery.

I peeped out of the curtain.

People were weeping and cursing the Roman Gnaeus Calpurnius Piso, cursing him and his wife, Placina. Why? I didn't much like either one of them, but what was all this?

Jacob shouted again at my bearer to hurry.

We were rushed through the gates and into the vestibule of a sizable house no different in design or color than my own in Rome, only much smaller. I could see the same refinements, the distant peristyle, clusters of weeping slaves.

The litter was promptly set down and I stepped out, deeply concerned that they had not stopped me at the doors to wash my feet, as was proper. And my hair, it had all fallen down in waves.

But no one noticed me. I turned round and round, amazed at the Oriental curtains and tassels that hung over the doorways, the caged birds everywhere singing in their little prisons. The woven carpets lying all over the floor, one heaped upon another.

Two obvious ladies of the house came towards me.

"What's the matter!" I asked.

They were as fashionable as any rich woman in Rome, drenched in bracelets and wearing gold-trimmed gowns.

"I implore you," said one of the women, "for your own sake, go! Get back into the litter!"

They tried to push me inside the curtained cell of the litter. I wouldn't go. I became furious.

"I don't know where I am," I said. "And I don't know who you are! Now, stop pushing me!"

The Master of the House, or someone who certainly appeared to be such, came dashing towards me, with tears streaming down his cheeks and his short tousled gray hair a mess—torn as if in mourning. He'd ripped his long tunic. He'd smeared dirt on his face! He was old with a bent back and a massive head, loaded with skin and wrinkles.

"Your Father was my young colleague," he said to me in Latin. He grabbed me by the arms. "I dined in your house when you were a baby. I saw you when you crawled on all fours."

"Tender," I said quickly.

"Your Father and I studied in Athens, slept under the same roof."

The women stood panic-stricken with their hands over their mouths.

"Your Father and I fought with Tiberius on his first campaign. We fought those lurid barbarians."

"Very brave," I said.

My black outer cloak fell down, revealing my unkempt wild long hair and plain dress. Nobody cared.

"Germanicus dined in this house because your Father spoke of me!"

"Oh dear, I see," I said.

One of the women motioned for me to get in the litter. Where was Jacob? The old man wouldn't let me go.

"I stood with your Father and with Augustus when news came to us of the massacre of our troops in the Teutoburg Forest, that General Varus and all his men were slain. My sons fought with your brothers in the legions of Germanicus when he punished those Northern tribes! Oh, God!"

"Yes, very marvelous, indeed," I said gravely.

"Get back in the litter and get out," said one of the women.

The old man clutched me.

"We fought the madman, King Arminius!" said the old man. "We could have won! Your brother Antony wasn't for giving up and coming back, was he?"

"I . . . no . . ."

"Get her out of here!" screamed a young patrician man, who had also been weeping. He came forward and shoved me towards the litter.

"Stand back, you imbecile!" I said to him. I slapped his face.

All this while, Jacob had been talking to the slaves, getting the scoop.

Jacob appeared beside me, as the gray-haired Greek sobbed and kissed my cheeks.

Jacob took over, guiding me into the litter.

"Germanicus has just been murdered," Jacob said

in my ear. "Everybody loyal to him is convinced that the Emperor Tiberius put the Roman Governor Piso up to the murder. It was done with poison. Word is spreading through the city like fire."

"Tiberius, you idiot!" I whispered, rolling my eyes. "One cowardly step after another!"

I sank back into the darkness. The litter was being lifted.

Jacob went right on: "Gnaeus Calpurnius Piso has allies here, naturally. Everybody's fighting everybody else. Settling scores. Mayhem. This Greek family traveled with Germanicus to Egypt. There are riots already. We go!"

"Farewell, friend," I cried to the old Greek, as I was carried from the house. But I don't think he heard me. He had gone down on his knees. He cursed Tiberius. He screamed of suicide and begged for the dagger.

We were outside once more, hurrying through the street.

I lay askew in the litter, thinking dully in the darkness. Germanicus dead. Poisoned by Tiberius!

I knew that this recent trip of Germanicus to Egypt had made Tiberius very angry. Egypt was like no other Roman province. Rome was so dependent upon it for grain that Senators could not go there. But Germanicus had gone, "just to see the ancient relics," his friends had said in the streets of Rome.

"A mere excuse!" I thought in desperation. "Where was the trial? The sentence? Poison!"

My bearers were running. People were screaming

and sobbing around us. "Germanicus, Germanicus! Give us back our beautiful Germanicus!"

Antioch had gone mad.

At last, we were obviously in a small narrow street that was little more than an alleyway—you know the kind, for a grid of them was uncovered in the ruins of Pompeii in Italy. You could smell the male urine collected in the jugs on the corner. You could smell food cooking from high chimneys. My bearers were running and stumbling over rough cobblestones.

Once we were all thrown to the side as a chariot came crashing through the narrow place, its wheels no doubt finding the ruts in the stone intended for it.

My head had hit the wall. I was furious and frightened. But Jacob said, "Lydia, we are with you."

I covered up all over with the cloak, so that only one eye allowed me to see the seams of light between the curtains on either side of me. I had my hand on my dagger.

The litter was set down. It was a cool indoor place. I heard Jacob's father, David, arguing. I knew no Hebrew. And I wasn't even sure that he was speaking in Hebrew.

Finally, Jacob took over in Greek, and I realized that they were purchasing outright a proper house for me which came with all fine appointments, including much fine furniture, left recently by a rich widow who had lived there alone, but alas, the slaves had been sold off. No slaves. This was a quick cash deal.

Finally, I heard Jacob say in Greek:

"You damn well better be telling me the truth."

As the litter was lifted I beckoned to him. "I owe you my life twice over now. That Greek family who was to shelter me? They are truly in danger?"

"Of course," he said. "When a riot starts, who cares? They went with Germanicus to Egypt! Piso's men know that! Anybody with the slightest excuse will attack, murder and plunder someone else. Look, fire." He told the men to hurry.

"All right," I said. "Never say my real name again. From now on say this name: My name is Pandora. I am a Greek from Rome. I paid you to bring me here."

"You have it, my dear Pandora," he replied. "You are some strong woman. The Deed to your new house is made up in a fake name with less charm. But the Deed verifies you are widowed, emancipated and a Roman Citizen. We'll get the Deed when we pay up the gold, which we won't do until we are in the house. And if the man does not give me that Deed with everything written out in full to protect you, I'll strangle him!"

"You're very clever, Jacob," I said wearily.

On and on went this dark bouncing journey in the litter until at last it came to a halt. I could hear the metal key turning in the lock of the gate, and then we were brought into the large vestibule of the house itself.

I should have waited out of consideration for my guardians, but frantically I climbed out of this miserable little black veiled prison, throwing off the cloak and taking a deep breath.

We were in the broad vestibule of a fine house,

with great charm to it and much ingenuity in its decoration.

Even now, my thoughts scattered, I saw the lion-head fountain right near the gate through which we'd just come, and I washed my feet in the cool of the water.

The receiving room, or atrium, was huge, and beyond it I saw the rich couches of the dining room on the far side of a rather large enclosed garden—the peristyle.

It was not my massive ancient opulent old home on the Palatine Hill, which had grown new corridors and rooms over many generations, penetrating its broad gardens.

It was a bit too glossy. But it was grand. All the walls were freshly painted with a more Oriental bent, I think—more swirls and serpentine lines. How could I judge? I could have fainted from relief. Would people really leave me alone here?

There sat the desk in the atrium, and near it books! Along the porticoes flanking the garden, I saw the many doors; I looked up and saw the second-story windows closed on the porches. Splendor. Safety.

The mosaic floors were old; I knew the style, the festive figures of the Saturnalia on parade. They had to have been brought here from Italy.

Little real marble, plastered columns, but so many well-executed murals full of the requisite happy nymphs.

I went out into the soft wet grass of the peristyle and looked up at the blue sky.

I wanted only to breathe, but now came the moment of truth regarding my belongings. I was too dazed to ask about what was mine. And as it turned out, no such thing was necessary.

Jacob and David first did an entire inventory of the household furnishings they were purchasing for me, as I stood there staring at them in near disbelief at their patience with detail.

And when they'd found every room quite fine, and a bedchamber down the hall to the right, and a small open garden somewhere to the left, beyond the kitchen, they went upstairs, found things proper and then unloaded my possessions. Trunk followed trunk.

Then to my utter shock, Jacob's father, David, drew out a scroll and actually started taking a full inventory of everything that belonged to me, from hairpins to ink and gold.

Jacob was meantime sent on an errand!

I could see the hasty writing of my Father on this inventory that David read under his breath.

"Personal toilet articles," David said in final summation of one portion of this examination. "Clothes, one, two, three trunks—to the largest bedroom, go! Household plate to the kitchen. Books here?"

"Yes, please." I was too shocked at his honesty and meticulousness to speak.

"Ah, so many books!"

"Fine, don't count them!" I said.

"I cannot, you see, these fragile . . ."

"Yes, I know. Carry on."

"You want your ivory and ebony shelves assembled here in the front room?"

"Magnificent."

I slumped down on the floor, only to be lifted at once by two helpful Asian slaves and settled in an amazingly soft cross-legged Roman chair. I was given a cup of fresh clean-smelling water. I drank it down, thought of blood. Closed my eyes.

"Ink, writing materials on the desk?" asked the old man.

"If you will," I sighed.

"Now, everybody out," said the old man, dispensing coins quickly and generously to these Asian slaves, who bowed from the waist and backed out of the room, nearly stumbling over each other.

I was about to try to form some sensible words of gratitude when a fresh brace of slaves rushed in—nearly colliding with the departing crew—carrying baskets of everything edible that a marketplace could yield, including at least nine kinds of bread, jugs of oil, melons, green vegetables and much smoked food that would last for days—fish, beef and exotic sea creatures dried out to look like parchment.

At once to the kitchen, save for a plate of olives and cheese and bread at once for the lady on that table to her left. Fetch the lady's wine, which her Father has sent.

Oh, how incredible. My Father's wine.

Then everyone was ordered out again with lots of coins freely given and the old man at once returned to his inventory.

"Jacob, come here, count for me this gold as I read off the list to you! Plate, coin, more coin, jewels of exceptional value? Coin, bars of gold. Yes . . ."

On and on they went, rushing at it.

Where had my Father hidden all this gold? I couldn't imagine it.

What was I going to do with it? Were they really going to let me keep this? They were honest men but this was such a fortune.

"You must wait until everyone is gone," said David, "and then hide this gold yourself in various places about the house. You will find such places. We cannot do that for you, for then we would know where it was. Your jewels? Some I leave here to be hidden for they are much too valuable to be flashed abroad among the populace in your first days." He opened a casket of gems. "See this ruby? It is superb. Look at the size of it. This can feed you for the rest of your life if sold to an honest man for half of its worth. Every jewel in this box is exceptional. I know jewels. These are hand-picked from the finest. See these pearls? Perfection." He returned the ruby and the pearls to the casket and shut the lid.

"Yes," I said weakly.

"Pearls, more gold, silver, plate . . ." he muttered. "It's all here! We should take more care but . . ."

"Oh, no, you have done wonders," I declared.

I stared at the bread and the wine in the cup. My Father's wine bottle. My Father's amphorae around the room.

"Pandora," said Jacob, addressing me most seriously. "Here in my hand is the Deed to this house. And another paper which describes your official entry into the port under your new made-up name, Julia, La, La, La and so forth. Pandora, we have to leave you."

The old man shook his head and bit his lip.

"We have to sail for Ephesus, child," he said. "I am ashamed that I must leave you, but the harbor will soon be blocked!"

"There are ships on fire already in the harbor," said Jacob under his breath. "They've pulled down the statue of Tiberius in the Forum."

"The transaction is closed," said the old man to me. "The man who sold the house has never laid eyes on you and does not know your real name, and there is no evidence of it remaining here. Those were not his slaves who brought you here."

"You've done miracles for me," I said.

"You are on your own, my beautiful Roman princess," Jacob said. "It hurts my soul to leave you like this."

"We must," said the old man.

"Don't go out for three days," said Jacob, coming near to me, about as near as he could, as if he even meant to break all the rules and kiss my cheek. "There are enough legions here to quell this riot, but they will let it burn itself out, rather than slaughter Roman citizens. And forget those Greek friends. Their house is already an inferno."

They turned to leave!

"Were you well paid for all this?" I asked. "If not, take from my gold now, freely. I insist!"

"Don't even think of such things," said the old man. "But for your peace of mind, know this: your Father staked me twice after my ships were captured by pirates in the Adriatic. Your Father put his money in with mine and I made profits for both of us. The Greek owed your Father money. Worry about those matters no more. But we must go!"

"God be with you, Pandora," said Jacob.

Jewels. Where were the jewels? I leapt up and opened the casket. There were hundreds of them, flawless, dazzlingly clear and exquisitely polished. I saw their value, their clarity and the care of the polishing. I took the big egg-shaped ruby David had shown to me and then another just like it and thrust them at the two men.

They put up their hands to say No.

"Oh, but you must," I said. "Give me this respect. Confirm for me that I am a free Roman woman and that I shall live as my Father told me to do! It will give me courage! Take this from me."

David shook his head sternly, but Jacob took the ruby.

"Pandora, here, the keys. Follow us and lock the gate at the street and then the doors to the vestibule. Don't fear. There are lamps everywhere. Plenty of oil—"

"Go!" I said as they passed over the threshold. I locked the gate and held to the bars, staring at them.

"If you can't get out, if you need me, come back here," I said.

"We have our own people here," Jacob said soothingly. "Thank you from my heart for the beautiful ruby, Pandora. You will survive. Go back in, bolt the doors."

I made it to the chair but I did not sit in it. Rather I collapsed and prayed, "*Lares familiares* . . . spirits of the house, I should find your altar. Welcome me, please, I bring no ill will to anyone. I will heap your altar with flowers and light your fire. Give me patience. Let me . . . rest."

Yet I did nothing but sit in shock on the floor, my hands limp, for hours as the daylight waned. As the strange little house grew dark.

A blood dream began, but I wouldn't have it. Not that alien Temple. Not the altar, no! Not the blood. I banished it and imagined I was home.

I was a little girl. Dream of that, I told myself, of listening to my eldest brother, Antony, talk of war in the North, driving the mad Germans back to the sea! He had so loved Germanicus. So had my other brothers. Lucius, the young one, he was so weak by nature. It broke my heart to think of him crying out for mercy as soldiers cut him down.

The Empire was the world. All that lay beyond was chaos and misery and struggle and strife. I was a soldier. I could fight. I dreamt I was putting on my armor. My brother said, "I am so relieved to discover you are a man, I always thought so."

I didn't waken till the following morning.

And then it was that grief and pain made themselves known to me as never before.

Note this. Because I knew the full absurdity of Fate and Fortune and Nature more truly than a human can bear to know it. And perhaps the description of this, brief as it is, may give consolation to another. The worst takes its time to come, and then to pass.

The truth is, you cannot prepare anyone for this, nor convey an understanding of it through language. It must be known. And this I would wish on no one in the world.

I was alone. I went from room to room of this small house, banging upon the walls with my fists and crying with my teeth clenched, and whirling. There was no Mother Isis.

There were no gods. Philosophers were fools! Poets sang lies.

I sobbed and tore at my hair; I tore at my dress as naturally as if it had been a newborn custom. I knocked over chairs and tables.

At times I felt a huge exhilaration, a freedom from all falsehoods and conventions, all means by which a soul or body can be held hostage!

And then the awesome nature of this freedom spread itself out around me as if the house did not exist, as if the darkness knew no walls.

Three nights and days I spent in this agony.

I forgot to eat food. I forgot to drink water.

I never lighted a lamp. The moon nearing her fullness gave enough light to this meaningless labyrinth of little painted chambers.

Sleep was gone from me forever.

My heart beat fast. My limbs clenched, then slackened, only to clench again.

At times, I lay on the moist good Earth of the courtyard, for my Father, because no one had laid his body on the moist good Earth, as it should have been done, right after his death and before any funeral.

I knew suddenly why this disgrace was so important, his body rent with wounds and not placed on the Earth. I knew the gravity of this omission as few have ever known the meaning of anything. It was of the utmost importance because it did not matter at all!

Live, Lydia.

I looked at the small leafy trees of the garden. I felt a strange gratitude that I had opened human eyes in this darkness on Earth long enough to see such things.

I quoted Lucretius:

"That which comes from Heaven ascends to Heaven"?

Madness!

Alas, as I said, I wandered, crawled, wept and cried for three nights and days.

4

INALLY, one morning, when the sun came spilling down through the open roof, I looked at the objects in the room and I realized I didn't know what they were, or what they'd been made for. I didn't know their common names. I was removed from their definitions. I didn't even know this place.

I sat up and realized I was looking at the Lararium, the shrine of the household gods.

This was the dining room of course, and those were the couches, and there the glorious conjugal bed!

The Lararium was a high three-sided shrine, a little temple with three pediments, and inside stood figures of old household gods. No one in this profane city had even taken them away with the dead woman.

The flowers were dead. The fire had simply gone out. No one had quenched it with wine, as should have been done.

On hands and knees I crawled in my torn dress around the garden of the peristyle, gathering flowers for these gods. I found the wood and made their sacred fire.

I stared at them. I stared for hours. It seemed I would never move again.

Night fell. "Don't sleep," I whispered. "Keep watch with the night! They wait for you by dark, those Egyptians! The moon, look, it's almost full, only a night or so from being full."

But the worst of my agony had passed and I was exhausted, and sleep rose to embrace me. Sleep rose as if to say, "Care no more."

The dream came.

I saw men in gilded robes. "You will be taken now in the sanctum." But what's there? I didn't want to see. "Our Mother, our beloved Mother of Sorrows," said the Priest. The paintings on the walls were rows upon rows of Egyptians in profile, and words made of pictures. Myrrh burned in this place.

"Come," said those who held me. "All the impurities have gone from you now, and you will partake of the sacred Fount."

I could hear a woman crying and moaning. I peeped into the great room before I entered it. There they were, the King and the Queen on their thrones, the King still and staring as in the last dream, and the Queen struggling against her golden fetters. She wore the crown of Upper and Lower Egypt. And pleated linen. Her hair was not a wig but real plaits. She cried and her white cheeks were stained in red. Red stained her necklace and her breasts. She looked soiled and ignominious.

"My Mother, my goddess," I said. "But this is an abomination."

I forced myself to wake.

I sat up and I laid my hand on the Lararium, and looked at the spiderwebs in the trees of the garden, made visible by the climbing sun.

I thought I heard people whispering in the ancient Egyptian tongue.

I was not going to allow this! I would not go mad.

Enough! The only man I had ever loved, my Father, said, "Live."

It was time for action. To get up and get going. I was suddenly all strength and purpose.

My long nights of mourning and weeping had been equivalent to the initiation in the Temple; death had been the intoxicant; comprehension had been the transformation.

It was over now, and the meaningless world was tolerable and need not be explained. And never would it be, and how foolish I had ever been to think so.

The facts of my predicament warranted action.

I poured out a cup of wine, and took it with me to the front gate.

The city seemed quiet. People walked to and fro, casting their eyes away from a half-dressed, ragged woman in her vestibule.

At last a workman trudging under his burden of bricks.

I thrust forth the wine. "I have been ill for three days," I said. "What of the death of Germanicus? How goes it in the city?"

The man was so grateful for the wine. Labor had made him old. His arms were thin. His hands shook.

"Madam, thank you," he said. He drained the cup, as if he could not stop himself. "Our Germanicus was laid out in the public square for all to see. How beautiful he was. Some compared him to the great Alexander. People could not determine. Had he been poisoned or not? Some said Yes, some said No.

"His soldiers loved him. Governor Piso, thank the gods, is not here and dares not come back. Germanicus's wife, the gracious Agrippina, has the ashes of Germanicus in an urn she carries next to her breast. She sails for Rome, seeking justice for Tiberius."

He handed me the cup. "I humbly thank you."

"The city is as usual again."

"Oh, yes, what could stop this glorified marketplace?" he declared. "Business goes on as always. The loyal soldiers of Germanicus keep the peace, waiting for justice. They will not let the murderous Piso return, and Sentius gathers to himself here all who served under Germanicus. The city is happy. The flame burns for Germanicus. If there is war, it won't be here. Don't worry."

"Thank you, you have helped me marvelously much."

I took the cup, locked the gate, shut the door and went into action.

Nibbling on enough bread to give me strength, and murmuring aloud the common sense of Luretius, I surveyed the house. It had a large luxurious bath on the right side of the courtyard. Full of light.

Water flowed steadily from the seashells of the nymphs into the plastered basin, and the water was fine. There was no need to light a fire for it.

In the bedchamber were my clothes.

Roman dresses were simple, as you know, just long shifts or tunics, and we wore two or three of them, plus an outdoor cover-up tunic, the stola, and finally the palla, or mantle, which hung to the ankles and belted below the breasts.

I chose the finest tunics, composing three layers of gossamer silk, and then a brilliant red palla that covered me from head to toe.

In all my life, I had never had to put on my own sandals. This was hysterically funny and annoying!

All my toilet articles had been laid out on tables which held burnished mirrors. What a mess!

I sat down in one of the many gilded chairs, pushed the burnished metal mirror close, and tried to work with the paints as my slaves had always done.

I managed to darken my eyebrows, but my horror of the painted Egyptian eyes stopped me. I rouged my lips, put some white powder on my face, but that was it. I couldn't attempt powdering my arms, as would have been done for me in Rome.

I don't know what I looked like. Now I had to braid this damned hair, and I managed it, and fixed the braids in a big coil on the back of my head. I used enough pins for twenty women. Dragging down the loose curls around my face, on my forehead and cheeks, I saw in the mirror a Roman woman, modest and acceptable, I thought, her brown hair parted in the middle, her eyebrows black and her lips rosy red.

Gathering up all this drapery was the biggest nuisance. I attempted to match length with length. I tried to get the silk stola straight and then belt it tightly beneath my breasts. I mean, all this folding, all this drapery and fastening. I'd always had slave girls around me. Finally with two undertunics and a long, fine red stola, I snatched up a silk palla, a very large one, fringed and decorated all over with gold.

I put on rings, bracelets. But I intended to hide under this mantle as much as possible. I could remember my Father cursing every day of his life that he had to wear the toga, the official outer garment of the highborn Roman male. Well, only prostitutes wore togas. At least I didn't have to cope with that.

I headed straight for the slave markets.

Jacob was right about the population here. The city was filled with men and women of all nations. Many women walked in pairs, arm in arm.

Loose Greek cloaks were entirely acceptable here, and so were long exotic Phoenician or Babylonian gowns, both for men and women. Long hair among the men was common, as were heavy beards. Some women went about in tunics no longer than a man's. Others were completely veiled, revealing only the eyes, as they walked, accompanied by guards and servants.

The streets were cleaner than they might have been in Rome, the sewage flowing to wider gutters in the center and more swiftly to its destination.

Long before I reached the Forum, or the central plaza, I had passed three different doors in which rich courtesans stood arguing sarcastically over price with wealthy young Greeks and Romans.

One said, as I passed, to a handsome young man, "You want me in bed? You're dreaming. Any of the girls you can have, as I told you. If you want me, go home and sell everything you own!"

Rich Romans in their full togas stood at the corner wine shops, and respected my quick glance away with a simple nod as I passed.

Pray none of them would recognize me! It was not a likely thing, by any means, and we were so far from Rome, and I had lived so long in my Father's house, happily reprieved by him from banquets and suppers, and even ceremonial gatherings.

The Forum was far larger than I had remembered from my brief glimpse. When I came to the edge of it and beheld the huge square flooded with sun, flanked on all sides with porticoes or Temples or Imperial buildings, I was amazed.

In the canopied markets, everything was for sale, silversmiths grouped together, the weavers in their own place, the silk merchants in a row, and I could see down the side street that came in to my right that it was dedicated to the sale of slaves—the better slaves, who might never have to go to an auction block.

Far away I saw the high masts of the ships. I could smell the river. There stood the Temple of Augustus, its fires burning, its uniformed Legionnaires in lazy readiness.

I was hot and anxious, because my mantle kept slipping, in fact, all this silk seemed to slip and to slide, and there were many open wine gardens where women gathered in groups, chatting. I could have found a place near enough to someone to have a drink.

But I had to have a household. I had to have loyal slaves.

Now, in Rome, of course I had never gone to a slave market. I would never have had to do such a thing. Besides, we had so many families of slaves on our land in Tuscany and in Rome that we seldom if ever bought a new slave. On the contrary, my Father had a habit of inheriting the decrepit and wise from his friends, and we had often teased my Father about the Academy, which did nothing in the slaves' garden but argue about history.

But now I had to act the shrewd woman of the world. I inspected every quality household slave on display, quickly settled upon a pair of sisters, very young and very frightened that they were going to be auctioned at noon and go to a brothel. I sent for stools and we sat together.

We talked.

They came from a small fine family household in Tyre; they'd been born slaves. They knew Greek and Latin well. They spoke Aramaic. They were angelic in their sweetness.

They had immaculate hands. They demonstrated

every skill I required. They knew how to dress hair, paint a face, cook food. They rattled off recipes for Eastern dishes of which I'd never heard; they named different pomades, rouges. One of them flushed with fear, and then said, "Madam, I can paint your face for you, and very quickly and perfectly!"

I knew this meant I had made a mess of the job.

I also knew that, coming from a small household, they were far more versatile than our slaves at home.

I bought them both, the answer to their prayers; I demanded clean tunics of modest length for both of them, got the tunics, made of blue linen, though they weren't very fine, then found a roaming merchant with an armful of pallae. I brought each sister a blue mantle. They were in such happiness. They were reticent and wanted their heads covered.

I had no doubt of them. They would have died for me.

It didn't occur to me that they were starving until, while searching for other slaves, I heard a nasty slave dealer remind an impudent educated Greek that he would get no food until he was sold.

"Horrors," I said. "You girls, you're probably hungry. Go to the cookshop in the Forum. Look down the street. See there, the scattering of benches and tables."

"Alone?" they said in dismay.

"Listen, girls. I have no time to feed you like birds from my hand. Don't look any man in the eye; eat and drink what you want." I gave them a seemingly shocking amount of money. "And don't leave the cookshop till I come for you. If a man comes to you, pretend to be in terror, bow your heads and protest as best you can that you don't speak his language. If worst comes to worst, go to the Temple of Isis."

They ran together down the narrow street towards the distant banquet, their mantles such a beautiful blue as they ballooned in the breeze that I can see it even now, the color of the sky streaking through the tight sweaty crowds beneath the jumble of canopies. Mia and Lia. Not hard to remember, but I could not tell them apart.

A low derisive laughter surprised me. It was the Greek slave who had just been threatened with starvation by his Master.

He said to his Master:

"All right, starve me. And then what will you have to sell? A sickened and dying man, instead of an unusual and great scholar."

Unusual and great scholar!

I turned and looked at the man. He sat on a stool and did not rise for me. He wore nothing but a filthy loincloth, which was plain stupidity on the part of the merchant, but this neglect certainly revealed that this slave was one very handsome man, beautiful in face, with soft brown hair and long almond-shaped green eyes, and a sarcastic expression to his pretty mouth. He was maybe thirty years old, perhaps a little younger. He was fit for his age, as Greeks like to be, having a sound musculature.

His brown hair was filthy, had been hacked off, and around his neck by a rope was the most wretched small board I ever beheld, crowded with tiny cramped letters in Latin.

Pulling up the mantle again, I stepped up very close to his gorgeous naked chest, a little amused by his audacious stare, and tried to read all this.

It seemed he could have taught all philosophy, all languages, all mathematics, could sing everything, knew every poet, could prepare whole banquets, was patient with children, had known military service with his Roman Master in the Balkans, could perform as an armed guard, was obedient and virtuous and had lived all his life in Athens in one house.

I read this a bit scornfully. He glared at me impertinently when he saw this scorn. Impudently, he folded his arms just below this little plaque. He leaned back against the wall.

Suddenly I saw why the merchant, hovering near, had not made the Greek rise. The Greek had only one good leg. The left leg below the knee was made of well-carved ivory, complete with carefully engraved foot and sandal. Perfect toes. Of course it had been pieced together, this fine ivory leg and foot, but in three proportionate sections, each girded with decorative work, and separate parts for the feet, nails defined and sandal straps exquisitely carved.

I had never seen such a false limb, such a surrender to artifice rather than a meager attempt to imitate nature.

"How did you lose your leg?" I asked him in Greek. No answer. I pointed to the leg. No answer.

I asked again in Latin. Still no answer.

The slave trader was rising on his toes in his anxiety and wringing his hands.

"Mistress, he can keep records, run any business; he writes in perfect hand, keeps honest numbers."

Hmmm. So no mention of tutoring children? I did not look like a wife and mother. Not good.

The Greek sneered and looked away. He said softly under his breath in piercing Latin that if I did spend money for him, I was spending it for a dead man. His voice was soft and beautiful, though weary and full of contempt, his enunciation unaffected and refined.

I threw off all patience. I spoke quickly in Greek.

"Learn from me, you arrogant Athenian idiot!" I said, red in the face, and furious to be so misjudged both by a slave and a slave dealer. "If you can write Greek and Latin at all, if you have in fact studied Aristotle and Euclid, whose name you misspelled, by the way, if you have been schooled in Athens and have seen battle in the Balkans, if even half of this great epic is true, why wouldn't you want to belong to one of the most keenly intelligent women you'll ever meet, who'll treat you with dignity and respect in exchange for your loyalty? What do you know of Aristotle and Plato that I don't? I've never struck a slave in my life. You pass up the one mistress to whom your loyalty might earn you any reward of which you could dream. That tablet is a pack of lies, isn't it?"

The slave was stunned, but not angered. He sat

forward, trying to appraise me further, without being obvious. The merchant gestured furiously for the slave to rise to his feet, which the slave did, giving him an admirable height over me. His legs were sound and strong up to the ivory limb.

"What about telling me the real truth as to what you can do?" I said, switching to Latin.

I turned to the slave dealer. "Get me a pen to correct this, the spelling of these names. If this man has any chance of becoming a teacher, these misspellings destroy it. He looks like a fool for writing such."

"I didn't have space enough to write!" declared the slave suddenly, whispering in perfect Latin fury. He bent towards me, as if I should understand.

"Look at this little tablet, if you're so keenly intelligent! Do you realize the ignorance of this dealer here. He has not sense enough to know he has an emerald, and thinks it a piece of green glass! This is wretched. I crammed here what generalities I could."

I laughed. I was seduced and thrilled. I couldn't stop laughing. This was too funny! The slave merchant was confused. Chastise the slave and lower his value? Or let the two of us work this out?

"What was I to do," he demanded in the same confidential whisper, only this time in Greek, "shout to every man passing, 'Here sits a great teacher, here sits a philosopher!'?" He grew a little calm, having thus released this rage. "The names of my grandfathers are carved on the Acropolis at Athens," he said.

The merchant was mystified.

But I was so obviously delighted and interested.

My mantle slipped again and I gave it a hard jerk. These clothes. Had no one ever told me silk slides on silk?

"And what about Ovid?" I said, taking a deep breath. I almost laughed myself into tears. "You wrote Ovid's name here. Ovid. Is Ovid popular here? Nobody would dare write that on your card in Rome, I can tell you. You know, I don't even know if Ovid is still alive, and it's a shame. Ovid taught me to kiss when I was ten years old, when I read the *Amores*. You ever read the *Amores*?"

His entire demeanor altered. He softened and I could see he was just on the verge of hope, hope that I might be a good mistress for him. But he couldn't let himself believe it.

The merchant was waiting for the slightest signal as to what he might do. Clearly he could follow our exchanges.

"Look, you insolent one-legged slave," I said. "If I thought you could even read Ovid to me in the evenings, I'd buy you in a moment. But this tablet here makes you a glorified Socrates and Alexander the Great smashed in one. In what war in the Balkans did you carry arms? Why are you dumped in the hands of this lowly merchant rather than taken at once to some fine house? How could anyone believe all this? If blind Homer had sung such a preposterous tale, people would have gotten up and left the tavern."

He grew angry, frustrated.

The merchant put out his hand in warning, as if to control the man.

"What the hell happened to your leg?" I asked. "How did you lose it? Who made you this glorious replacement?"

Lowering his voice to an angry yet eloquent whisper, the slave declared slowly and patiently:

"I lost it in a boar hunt, with my Roman Master. He saved my life. We hunted often. It was on Pentelikon, the mountain . . ."

"I know where Pentelikon is, thank you," I said.

His facial expressions were elegant. He was utterly confused. He licked his parched lips and said:

"Just make this merchant fetch the parchment and the ink." He spoke his Latin with such beauty, the beauty of an actor or rhetorician, yet with no effort. "I'll write the *Amores* of Ovid from memory for you," he said, gently pleading through clenched teeth, which is no mean feat. "And then I'll copy out all of Xenophon's history of the Persians for you, if you have the time, in Greek, of course! My Master treated me like a son; I fought with him, studied with him, learned with him. I wrote his letters for him. His education I made my education because he wanted it so."

"Ah," I said in proud relief.

He looked the full gentleman now, angered, caught in impossible circumstance yet dignified, and reasoning with just enough spirit to strengthen his own soul.

"And in bed? Can you do it in bed?" I asked. I can't say what rage or desperation prompted this question.

He was genuinely shocked. Good sign. His eyes really widened. He furrowed his brow.

Meantime the slave trader emerged with the table, stool, parchment, ink, and set it all down on the hot cobblestones.

"Here, write," he said to the slave. "Make letters for this woman. Add sums. Or I'll kill you and sell your leg."

I broke again into helpless laughing. I looked at the slave, who still stood dazed. He broke away from my gaze to cast a disdainful look on the merchant.

"Are you safe around the slave girls?" I said patronizingly. "Are you a lover of boys?"

"I am completely trustworthy!" the slave said. "I am not capable of crimes for any Master."

"And what if I desire you in my bed? I'm the Mistress of the house, twice widowed and on my own, and I am Roman."

His face darkened. I couldn't name the emotions that seemed to pass over his expression, the sadness, indecision, confusion and ultimate perplexity that transformed him.

"Well?" I asked.

"Let's put it this way, Madam. You would be much more pleased with my recitation of Ovid than with any attempted enactment of his verses by me."

"You like boys," I said with a nod.

"I was a born a slave, Madam. I made do with

boys. I know nothing else. And I need neither." His face was crimson now, and he had lowered his eyes.

Lovely Athenian modesty.

I gestured for him to sit down.

This he did with amazing simplicity and grace, considering the circumstances: the heat, the dirt, crowds, the fragile stool and the wobbling table.

He picked up the pen and quickly wrote in flawless Greek, "Have I foolishly offended this great lady of learning and exceptional patience? Have I brought about, through rashness, my own doom?" He wrote on in Latin, "Does Lucretius tell us the truth when he says that death is nothing to fear?" He thought for a moment, and then he wrote in Greek again, "Are Virgil and Horace really equal to our great poets? Do the Romans truly believe this, or only hope it is true, knowing their achievements shine in other arts?"

I read this all very thoughtfully, smiling most agreeably. I had fallen in love with him. I looked at his thin nose, his cleft chin, and I looked into the green eyes that looked up at me.

"How did you come to this?" I asked. "A slave shop in Antioch? You're Athenian-bred, just as you say."

He tried to stand to answer. I pushed him to sit down.

"I can tell you nothing of that," he said. "Only that I was much beloved by my Master, that my Master died in his bed with his family around him. And that here I am."

"Why didn't he set you free in his will?"
"He did, Madam, and with means."
"What happened?"
"I can tell you no more."
"Why not? Who sold you, why?"
"Madam," he said, "please place a value upon my loyalty to a house in which I served all my life. I cannot speak more. If I become your servant, you will have the same loyalty from me. Your house will become my house, and sacred to me. What happens within your walls will remain within your walls. I speak of virtue and kindness in my Master because this is proper to say. Let me say no more."
Sublime old-Greek morality.
"Write more, hurry!" said the slave merchant.
"Be quiet," I told him. "He's written quite enough."
The handsome brown-haired slave, this enticingly beautiful one-legged man, had fallen into some deep pit of woe and looked towards the distant Forum, flash of figures back and forth over the mouth of the street.
"What would I do as a free man?" he said to me, looking up at me from a position of utter careless loneliness. "Copy all day for a pittance at the booksellers? Write letters for coins? My Master risked his own life to save me from that boar. In battle I served under Tiberius in Illyricum, where with some fifteen legions he put down all revolts. I chopped the head off a man to save my Master. What am I now?"
I was filled with pain.
"What am I now?" he repeated the question.

"If I were free, I would live hand to mouth, and when I slept in some filthy tenement, my ivory leg would be severed and stolen!"

I gasped and put my hand to my lips.

His eyes filled with tears as he looked at me, and his voice became all the more softer, yet sharply articulate:

"Oh, I could teach philosophy beneath the arches out there, you know, prattle on about Diogenes, and pretend that I liked wearing rags, as do his followers these days. What a circus out there, have you seen it? I have never seen so many philosophers in my life as in this city! Take a look when you go back. You know what it takes to teach philosophy here? You have to lie. You have to fling meaningless words as fast as you can at young people, and brood when you can't answer, and make up nonsense and ascribe it to the old Stoics."

He broke off, and tried to gain command of himself.

I was almost in tears as I looked down at him.

"But you see, I have no skill at lying," he said. "That has been my undoing with you, Great Lady."

I was shattered inside, my wounds silently opened. The nerve which had carried me out of confinement was ebbing away. But surely he saw my tears.

He looked towards the Forum again.

"I dream of an honorable Master or Mistress, a house with honor. Can a slave through the contemplation of honor thereby have honor? The law says not. So any slave called to testify in a court trial must be tortured, for he has no honor! But reason says otherwise. I have learned and I can teach both bravery and honor. And yes, all of this tablet is true. I didn't have time or opportunity to temper its boastful style."

He bowed his head and looked again towards the Forum, as though towards the lost world. He drew himself up in the chair, for bravery's sake. Again, he tried to stand.

"No, sit," I said.

"Madam," he said, "if you seek my services for a house of ill repute, let me tell you now . . . if it is to torture and force young girls such as those you just purchased, if you order me to advertise their charms abroad, I won't do it. It is as dishonorable to me as to steal or to lie. Why do you want me?"

The tears were halted, merely resting between him and his vision of the world around him. His face was serene.

"Do I look as if I am a whore?" I asked him with shock. "Yea gods, I wore all my best clothes. I'm doing my best to look revoltingly respectable in all these fancy silks! Do you see cruelty in my eyes? Can't you believe that it is perhaps the tempered soul that survives grief? One need not fight on a battlefield to have courage."

"No, Madam, no!" he said. He was so very sorry.

"Then why fling these insults at me now?" I said, full of hurt. "And no, I agree with you, what you've written there, our Roman poets are not the equals of the Greeks. I don't know our destiny as an Empire and this weighs as heavily on me as it ever did on my Father and his Father! Why? I don't know!" I turned as if to go, but I had really no intention of going! His insults had simply gone too far.

He bent towards me over the writing table.

"Madam," he said whispering even lower and with greater solicitude. "Forgive me my rash words. You are absolutely a paradox. Your face is eccentrically painted, and I think the lip rouge is not properly set. You have rouge on your teeth. You have no powder on your arms. You wear three dresses of silk and I can see through all of them! Your hair is in two barbarian-style braids lying on your shoulders, and you are raining little silver and gold pins galore. Look at these little pins falling. Madam, you will be hurt by these pins. Your mantle, more appropriate for evening, has fallen on the ground. Your hems drag in the dirt."

Not missing a beat of his speech, he reached down deftly and picked up the palla, standing at once to offer it to me, coming round the table with a heavy shift of his leg, to lay the palla on my shoulders.

"You speak with miraculous speed, and stunning gibes," he went on, "yet you carry a huge dagger in your girdle. It should be hidden on your forearm under your mantle. And your purse. You take gold out of it to pay the girls. It's huge, carelessly visible. And your hands, your hands are beautiful, fine as your Latin and your Greek, but they are deeply creased with dirt as though you have been digging in the Earth itself."

I smiled. I had stopped my tears.

"You are very observant," I said cheerfully. I was charmed. "Why did I have to cut you so deeply to find your soul? Why can't we simply reveal ourselves to one another? I need a strong steward, a guardian who can bear arms, run my house and protect it because I am alone. Can you really see through all this silk?"

He nodded. "Well, now that the mantle is over your shoulders and hiding the . . . the dagger and the girdle—" He blushed. Then as I smiled at him, trying to regain my calm, trying to fight back the engulfing darkness that would take away all confidence from me, all faith in any task, he spoke on.

"Madam, we learn to hide our souls because we are betrayed by others. But I would entrust to you my soul! I know it, if you would reconsider your judgment! I can protect you, I can run your house. I will not molest your little girls. But mark, for all my time fighting in Illyricum I have one leg. I came home from three years of bloody constant battle to lose it to a boar because a spear, poorly tempered and made, broke as I thrust it into the boar."

"What's your name?" I asked.

"Flavius," he answered. This was a Roman name.

"Flavius," I said.

"Madam, the palla is slipping again from your head. And these little pins, they are sharp, they are everywhere, they'll hurt you."

"Never mind that," I said, though I let him drape me again properly as if he were Pygmalion, and I his

Galatea. He used the tips of his fingers. But the mantle was already soiled.

"Those girls," I said, "whom you glimpsed. They are my household, as of the past half-hour. You have to be their loving master. But if you lie in any woman's bed under my roof, the bed had better be mine. I am flesh and blood!"

He nodded, at a total loss for words.

I pulled open my purse and took out what I thought to pay, a reasonable price in Rome, I thought, where slaves were always bragging about how much they had cost. I laid down the gold, oblivious to the imprint of the coin, only gauging the value.

The slave stared at me with ever increasing fascination, then his eyes whipped the merchant.

The slimy, merciless, weasling slave trader puffed up like a toad and told me this priceless Greek scholar was to be auctioned for a high price. Several rich men had expressed interest. An entire school class was to question him within the hour. Roman officers had sent their stewards to inspect him.

"I have no more stamina for it," I said, and reached in my purse again.

At once, my new slave Flavius put his hand out gently to prevent me.

He glared at the merchant with great authority and fearless contempt.

"For a man with one leg!" said Flavius between his teeth. "You thief! You charge my Mistress that, here in Antioch, where slaves are so plentiful the ships take them on to Rome, for it's the only way to cut their losses!"

I was quite impressed. All had gone so well. The darkness flowed back away from me, and there seemed for the moment a divine meaning in the warmth of the sun.

"You cheat my Mistress and you know it! You're the scum of the Earth!" he went on. "Madam, do we ever purchase from this scoundrel again? I advise never!"

The slave trader broke into an inane smile, a hideous grimace of cowardice and stupidity, bowed and gave me back a third of what I'd given him.

I could hardly keep from another burst of laughing. I had to fetch the mantle from the ground again. Flavius did it. This time, I knotted it properly in front.

I looked at the gold which had been returned, scooped it up, entrusted it to Flavius and off we went.

When we had plunged into the thick crowd in the center of the Forum I did laugh and laugh at the whole affair.

"Well, Flavius, you're protecting me already, saving me money, giving me excellent advice. If there were more men like you in Rome, the world might be better for it."

He was choked up. He couldn't talk. It was an effort to whisper:

"Lady, you have on trust my body and soul forever."

I went up on tiptoe and kissed his cheek. I realized

that his nakedness, the filth of the loincloth, all this was a disgrace he bore without a sign of protest.

"Here," I said, giving him some money. "Take the girls home, put them to work, then you go to the baths. Get clean. Get Roman clean. Have a boy if you want. Have two. Then buy fine clothes for yourself, not slave clothes, mind you, but clothes that you would buy for a rich young Roman Master!"

"Madam, please hide that purse!" he said as he took the coins. "And what is my Mistress's name? To whom shall I say I belong, if asked."

"To Pandora of Athens," I said. "Though you shall have to fill me in on the current state of my birthplace, because I have never actually been there. But a Greek name serves me well. Now, go. See, the girls watch!"

Lots of people were watching. Oh, this red silk! And Flavius was such a splendid figure of a male.

I kissed him again, and whispered in his ear, calculatingly, devil that I am, "I need you, Flavius."

He looked down at me, awestruck. "I am yours forever, Madam," he whispered.

"Are you sure you can't do with me in bed!"

"Oh, believe me, I have tried!" he confessed, flushing again.

I made my hand into a fist and punched his muscular arm.

"Very well," I said.

The damsels had already risen, at my gesture. They knew I sent him to them.

I gave him my key, the directions to my house, described the particularities of its gate, and the old bronze lion fountain right inside the gate.

"And you, Madam?" he asked. "You're going in the crowd unaccompanied? Madam, the purse is huge! It's full of gold."

"Wait till you see the gold in the house," I said. "Appoint yourself the only one who can open chests, and then hide them in obvious places. Replace all the furniture I've smashed in my . . . my solitude. There are many pieces stored in rooms above."

"Gold in the house!" He was alarmed. "Chests of gold!"

"Now, don't worry about me," I said. "I know where to seek help now. And if you betray me, if you steal my legacy and I find my house ruined when I return, I suppose I shall have deserved it. Cover up the chests of gold with carpets. The place has heaps of little Persian carpets. Look upstairs. And tend to the Shrine!"

"I shall do everything you ask and more."

"So I thought. A man who cannot lie cannot steal. Now the sun is intolerable here. Go to the girls. They wait."

I turned.

He caught me by coming round in front of me.

"Madam, there is something I must tell you."

"What!" I said with an ominous face. "Not that you're a eunuch," I said. "Eunuchs don't grow muscles in their arms and legs like that."

"No," he said. Then he took on a sudden gravity. "Ovid, you spoke of Ovid. Ovid is dead. Ovid died two years ago in the wretched town of Tomis on the upper rim of the Black Sea. It was a miserable choice of exile, a barbarian outpost."

"No one told me this. What a revolting silence." I threw up my hands over my face. The mantle fell. He retrieved it. I scarce noticed. "I had so prayed that Tiberius would let Ovid come back to Rome!" I told myself I had no time to stop for this. "Ovid. No time to weep for him now . . ."

"His books are no doubt plentiful here," Flavius said. "They are very easily found in Athens."

"Good, perhaps you will have time to find some for me. Now, I'm off; pins or tumbled braids or sliding mantle, I do not care. And don't look so worried. When you leave the house, just lock up the girls and the gold."

When I finally turned around he was making his way rather gracefully towards the girls. The sun rippled prettily on his well-muscled back. His hair was curly and brown, rather like my own. He stopped for one moment when a vendor attacked him with an armful of cheaply made tunics, cloaks and whatnot, more than likely stolen goods, full of dye that would run in the first rain, but who knows? He bought a tunic hastily and slipped it over his head, and purchasing a red sash, tied it around his waist.

Such a transformation. The tunic went halfway to his knees. That must have been a great relief to him, to have on something clean. I should have thought of this before I left him. Stupid.

I admired him. Naked or clothed, you can't carry such beauty and dignity unless you have been cherished. He wore the raiment of the affection bestowed on him and inscribed in the art of his ivory leg.

In our brief encounter, a bond had been forged forever.

He greeted the girls. With his arms around them, he guided them out of the crowd.

I went straight to the Temple of Isis, and thereby, unwittingly, took the first firm step towards a larcenous immortality, an inglorious and unearned supernature, a never ending and utterly useless doom.

5

S SOON as I entered the Temple Compound I was received by several rich Roman women, who welcomed me generously. They were all properly painted with white on their arms and their faces, well-drawn eyebrows, lip color—all the details of which I'd made a hash that morning.

I explained that though I had means, I was on my own. They were for helping me in every way. When they heard I had been actually initiated in Rome, they were in awe.

"Thank Mother Isis they didn't discover you and execute you," said one of the Roman women.

"Go in and see the Priestess," they said. Many of them had not yet undergone the secret ceremonies and were waiting to be called by the goddess for this momentous event.

There were many other women here, some Egyptian, some Babylonian perhaps. I could only guess. Jewels and silks were the order of the day. Fancy painted gold borders lined their mantles; some wore simple dresses.

But it seemed to me that all of them spoke Greek.

I couldn't bring myself to enter the Temple. I looked up and saw in my mind our crucified Priests in Rome.

"Thank God you were not identified," said one.

"Quite a few people fled to Alexandria," said another.

"I raised no protest," I said dismally.

There came a chorus of sympathy. "How could you, under Tiberius? Believe me, every one who could escaped."

"Don't be laden with misery," said a young blue-eyed Greek woman, very properly dressed.

"I'd fallen away from the worship," I said.

Again came a comforting round of soft voices.

"Go in now," said one woman, "and ask to pray in the very sanctuary of Our Mother. You are an initiate. Most of us here are not."

I nodded.

I went up the steps of the Temple and entered inside it.

I paused to shake from my mantle the mundane, that is, all the trivia I had discussed. My mind was focused upon the goddess, and desperate to believe in her. I loathed my hypocrisy, that I used this Temple and this worship, but then it didn't seem significant. My despair of the three nights had penetrated too deep.

What a shock awaited me as I found myself inside.

The Temple was far more ancient than our Temple in Rome, and Egyptian paintings covered its walls. A shiver at once went through me. The columns were in the Egyptian style, not fluted but smoothly round, and brightly painted in orange, and rising to giant lotus leaves at the capitals. The smell of the incense was overpowering and I could hear music emanating from the Sanctuary. I could hear the thin notes of the lyre, and of the wires of the sistrum being plucked, and I could hear a litany being chanted.

But this was a thoroughly Egyptian place, which enveloped me as firmly as my blood dreams. I almost fainted.

The dreams came back—the deep paralytic sense of being in some secret Sanctuary in Egypt, my soul swallowed within another body!

The Priestess came to me. This too was a shock.

In Rome, her dress would have been purely Roman, and she might have worn a small exotic headdress, a little cap to her shoulders, perhaps.

But this woman wore Egyptian clothes of pleated linen, in the old style, and she wore a magnificent Egyptian headdress and wig, the broad mass of long black braids falling down stiffly over her shoulders. She looked as extravagant perhaps as Cleopatra had ever looked, for all I knew.

I had only heard stories of Julius Caesar's love of Cleopatra, then her affair with Mark Antony and Cleopatra's death. All that was before my birth.

But I knew that Cleopatra's fabulous entrance

into Rome had much affrighted the old Roman sense of morality. I had always known the old Roman families feared Egyptian magic. In the recent punitive Roman massacre, which I've described, there was a lot of shouting about license and lust; but beneath it, there had been an unspoken fear of the mystery and the power hidden behind the Temple doors.

And now as I gazed at this Priestess, at her painted eyes, I felt in my soul this fear. I knew it. Of course this woman seemed to have stepped from the dreams, but it was not that which struck me so much, for after all, what are dreams? This was an Egyptian woman—wholly alien and inscrutable to me.

My Isis had been Greco-Roman. Even her statue in the Roman Sanctuary had been clothed in a gorgeously draped Greek dress and her hair had been done softly in the old Greek style, with waves around her face. She had held her sistrum and an urn. She had been a Romanized goddess.

Perhaps the same had happened with the goddess Cybele in Rome. Rome swallowed things and made them Roman.

In a very few centuries, though I had no thought of it then—how could I—Rome would swallow and shape the followers of Jesus of Nazareth, and make of his Christians the Roman Catholic church.

I suppose you are familiar with the modern expression, "When in Rome, do as the Romans do."

But here, in this reddish gloom, among flickering lights and a deeper muskier incense than I had ever smelled, I resented my timidity in silence. Then the dreams did descend, like so many veils lowered one by one to enclose me. In a flash I saw the beautiful Queen weeping. No. She screamed. Cried for help.

"Get away from me," I whispered to the air around me. "Fly from me, all things that are impure and evil. Get away from me as I enter the house of my Blessed Mother."

The Priestess took me in hand. I heard voices from my dream in violent argument. I strained to clear my vision, to see the worshipers coming and going towards the Sanctuary to meditate or to make sacrifice, to ask for some favor. I tried to realize it was a big busy crowd, very little different from Rome.

But the touch of the Priestess enfeebled me. Her painted eyes struck terror. Her broad necklace caused me to blink my eyes. Row upon row of flat stones.

I was taken into a private apartment of the Temple by her, offered a sumptuous couch. I lay back exhausted. "Fly from me, all things evil," I whispered. "Including dreams."

The Priestess sat beside me and enfolded me in her silken arms. I looked up into a mask!

"Talk to me, suffering one," she said in Latin with a thick accent. "Speak all that must come forth."

Suddenly—uncontrollably—I poured out my whole family story, the annihilation of my family, my guilt, my travails.

"What if I was the cause of my family's downfall—my worship at the Temple of Isis? What if Tiberius had remembered it? What have I done? The Priests were crucified and I did nothing. What does Mother Isis want of me? I want to die."

"That she does *not* want of you," said the Priestess, staring at me. Her eyes were huge, or was it the paint? No, I could see the whites of her eyes, so glistening and pure. Her painted mouth let loose words like a tiny breeze in a monotone.

I was fast becoming delirious and totally unreasonable. I murmured what I could about my initiation, what details I could tell a Priestess, for all these things were highly secret, you know, but I confirmed for her that I had been reborn in the rites.

All the stored-up weakness in me was cut loose in a flood.

Then I lay down my guilt. I confessed that I had, early on, left the Cult of Isis, that in recent years, I had walked only in the public processions to the sea, when the goddess was carried to the shore to bless the ships. Isis, the goddess of Navigation. I had not lived a life of devotion.

I had done nothing when the Priests of Isis were crucified, except speak out with many others behind the Emperor's back. There had been a solidarity between me and those Romans who thought Tiberius was a monster, but we had not raised our voices in defense of Isis. My Father had told me to remain silent. So I had. This was the same Father who had told me to live.

I turned over and slipped down off this couch and I lay on the tiled floor. I don't know why. I pressed my cheek to the cold tile. I liked the coldness against my face. I was in a state of madness, but not an uncontrollable state. I lay staring.

I knew one thing. I wanted to get out of this Temple! I didn't like it. No, this had been a very bad idea.

I hated myself suddenly for having become so vulnerable to this woman, whatever sort she was, and the atmosphere of the blood dreams beckoned to me.

I opened my eyes. The Priestess bent over me. I saw the weeping Queen of my nightmares. I turned away and shut my eyes.

"Be at peace," she said in her calculated and perfected voice. "You did nothing wrong," said the Priestess.

It seemed preposterous that such a voice should issue from such a painted face and form, but the voice was definite.

"First," the Priestess said, "you must understand that Mother Isis forgives anything. She is the Mother of Mercy." Then she said, "You have been more fully initiated by your description than most here or anywhere. You made a long fast. You bathed in the sacred blood of the bull. You must have drunk the potion. You dreamed and saw yourself reborn."

"Yes," I said, trying to revive the old ecstasy, the priceless gift of belief in something. "Yes. I saw the stars and great fields of flowers, such fields . . ."

It was no good. I was scared of this woman and I wanted to get out of there. I'd go home and confess all this to Flavius and make him let me weep on his shoulder.

"I am not pious by nature," I confessed. "I was young. I loved the free women who went there, the women who slept with whom they chose, the whores of Rome, the keepers of the houses of pleasure, I liked women who thought for themselves, and followed the goings-on of the Empire."

"You can enjoy such company here as well," said the Priestess, without batting an eye. "And don't fear that your old ties to the Temple caused your downfall in Rome. We have plenty of news to confirm that the highborn were not persecuted by Tiberius when he destroyed the Temple. It is always the poor who suffer: the street whore and the simple weaver, the hairdresser, the bricklayer. No noble family was persecuted in the name of Isis. You know that. Some women fled to Alexandria because they would not give up the worship, but they were never in danger."

The dreams approached. "Oh, Mother of God," I whispered.

The Priestess went on talking.

"You, like Mother Isis, have been the victim of tragedy. And you, like Mother Isis, must take strength and walk alone, as Isis did when her husband, Osiris, was slain. Who helped her when she searched all over Egypt for the body of her murdered husband, Osiris? She walked alone. She is the greatest of the goddesses. When she recovered the body of her husband, Osiris, and could find no organ of generation for him with which she might be impregnated, she drew the semen right from his spirit. Thus, the god Horus was born of a woman and a god. It was the power of Isis who drew the spirit from the dead man. It is Isis who tricked the god Ra into revealing his name."

That was the old tale all right.

I looked away from the Priestess. I was unable to look at her decorated face! Surely she felt my revulsion. I must not hurt her. She meant well. It wasn't her fault that she looked to me like a monster. Why in hell had I come here!

I lay dazed. The room had a soft golden light coming mainly through its three doors, and they were cut Egyptian-style, these doors, wider at the base than at the top, and I let this light make a blur of my vision. I asked the light to do this.

I felt the Priestess's hand. Such silken warmth. So lovely, her touch, her sweetness.

"Do you believe all of it!" I suddenly whispered.

She completely ignored this question. Her painted mask gave forth the creed.

"You must be like Mother Isis. Depend on no one. You don't have the burden of recovering a lost husband or father. You are free. Receive into your house men with love as you choose. You belong to no one but Mother Isis. Remember, Isis is the goddess who loves, the goddess who forgives, the goddess of infinite understanding because she herself has suffered!"

"Suffered!" I gasped. I moaned, a very uncommon sound for me, most of my life. But I saw the weeping Queen of my nightmares, bound to her throne.

"Listen to this," I said, "the dreams I will now recount, and then tell me why it is happening." I knew my voice sounded angry. I was sorry for it. "These dreams don't come from wine or potions, or after long periods of wakefulness that twist the mind."

Then I launched into another totally unplanned confession.

I told this woman of the blood dreams, the dreams of ancient Egypt in which I had drunk blood—the altar, the Temple, the desert, the sun rising.

"Amon Ra!" I said. This was the Egyptian name for the sun god, but I had never spoken it to my knowledge. I said it now. "Yes, Isis tricked him into revealing his name, but he killed me and I was her blood drinker, do you hear me, a thirsty god!"

"No!" said the Priestess. She sat motionless.

She thought for a long while. I had scared her and now this scared me all the more.

"Can you read the ancient picture writing of Egypt?" she asked.

"No," I said.

Then she said, in a more relaxed and vulnerable tone:

"You speak of very old legends, legends buried in the history of our worship of Isis and Osiris; that they once did indeed take the blood of their victims as sacrifice. There are scrolls here that tell of this. But nobody can really decipher them, except for one . . ."

Her voice trailed off.

"Who is the one?" I asked. I sat up on my elbows. I realized the plaits of my hair had come undone. Good. It felt good because it was free now and clean. I raked my hair with both hands.

What did it feel like to be entombed in paint and wig like this Priestess?

"Tell me," I said, "who is the one who can read these legends. Tell me!"

"These are evil tales," she said, "that Isis herself and Osiris live on, somewhere, in material form, taking blood even now." She made an expression of denial and disgust. "But this is not our worship! We sacrifice no humans here! Egypt was old and wise before Rome was born!"

Who was she trying to convince? Me?

"I've never had such dreams, in a string like this, with the same theme."

She became very worked up with her declarations.

"Our Mother Isis has no taste for blood. She has conquered death and set her husband Osiris as King of the Dead, but for us, she is life itself. She didn't send you these dreams."

"Probably not! I agree with you. But then who did? Where do they come from? Why did they pursue me at sea? Who is this one who can read the old writing?"

She was shaken. She had let go of me and she stared off, her eyes taking on a deceptive ferocity due to the black lining.

"Perhaps somewhere in childhood you heard an old tale, maybe an old Egyptian Priest told it to you. You forgot it, and now it flames in your tortured mind. It feeds on fires to which it has no right—your Father's death."

"Yes, well, I certainly hope so, but I've never known an old Egyptian. At the Temple, the Priests were Roman. Besides, if we take the dreams and lay them out, what is the pattern there? Why is the Queen weeping? Why does the sun kill me? The Queen is in fetters. The Queen is a prisoner. The Queen is in agony!"

"Stop." The Priestess shuddered. Then she put her arms around me, as if it was she who needed me. I felt her stiff linen and the thick hair of her wig, and beneath it the hurried pounding of her heart. "No," she said. "You're possessed of a demon, and we can drive this demon out of you! Maybe the way was opened for this wretched demon when your Father was attacked at his own Hearth."

"You really believe it's possible?" I asked.

"Listen," she said as casually now as one of the women outside. "I want you to be bathed, to have fresh garments. This money, what portion can you give me? If none, we will provide all for you. We are rich here."

"Here's plenty. I don't care." I pulled the purse loose from my girdle.

"I will have everything done for you. Fresh clothes. This silk is too fragile."

"You are telling me!" I said.

"This mantle is torn. Your hair is uncombed."

I spilled out a dozen or so gold coins, more than I had paid for Flavius.

It shocked her, but she covered up the shock very quickly. Suddenly she stared at me, and her painted mask managed to make a flexible expression, a frown. I thought it might crack.

I thought she might weep. I was becoming a regular expert in making people weep. Mia and Lia had wept. Flavius had wept. Now she was going to cry. The Queen in the dream was crying!

I laughed in madness, throwing back my head, but then I saw the Queen! I saw her in distant wavery recollection, and I felt such sorrow that I too could have cried. My mockery was blasphemy. It was a lie unto myself.

"Take the gold for the Temple," I said. "Take it for new clothes, for all I need. But my offering to the goddess, I want it to be flowers, and bread, warm from the oven, a small loaf."

"Very good," she said with an eager nod. "That is what Isis wants. She wants no blood. No! No blood!"

She started to help me up.

I paused. "In the dream, you understand that she weeps. She is not happy with these blood drinkers, she protests, she objects. She herself is not the one who drinks blood."

The Priestess was confounded, and then she nodded. "Yes, that is obvious, is it not?"

"I too protest and suffer," I said.

"Yes, come," she said leading me through a thick tall door. She left me in the hands of the Temple slaves. I was relieved. I was weary.

I was taken into the ceremonial bath, cleansed by Temple maidens and re-dressed carefully by Temple maidens.

What a pleasure to have it all done right.

For a little while I wondered helplessly if they would frame me in white pleats and black plaits but they used the Roman style.

My hair was properly done by these girls in a correct circlet that would hold, leaving a generous frame of ringlets around the face.

The clothes given me were new and made of fine linen. Flowers had been stitched along the borders. This finery, so precise, so minute, seemed more valuable than gold.

It certainly gave more joy to me than gold.

I felt so tired! I was so grateful.

The girls then made up my face more artfully than I could have done it, and more in the Egyptian style, and I flinched when I saw myself in the mirror. Flinched. It wasn't the full paint of the Priestess, but my eyes were rimmed with black.

"How dare I complain?" I whispered.

I put down the mirror. One doesn't have to see oneself, fortunately.

I emerged into the great hall of the Temple, a proper Roman woman, with the extravagant face paint of the East. A common sight in Antioch.

I found the Priestess with two others, as formally dressed as she, and a Priest who wore the same old-fashioned Egyptian headdress, only he wore no wig, just a striped hood. His tunic was short, pleated. He turned and glared at me as I came forward.

Fear. Crushing fear. Flee this place! Forget about the offering, or have them make it for you. Go home. Flavius is waiting. Get out!

I was struck dumb. I let the Priest draw me aside.

"Pay attention," he said to me gently. "I will take you now into the holy place. I will let you talk to the Mother. But when you come out, you must come to me! Don't leave without coming to me. You must promise me, you will return each day, and if you have more of these dreams, you will lay them before us. There is one to whom they should be told, that is, unless the goddess drives them from your mind."

"Of course I will tell anyone who can help," I said. "I hate these dreams. But why are you so anxious? Are you afraid of me?"

He shook his head. "I don't fear you, but there is something I must confide to you. I must talk to you either today or tomorrow. I must speak with you. Go now to the Mother, then come to me."

The others led me to the chamber of the Sanctuary; there were white linen curtains before the shrine. I saw my sacrifice lying there, a great garland of sweet-smelling white flowers, and the warm loaf of bread. I knelt. The curtains were pulled back by unseen hands and I found myself alone in the chamber kneeling before the *Regina Caeli*, the Queen of Heaven.

Another shock.

This was an ancient Egyptian statue of our Isis, carved from dark basalt. Her headdress was long, narrow, pushed behind her ears. On her head she wore a great disk between horns. Her breasts were bare. On her lap sat the adult Pharaoh, her son Horus. She held her left breast to offer him her milk.

I was struck with despair! This image meant nothing to me! I groped for the essence of Isis in this image.

"Did you send me the dreams, Mother!" I whispered.

I laid out the flowers. I broke the bread.

I heard nothing in the silence from the serene and ancient statue.

I prostrated myself on the floor, stretching out my arms. And from the depths of my soul, I struggled to say, I accept, I believe, I am yours, I need you, I need you!

But I wept. All was lost to me. Not merely Rome and my family, but even my Isis. This goddess was the embodiment of the faith of another nation, another people.

Very slowly a calm settled over me.

Is it so, I thought. The Cult of my Mother is in all

places, North and South and East and West. It is the spirit of this Cult which gives it power. I need not literally kiss the feet of this effigy. That is not the point.

I raised my head slowly, then sat back on my heels. A real revelation came upon me. I cannot fully record it. I knew it, fully, in an instant.

I knew that all things were symbols of other things! I knew that all rituals were enactments of other happenings! I knew that out of our practical human minds we devised these things with an immensity of soul that would not allow the world to be devoid of meaning.

And this statue represented love. Love above cruelty. Love above injustice. Love above loneliness and condemnation.

That was what mattered, that single thing. I stared up at the face of the goddess and I knew her! I stared at the little Pharaoh, the proffered breast.

"I am yours!" I said coldly.

Her stark primitive Egyptian features were no obstacle to my heart; I looked at the right hand which held her breast.

Love. This requires strength from us; this requires endurance; this requires an acceptance of all that is unknown.

"Take the dreams away from me, Heavenly Mother," I said. "Or reveal their purpose. And the path I must follow. Please."

Then in Latin I said an old litany:

You are she who has separated the Heavens and the Earth.
You are she who rises in the Dog Star.
You are she who makes strong the right.
You are she who makes the children to love their parents.
You are she who decreed mercy for all who ask for it.

I believed these words, but in a wholly profane way. I believed them because I saw her worship as having collected together from the minds of men and women the best ideas of which men and women were capable. That was the function for which a goddess existed; that was the spirit from which she drew her vitality.

The lost phallus of Osiris exists in the Nile. And the Nile inseminates the fields. Oh, it was so lovely.

The trick was not to reject it, as Lucretius might have suggested, but to realize what her image meant. To extract from that image the best in my own soul.

And when I looked down at the beautiful white flowers, I thought, "It is your wisdom, Mother, that these bloom." And I meant by that only that the world itself was filled with so much to be cherished, preserved, honored, that pleasure itself was resplendent—and she, Isis, embodied these concepts that were too deep to be called ideas.

I loved her—this expression of goodness which was Isis.

The longer I looked at her stone face, the more it seemed she saw me. An old trick. The more I knelt there, the more it seemed she spoke to me. I allowed this to happen, fully aware that it meant nothing. The dreams were remote. They seemed a puzzle which would find its idiot resolution.

Then with true fervor, I crawled towards her and kissed her feet.

My worship was over.

I went out refreshed, jubilant.

I wasn't going to have those dreams anymore. There was still daylight. I was happy.

I found many friends in the courtyard of the Temple, and sitting down with them under the olive trees, I drew out of them all the information I needed for practical life, how to get caterers, hair-dressers, all that. Where to buy this thing and the other.

In other words, I was armed by my rich friends with full equipment to run a fine house without actually cluttering it up with slaves I didn't want. I could stick with Flavius and the two girls. Excellent. Anything else could be hired or bought.

Finally, very tired, with my head full of names to remember and directions to recall, and very amused with the jokes and stories of these women, delighted by their ease in speaking Greek—which I had always loved—I sat back and thought, I can go home now.

I can begin.

The Temple was still very busy. I looked at the doors. Where was the Priest? Well, I would come back tomorrow. I didn't want to revive those dreams now, that was certain. Many people were coming and going with flowers and bread and some with birds to be set free for the goddess, birds that would take wing out of the high window of her Sanctuary.

How warm it was here. What a blaze of flowers covered the wall! I had never thought there could be a place as beautiful as Tuscany, but maybe this place was beautiful too.

I went out of the courtyard, before the steps, and into the Forum.

I approached a man under the arches who was teaching a group of young boys all of what Diogenes has espoused, that we give up the flesh and all its pleasures, that we live pure lives in denial of the senses.

It was so much as Flavius had described it. But the man meant his words, and was well versed. He spoke of a liberating resignation. He caught my fancy. For this is what I thought had come to me in the Temple, a liberating resignation.

The boys who listened were too young to know this. But I knew it. I liked him. He had gray hair and wore a simple long tunic. He was not ostentatiously in rags.

I at once interrupted. With a humble smile I offered the counsel of Epicurus, that the senses wouldn't have been given us were they not good. Wasn't this so? "Must we deny ourselves? Look, back at the courtyard of the Temple of Isis, look at the flowers covering the top of the wall! Is this not something to savor? Look at the roaring red of those flowers! Those flowers are in themselves enough to lift a person out of sorrow. Who is to say that eyes are wiser than hands or lips?"

The young men turned to me. I fell into discussions with several of them. How fresh and pretty they were. There were long-haired men from Babylon and even highborn Hebrews here, all with very hairy arms and chests, and many colonial Romans who were dazzled by the points I made, that in the flesh and in the wine, we find the truth of life.

"The flowers, the stars, the wine, the kisses of one's lover, all is part of Nature, surely," I said. I was of course on fire, having just come from the Temple, having just unburdened all fears and having resolved all doubts. I was for the moment invincible. The world was new.

The Teacher, whose name was Marcellus, came from under the arch to greet me.

"Ah, Gracious Lady, you amaze me," he said. "But from whom did you really learn what you believe? Was it from Lucretius? Or was it from experience? You realize that we must not ever encourage people to abandon themselves to the senses!"

"Have I said anything about abandon?" I asked. "To yield is not to abandon. It is to honor. I speak of a prudent life; I speak of listening to the wisdom of our bodies. I speak of the ultimate intelligence of kindness, and enjoyment. And if you will know,

Lucretius didn't teach me as much as one might think. He was always too dry for me, you know. I learned to embrace the glory of life from poets like Ovid."

The crowd of boys cheered.

"I learnt from Ovid," came shout after shout.

"Well, that's fine, but remember your manners as well as your lessons," I said firmly.

More cheering. Then the young men began tossing out verses from Ovid's *Metamorphoses*.

"That's splendid," I declared. "How many here? Fifteen. Why don't you come to my house for a supper?" I asked. "Five nights from now, all of you. I need the time to prepare. I have many books I want to show you. I promise you, I will show you what a delicious feast can do for the soul!"

My invitation was accepted with amusement and laughter. I disclosed the location of my house.

"I am a widow. My name is Pandora. I invite you with all propriety, and the feast awaits you. Don't expect dancing boys and girls, for you will not find them under my roof. Expect delicious food. Expect poetry. Which of you can sing the verses of Homer? Truly sing them? Which of you sings them now from memory for pleasure!"

Laughter, conviviality. Victory. It seemed everybody could do this, and welcomed the opportunity. Someone made a soft mention of another Roman woman who would be most jealous when she discovered she had competition in Antioch.

"Nonsense," said another, "her table is overcrowded. Lady, may I kiss your hand?"

"You must tell me who she is," I said. "I'll welcome her. I want to know her, and what I can learn from her."

The Teacher was smiling. I slipped him some money.

It was getting dusk. I sighed. Look. The rising stars of the tinted evening that precedes blackness.

I received the boys' chaste kisses and confirmed our feast.

But something had changed. It was as quick as the opening of one's eyes. Ah, painted eyes, no.

Perhaps it was only the awful pall of twilight.

I felt a shudder. *It is I who summoned you.* Who spoke those words? *Beware, for you would be stolen from me now and I will not have it.*

I was dumbstruck. I held the teacher's hand warmly. He talked about moderation in living. "Look at my plain tunic," he said. "These boys have so much money, they can destroy themselves."

The boys protested.

But this was dim to me. I tried to listen. My eyes roved. Whence came that voice! Who spoke those words! Who summoned me and who would attempt the theft?

Then to my silent astonishment I saw a man, his head covered by his toga, watching me. I knew him immediately, by his forehead and his eyes. I recognized his walk now as he moved steadily away.

This was my brother, the youngest, Lucius, the one I despised. It had to be him. And behold the sly manner in which he fled from notice into the shadows.

I knew the whole person. Lucius. He waited at the end of the long portico.

I couldn't move, and it was getting dark. All the merchants who are open only in the day were gone. The taverns were putting out their lanterns or torches. One bookseller remained open, with great displays of books under the lamps above.

Lucius—my much detested youngest brother—not coming to welcome me with tears but gliding in the shadows of the portico. Why?

I feared I knew.

Meantime, the boys were begging me to go to the nearby wine garden with them, a lovely place. They were fighting over who would pay for my supper there.

Think, Pandora. This sweet little invitation is some keen test of the degree of my daring and freedom. And I should not go to a common tavern with the boys! But within moments I would be alone.

The Forum grew quiet. The fires blazed before the Temples. But there were great spaces of darkness. The man in the toga waited.

"No, I must be off now," I said. Desperately I thought, what I shall I do for a torchbearer? Dare I ask these youths to see me home? I could see their slaves waiting about, some already lighting their torches or lanterns.

Singing came from the Temple of Isis.

It was I who summoned you. Beware . . . for me and my purpose!

"This is madness," I muttered, waving goodnight to those who left in pairs or trios. I forced smiles and kind words.

I glared at the distant figure of Lucius, who now slouched at the end of the portico in front of doors closed for the night. His very posture was furtive and cowardly.

Quite suddenly, I felt a hand on my shoulder. I brushed it off immediately, wishing to lay down limits to such familiarity, and then I realized a man was whispering in my ear:

"The Priest at the Temple begs for you to come back, Madam. He needs to talk with you. He did not mean for you to leave without talking."

I turned to see a Priest there beside me, in full Egyptian headdress and impeccable white linen and wearing a medallion of the goddess around his neck.

Oh, thank Heaven.

But before I could recover myself or answer, another man had stepped up boldly, heaving forward his ivory leg and foot. Two torchbearers accompanied him. We were embraced by a warm light.

"Does my Mistress wish to talk to this Priest?" he asked.

It was Flavius. He had followed my commands. He was wonderfully dressed as a Roman gentleman in the long tunic and a loose cloak. As a slave, he couldn't wear a toga. His hair was neat and trimmed and looked as impressive as any free man's. He was shining clean and appeared completely confident.

Marcellus, the Philosopher-Teacher, lingered. "Lady Pandora, you are most gracious, and let me assure you that the tavern these boys frequent may give rise to another Aristotle or Plato but it is not a fit place for you."

"I know that," I said. "Don't worry."

The Teacher looked warily at the Priest and at the handsome Flavius. I slipped my arm about Flavius's waist. "This is my steward, who will welcome you the night you come to me. Thank you for letting me disrupt your teaching. You're a kind man."

The Teacher's face stiffened. Then he leaned closer. "There's a man under the portico; don't look at him now, but you need more slaves to protect you. This city is divided, dangerous."

"Yes, so you see him too," I said. "And his glorious toga, the mark of his genteel birth!"

"It's getting dark," Flavius said. "I'll hire more torchbearers now and a litter. Right over there."

He thanked the Teacher, who reluctantly slipped away.

The Priest. He was still waiting. Flavius gestured for two more torchbearers and they came trotting to join us. We now had a plenitude of light.

I turned to the Priest. "I will come to the Temple directly, but I must first talk with that man over there! The man in the shadows?" I pointed quite visibly. I stood in a flood of light. I might as well have been on a stage.

I saw the distant figure cringe and try to fade into the wall.

"Why?" Flavius asked with about as much humility as a Roman Senator. "Something is very wrong about that man. He's hovering. The Teacher was right."

"I know," I answered. I heard the dim, echoing laughter of a woman! Yea gods, I had to stay sane long enough to get home! I looked at Flavius. He had not heard the laughter.

There was one sure way to do this. "You torch-bearers, all of you, come with me," I said to the four of them. "Flavius, you stand here with the Priest and watch as I greet this man. I know him. Come only if I call."

"Oh, I don't like it," said Flavius.

"Neither do I," said the Priest. "They want you in the Temple, Madam, and we have many guards to escort you home."

"I won't disappoint you," I said, but I walked straight towards the toga-clad figure, crossing yard after yard of paved squares, the torches flaring around me.

The toga-clad man gave a violent start, with his whole body, and then he took a few steps away from the wall.

I stopped, still out in the square.

He had to come closer. I wasn't going to move. The four torches gasped and blew in the breeze.

Anybody anywhere near could see us. We were the brightest thing in the Forum.

The man approached. He walked slow, then fast. The light struck his face. He was consumed with rage.

"Lucius," I whispered. "I see you, but I can't believe what I see."

"Nor can I," he said. "What the hell are you doing here?" he said to me.

"What?" I was too baffled to answer.

"Our family is in disgrace in Rome and you're making a spectacle of yourself in the middle of Antioch! Look at you! Painted and perfumed and your hair full of ointment! You are a whore."

"Lucius!" I cried. "What in the name of the gods are you thinking? Our Father is dead! Your own brothers may be dead. How did you escape? Why aren't you glad to see me? Why don't you take me to your house?"

"Glad to see you!" he hissed. "We are in hiding here, you bitch!"

"How many of you? Who? What about Antony? What happened to Flora?"

He sneered with exasperation.

"They are murdered, Lydia, and if you do not get yourself to some safe corner where no roaming citizen of Rome can find you, you are dead too. Oh, that you would turn up here, spouting philosophy! Everybody in the taverns was talking about you! And that slave with the leg made of ivory! I saw you at noon, you wretched and infernal nuisance. Damn you, Lydia!"

This was pure unadulterated hate.

Again, came that distinct echoing laughter. Of course he did not hear it. Only I could hear it.

"Your wife, where is she. I want to see her! You *will* take me in!"

"I will not."

"Lucius, I am your sister. I want to see your wife. You're right. I've been foolish. I didn't think things through very well. There are so many miles of sea between here and Rome. It never occurred to me—"

"That's just it, Lydia, you never really think of anything sensible or practical. You never did. You're an uncompromising dreamer, and stupid on top of it."

"Lucius, what can I do?"

He turned from right to left, sizing up the torchbearers.

He narrowed his eyes. I could feel his hatred. Oh, Father, do not see this from Heaven or the Underworld. My brother wants me dead!

"Yes," I said, "four torchbearers and we are in the middle of the Forum. And don't forget about the man with the ivory leg over there and the Priest," I said softly. "And do regard the soldiers outside the Emperor's Temple. Take note. How goes it with your wife? I must see her. I'll come in secret. She'll be happy that I am alive, surely, for I love her like a sister. I will never connect myself with you in public. I've made a grievous error."

"Oh, knock it off," he said. "Sisters! She's dead!"

He looked from right to left again. "They were all massacred. Don't you understand? Get away from me." He took a few steps back but I moved forward, drawing the light around him again.

"But who is with you, then? Who escaped with you? Who else is alive?"

"Priscilla," he said, "and we were damned lucky to get away when we did."

"What? Your mistress? You came here with your mistress? The children, they are all dead?"

"Yes, of course, they must be. How could they have escaped? Look, Lydia, I give you one night to get out of this city and away from me. I am lodged here comfortably and will not tolerate you. Get out of Antioch. Go by sea or land, I don't care, but go!"

"You left your wife and children to die? And came here with Priscilla?"

"How the hell did you get away, you stinking bitch in heat, answer me that! Of course you had no children, the great famous barren womb of our family!" He looked at the torchbearers. "Get away from here!" he shouted.

"Stay right where you are."

I put my hand on my dagger. I moved the mantle so that he could see the flash of the metal.

He looked genuinely surprised and then gave a ghastly false smile. Oh, revolting!

"Lydia, I wouldn't hurt you for the world!" he said as if insulted. "I am only worried for us all. Word came from the house. Everyone had been killed. What was I to do, go back and die for nothing?"

"You're lying. And don't you call me a bitch in heat again unless you want to become a gelding. I know you lie. Somebody tipped you off, and you got out! Or it was you who betrayed us all."

Ah, how sad for him that he was not more clever, more quick. He did not take umbrage at these loathsome charges as he should have. He just tilted his head and said:

"No, that's not true. Look, come with me now. Send these men away, get rid of that slave, and I will help you. Priscilla adores you."

"She's a liar and slut! And how calm you have become in the face of my suspicions. Nothing as steamed as when you saw me! I just accused you of betraying our family to the *Delatores*. I accused you of abandoning your wife and children to the Praetorian Guard. Can you hear these words?"

"It's utter stupidity, I would never do such a thing."

"You reek of guilt. Look at you. I should kill you now!"

He backed up. "Get out of Antioch!" he said. "I don't care how you judge me or what I had to do to save myself and Priscilla. Get out of Antioch!"

There were no words for my judgment. It was harsher than my soul could hold.

He backed away, and then walked fast into the darkness, disappearing before he reached the portico. I listened to his steps as they echoed down the street.

"Dear Heaven!" I whispered. I was about to cry. My hand was still on the dagger, however.

I turned around. The Priest and Flavius stood much closer than ordered. I was frankly utterly baffled, stopped.

I didn't know what to do.

"Come to the Temple at once," said the Priest.

"All right," I said. "Flavius, you come with me, stand watch with the four torchmen, I want you right by the Temple guards, and keep an eye out for that man."

"Who is he, Madam," Flavius whispered as I strode towards the Temple, leading them both.

How regal he looked. He had the presence of a free man. And his tunic was beautiful thin wool, striped in gold, belted in gold, well fitted across his chest. Even his ivory leg had been polished. I was more than pleased. But was he armed?

Beneath his quiet demeanor, he was deeply protective of me.

In my misery, I couldn't form words to answer him.

Several litters were now crisscrossing the square, carried on the shoulders of hurrying slaves, and other slaves carried the torches beside them. A kind of soft glow rose from the commotion. People were on their way to dinners or private ceremonies. Something was happening in the Temple.

I turned to the Priest. "You will guard my slave and my torchbearers?"

"Yes, Madam," he said.

It was full night. The breeze was sweet. A few lanterns had been lighted under the long porticoes. We drew near to the braziers of the goddess.

"Now I must leave you," I said. "You have my permission to protect my property, as you so eloquently put it earlier, unto death. Don't move from these doors. I won't leave here without you. I won't stay long. I don't want to. But have you a knife?"

"Yes, Madam, but it's untried. It was among your possessions, and when you did not come home and it grew dark . . ."

"Don't recount the history of the world," I said. "You did the right thing. You probably will always do the right thing."

I turned my back to the square and said, "Let me see it. I'll know if it's decorative or sharp."

When he drew it from the forearm sling, I touched it with my finger and blood came from the cut. I returned it. This had belonged to my Father. So my Father had filled my trunk with his weapons as well as his wealth, so that I might live!

Flavius and I exchanged one last slow glance.

The Priest grew very anxious. "Madam, please come inside," he said.

I found myself ushered right through the tall doors into the Temple, and with the Priestesses and the Priest of earlier that afternoon.

"You want something of me?" I asked. I was out of breath. I was faint. "I have much on my mind, things that must be done. Can this wait?"

"No, Lady, it cannot!" said the Priest.

I felt a shudder in my limbs as if I were being watched by someone. The tall shadows of the Temples were too concealing.

"All right," I said. "It's about those awful dreams, isn't it?"

"Yes," said the Priest. "And more than that."

6

E WERE taken into another chamber, and this one had only one dim light.

I couldn't see well in the flickering of the flame and I realized I could not make out the faces of the other Priest and Priestess. An Oriental screen, a screen of worked ebony, partitioned off the end of this room, and I felt certain someone was behind it.

But I felt nothing but gentleness emanating from all of these gathered here. I looked around. I was so miserable over my brother, and so impatient that I couldn't find polite words.

"Please, you must forgive me," I said. "A dire matter requires me to hurry." I was becoming afraid for Flavius's safety. "Do send guards to flank my slave outside, now."

"Done, Lady," said the Priest, the one I knew. "I beg you to stay and recount your story again."

"Who is there!" I pointed. "Behind that screen. Why is this person concealed?" This was very rude and irreverent, but I was in a full state of alarm.

"That is one of our most devoted supporters," said the Priest who had escorted me to the shrine of Isis earlier. "This one often comes by night to pray at the shrine and has given much money to the Temple. He only wants to hear what we have to say."

"Well, I'm not so sure of that. Tell him to come out!" I said. "Besides, what is it we're supposed to say?"

I was infuriated suddenly that they might have betrayed my confidences. I hadn't told them my true Roman name, only of my tragedy, but the Temple was sacred.

They became all flustered in their gentleness.

The figure, draped in the toga, much taller than my brother, in fact, remarkably tall, stepped out from behind the screen. The toga was dark, but nevertheless the classical garment. His face was hidden by the toga. I could only see his lips.

He whispered:

"Don't be afraid. You told the Priest and Priestesses this afternoon of blood dreams."

"This was in confidence!" I said indignantly. I was completely suspicious, for I had told a good deal more than blood dreams to these people.

I tried better to see the figure. There was something distinctly familiar about the figure—the voice, even in a whisper . . . something else.

"Lady Pandora," said the Priestess who had so consoled me earlier. "You talked to me of an old legendary worship, worship which we oppose and condemn. A worship of our Beloved Mother which once involved human sacrifice. I told you that we abhor such things. And we do."

"However," said the Priest, "there is someone afoot in the city of Antioch who does drink blood from humans, draining them until they are dead. Then he flings the bodies before dawn on our steps. The very steps of our Temple." He sighed. "Lady Pandora, I am entrusting you with a powerful confidence."

All thought of my evil brother left me. The hound of the dreams bore down upon me with its evil breath. I tried to gather my wits. I thought again of the voice I'd heard in my head: *It is I who summoned you.* The feminine laughter.

"No, it was a woman's laughter," I murmured.

"Lady Pandora?"

"You tell me there is someone afoot in Antioch who drinks blood."

"By night. He cannot walk in the day," said the Priest.

I saw the dream, the rising sun, knowing I the blood drinker would die in the rays of the sun.

"You're telling me that these blood drinkers I saw in my dream exist?" I asked. "That one of them is here."

"Someone wants us to believe this," said the Priest, "that the old legends have truth, but we don't know who it is. And we are leery of the Roman authorities. You know what happened in Rome. You came speaking of dreams in which the sun killed you, in which you were a blood drinker. Lady, I'm not betraying your confidences here. This one—"

He gestured to the tall man. "This is the one who reads the ancient writing. He's read the legends. Your dreams echo the legends."

"I am sick," I said. "I need a chair. I have enemies to worry about."

"I'll protect you from your enemies," said the mysterious tall man in the toga.

"How can you? You don't even know who they are."

There came a silent voice from the tall man in the toga:

Your brother Lucius betrayed the entire family. He did it out of jealousy of your brother Antony. He sold out everybody to the Delatores *for a guaranteed one-third of the family's wealth and left before the killing began. He had the cooperation of Sejanus of the Praetorian Guard. He wants to kill you.*

I was shocked but also not about to let this person overwhelm me.

You speak just like the woman, I said silently. *You speak right to my thoughts. You speak like the woman who said to me in my head, "It is I who summoned you."*

I could feel his shock at this. But I too slumped as if dealt a mortal blow. So this creature knew all about my brothers, and Lucius had betrayed us. And this creature knew.

What are you? I fired off to the mind speaker, the tall one. *Are you a magician?*

No answer.

The Priest and Priestess, unable to hear this silent exchange, pursued their course.

"This blood drinker, Lady Pandora, he leaves human victims on the steps of the Temple before dawn. He writes an old name in Egyptian on his victims with their blood. Should the government discover this, our Temple might be held accountable. This is not our worship.

"Will you recount again for us—for our friend here—your dreams? We must protect the worship of Isis. We did not believe in these old legends . . . until this creature appeared and began his killing, then comes out of the sea a beautiful Roman woman who speaks of similar beings who are in her dreams."

"What name does he write on his victims?" I asked. "This blood drinker. Is it Isis?"

"It's meaningless, it's forbidden, it's old Egyptian. It is one of the names by which Isis was once called, but never by us."

"What is it?"

None of them, including the silent one, answered me.

In the silence, I thought of Lucius and I almost wept. Then hatred came over me, deep hatred, as it had in the Forum when I spoke with him, saw his cowardly rage. Betrayed the entire family. To be weak is a dangerous thing. Antony and my Father had been such strong men.

"Lady Pandora," said the Priest. "Tell us what you might know of this creature in Antioch. Have you dreamed of him?"

I thought of the dreams. I tried to respond in

depth to what these people in this Temple were telling me.

The tall distant Roman spoke:

"Lady Pandora knows nothing about this blood drinker. She is telling you the truth. She knows only the dreams and there have been no names spoken in her dreams. In her dreams she sees an earlier time of Egypt."

"Well, thank you, Gracious Lord!" I said furiously. "And just how have you arrived at that conclusion?"

"By reading your thoughts!" the Roman said, quite unruffled. "The same as I have regarding those who would put you in danger here. I'll protect you from your brother."

"Indeed. You had better leave that to me. It is I who will settle that score with him. Now, let us leave the question of my personal misfortune. And you explain to me, most clever one, why I am having these dreams! Fork up some useful magic from your mind reading. You know, a man with your gifts should post yourself at the courthouse, and determine cases for the judges if you can read minds. Why don't you go to Rome and become the advisor to the Emperor Tiberius?"

I could feel, positively feel, the little tumult in the heart of the distant concealed Roman. Again, there came that sense of something familiar about this creature. Of course I was no stranger to necromancers, astrologists or oracles. But this man had mentioned specific names—Antony, Lucius. He was an astounder.

"Tell me, oh, mysterious one," I said. "How close do my dreams come to what you've read in the old writing? And this blood drinker, the one that's roaming Antioch, is he a mortal man?"

Silence.

I strained to see the Roman more clearly but couldn't. He had in fact receded somewhat into the darkness. My nerves were on the breaking point. I wanted to kill Lucius; in fact, I had no choice.

The Roman said softly, "She knows nothing of this blood drinker in Antioch. Tell her what you know of him—for it may be he, this blood drinker, who is sending her the dreams."

I was confused. The woman's voice had been so clear in my head earlier, *It is I who summoned you.*

This was causing confusion in the Roman; I could feel it like a little turbulence in the air.

"We've seen him," said the Priest. "Indeed, we watch, in order to collect these poor drained corpses before anyone finds them and blames the deed on us. He is burned, burned all over his body, blackened. He cannot be a man. He is an old god, burnt black as if in an inferno."

"Amon Ra," I said. "But why didn't he die? In the dreams, I die."

"Oh, it is a horror to behold," said the Priestess suddenly, as if she could contain herself no longer. "This thing cannot be human. Its bones show through its blackened skin. But it is weak and its victims are weak. It barely staggers, yet it can drain the blood from the poor maimed souls upon whom it feeds. It crawls away in the morning as if it hasn't the strength to walk."

The Priest seemed impatient.

"But he's alive," said the Priest. "Alive, god or demon or man, he lives. And each time he drinks blood from one of these weaklings, he grows a little stronger. And he is straight from the old legends, and you have dreamed of them. He wears his hair long in the old Egyptian style. He is in agony from his burns. He spits curses at the Temple."

"What kind of curses?"

The Priestess interjected at once. "He seems to think that Queen Isis has betrayed him. He speaks in old Egyptian. We barely understand him. Our Roman friend here, our benefactor, has translated the words for us."

"Stop!" I demanded. "My head is reeling. Don't say anymore. The man over there has told the truth. I know nothing of this bloody burnt creature. I don't know why I have the dreams. I think a woman is sending the dreams to me. It may be the Queen I described to you, the Queen on the throne, in fetters, who weeps, I don't know why!"

"You have never seen this man?" asked the Priest.

The Roman answered for me. "She has not."

"Oh, your marvelous talents as spokesman again!" I said to the Roman. "I am so delighted! Why are you hiding behind your toga? Why do you stand over there, so far away that I can't see you? Have you seen this blood drinker?"

"Be patient with me," he said. It was spoken with

such charm that I couldn't bring myself to say more to him. I turned on the Priest and the Priestess.

"Why don't you lie in wait for this black burnt thing," I said, "this weakling? I am hearing voices in my head. But it's the words of a woman that come to me, warning me of danger. It's a woman laughing. I want to leave now. I want to go home. I have something that must be done, and must be done cleverly. I need to go."

"I will protect you from your enemy," said the Roman.

"That's charming," I answered. "If you can protect me, if you know who my enemy is, then why can't you lie in wait for this blood drinker? Catch him in a gladiator's net. Sink five tridents into him. Five of you can hold him. All you have to do is hold him till the sun rises, the rays of Amon Ra will kill him. It may take two days, even three, but they'll kill him. He'll burn like I did in the dream. And you, mind reader, why don't you help?"

I broke off, shocked and disoriented. Why was I so certain of this. Why was I using the name Amon Ra so casually, as if I believed in the god? I scarcely knew his fables.

"The creature knows when we are lying in wait," said the Priest and Priestess. "He knows when the tall friend is here, and does not come. We are vigilant, we are patient, we think we will see no more of him, and then he comes. And now you have come with the dreams."

A vivid garish flash of the dream returned. I was

a man. I argued and cursed. I refused to do something which I had been ordered to do. A woman was weeping. I fought off those who tried to stop me. But I had not foreseen that I would, as I ran away, come to a desert place where I could find no shelter.

If the others spoke, I took no note of it. I heard the woman of the dream crying, the fettered Queen, and the woman was a blood drinker too. "You must drink from the Fount," said the man in my dream. And he wasn't a man. I wasn't a man. We were gods. We were blood drinkers. That's why the sun destroyed me. It was the force of a more powerful god. Layers upon layers of the dream lay below this polished bit of remembrance.

I came to my senses, or back to an awareness of the others, when someone placed a cup of wine in my hands. I drank it. It was excellent wine, from Italy, and I felt refreshed, though at once tired. It would make the walk home much too tiring if I drank any more. I needed my strength.

"Take this away," I said. I looked at the Priestess. "In the dream, I told you, I was one of them. They wanted me to drink from the Queen. They called her 'the Fount.' They said she did not know how to rule. I told you."

The Priestess burst into tears and turned her back, hunching up her narrow shoulders.

"I was one of the blood drinkers," I said. "I was thirsty for blood. Listen, I am no lover of blood sacrifice. What do you know here? Does Queen Isis exist somewhere, within this Temple, bound in fetters—"

"No!" cried the Priest. The Priestess turned around, echoing the same horrified denial.

"All right, then, but you said there were legends that she did exist somewhere in material form. Now, what do you think is happening? She has summoned me here to assist this one, this burnt-up weakling? Why me? How can I do it? I'm a mortal woman. Remembering dreams of a past life does not enhance my power. Listen! It was a woman's voice, I told you, which spoke in my head to me, not an hour ago out there in the Forum, and she said 'It is I who summoned you,' I heard this, and she swore she would not have me stolen from her. Then up comes this mortal man who's more of a threat to me than anything in my head. The voice in my head had warned me of him! I don't want any of your mysterious Egyptian religion. I refuse to go mad. It is you, all of you—especially the talented mind reader—who must find this thing before he makes any more trouble. Allow me to go on."

I stood up and began to walk out of the chamber.

The Roman spoke behind me, most gently, "Are you really going out into the night alone, knowing full well what awaits you—that you have an enemy who wants to kill you, and that you have in your dreams knowledge that may draw this blood drinker to you?"

This was such a change of pace for the lofty mind reader, such a slip into semi-sarcastic vernacular, that I almost laughed.

"I'm going home now!" I said firmly.

They all pleaded, in different modes and tones. "Stay in the Temple."

"Absolutely not," I said. "If the dreams return I'll write them down for you."

"How can you be so foolish!" said the Roman with genteel impatience. You would have thought *he* was my brother!

"That is an unforgivable impertinence," I said. "Are not magicians and mind readers bound by manners?" I looked to the Priest and Priestess. "Who is this man?"

I went out and they followed me. I hurried to the door.

In the light I saw the Priestess's face. "We know only that he's our friend. Please listen to his advice. He has never done anything but good for the Temple. He comes to read the Egyptian books we have here. He buys them up from the shops as soon as the sea brings them to us. He is wise. He can read minds, as you see."

"You promised an escort of guards," I said.

And I will be with you. The voice came from the Roman, though I did not know where he was now at all. He was not in the great hall.

"Come, live within the Temple of Isis, and nothing can harm you," said the Priest.

"I'm not quite the woman for living in the Temple Compound," I said, trying to sound as humble and grateful as I could. "I'd drive you mad in a week. Please open the door."

I slipped out. I felt I had escaped from a dark corridor of spiderwebs, back into the Roman night, among Roman columns and Roman temples.

I discovered Flavius pressed against the column beside me, staring down into the stairs. Our four torchbearers were gathered next to us, very much alarmed.

There were men who were obviously Temple guards, but they stood cleaving to the doors, as did Flavius.

"Madam, go back in!" whispered Flavius.

At the foot of the stairs stood a group of helmeted Roman soldiers in full military dress with polished muscled breastplates and short red cloaks and tunics. They carried their deadly swords as if they were in battle. Their bronze helmets shone in the light of the Temple braziers.

Battle dress within the city. Everything but shields. And who was the leader?

Lucius, my brother, stood beside the leader. Lucius wore his battle tunic of red, but no breastplate or sword. His toga was doubled and redoubled over his left arm. He was clean, with shining hair, exuding money. A jeweled dagger was on his forearm; another dagger was in his belt.

Trembling, he pointed at me.

"There she is," said Lucius. "Of the entire family,

she escaped the order of Sejanus. It was a plot to kill Tiberius and somehow she bribed her way out of Rome!"

I quickly sized up the soldiers. There were two young Asiatics but the others were *old* and *Roman*; six in number. Yea gods, they must have thought I was Circe!

"Go back in," said my beloved and loyal Flavius, "seek sanctuary."

"Be still," I said. "There's always time for that."

The leader, he was the key, and I saw that he was an older man, older than my brother Antony, yet not as old as my Father. He had thick gray eyebrows and was impeccably clean shaven.

He wore battle scars proudly, one on his cheek, another on his thigh. He was exhausted. His eyes were red and he shook his head as if to clear his vision.

This man's arms were very tanned, yet he was well muscled. This meant war—lots and lots of war.

Lucius declared, "The entire family stands condemned. She should be executed on the spot!"

I decided my strategy as if I were Caesar himself. I spoke up at once, proceeding two steps down:

"You are the Legate, are you not? How tired you must be!" I took his hand in both of mine. "Were you under the command of Germanicus?"

He nodded.

First blow struck!

"My brothers fought with Germanicus in the

North," I said. "And Antony, the eldest, after the Triumphal March in Rome, lived long enough to tell us of the bones found in the Teutoburg Forest."

"Ah, Madam, to see that field of bones, an entire army ambushed and the bodies left to rot!"

"Two of my brothers died in the battle. It was in a storm, in the North Sea."

"Madam, you never saw such a disaster, but do you think the Barbarian God, Thor, could frighten our Germanicus?"

"Never. And you came here with the General?"

"Went everywhere with him, from the banks of the Elbe in the North to the South end of the River Nile."

"How marvelous, and you are so tired, Tribune, look at you, you need sleep. Where is the famous Governor Gnaeus Calpurnius Piso? Why did it take him so long to quiet the city?"

"Because he's not here, Madam, and he doesn't dare to come back. Some say he makes a mutiny in Greece, others that he flees for his life."

"Stop listening to her!" shouted Lucius.

"He was never much loved in Rome, either," I said. "It was Germanicus whom my brothers loved and my Father praised."

"Indeed, and if we had been given one more year—one more year, Madam—we could have extinguished the fire of that bloody upstart King Arminius forever! We didn't even need that long! You spoke of the North Sea. We fought on all terrain."

"Oh, yes, in the thick of the forest, and tell me this, were you there, Sir, when they found the lost standard of General Varus's legions? Is the story true!"

"Ah, Madam, when that golden eagle was raised, you never heard such cries as from the soldiers."

"This woman is a liar and a traitor," shouted Lucius.

I turned on him. "Don't push me too far! You're past all patience now. Do you even know the numbers of the Legions of General Varus who were ambushed in the Teutoburg Forest? I thought not! They were the Seventh, the Eighth and the Ninth."

"Right, correct," said the Legate. "And we could have wiped out those tribes completely. The Empire would reach to the Elbe! But for some reason, and mine is not the place to question, our Emperor Tiberius called us back."

"Hmmm, and then condemns your beloved leader for going to Egypt."

"Madam, it was no trip to seize power, Germanicus's trip to Egypt. It was because of a famine."

"Yes, and Germanicus had been declared *Imperium Maius* of all the Eastern provinces," I said.

"And there was so much trouble!" said the Legate. "You can not imagine the morale, the habits of the soldiers here, but our General never slept! He went directly when he heard of the famine."

"And you with him?"

"All of us, his cohorts. In Egypt he delighted in seeing the old monuments. So did I."

"Ah, how marvelous for him. You must tell me about Egypt! You know that I, as a Senator's daughter, cannot go to Egypt any more than can a Senator. I would so love—"

"Why is that, Madam?" asked the Legate.

"She's lying to you!" roared Lucius. "Her whole family was murdered."

"Very simple reason, Tribune," I said to the Legate. "It's no state secret. Rome is so dependent upon Egypt for corn that the Emperor wants to prevent the country from ever falling under the control of a powerful traitor. Surely you grew up as I did in dread of another Civil War."

"I put my faith in our Generals," said the Legate.

"You are right to do so. And you saw nothing from Germanicus but loyalty, is that not so?"

"It is absolutely so. Ah, Egypt. We saw such Temples and statues!"

"The singing statues," I asked, "did you see them, the colossal man and woman who wail in the rising of the sun."

"Yes, I heard it, Madam," he said, nodding furiously. "I heard the sound! It is magical. Egypt is full of magic!"

"Hmmm." A tremor ran through me. I banished it. In a flash I saw two images mixed: that of the tall Roman in his toga, and that of a burnt and cunning creature! Think straight, Pandora!

"And in the Temple of Ramses the Great," said the Legate, "one of the Priests read the writing on the walls. All about victory? All about battle? We laughed because nothing really changes, Madam."

"And Governor Piso, do you believe these rumors? Can we not speak safely of them, of rumors as if rumors were not things?"

"Everyone here despises him!" said the Legate. "He was a bad soldier, plain and simple! And Agrippina the Elder, Germanicus's beloved wife, is on her way to Rome now with the General's ashes. She will officially accuse the Governor before the Senate!"

"Yes, how courageous of her, and that is how it should be done. If families are judged without trial, then we have fallen into tyranny, haven't we? Here, our friendly lunatic, don't you agree to that?"

Lucius was speechless. He turned red.

"And in the Teutoburg Forest," I said tenderly, "that gloomy arena for our doom, did you see all the bones of our lost legions, scattered about?"

"Buried them, Madam, with these hands!" The Legate held up his weathered callused palms. "For who could tell what bones were ours and what bones were theirs? And Madam, the platform of that cowardly, sneaking King was still standing, from which the loathsome long-haired slob had ordered the sacrifice to his pagan gods of our men."

Nods and noble mumbles came from the other soldiers.

"I was but a small child," I said, "when word came of the ambush of General Varus. But I remember our Divine Emperor Augustus—how he let his hair grow long in mourning and how he would pound his head on the walls, crying, 'Varus, bring me back my legions.' "

"You actually saw him this way?"

"Oh, many a time, and was present one night when he discussed his often mentioned thoughts—that the Empire must not try to push further. Rather it should police the states which it now contains."

"Then Caesar Augustus did say this!" said the Legate in fascination.

"He cared about you," I said to the Legate. "How many years have you been in the field? Do you have a wife?"

"Oh, how I long to go home," said the Legate. "And now that my General has fallen. My wife is gray-haired as I am. I see her when we go to Rome for parades."

"Yes, and compulsory service was only six years under the Republic, but now, you must fight for what? Twelve? Twenty? But who am I to criticize Augustus, whom I loved as I loved my Father and all my dead brothers?"

Lucius could see what was happening. He sputtered when he spoke:

"Tribune, read my Safe Conduct! Read it!"

The Legate looked truly annoyed.

My brother marshaled what he could of his rhetoric, which wasn't much. "She lies. She is condemned. Her family is dead. I was compelled to bear witness to Sejanus because they sought to kill Tiberius himself!"

"You turned on your own family?" asked the soldier.

"Oh, don't wear yourself out with this," I said. "The man has harried me all day. He has discovered that I am a woman alone, an heiress, and thinks that this is some uncivilized outpost of the Empire where he can bring a charge against a Senator's daughter with no proof. Dear lunatic, do pay attention. Julius Caesar gave Antioch its municipal standing less than one hundred years ago. There are legions stationed here, are there not?"

I looked at the Legate.

The Legate turned and glowered at my trembling brother.

"What is this Safe Conduct?" I asked. "This bears the name Tiberius."

The Legate snatched it from Lucius before Lucius could respond and handed the scroll to me. I had to take my hand off my dagger to unroll the paper.

"Ah, Sejanus of the Praetorian Guard! I knew it. And the Emperor probably knows nothing of it. Tribune, do you know those palace guards make one and one half times what a Legionnaire makes? And now they have these *Delatores*, given incentive to charge others with crimes for one-third of the condemned man's property!"

The Legate was now sizing up my brother and every flaw in Lucius shone in the light; his cowardly posture, his trembling hands, his shifty eyes, his growing desperation in the pursing of his lips.

I turned to Lucius.

"Do you realize, you madman, whoever you are, what you are asking of this seasoned and wise Roman officer? What if he should believe your insane lies? What will become of him when the letter arrives from Rome inquiring into my whereabouts and the disposition of my fortune!"

"Sir, this woman is a traitor!" shouted Lucius. "On my honor I swear—"

"What honor is that?" asked the soldier under his breath. His eyes fixed on Lucius.

"If Rome were such," I said, "that families as old as mine could be so easily dispatched as this man asks you now to do with me, then why would the widow of Germanicus dare to go before the Senate for a trial?"

"They are all executed," said my brother, who was at his worst and most solemn, and seemed to have lost all touch with the effect of his words, "every one of them, because they were in a plot to kill Tiberius and I was given Safe Conduct and passage out for reporting them, as was my duty, to the *Delatores*, and to Sejanus, with whom I spoke myself!"

The possibilities were making themselves known slowly to the Legate.

"Sir," I said to Lucius, "have you anything else on your person that identifies you?"

"I don't need anything else!" said Lucius. "Your fate is death."

"Same as it was for your Father?" asked the Legate, "and your wife? Had you children?"

"Throw her into prison tonight, and write to Rome!" declared Lucius. "You'll see that I speak the truth!"

"And where will you be, whoever you are, while I am in prison? Looting my house?"

"You slut!" shouted Lucius. "Don't you see this is all feminine wiles and lurid distraction!"

There was shock among the soldiers, revulsion in the face of the Legate. Flavius moved next to me.

"Officer," asked Flavius with tempered dignity, "what am I allowed to do on behalf of my Mistress against this madman?"

"You use such words again, Sir," I said firmly to Lucius, "and I'll lose my patience."

The Legate took Lucius's arm. Lucius's right hand went to his dagger.

"Just who are you?" the Legate demanded. "Are you one of the *Delatores*? You tell me you turned on your whole family?"

"Tribune," I said, laying the gentlest touch yet on his arm. "My Father's roots went back to the time of Romulus and Remus. We know no origins other than those in Rome. It was the same with my Mother, who was herself the daughter of a Senator. This man is saying rather . . . horrible things."

"So it seems," said the Legate, narrowing his gaze, as he inspected Lucius. "Where are your friends here, your companions; where do you live?"

"You can't do anything to me!" said Lucius.

The Legate glared at Lucius's hand on the dagger.

"You prepare to draw that against me!" asked the Legate.

Lucius clearly was at a loss.

"Why did you come to Antioch?" I demanded of Lucius. "Were you the bearer of the poison that killed Germanicus?"

"Arrest her!" shouted Lucius.

"No, I don't believe my own accusation. Not even Sejanus would put such treachery in the hands of a petty scoundrel like you! Come now, what else do you have on your person to connect you with this family, this Safe Conduct which you say came from the pen of Sejanus?"

Lucius was utterly baffled.

"I certainly have nothing belonging to me to connect me to your wild and bloody sagas and tales," I said.

The Legate interrupted me. "Nothing to connect you to this name?" He took the Safe Conduct from my hand.

"Absolutely nothing," I said, "nothing but this madman here who is spouting horrors, and would lead the world to believe that our Emperor has lost his wits. Only he connects me with his bloody plot without witness or verification, and hurls insults at me."

The Legate rolled up the Safe Conduct. "And your purpose here, Madam?" he asked in a whisper.

"To live in peace and quiet," I said softly. "To live in safety and under the true shelter of Roman rule."

Now I knew the battle had been won. But something else was required to seal the victory. I took another gamble.

Slowly I reached for my dagger and slowly I brought it out of its sling.

Lucius leapt back at once. He drew his dagger and lunged at me. He was immediately stabbed by the Legate and at least two of the soldiers.

He hung there bleeding on their weapons, staring from right to left, and then he spoke, but his mouth was too full of blood. His eyes widened; it seemed again he would speak. Then, as the soldiers withdrew their daggers, his body folded up on the cobblestones at the foot of the stairs.

My brother Lucius was quite mercifully dead.

I looked at him and shook my head.

The Legate looked at me. This was a significant moment, and I knew it.

"What is it, Tribune," I asked, "that separates us from the long-haired barbarians of the North? Is it not law? Written law? Traditional law? Is it not justice? That men and women are called to account for what they do?"

"Yes, Madam," he said.

"You know," I went on in a reverent voice, staring at this heap of blood and clothes and flesh that lay on the stones, "I saw our great Emperor Caesar Augustus on the day of his death."

"You saw him? You did?"

I nodded. "When they were certain he was to die, we were rushed to him with a few other close friends. It was his hope to put down rumors in the capital that might lead to unrest. He had sent for a mirror and combed his hair. He was primly propped up. And he asked us as we entered the room: Didn't we think he'd played his part well in the comedy of life?

"I thought, what courage! And then he made some further joke, the old theatrical line they say after plays:

> If I have made you happy, kindly let me know
> your appreciation with a warm goodbye.

"I could tell you more, but—"

"Oh, please do," said the Legate.

"Well, why not?" I asked. "It was told to me that the Emperor said of Tiberius, his chosen successor, 'Poor Rome, to be chewed slowly by those sluggish jaws!' "

The Legate smiled. "But there wasn't anyone else," he said under his breath.

"Thank you, Tribune, for all your assistance. Would you allow me to take from my purse sufficient funds to treat you and your soldiers to a fine dinner—"

"No, Madam, I wouldn't have it be said I or any man here was bribed. Now this dead man. Do you know anything more of him?"

"Only this, Officer, that his body probably belongs in the river."

The soldiers all laughed among themselves.

"Good night, Gracious Lady," said the soldier.

And off I went, striding across the blackness of the Forum, with my beloved one-legged Flavius at my side and the torchbearers round us.

Only now did I shake all over. Only now did the sweat cover my whole body.

When we had plunged deeply into the unbroken darkness of a small alleyway, I said, "Flavius, let these torchbearers go. There is no reason for them to know where we are headed."

"Madam, I don't have any lantern."

"The night's full of stars and has a near full moon. Look! Besides, there are others from the Temple who are following us."

"There are?" he asked. He paid off the torch-bearers and they ran back towards the mouth of the street.

"Yes. There is one watching. And besides, we can see well enough by the lighted windows and Heaven's light, don't you think? I am tired, so tired."

I walked on, reminding myself again and again that Flavius could not keep up. I began to weep.

"Tell me something with your great philosophical knowledge," I said as I walked on, determined to make the tears stop. "Tell me why evil people are so stupid? Why are so many of them just plain stupid?"

"Madam, I think there are quite a few evil people who are quite clever," he said. "But never have I seen such skilled rhetoric on the part of anyone, either bad or good, as your talents revealed just now."

"I'm delighted that you know that that is all it was," I said. "Rhetoric. And to think he had the same teachers as I, the same library, the same Father—" My voice broke.

He put his arm gingerly about my shoulder and this time I didn't tell him to move away. I let him steady me. We walked faster as a pair.

"No," I said, "Flavius, the majority of the evil are just plain dumb, I've seen it all my life. The true crafty evil person is rare. It's bumbling that causes most of the misery of the world, utter stupid bumbling. It's underestimation of one's fellow man! You watch what happens with Tiberius. Tiberius Caesar and the Guard. Watch what happens to that damned Sejanus. You can sow the seeds of distrust everywhere, and lose yourself in an overgrown field."

"We are home, Madam," he said.

"Oh, thank God, you know it. I could never have told you this was the house."

Within moments, he stopped and turned the key in a lock. The smell of urine was everywhere overpowering, as it always was in the back streets of ancient cities. A lantern threw a dim light on our wooden door. The light danced in the jet of water which fell from the lion's mouth in the fountain.

Flavius gave a series of knocks. It sounded to me as if the women answering the inner door were crying.

"Oh, Lord, now what?" I said. "I am too sleepy. Whatever it is, tend to it."

I went inside.

"Madam," squealed one of the girls. I couldn't remember her name. "I didn't let him in. I swear I never unbolted the door. I have no key to the gate. We had this house, all this, ready for you!" She sobbed.

"What on Earth are you talking about?" I asked.

But I knew. I'd seen in the corner of my eye. I knew. I turned and saw a very tall Roman sitting in my newly refurbished living room. He sat relaxed with ankle on knee in a gilded wooden chair.

"It's all right, Flavius," I said. "I know him."

And I did. Because it was Marius. Marius the tall Keltoi. Marius, who had charmed me in childhood. Marius, whom I had almost identified in the shadows of the Temple.

He rose at once.

He came towards me, where I stood in the darkness on the edges of the atrium, and he whispered, "My beautiful Pandora!"

7

E STOPPED just short of touching me.

"Oh, do, please," I said. I moved to kiss him, but he moved away. The room had scattered lamps. He played the shadows.

"Marius, of course, Marius! And you look not one day older than when I saw you in my girlhood. Your face is radiant, and your eyes, how beautiful are your eyes. I would sing these praises to the accompaniment of a lyre if I could."

Flavius had slowly withdrawn, taking the distressed girls with him. He made not a sound.

"Pandora," Marius said, "I wish I could take you in my arms, but there are reasons why I cannot, and you mustn't touch me, not because I want it so much, but because I'm not what you think. You don't see the evidence of youth in me; it is something so far afield of the promises of youth that I've only just begun to understand its agonies."

Suddenly he looked off. He raised his hand for my silence and patience.

"That thing is abroad," I said. "The burnt blood drinker."

"Don't think on your dreams just now," he said to me directly. "Think on our youth. I loved you when you were a girl of ten. When you were fifteen I begged your Father for your hand."

"You did? He never told me this."

He looked away again. Then he shook his head.

"The burnt one," I said.

"I feared this," he cursed himself. "He followed you from the Temple! Oh, Marius! You are a fool. You have played into his hands. But he is not as clever as he thinks."

"Marius, was it you who sent me the dreams!"

"No, never! I would do anything in my power to protect you from myself."

"And from the old legends?"

"Don't be quick of wit, Pandora. I know your immense cleverness served you well back there with your loathsome brother Lucius and the gentleman Legate. But don't think too much about . . . dreams. Dreams are nothing, and dreams will pass."

"Then the dreams came from him, this hideous burnt killer?"

"I can't figure it!" he said. "But don't think on the images. Don't feed him now with your mind."

"He reads minds," I said, "just as you do."

"Yes. But you can cloak your thoughts. It's a mental trick. You can learn it. You can walk with your soul locked up in a little metal box in your head."

I realized he was in much pain. An immense sadness came from him. "This cannot be allowed to happen!" he insisted.

"What is that, Marius? You speak about the woman's voice, you—"

"No, be quiet."

"I will not! I will get to the bottom of this!"

"You must take my instructions!" He stepped forward and again he reached to touch me, to take me by the arms, as my Father might have done, but then he did not.

"No, it is you who must tell me everything," I said.

I was amazed at the whiteness of his skin, its utter blemishless perfection. And once again the radiance of his eyes seemed almost impossible. Inhuman.

Only now did I see the full glory of his long hair. He did look like the Keltoi, who had been his ancestors. His hair touched his shoulders. It was a gleaming gold, overly bright, yellow as corn and full of soft curls.

"Look at you!" I whispered. "You're not alive!"

"No, take your last look, for you are leaving here!"

"What?" I said. "Last look?" I repeated his words. "What are you talking about! I've only arrived, laid my plans, rid myself of my brother! I am not leaving here. Do you mean to say you are leaving me?"

There was a terrible anguish in his face, a courageous appeal that I had never seen in any man, not even in my Father, who had worked swiftly in those last fatal moments at home, as if he were merely intent on sending me on an important appointment.

Marius's eyes were filmed with blood. He was crying, and his eyes were sore with the tears! No! These were tears like the tears of the magnificent Queen in the dream, who, bound to her throne, wept and stained her cheeks and her throat and her linen.

He wanted to deny it. He shook his head, but he knew I was quite convinced.

"Pandora, when I saw it was you," he said, "when you came into the Temple and I saw it was you who had had these blood dreams, I was beside myself. I must get you far from this, far from all danger."

I separated myself from his spell, from the aura of his beauty. I beheld him with a cold eye, and I listened as he went on, noting all about him, from the glitter of his eyes to the way that he gestured.

"You have to leave Antioch at once," he said. "I will stay here the night with you. Then in the day, you pick up your faithful Flavius and your two girls, they are honest, and you take them with you. You put miles between you and this place by day, and this thing can't follow you! Don't tell me now where you mean to go. You can discuss all this at the docks in the morning. You have plenty of money."

"You are the one who is dreaming now, Marius; I am not going. Who is it precisely that you want me to flee? The weeping Queen on her throne? Or the prowling, burnt one? The former reaches me over miles and miles of sea with her summons. She warns me against my evil brother. The other I can easily dispatch. I have no fear of him. I know what he is from the dreams, and I know how the sun has hurt him, and I will myself pin him to the wall in the sun."

He was silent, biting his lip.

"I will do that for her, for the Queen in the dreams, to avenge her."

"Pandora, I am begging you."

"In vain," I said. "Do you think I have come so far only to run again? And the woman's voice—"

"How do you know it was this Queen of whom you dreamt? There could be other blood drinkers in this city. Men, women. They all want the same thing."

"And you fear them?"

"Loathe them! And I must keep clear of them, not give them what they want! Never give them what they want."

"Ah, I see it all," I said.

"You do not!" he said, scowling down at me. So fierce, so perfect.

"You are one of them, Marius. You are whole. You are unburnt. They want your blood to heal themselves."

"How could you think of such a thing?"

"In my dreams, they called the Queen 'the Fount.' "

I flew at him and imprisoned him in my arms! He was powerfully strong, solid as a tree! I never felt such hardness of muscle in a man. I lay my head on his shoulder, and his cheek against the top of my head was cold!

But he enfolded me gently with both arms, stroking my hair, pulling it down out of all the pins and letting it flow down my back. I felt a rich tingling all over the surface of my skin.

Hard, so hard, yet with no pulse of life. No warmth of human blood in his gentle, sweet gestures.

"My darling," he said, "I don't know the source of your dreams, but I know this. You will be protected from me and from them. You will never become part of this old tale that goes on verse by verse no matter how the world changes! I won't allow it."

"Explain these things to me. I will not cooperate with you until you explain everything. Do you know the anguish of the Queen of the dream? Her tears are like yours. Look. Blood. You stain your tunic! Is she here, this Queen; has she summoned me?"

"And what if she has and she wants to punish you for this former life you dreamt in which the evil gods kept her fettered. What if that is so!"

"No," I said. "That is not her intention. Besides, I wouldn't do what the dark gods of the dream said. I wouldn't drink from 'the Fount.' I ran and that's why I died in the desert."

"Ah!" He threw up his hands! And walked away. He stared out into the dark peristyle. Only the stars lighted the trees there. I saw a faint glow coming from the far dining room on the other side of the house.

I looked at him, at his great height and the straightness of his back, and the way his feet were so firmly fixed on the mosaic floor. The lamps made his blond hair glorious.

I heard him, though he whispered with his back to me.

"How could this stupid thing have happened!"

"What stupid thing!" I demanded. I came to his side. "You mean that I am here, in Antioch. I'll tell you how. My Father arranged my escape, that's how . . ."

"No, no, I don't mean that. I want you to be safe, alive, out of all danger, protected, so that you flower as you are meant to do. Your petals aren't even bruised at the edges, look at you, and your boldness heats your beauty! Your brother had no chance against your learning or your rhetoric. And yet you charmed the soldiers and made slaves of them with your superiority, never once rousing their resentment. You have years of life in you! But I must think of some way to make you safe. Look. This is the heart of it. You have to leave Antioch during the day."

" 'Friend of the Temple,' that's what the Priest and Priestess called you. They said you could read the old script. They said you bought up all the Egyptian books when they came into the port. Why? If you seek her, the Queen, then seek her through me, because it is she who said that she had summoned me."

"She didn't speak in the dreams! You don't know

who spoke the words! What if the dreams do have their root in your migrant soul? What if you have lived before? And now you come to the Temple and there is one of these loathed ancient gods on the prowl and you are in danger. You must get away, from here, from me, from this wounded hunter, whom I will find."

"You're not telling me all you know! What happened to you, Marius! What happened! Who did this to you, this miracle of your radiance. This is no cloak; the light comes from within!"

"Damn it, Pandora, do you think I wanted my life foreshortened and my destiny extended forever!" He was suffering. He looked at me, unwilling to speak, and I felt such pain coming from him, such loneliness, that for a moment it was unbearable.

I felt a wave of my own anguish of the long night before, when the utter vacuity of all religions and creeds had struck me hard and the sheer effort of a good life seemed a fool's trap, and nothing more.

He suddenly closed his arms around me, surprising me, holding me firmly and rubbing his cheek gently against my hair, and kissing my head. Silken, polished, gentle beyond words. "Pandora, Pandora, Pandora," he said. "The beautiful little girl grown into the marvelous woman."

I held this hard effigy of the most spectacular and singular man I had ever known or seen: I held it and this time heard the beating of his heart, the distinct rhythm of it. I laid my ear on his chest.

"Oh, Marius, if only I could lay my head to rest

next to yours. If I could only yield to your protection. But you are driving me away! You don't promise guardianship, you ordain flight for me, wandering and more nightmares, and mystery, and despair. No. I can't."

I turned away from his caresses. I could feel his kisses on my hair.

"Don't tell me that I'll never see you again. Don't think I can bear that along with everything else that's happened. I have no one here, and then who comes but one who left such a stamp on my girlish heart that the details are as deep as the finest coin. And you say you will never see me again, that I must go."

I turned around.

It was lust shining in his eyes. Yet he checked it. In a soft voice, he confessed with a little smile:

"Oh, how I admired your work with the Legate. I thought the two of you would plan out the whole conquest of the Germanic tribes on your own." He sighed. "You must find a good life, a rich life, a life where your soul and body are fed." The color flared in his face. He looked at me, at my breasts, at my hips and then at my face. Ashamed and trying to conceal it. Lust.

"Are you a man still?" I asked.

He didn't answer me. But his expression grew chilly.

"You will never know the full extent of what I am!" he said.

"Ah, but not a man!" I said. "Am I right? Not a man."

"Pandora, you are deliberately taunting me. Why? Why do this?"

"This transformation, this induction into the blood drinkers; it's added no inches to your height. Did it add any inches anywhere else?"

"Please stop this," he said.

"Want me, Marius. Say that you do. I see it. Confirm it in words. What does that cost you?"

"You are infuriating!" he said. His face colored deeply with his rage, and pressed his lips together so hard that they went white. "Thank the gods that I don't want you! Not enough to betray love for brief and bloody ecstasy."

"The Temple people, they don't really know what you are, do they?"

"No!" he said.

"And you will not lay open your heart to me."

"Never. You will forget me and these dreams will fade. I wager I can make them fade, myself, through prayer for you. I will do it."

"That's a pious tack," I said. "What grants you such favor with the ancient Isis, who drank blood and was the Fount?"

"Don't say those words; it's all lies, all of it. You do not know that this Queen you saw was Isis. What did you learn in these nightmares? Think. You learned that this Queen was the prisoner of those who drank blood and she condemned them! They were evil. Think. Go back into the dream. Think. You thought them evil, evil then, and you think them evil now. In the Temple, you caught the scent of evil. I know you did. I watched you."

"Yes. But you're not evil, Marius, you can't convince me of this! You have a body like marble, you're a blood drinker, but like a god, but not evil!"

He was about to protest when he stopped again. He looked out of the corner of his eye. And then slowly turned his head and let his gaze drift up through the roof of the peristyle.

"Is it the dawn coming," I asked, "the rays of Amon Ra?"

"You are the most maddening human being I've ever known!" he said. "If I had married you, you would have put me in an early grave. I would have been spared all of this!"

"All of what?"

He called out for Flavius, who had been close all the while, listening to everything.

"Flavius, I'm leaving now," he said. "I must. But guard her. When night falls, I'll be here again, as quickly as I can. Should anything precede me, any badly scarred and frightening assailant, go for its head with your sword. The head, remember? And of course your Mistress here will no doubt be quite able to lend a hand in defending herself."

"Yes, sir. Must we leave Antioch?"

"Watch your words, my faithful Greek," I said. "I am Mistress here. We are not leaving Antioch."

"Try to persuade her to prepare," said Marius.

He looked at me.

A long silence fell between us. I knew he read my

thoughts. Then a shudder of the blood dreams passed over me. I saw his eyes brighten. Something quickened in his expression. I shook off the dream, filled with terror. I am no hostess to terror.

"It's all interwound," I murmured, "the dreams, the Temple, you being there, their calling on you for help. What are you, some white god put on Earth to hunt the dark blood drinkers? Does the Queen live?"

"Oh, I wish I were such a god!" he said. "I would be if I could be! That no more blood drinkers will ever be made, of that I am certain. Let them lay flowers on an altar before a statue of basalt!"

I felt such love for him and rushed to him suddenly. "Take me with you now, wherever you are going."

"I can't!" he said. He blinked as though something hurt his eyes. He couldn't fully lift his head.

"It's the coming light, isn't it? You are one of them."

"Pandora, when I come to you, be ready to leave this place!" he said.

And he vanished.

Like that, he vanished. Like that, he was gone from my arms and from my living room and from my house.

I turned away and walked slowly about the shadowy living room. I looked at the murals on the walls; the happy dancing figures with their laurels and their crowns of leaves—Bacchus and his nymphs, so modestly covered for such a riotous crew!

Flavius spoke. "Madam, a sword which I found among your possessions, may I have it in readiness?"

"Yes, and daggers galore, and fire, do not forget fire. It will run from fire." I sighed. How did I know this? I did. So much for it. "But Flavius." I turned around. "It won't come until dark. There is only a small margin of the night left. We can both sleep as soon as we see the sky turn purple." I lifted my hand to my forehead. "I am trying to remember . . ."

"What, Madam?" Flavius said. He looked no less splendid after the spectacle of Marius, simply a man of different proportion but equally fine, and with warm human skin.

"Whether the dreams ever came by day. Was it always night? Oh, I am sleepy and they summon me. Flavius, put a light in my bath. But I'm going to bed. I am drowsy. Can you watch?"

"Yes, Madam."

"Look, the stars have all but faded. What is it like to be one of them, Flavius, to be admired only in the darkness, when men and women live with candles and lamps. To be known and described, only in the heaviness of night, when all the business of day has ended!"

"You are truly the most resourceful woman I've ever known," he said. "How you brought justice to the man who accused you." He took my arm, and we moved towards the bedchamber where I had dressed that morning.

I loved him. An entire lifetime of crises could not have made it stronger.

"You will not sleep in the great bed of the house, in the dining room?"

"No," I said. "That is for the display of marriage, and I will never know marriage again. I want to bathe, but I'm so sleepy."

"I can wake the girls."

"No, to the bed. You have a chamber proper?"

"Yes," he led the way. It was still quite dark. I thought I heard a rustling noise. Realized it was nothing.

And there lay the bed with its small lamp, and on the bed so many pillows in the Oriental style, a soft soft nest into which I fell, like a Persian.

At once, the dream:

We blood drinkers stood in a vast Temple. It was meant to be dark. We could see this dark, as certain animals must see in the dark. We were all bronze-skinned, or tanned, or golden. We were all men.

On the floor lay the Queen screaming. Her skin was white. Pure white. Her long hair was black. Her crown bore the horns and the sun! The crown of Isis. She was the goddess! It took five blood drinkers on either side to hold her down. She thrashed her head from side to side, her eyes seeming to crackle with Divine Light.

"I am your Queen! You cannot do this to me!" How purely white she was, and her screams grew ever more desperate and imploring. "Great Osiris, save me from this! Save me from these blasphemers! Save me from the profane!"

The Priest beside me sneered at her.

The King sat motionless on the throne. But it was not to this King that she prayed. She prayed to an Osiris beyond.

"Hold her more tightly."

Two more came to secure her ankles.

"Drink!" said the Priest to me. "Kneel down and drink from her blood. Her blood is more powerful than any blood that exists in the world. Drink."

She cried softly.

"Monsters, demon children!" she sobbed.

"I won't do it," I said.

"Do it! You must have her blood!"

"No, not against her will. Not like this! She's our Mother Isis!"

"She is our Fount and our prisoner."

"No," I said.

The Priest shoved me forward. I knocked him down to the floor. I looked at her.

She looked at me as indiscriminately as she looked at the others. Her face was delicate and exquisitely painted. Her rage did not distort her features. Her voice was low and full of hatred.

"I will destroy you all," she said. "Some morning, I will escape and walk into the sun's light and all of you will burn! All of you will burn! As I burn! Because I am the Fount! And the evil in me will be burnt and extinguished in all of you forever. Come, you miserable fledgling," she said to me. "Do as they say. Drink, and wait my vengeance.

"The god Amon Ra will rise in the East and I will walk towards him, and his deadly rays will kill me. I shall be a sacrifice of fire to destroy every one of you who has been born of me, transformed by my blood! You greedy wanton gods who would use the power we possess for gain!"

Then a hideous transformation befell the entire dream. She rose to her feet. She was pristine and freshly adorned. Torches burst into flame around her, one and two and three and then many and more, flaring as if they'd just been ignited, till she was surrounded by flame. The gods were gone. She smiled and beckoned to me. She lowered her head; the white beneath her eyes shone as she looked up at me. She smiled. She was cunning.

I woke up screaming.

I was in my bed. Antioch. The lamp burned. Flavius held me. I saw the light shine on his ivory leg as it was stretched out. I saw the light shine on the carved toes.

"Hold onto me, hold me!" I said. "Mother Isis! Hold me.

"How long have I been asleep?"

"Only moments," he said.

"No."

"The sun has just risen. Do you want to go out, lie in the warm sun perhaps?"

"No!" I screamed.

He tightened his warm, desperate comforting grip. "It was only a bad dream, my beautiful lady," he said. "Close your eyes. I'll sleep by your side, with my dagger here."

"Oh, yes, please, please, Flavius. Don't let me go. Hold me," I cried.

I lay down and he snuggled next to me, his knees behind mine, his arm over me.

My eyes opened. I heard Marius's voice again:

"Thank the gods that I don't want you! Not enough to betray love for brief and bloody ecstasy."

"Oh, Flavius," I said. "My skin! Is my skin burning!" I started to rise. "Put out the light. Put out the sun!"

"No, Madam, your skin is as beautiful as it always was. Lie down. Let me sing to you."

"Yes, sing . . ." I said.

I followed his song, it was Homer, it was Achilles and Hector, and I loved the way he sang it, the pauses he made, I pictured those heroes, and the high walls of doomed Troy, and my eyes grew heavy. I drifted. I rested.

He placed his hand over my head, as if to keep the dreams out, as if to be a human dream catcher. And I sighed as he smoothed my hair.

I pictured Marius, the sheen of his skin. It had been so like that of the Queen, and the dazzle of his eyes, so truly like that of the Queen, and I heard him say, "Damn it, Pandora, do you think I wanted my life foreshortened and my destiny extended forever!"

And there followed, before unconsciousness, the utter despair, the sense of worthlessness of all striving. Better that we be no more than beasts, like the lions in the arena.

8

I AWOKE. I could hear the birds. I wasn't sure. I calculated that it was still morning, midmorning.

I walked barefoot into the next room, and through it into the peristyle. I walked on the tiled edge of the Earth and looked up at the blue sky. The sun had not yet risen high enough to be seen directly above.

I unbolted the door and went barefoot to the gate. To the first man I saw, a man of the desert, wearing a long head veil, I said:

"What time is it? Noon?"

"Oh, no, Madam," he said. "Not by half. Have you overslept? How lucky for you." He nodded and went on.

A lamp burned in the living room. I walked into the living room and saw that the lamp stood on the desk which my servants had prepared for me.

The ink was there and so were the pens, and so were sheets of clean parchment.

I sat down and I wrote down everything that I

could remember of the dreams, my eyes straining to see by the miserable little lamp in the shadows, too far from the light that filled the fresh green garden of the peristyle.

My arm hurt finally from the speed with which I scratched at the parchment. In detail I described the last dream, the torches, the Queen's smile, her beckoning to me.

It was done. All the while, I had set aside the pages to dry all about me on the floor. There was no breeze or wind to threaten them. I gathered them up.

I went to the edge of the garden deliberately to look at the blue sky, this sheaf of papers close to my breast. Blue and clear.

"And you cover this world," I said. "And you are changeless, save for one light that rises and sets," I said to the sky. "Then comes the night with deceptive and seductive patterns!"

"Madam!" It was Flavius behind me, and very sleepy. "You've scarcely slept at all. You need rest. Go back to bed."

"Go get my sandals now, hurry," I said.

And as he disappeared, so did I—out the front gate of the house, walking as fast as I could.

I was halfway to the Temple of Isis when I realized the discomfort of confronting this filthy street in bare feet. I realized I wore the rumpled linen dresses in which I'd slept. My hair streamed. I didn't slow my pace.

I was elated. I was not helpless as when I had fled my Father's house. I was not edgy and in deep danger as when Lucius had pointed me out to the Roman soldiers last night.

I was not gripped in fear as I had been when the Queen smiled to me in the dream. Nor shivering as I had been upon waking.

I walked on and on. I was in the grip of an immense drama. I would see it through to the last act.

People passed—laborers of the morning, an old man with a crooked stick. I barely saw these people.

I took a cold small delight in the fact that they noticed my loose, free hair and my wrinkled gowns. I wondered what it must be like to separate oneself from all civilization and never worry again about the position of a fastening or a pin, to sleep on grass, to fear nothing!

Fear nothing! Ah, that was so beautiful to me.

I came to the Forum. The markets were busy; the beggars were out in full force. Curtained litters were being carried every which way. The philosophers were teaching under the porticoes. I could hear those huge strange noises that always come from a harbor—of the cargo being dropped, perhaps, I didn't know. I smelled the Orontes. I hoped Lucius's body was floating in it.

I went up the steps and right into the Temple of Isis.

"The High Priest and Priestess," I said. "I must see them." I walked past a confused and distinctly virginal-looking young woman and went into the side chamber where they had first spoken to me. No table. Only the couch. I went into another apartment of the Temple. A table. Scrolls.

I heard feet rushing. The Priestess came to me. She was already painted for the day and her wig and ornaments were in place. I felt no shock as I looked at her.

"Look," I said. "I had another dream." I pointed to the sheets which I had piled neatly on the table. "I've written down everything for you."

The Priest arrived. He approached the table and stared at the sheets.

"Read it all, every word. Read it now. Bear witness lest something happens to me!"

The Priest and Priestess stood on opposite sides of me, the Priest carefully lifting the pages to study each one, while not actually turning over the stack.

"I am a migrant soul," I said. "She wants some reckoning or favor of me, I don't know which, but she lives! She is no mere statue."

They stared at me.

"Well? Speak up? Everyone comes to you for guidance."

"But Madam," said the Priest, "we can't read any of this."

"What?"

"It's written in the most ancient and ornate form of the old picture writing."

"What!"

I stared down at the pages. I saw only my own words as they had flowed in a cadence from my mind, through my hand, through my pen. I couldn't make my eyes fix upon the form of the letters.

I lifted the last page and read aloud, "Her smile was cunning. It filled me with fear." I held out the page.

They shook their heads in firm denial.

Suddenly there was a little ruckus and Flavius, much out of breath and red in the face, was admitted to the room. He had my sandals. He took one look at me and rested back against the wall in great and obvious relief.

"Come here," I said.

He obeyed.

"Now look at these pages, read them, are they not in Latin?"

Two slaves came timidly, hastily washing my feet and fastening on my sandals. Above me Flavius looked at the pages.

"This is ancient Egyptian writing," Flavius said. "The oldest form I've ever seen. This would fetch a fortune in Athens!"

"I just wrote it!" I said. I looked at the Priest, then the Priestess. "Summon your tall blond-haired friend," I said. "Get him here. The mind reader, the one who can read the old script."

"We can't, Madam." The Priest looked helplessly at the Priestess.

"Why not? Where is he? He only comes after dark, doesn't he?" I asked.

They both nodded.

"And when he shops for books, all the books on

Egypt, he does this by the light of lamps too?" I asked. I already knew the answer.

They looked at one another helplessly.

"Where does he live?"

"Madam, we do not know. Please don't try to find him. He will be here as soon as the light fades. He cautioned us last night that you were most precious to him."

"You don't know where he lives."

I stood up.

"All right," I said, I picked up the sheaf of my pages, my spectacular ancient writing.

"Your burnt one," I said, as I walked out of the room, "your murdering blood drinker. Did he come last night? Did he leave you an offering?"

"Yes," said the Priest. He looked humiliated. "Lady Pandora, rest and take some food."

"Yes," said my loyal Flavius, "you must."

"Not a chance," I said. Clutching the pages, I walked across the great hall to the front doors. They pleaded with me. I ignored them.

I went out into the heat of the day. Flavius followed. The Priest and Priestess pleaded with us to remain.

I scanned the enormous marketplace. The good booksellers were all grouped at the far left end of the Forum. I walked across the square.

Flavius struggled to keep up. "Madam, please, what are you going to do? You've lost your mind."

"I have not and you know it," I said. "You saw him last night!"

"Madam, wait for him at the Temple, as he asked," Flavius said.

"Why? Why should I do that?" I asked.

The bookshops were numerous, containing manuscripts in all languages. "Egypt, Egypt!" I cried out, both in Latin and Greek. There was lots of noise, many buyers and sellers. Plato was everywhere, and Aristotle. There was a whole stack of the book of his life by Caesar Augustus, which he had completed in the years before his death.

"Egypt!" I cried out. Merchants pointed to old scrolls. Fragments.

The canopies flapped in the breeze. I looked into one room after another, at rows of slaves busily copying, slaves dipping their pens, who did not dare to look up from their work.

There were slaves outside, in the shade, writing letters dictated by humble men and women. It was all very busy.

Trunks were being brought into one shop. The owner, an elderly man, came forward.

"Marius," I said. "I come from Marius, the tall blond one who comes to your shop only by night."

The man said nothing.

I went into the next shop. Everything was Egyptian, not merely the scrolls rolled out for display but the fragments of painting on the walls, the chunks of plaster holding still the profile of a King or Queen, rows of little jars, figures from some long-defiled tomb. How the Egyptians loved to make those tiny wooden figures.

And there I beheld just the sort of man I sought, the true antiquarian. Only reluctantly did he look up from his book, a gray-haired man, the book a codex in modern Egyptian.

"Nothing that would interest Marius?" I asked, walking into the shop. Trunks and boxes blocked me at each turn. "You know, the tall Roman, Marius, who studies the ancient manuscripts, buys the most prized of them? You know the man I mean. Very blue eyes. Blond hair. He comes by night; you stay open for him."

The man nodded. He glanced at Flavius and said with a lift of his eyebrows, "Quite an ivory leg there." Cultured Greek. Excellent. "Grecian, Oriental and perfectly pale."

"I come on Marius's behalf," I said.

"I save everything for him, as he asks," said the man with a little shrug. "I sell nothing that isn't offered first to Marius."

"I'm sure you do. I come on his behalf." I looked around. "May I sit down?"

"Oh, please do, forgive me," said the man. He gestured to a sturdy trunk. Flavius stood perplexed. The man sat back down at his cluttered table.

"I wish I had a proper table. Where is my slave? I know I have some wine around here. I just . . . I was reading in this text the most amazing story!"

"Really," I said. "Well, take a look at this!" I thrust the pages into his hand.

"My God, but this is beautiful copying," he said, "and so fresh!" He whispered under his breath. He could make out many of the words. "Marius will be very interested in this. This is about the legends of Isis, this is what Marius studies."

I drew back the papers gently. "I've written this for him!"

"You wrote it?"

"Yes, but you see, I want to surprise him with something, a gift! Something newly arrived, something he hasn't seen yet."

"Well, there's quite a lot."

"Flavius, money."

"Madam, I don't have any."

"That's not true, Flavius; you wouldn't leave the house without the keys and some money. Hand it over."

"Oh, I'll take it on credit if it's for Marius," said the old man. "Hmmm, you know, several things came onto the market this very week. It's because of the famine in Egypt. People were forced to sell, I suppose. You never know where an Egyptian manuscript comes from. But here—" He reached up and took a fragile papyrus from its niche in the dusty crisscross of wooden shelves.

He laid it down reverently and most cautiously opened it. The papyrus had been well preserved, but it was flaking at the edges. The thing would disintegrate if not handled with care.

I stood to look at it over his shoulder. A dizziness overcame me. I saw the desert and a town of huts with roofs of palm branches. I strained to open my eyes.

"This is," said the old man, "positively the oldest manuscript in Egyptian which I have ever seen! Here, steady yourself, my dear. Lean upon my shoulder. Let me give you my stool."

"No, not necessary," I said gazing at the letters. I read aloud, "To my Lord, Narmer, King of Upper and Lower Egypt, who are these enemies of me that say I do not walk in righteousness? When has Your Majesty ever known me not to be righteous? Indeed I seek to do always more than what is asked of me or expected. When have I not heard every word of the accused so that he may be judged in fairness, as would Your Majesty? . . ."

I broke off. My head swam. Some brief recollection. I was a child and we were all going up into the mountains over the desert to ask the god Osiris, the blood god, to look into the heart of the evildoer. "Look," said those around me. The god was a man of perfection, bronze of skin and under the moon; he took the condemned and slowly drew out his blood. Beside me a woman whispered that the god had made his judgment and rendered punishment and the evil blood would go back now to be cleansed and reborn in another in which it would do no harm.

I tried to banish this vision, this sense of enclosing remembrance. Flavius was greatly concerned and held me by the shoulders.

I stood suspended in two worlds. I gazed out at the bright sun striking the stones of the Forum, and I lived somewhere else, a young man running up a mountain, declaring my innocence. "Summon the old blood god! He will look into my husband's heart and see that the man lies. I never lay with another." Oh, sweet darkness, come, I needed it to shroud the mountains because the blood god slept by day, hidden, lest Ra, the sun god, find him and destroy him out of jealousy.

"Because she had conquered them all," I whispered. I meant Queen Isis. "Flavius, hold me."

"I have you, Madam."

"There," said the old man, who had risen and pushed me down on his stool.

The night over Egypt filled with stars. I saw it as distinctly as I saw this shop around me in Antioch at midday. I saw the stars and knew I had won. The god would rule. "Oh, come forth, please, from this mountain, our beloved Osiris, and look into my husband's heart and my heart, and if you find me in the wrong, then my blood is yours, I pledge it." He was coming! There he was, as I had seen him in childhood before the Priests of Ra had forbidden the old worship. "Righteousness, righteousness, righteousness!" the crowd chanted. The man who was my husband cowered as the god pointed his finger in judgment at him. "Give me this evil blood and I shall devour it," said the god. "Then bring back my offerings. Do not be cowards in the face of a rich priesthood. You stand before a god." He pointed at each of the villagers and pronounced his or her name. He knew trades. He could read their minds! He drew back his lips and showed his fangs. The vision dissolved. I stared at common objects as though they had life and venom.

"Oh, yea gods," I said in genuine distress. "I must reach Marius. I must reach him now!" When he heard these things, Marius would draw me into the truth with him. He had to do it.

"Hire a litter for your Mistress," said the old bookseller to Flavius. "She is overtired, and it's too long a walk up that hill!"

"Hill?" I perked up. This man knew where Marius lived! I quickly went faint again, bowing my head, and with a weary gesture said, "Please, old gentleman, tell my steward precisely how to reach the house."

"Of course. I know two short cuts, one slightly more difficult than another. We deliver books to Marius all the time."

Flavius was staring aghast.

I tried to suppress my smile. This was going much better than I had ever hoped. But I was torn and bruised from the visions of Egypt. I hated the look of the desert, the mountains, the thought of blood gods.

I rose to go.

"It's a pink villa on the very edge of the city," said the old man. "It's just within the walls, overlooking the river, the last house. Once it was a country house outside the walls. It is on a mountain of stones. But no one will answer Marius's gate by day. All know how he wants to sleep all day and study all night, as is his custom. We leave our books with the boys."

"He'll welcome me," I said.

"If you wrote that, most likely he will," said the old man.

Then we were off. The sun had fully risen. The square was filled with shoppers. Women carried baskets on their heads. The Temples were thriving. It was a game, darting through the crowd, one way and then another.

"Come on, Flavius," I said.

It was a torture keeping to Flavius's slow pace as we mounted the hill, turn by turn, drawing ever closer.

"You know this is madness!" said Flavius. "He can't be awake during the light of day; you've proven this to me and to yourself! I, the incredulous Athenian, and you the cynical Roman. What are we doing?"

Up and up we climbed, passing one sumptuous house after another. Locked gates. The bark of guard dogs.

"Hurry up. Must I listen to this lecture forever? Ah, there, look, my beloved Flavius. The pink house, the last house. Marius lives in style. Look at the walls and the gates."

At last I had my hands on the iron bars. Flavius collapsed on the grass across the small road. He was spent.

I pulled on the bell rope.

Trees laid down heavy limbs over the top of the walls. Through the mesh of leaf, I could make out a figure that came out on the high porch of the second floor.

"No admittance!" he cried out.

"I have to see Marius," I said. "He's expecting me!" I cupped my hands and shouted. "He wants me to come. He told me to come."

Flavius said a quick prayer under his breath. "Oh, Mistress, I hope you know this man better than you knew your own brother."

I laughed. "There is no comparison," I said. "Stop complaining."

The figure had disappeared. I heard running feet.

Finally two dark-headed young boys appeared before me, little more than children, beardless, with long black curls, and beautifully dressed in gold-trimmed tunics. They looked Chaldean.

"Open the gate, hurry!" I said.

"Madam, I can't admit you," said the speaker of the two. "I cannot admit anyone to this house until Marius himself comes. Those are his orders."

"Comes from where?" I asked.

"Madam, he appears when he wishes, then he receives who he will. Madam, please, tell me your name and I will tell him that you have called."

"You either open the gate or I will climb over the wall," I said.

The boys were horrified. "No, Madam, you can't do that!"

"Well? Aren't you going to shout for help?" I asked.

The two slaves stared amazed. They were so pretty. One was slightly taller than the other. Both wore exquisite bracelets.

"Just as I thought," I said. "There's no one else here

but you." I turned and tested the thick snaggle of vine that rose over the plastered brick. I leapt up and planted my right foot as high as I could in the thick mesh and rose in one leap to throw my arms over the top of the wall.

Flavius had risen from the grass and rushed to me.

"Madam, I beg you not to do this," said Flavius. "Madam, this is bad, bad, bad! You can't just climb this man's wall."

The servants within were chattering frantically with one another. I think it was in Chaldean.

"Madam, I fear for you!" cried Flavius. "How can I protect you from such a man as this Marius? Madam, the man will be angry with you!"

I lay on the top of the wall, on my stomach, catching my breath. The garden inside was vast and lovely. Ah, what marble fountains. The two slaves had backed up and were staring at me as if I were a powerful monster.

"Please, please!" both boys pleaded with me at once. "He'll exact a terrible vengeance! You don't know him. Please, Madam, wait!"

"Hand me the sheets of paper, Flavius, hurry. I have no time for disobedience!"

Flavius complied. "Oh, this is wrong, wrong, wrong!" he said. "Nothing can come of this but the most fearful misunderstandings."

Then I slid down the inside of the wall, tickled all over by the thick overlay of bristling and brilliant leaves, and I lay my head in the matted tendrils and blossoms. I didn't fear the bees. I never have. I rested. I held tight to my written pages. Then moved to the gate so I could see Flavius.

"You let me handle Marius," I said. "Now, you didn't come out without your dagger."

"No, I did not," he said, lifting his cloak to reveal it, "and with your permission I would like to plunge it through my heart now so that I will be most assuredly stone-cold dead before the Master of this house arrives home to find you running rampant in his garden!"

"Permission denied," I said. "Don't you dare. Haven't you heard all that has been said? You are on guard not against Marius but against a shriveled limping demon of burnt flesh. He'll come at dark! What if he reaches here before Marius?"

"Oh, yea gods, help me!" His hands flew to his face.

"Flavius, straighten up. You are a man! Do I have to remind you of this perpetually? You are watching for this dreaded burnt bag of bones, and he is weak. Remember what Marius said. Go for his head. Stab him in the eyes, just cut him and cut him and shout for me, and I will come. Now go to sleep until dark. He can't come till then, if he even knows to come here! Besides, I think Marius will arrive first."

I turned and walked towards the open doors of the villa. The beautiful long-haired boys were in tears.

For a moment the tranquillity and moist cool air of the garden lulled all fear in me, and I seemed safe, among patterns I understood, far far from dark Temples, safe in Tuscany, in our own family gardens there, which had been so rich like this.

"Let me beg you one last time to come back out of this man's garden!" Flavius shouted.

I ignored him.

All the doors of this lovely plastered villa stood open to the porches above or the outdoors below. Listen to the trickling of the fountains. There were lemon trees, and many a marble statue of a lazy, sensuous god or goddess, round which flowers grew in rich purple or blue. Diana, the huntress, rose from a bed of orange blossoms, the marble old and pitted. And there, a lazy Ganymede, half-covered in green moss, marked some path that had been overgrown. Far off, I could see the naked bending Venus at her bath on the edge of a pool. Water flowed into the pool. I glimpsed fountains all around me.

The small common white lilies had gone wild, and there stood old olive trees with marvelously twisted trunks, so wondrous to climb in childhood.

A pastoral sweetness hung over all, yet nature had been kept at bay. The stucco of the walls was freshly painted, and so were the wooden shutters, opened wide.

The two boys were crying. "Madam, he'll be so angry."

"Well, not with you," I said, as I entered the house. I had come across the grass and left scarcely any footprint on the marble floor.

"Boys, do stop sobbing! You don't even have to plead with him to believe you. Isn't that true? He'll read the truth in your thoughts?"

This startled each in his own way. They looked at me warily.

I stopped just past the threshold. Something emanated from the house, not loud enough to be called a sound, but very like the rhythmic precursor of a sound. I had heard this very soundless rhythm before. When was it? In the Temple? When first I entered the room where Marius had hidden behind the screen?

I walked on marble floors from room to room. Breezes everywhere played with the hanging lamps. There were many lamps. And the candles. How many candles. And lamps on stands. Why, when this place was lighted up, it must have been bright as day!

And gradually I realized the entire lower floor was a library, except for the inevitable sumptuous Roman bath, and an enormous wardrobe of clothes.

Every other room was filled with books. Nothing but books. Of course there were couches for lying and reading, and desks for writing, but every wall had its prodigious stack of scrolls or shelves of bound books.

Also there were strange doors. They appeared to open onto concealed stairwells. But they had no locks and seemed to be made of polished granite. I found at least two of these! And one chamber of the first floor was totally enclosed in stone and locked in the same way, by impenetrable doors.

As the slaves trembled and sobbed I went outside and up the stairs to the second floor. Empty. Every room simply empty, except the room that obviously belonged to the boys! There were their beds, and their little Persian altars and gods, and rich rugs and tasseled pillows and the usual Oriental swirl of design.

I came down.

The boys sat at the main door, as if positioned like marble statues, each with his knees up, head down, weeping softly, perhaps getting a bit worn out.

"Where are the bedrooms of this house? Where is Marius's bedroom? Where is the kitchen? Where is the household shrine?"

One of them let out a soft choking cry. "There are no bedrooms."

"Of course not," I said.

"Our food is brought to us," wailed the other. "Cooked and most delicious. But I fear that, unwittingly, we have enjoyed our last meal."

"Oh, do take it easy. How can he blame you for what I've done? You're merely children and he's a gentle being, is he not? Here, put these pages on his desk, and weight them down so that they don't fly away."

"Yes, he is most gentle," said the boy. "But most set in his ways."

I closed my eyes. I sensed the sound again, the emanating encroaching sound. Did it want to be heard? I couldn't tell. It seemed impersonal, like the beat of a sleeping heart or the flow of the water in the fountains.

I walked over to a large beautiful couch, draped in fine silk with Persian designs. It was very wide and seemed to bear, despite much straightening, the imprint of a man's form. There was the pillow there, all fluffed and fresh, yet still I could see the indentation of the head, where the man had lain.

"Does he lie here?"

The boys leapt to their feet, curls flying.

"Yes, Madam, that is his couch," said the speaker of the two. "Please, please, don't touch it. He lies there for hours and reads. Madam, please! He is most particular that we do not lie on it playfully in his absence, though he gives us free rein in every other regard."

"He'll know if you even touch it!" said the other boy, speaking up for the first time.

"I'm going to sleep on it," I said. I lay down and closed my eyes. I rolled over and brought up my knees. "I am tired. I want only sleep. I feel safe for the first time in so long."

"You do?" asked one of the boys.

"Oh, come here and lie by me. Bring pillows for your heads, so that he will see me before he sees you. He knows me well. The pages I have brought, where are they, yes, on the desk, well, they will make it clear why I have come in. It's all changed now. Something is wanted from me. I have no choice. There is no road home. Marius will understand. I've come as close to him as possible for my protection."

I lay back right in the hollow of the pillow where he lay. I took a long deep breath. "The breeze is like music here," I whispered, "do you hear it?"

I slept the deep exhausted sleep which I had held off now for so many hours of both night and day.

Hours must have passed.

I woke with a start. The sky was purple. The slaves

were curled up next to the couch, just beneath me, like terrified little animals.

I heard the noise again, the sound, distinct, a pulse. I thought oddly of something I used to like to do as a child. It was this: I would put my ear to my Father's chest. And when I heard his heart, then I would kiss it. It had always made him happy.

I rose, realizing that I was not fully awake but certain this was no dream. I was in the beautiful villa of Marius in Antioch. The marble rooms opened one upon another.

I went to the last room, the room enclosed in stone. The doors were impossibly heavy. But suddenly, silently, they opened as if pushed from within.

I entered a massive chamber. Another pair of doors lay ahead of me. They too were made of stone. They had to lead to a stairwell, for the house ended just beyond.

These doors too suddenly opened, as if released by a spring!

Light from below.

A stairway went down from the threshold of the door. It was white marble, and newly made, with no wear of feet on it. So smooth, each slab, so clean.

A soft series of flames burned below, sending their antic shadows up the stairwell.

The sound now seemed louder. I closed my eyes. Oh, that all the world were these polished chambers and all that exists could be explained within.

Suddenly, I heard a loud cry.

"Lady Pandora!"

I spun around.

"Pandora, he is over the wall!"

The boys came screaming through the house, echoing Flavius's cry, "Lady Pandora!"

A great darkness gathered itself right before my eyes and then descended on me, throwing the helpless, beseeching boys to the side. I was almost pitched down the stairwell.

Then I realized I was in the grasp of the burnt thing. I looked down to see the black wrinkled arm, like old leather, that held me. Strong spices filled my nostrils. Fresh clothing covered the hideously thin leg I saw, the dried-up foot.

"Boys, get the lamps, set it on fire!" I shouted. I fought desperately, driving us both back from the stairwell, but I couldn't get loose from the creature. "Boys, the lamps downstairs!"

The boys clung to one another.

"I have you!" this creature said tenderly in my ear.

"No, you don't!" I said, and gave him one fine blow with my right elbow. It drove him off balance. He nearly toppled. But he didn't let me go. The whiteness of his tunic glowed in the shadows as he once more enclosed my arms, and rendered me almost helpless.

"Boys, downstairs, lamps full of oil!" I said. "Flavius!"

The creature hugged me as if he were a giant snake. I could scarce breathe.

"We can't go downstairs!" one of the boys cried.

"We're not allowed," said the other.

The creature laughed in my ear, a rich deep laugh.

"Not everyone is so bound to rebellion as you are, beautiful woman, outwitting your brother at the foot of the Temple steps."

It was shocking to hear this clear articulate voice coming from a body which seemed burnt beyond all hope of life. I watched the blackened fingers moving over my own. I felt the touch of something cold on my neck. Then I felt the punctures. His fangs.

"No!" I cried. I thrashed back and forth in his grip, then threw all of my weight against him so that he almost toppled again but didn't fall.

"Stop it, bitch, or I'll kill you now."

"Why don't you?" I demanded.

I twisted to see his face. It was like that of a long-dead corpse dried in the desert, burnt black with a spine of a nose, and arched lips that seemed quite unable to close over white teeth and the two fangs he bared now as he looked at me.

His eyes were full of blood, as Marius's eyes had been. His hair was a fine black mop, very thick, fresh and clean, as though it had sprung from his body, renewing itself like magic.

"Yes," he said confidently. "That is just what happened. And very soon I will have the blood I need to renew all of me! I won't be this hideous monster you see. I'll be what I was before those Egyptian fools put her in the sun!"

"Hmmm, so she kept her promise," I said. "She walked into the rays of Amon Ra so you would all burn up."

"What do you know of it? She hasn't moved or

spoken in a thousand years. I was that old when they removed the stones that enclosed her. She couldn't have walked into the sun. She is a great sacred vial of blood, an enthroned source of power, that's all, and I will have that blood, which your Marius has stolen out of Egypt."

I pondered, searching desperately for a means to free myself.

"You came to me as a gift," said the burnt one. "You were all I needed to take on Marius! He wears his affections and weakness for you like bright silk garments for me to see!"

"I see," I said.

"No, you don't!" he said. My head was pulled back by my hair. I screamed in annoyance.

His sharp teeth went into my neck. A series of heated wires threaded me through and through.

I swooned. An ecstasy rendered me motionless. I tried to resist, but I saw visions. I saw him in his glory, a golden man of an Eastern land, in a Temple of skulls. He was dressed in bright green silk breeches with an ornamented band around his forehead. Face delicate of nose and mouth. Then I saw him, without explanation, burst into flames that sent his slaves screaming. He twisted and turned in these flames, not dying but suffering exquisitely.

My head was swimming, and I was weakening. My blood flowed from all parts of my body into his wretched form. I thought of my Father, of my Father saying, "Live, Lydia!" I wrenched my neck away from him and turned, poking him hard with my shoulder, and then pushed him with two hands so that he slid backwards on the floor. I brought my knee up against him. Nothing could get him off me!

I tried to reach for my dagger, but I was too dizzy, and besides, I didn't have my dagger. My only chance lay with the burning oil in the lamps at the foot of the stairs. I turned, reeling, and the monster caught me again with both hands by my long hair. He yanked me back.

"You demon!" I said. His strength had worn me out. He tightened his grip slowly. I knew that soon my arms would break.

"Ah," he said, twisting free of me, and holding tight as ever. "My purpose is served."

A brighter light suddenly filled up the stairway.

A torch was placed at the foot of the steps. Then Marius stepped into view.

He appeared utterly calm and he appeared to be looking past me into the eyes of my captor.

"And what will you do now, Akbar?" Marius asked. "Hurt her, violate her but one more time, and I shall kill you. Kill her, and you will die in agony. Let her go and you can run."

He mounted the steps one by one.

"You underestimate me," said the burnt thing, "you arrogant Roman bumbler, you think I don't know you keep the Queen and the King, that you stole them out of Egypt? It is known. The word is spread through the world, through the Northern woods, through the wild lands, through the lands of which you know nothing. You killed the Elder who guarded the King and the Queen and stole them! The King and Queen have not moved or spoken in a thousand years. You took our Queen from Egypt. You think you are a Roman Emperor? You think she is a Queen you can take captive, like Cleopatra! Cleopatra was a Greek whore. This is our Isis, our Akasha! You blaspheming fool. Now let me into Akasha's presence. Stand against me, and this woman, the only mortal whom you truly love, dies."

Marius came up step by step towards us.

"Akbar, did your informants tell you that it was the Elder in Egypt, her long keeper himself, who left the Royal Pair to stand in the sun?" asked Marius. He took another step upward. "Did they tell you that it was the Elder that caused the sun to strike them, the fire which destroyed hundreds of us, and spared the oldest only so they could live in agony as you do?"

Marius made a quick gesture. I felt the fangs deep in my neck. I couldn't get away. Again, I saw this creature in his former splendor, taunting me with his beauty, his jeweled feet as he danced, surrounded by painted women.

I heard Marius right beside me, but I couldn't make out the words.

The folly of it all went through my mind. I had led this creature to Marius, but was that what the Mother wanted? Akasha, that was the ancient name written on the bodies dumped on the steps of the Temple. I knew her name. I knew it in the dreams. I was losing consciousness. "Marius," I called out with all my strength.

My head fell forward, free of the fangs. I fought this total captivating weakness. I deliberately pictured the Emperor Augustus receiving us on his deathbed. "I shall not see the end of this comedy," I whispered.

"Oh, yes, you shall." It was Marius's calm voice right near us. I opened my eyes. "Akbar, don't risk it again, you've shown your determination."

"Don't reach for me again, Marius," said the burnt creature. "My teeth caress her neck. But one more drop and her heart is silent."

The rich dark of night brightened the torch below. That was all I could see. The torch. "Akasha," I whispered.

The burnt thing took a deep breath, his chest heaving against me. "Her blood is beautiful," he said. He kissed my cheek with the parched burnt lips. I closed my eyes. It was becoming harder and harder for me to breathe. I couldn't open my eyes.

He went on talking.

"You see, I have no fear to take her into death with me, Marius, for if I must die by your hand, why not with her as my consort?"

These words were distant, echoing.

"Pick her up in your arms," said Marius. He was very close to us. "And carry her gently, as if she were your only beloved child, and come down with me into the Shrine. Come and see the Mother. Kneel before Akasha and see what she will allow!"

I swooned again, but I heard the creature laugh. He did lift me now, under the knees, and my head fell back. We went down the steps.

"Marius," I said, "he's weak. You can kill him." My face fell against the chest of the burnt one as we descended. I could feel the bones of his chest. "Really, very weak," I said, scarcely able to remain conscious. Akasha, yes, her true name.

"Carefully, my friend," said Marius. "She dies and I destroy you. You've almost overplayed your hand. She narrows your chances with every labored breath. Pandora, be silent, please. Akbar is a great blood drinker, a great god."

I felt a cold firm hand clasp mine.

We had reached the lower floor. I tried to lift my head. I saw rows of lamps, splendid wall paintings hammered with gold, a ceiling veiled in gold.

Two great stone doors were opened. A chapel lay within, a chapel full of dense fluttering devotional light and the overpowering scent of lilies.

The blood drinker who held me let out a cry. "Mother Isis," he said piteously. "Oh, Akasha!"

He released me, setting me down on my feet, as Marius at once took hold of me, and the blistered and damaged one rushed towards the altar.

I stared, amazed. But I was dying. I couldn't breathe. I was falling to the floor. I tried to swallow air but I could not. I could not stand without Marius.

But oh, to leave the Earth and all its miseries with such a vision:

There they sat, The Great Goddess Isis and the King Osiris, or so it seemed, bronzed in skin, not white like the poor captive Queen in my dreams, but perfectly arrayed in garments of spun gold pleated and sewn in the fixed Egyptian style. Their black hair was long, plaited, real. The paint on their faces was fresh, the dark eye-lining and mascara, the reddened lips.

She wore no crown of the horns and sun disk. Her collar of gold and jewels was superb, shimmering and alive in my eyes.

"I must get the crown, restore the crown!" I said aloud, hearing this voice come from me as if it had been born elsewhere to instruct me. My eyes closed.

The black thing knelt before the Queen.

I couldn't see clearly. I felt Marius's arms, and then a gush of hot blood come into my mouth. "No, Marius, protect her!" I tried to speak. My words were washed away in this infusion of blood. "Protect the Mother!" Again it came filling my mouth so that I had to swallow. Immediately I felt the strength, the power of this blood, infinitely stronger than the pull of Akbar. The blood rushed like so many rivers to the sea, through my body. It would not be stopped. Another gush followed, as if a giant storm had driven the river even faster into its delta, its broken and random streams seeking every morsel of flesh.

A wide and wondrous world opened and would have welcomed me, sunlight in the deep forest, but I wouldn't see it. I broke free. "The Queen, save her from him!" I whispered. Did the blood drip from my lips? No, it was gone inside me.

Marius wouldn't listen to me. Again a bloody wound was pressed to my mouth, and the blood was driven ever faster. I felt the air fill my lungs. I could feel the length of my own body, sturdy, standing on its own. The blood brightened inside me like light, as though it had enflamed my heart. I opened my eyes. I was a pillar. I saw Marius's face, his golden eyelashes, his deep blue eyes. His long hair parted in the middle fell to his shoulders. He was ageless, a god.

"Protect her!" I cried. I turned and pointed.

A veil was lifted that had all my life hung between me and all things; now in their true color and shape, they gave forth their deliberate purpose: the Queen stared forward, immobile as the King. Life could not have imitated such serenity, such utter paralysis. I heard water dropping from the flowers. Tiny drops striking the marble floor, the fall of a single leaf. I turned and saw it, curled and rocking on the stones, this tiny leaf. I heard the breeze move under the golden canopied ceiling. And the lamps had tongues of flame to sing.

The world was a woven song, a tapestry of song. The multicolored Mosiacs gleamed, then lost all form, then even pattern. The walls dissolved into clouds of colored mist which welcomed us, through which we could roam forever.

And there she sat, The Queen of Heaven, reigning over all in supreme and unperturbed stillness.

All the yearning of my childish heart was fulfilled. "She lives, she is real, she reigns over Earth and Heaven."

The King and the Queen. They didn't stir. Their eyes beheld nothing. They did not look at us. They did not look at the burnt thing as he drew closer and closer to their throne.

The arms of the Royal Pair were covered in many inscribed and intricate bracelets. Their hands rested on their thighs. It was the manner of many an Egyptian statue. But there never has been a statue to equal either of them.

"The crown, she would have her crown," I said. With astonishing vigor I walked forward towards her.

Marius took my hand. Keenly, he watched the progress of the burnt one.

"She was before all such crowns," Marius said, "they do not mean anything to her."

The thought itself burst with the sweetness of a grape on my tongue. Of course she was there before. In my dreams, she had had no crown. She was safe. Marius kept her safe.

"My Queen," said Marius from behind me. "You have a supplicant. It is Akbar from the East. He would drink the royal blood. What is your will, Mother?"

His voice was so tranquil! He had no fears.

"Mother Isis, let me drink!" cried this burnt creature. He stood up, threw up his arms and created another dancing vision of his former self. He wore human skulls hanging from his belt. He wore a necklace of blackened human fingers! Another of blackened human ears! It was grisly and revolting, yet he seemed to think it seductive and overpowering. At once the image left him. The god from the faraway land was on his knees.

"I am your servant and always was! I slew only the

evildoer, as you commanded. I never abandoned your true worship."

How fragile and insignificant seemed this pleading one, so revolting, so easy to clear away now from her presence. I looked at the King Osiris, as remote and indifferent as the Queen.

"Marius," I said, "the corn for Osiris; doesn't he want the corn? He's the god of the corn." I was filled with visions of our processions in Rome, of people singing and bearing the offerings.

"No, he doesn't want the corn," said Marius. He laid his hand on my shoulder.

"They are true, they are real!" I cried out. "It is all real. Everything is changed. Everything is redeemed."

The burnt thing turned and glared at me. But I was quite beyond all reason. He turned back to the Queen and reached out for her foot.

How her toenails flashed in the light with the golden flesh beneath them. But she was stone-still, as was the crownless King, without seeming judgment or power.

The creature suddenly sprang up and tried to seize the Queen by the neck!

I screamed.

"Shameless, despicable."

Swiftly the frozen right arm of the Queen rose, her hand surrounding the burnt thing's skull and crushing it, the blood gushing down her as the monster gave his last fractured cry for mercy. She caught his body as it dropped over her waist. She hurled it in the air, and all its limbs broke loose from it, crashing to the floor like so much timber.

A gusting wind caught each remnant and gathered them all in one as a lamp fell from its three-legged stand to spill its burning oil on the remains.

"The heart, look," I said. "I can see its heart. The heart beats."

But the fire quickly consumed the heart, consumed the flexing fingers and the writhing toes. There was a great stirring, a dance in the fire of bones, bones whirling in the flames, and then the bones blackened, thinned, snapped to pieces, became fragments; all of this thing was reduced at last to smoking cinders, crisping and skittering on the floor.

Then came the breeze again, full of the breath of the garden, lifting these cinders and carrying them away, like so many fragile tiny black insects, into the shadows of the antechamber.

I was spellbound.

The Queen was as before, her hand in its old place. She and the King stared at nothing, as if nothing had taken place. Only the wretched stain on her gown bore witness.

Their eyes took no heed of Marius or of me.

Then there was only quiet in the chapel. Only sweet perfumed quiet. Golden light. I breathed deeply. I could hear the oil in the lamps turned to flame. The Mosiacs were peopled with finely made worshipers. I could see the slow minute beginnings of decay of the various flowers, and it seemed but another strain of the same song that expressed their growth, their browning edges but another color in no contradiction to their brilliant colors.

"Forgive me, Akasha," Marius said softly, "that I let him come so close. I was not wise."

I cried. Great gushing tears came from me.

"You summoned me," I said to the Queen through my tears. "You called me here! I will do all you want of me."

Slowly her right arm rose; it rose from her thigh and extended itself and her hand very gently curved in the beckoning gesture of the dream, but there was no smile, no change in her frozen face.

I felt something invisible and irresistible wrap itself around me. It came from her outstretching welcoming arm. It was sweet and soft and caressing. It made a flush of pleasure through all my limbs and my face.

I moved forward, wound up in its will.

"I beg you, Akasha!" Marius said softly. "I beg you under the name of Inanna, under the name of Isis, under the name of all goddesses, don't hurt her!"

Marius simply didn't understand! Marius had never known her worship! I knew. I knew that her blood drinker children had meant to be judges of the evildoer, and drink only from the condemned, according to her laws. I saw the god of the dark cave, whom I'd seen in my vision. I understood all.

I wanted to tell Marius. But I couldn't. Not now. The world was reborn, all systems built upon skepticism or selfishness were as fragile as spiderwebs and meant to be swept away. My own moments of despair had been nothing more than detours into an unholy and self-centered blackness.

"The Queen of Heaven," I whispered. I knew I was speaking in the ancient tongue. A prayer came to my lips.

"And Amon Ra, the Sun God, for all his power, shall never conquer the King of the Dead or his bride, for she is the ruler of the starry heavens, of the moon, of those who would bring the sacrifice of the evildoer. Cursed be those who misuse this magic. Cursed be those who seek to steal it!"

I felt myself, a human, held together by the intricate threads of blood which Marius had given me. I felt the design of its support. It had no weight, my body.

I was lifted towards her. Her arm came around me and pulled my hair back from my face. I put out my arms to embrace her neck because I could do nothing else. We were too close for any other possible sign of love.

I felt the soft silk of her real plaited hair, and the coldness and firmness of her shoulders, her arm. Yet she did not look at me. She was a petrified thing. Could she look at me? Did she choose to remain silent, staring forward? Did some evil spell hold her helpless, a spell from which a thousand hymns might waken her?

In my delirium I saw the words engraved in gold pieces among the jewels of her collar: "Bring to me the evildoer and I shall drink his blood."

It seemed I was in the desert and the necklace was tumbling over and over in the sand, in the wind, rather like the body of the burnt one had tumbled. Fallen, lost, to be remade.

I felt my head drawn to her neck. She had opened her fingers over my hair. She directed it, that my lips should feel this skin.

"It's what you want, isn't it?" I asked. But my words seemed remote from me, a pathetic expression of the fullness of my soul. "That I am to be your daughter!"

She tipped her head slightly, away from me, so that I saw her neck. I saw the vein displayed, the vein from which she wanted me to drink.

Her finger rose gently through my hair, never pulling it or hurting it, merely embracing my head, sending rampant ecstasy through me, and urging my head gently down so that my lips could no longer avoid her shimmering skin.

"Oh, my adored Queen," I whispered. I had never known such certainty, such ecstasy without limits or mundane cause. I had never known such bursting, triumphant faith as my faith in her.

I opened my mouth. Nothing human could bite through this hard flesh! Yet it gave, as though it were thin, and the blood pumped into me, "the Fount." I heard her heart driving it, a deafening force that vibrated in the drums of my ears. This was not blood. This was nectar. This was all that any created being could ever desire.

9

ITH the nectar flowing into me, there came another realm. Her ringing laughter filled the corridor; she ran ahead of me, girlish, feline, unencumbered by grandeur. She beckoned for me to follow. Out under the stars, Marius sat alone in his soft shapeless garden. She pointed to him. I saw Marius rise and take me in his arms. His long hair was such a fine adornment. I saw what she wanted. It was Marius I kissed in this vision as I drank from her; it was Marius with whom I danced.

A shower of flower petals descended upon us as upon a bridal couple in Rome, and Marius held my arm as though we had just been wed, and all around us people sang. There was a flawless happiness, a happiness so keen that perhaps there are those born who never even have the capacity for it.

She stood atop a broad black altar of diorite.

It was night. This was an enclosed place, filled with people, but it was dark and cool with the sandy wind off the valley floor, and she looked down at the one they offered up to her. He was a man, his eyes closed, his hands were bound. He didn't struggle.

She showed her teeth; a gasp rose from the worshipers who filled the place, and then she took the man by the throat and drank his blood. When she had finished, she let him fall and she held up her arms.

"All things are cleansed in me!" she cried out. Once again the petals fell, petals of all colors, and peacock feathers waved about us, and branches of palm, and there was singing in great lusty bursts, and the sound of a riotous drum, and she smiled looking down from where she stood, her face remarkably flushed and mobile and human, her black-painted eyes sweeping over her worshipers.

All began to dance, save she, who watched, and then her eyes rose slowly and she looked over their heads, out the high rectangular windows of this place, at the twinkling firmament. Pipes played. The dance had become a frenzy.

A weary and secretive darkness crept into her face, a distraction, as though her soul had traveled out of doors towards Heaven, and then she looked sadly down. She looked lost. Anger overcame her.

Then she cried out in a deafening voice, "The rogue blood drinker!" The crowd fell silent. "Bring him to me."

The crowd parted to let this struggling furious god be forced to her altar.

"You dare judge me!" he cried. He was Babylonian, with full long curly locks and beard and mustache. It took ten mortals to hold him.

"Into the burning place, in the mountains, in the sun, in the strongest fetters!" she cried. He was dragged away.

Once again she looked up. The stars grew big and age-old patterns were clear. We floated under the stars.

A boy in a delicate gilded chair argued with those around him. The men were old, half-invisible in the darkness. The lamp shone on the boy's face. We stood in the door. The boy was frail, his little limbs like sticks.

"And you say," said the incredulous boy, "that these blood drinkers are worshiped in the hills!"

I knew he was the Pharaoh by the sacred lock of hair that grew from his bald head, by the manner in which the others waited upon him. He looked up in horror as she approached. His guardians fled.

"Yes," she said, "and you will do nothing to stop it!"

She lifted him, this small fragile boy, and tore at his throat as an animal might do it, letting the blood flood from the fatal wound. "Little King," she said. "Little Kingdom."

The vision ended.

Her cold white skin was closed beneath my lips. I kissed her now. I no longer drank.

I felt my own form, felt myself fall back over her arm, felt myself slipping out of her embrace.

In the dim radiance, her profile remained as it had before, silent and without feeling. Stark, a face without a blemish or a line. I sank back into Marius's arms. Her arm and hand returned to their former rigid position.

Everything was brilliantly clear, the motionless King and Queen, the artful figures fixed in lapis lazuli in the gold mosaics.

I felt a sharp pain in me, in the heart, in the womb, as if someone had stabbed me. "Marius!" I cried out.

He picked me up and carried me from the chamber.

"No, I want to kneel at her feet," I said. The pain took the breath out of me. I tried not to scream from this pain. Oh, the world had just been reborn. And now this agony.

He set me down on the high grass, letting it be crushed under me. A flood of sour human fluid came out of my womb, even out of my mouth. I saw flowers right near me. I saw the friendly Heavens, vivid as in my vision. The pain was unspeakable.

I knew now why he had removed me from the Shrine.

I wiped at my cheek. I couldn't bear this filth. The pain devoured me. I struggled to see again what she had revealed to me, remember what she said, but there was too much obstruction in this pain.

"Marius!" I cried.

He covered me and kissed my cheek. "Drink from me," he said, "drink until the pain goes away. It's only the body dying, drink. Pandora, you are immortal."

"Fill me, take me," I said. I reached down between his legs.

"It doesn't matter now."

But it was hard, this organ I sought, the organ forever lost to the god Osiris. I guided it, hard and cold as it was, into my body. Then I drank and drank, and when I felt his teeth again on my neck, when he began to draw from me the new mixture that filled my veins, it was sweet suckling, and I knew him and loved him and knew all his secrets in one flash which meant nothing.

He was right. The lower organs meant nothing. He fed on me. I fed on him. This was our marriage. All around us, the grass was waving softly in the breeze, a majestic conjugal bed, and the smell of the green flooded me.

The pain was gone. I flung out my arm and felt the softness of flowers.

He tore off my fouled dress and lifted me. He carried me into the pool where the marble Venus stood forever with back bent, and one foot raised above the cool water.

"Pandora!" he whispered.

The boys stood at his side, offering him pitchers.

He dipped a pitcher and poured the water over me. I felt beneath my feet the tile at the bottom of the pool as the water ran down my skin. I had never known such sensation! Another pitcherful washed over me, deliciously. I feared for one instant the pain would return, but no, it was gone.

"I love you with all my heart," I said. "All my love belongs to them and to you, Marius. Marius, I can see in the darkness, I can see in the deep dark beneath the trees."

Marius held me. The boys slowly bathed us both, dipping their pitchers and pouring the silvery water over us.

"Oh, to have you with me," Marius said, "to have you here; not to be alone, but to be with you, my beauty, you of all souls! You." He stood back, and I gloried in him, drenched as I was, reached to touch his long wild foreign hair. He sparkled all over with droplets.

"Yes," I said. "It was exactly what she wanted."

His face stiffened. He scowled. He stared at me. Something had changed altogether, and for the worse. I could feel it.

"What?" he asked.

"It is what she wanted. She made it plain to me in the visions. She wanted me to be with you, so you wouldn't be alone."

He stood back. Was this anger?

"Marius, what is the matter with you? Can't you see what she's done?"

He stepped back again, away from me.

"You didn't realize that's what was happening?" I asked.

The boys thrust forth towels. Marius took one and wiped his face and his hair.

I did the same.

He was furious. He shook with anger.

This was a moment of mingled and inexplicable beauty and horror—his white body there, the shimmering pool, the lights falling gracefully from the open doors of the house, and above, the stars, her stars. And Marius angry and bristling, his eyes full of outrage.

I looked at him.

"I am her Priestess now," I said. "I'm to restore her worship. That's what she wants. But she brought me also for you, because you were alone," I said. "Marius, I saw all this. I saw our own wedding in Rome, as if it were the old days and our families were with us. I saw her worshipers."

He was plainly horrified.

I didn't want to see this. Surely I was misunderstanding him.

I stepped up on the grass. I let the boys dry my body. I looked up at the stars. The house with all its warm lamps seemed crude and fragile, a bumbled attempt to make an order of things, which could not compare to the making of one complete flower.

"Oh, how spectacular is the simple night," I said. "It seems an insult to the night to speak of purpose and intent, when this common moment is so brimming full of blessed design and tranquillity. All things follow their course."

I stood back and spun around, letting the water fly from me. I was so strong. No dizziness overcame when I stopped. I had a sense of infinite power.

One of the boys held out a tunic for me. It was a man's, but as I've said so often here, Roman clothes are very simple. It was just a short tunic. I put it on and let him tie the sash around my waist. I smiled at him. He trembled and stepped back from me.

"Dry my hair," I told him. Ah, such sensations.

Slowly I looked up. Marius too was dried and dressed. He was still looking at me with violent protest, and downright indignation.

"Someone has to go in," I said, "to change her golden gown. That blasphemer, he left her bloody."

"I will do that!" Marius said in plain anger.

"Oh, so it comes to this," I said. I looked around me, seduced by beauty to forget his altogether, to come back to him at some later hour after I had roamed beneath the olive trees and consorted with the constellations.

But his anger hurt me. The hurt was strange, and deep, without the various stages mortal flesh and mind command of pain.

"Oh, isn't it splendid!" I said. "I learn that the goddess reigns, that she is real, that she has made all things! That the world is not just a giant graveyard! But I learn this as I find myself in an arranged marriage! And behold the groom! How he nurses his own temper."

He sighed and bowed his head. Was I to see him cry again, this flawless familiar and beloved god among crushed flowers?

He looked up. "Pandora," he said. "She's not a goddess. She didn't make the world."

"How dare you say this!"

"I have to say it! I would have died for the truth when I was alive and will die for it now. But she will not let this happen. She needs me and she needs you to make me happy!"

"So very well!" I threw my hands. "I am happy to do it. And we will restore her worship."

"We will not!" he said. "How can you even think of such a thing."

"Marius, I want to sing it from the tops of mountains; I want to tell the world that this miracle exists. I want to run through the streets singing. We are to restore her to her throne in a great Temple in the very middle of Antioch!"

"You're talking madness!" he shouted.

The boys had run away.

"Marius, have you stopped up your ears to her commands? We are to hunt down and kill her renegade gods and see that new gods are born from her, gods who look into souls, gods who seek justice, not lies, gods who are not fantastical, lustful idiots or the drunken whimsical creatures of the Northern sky who hurl thunderbolts. Her worship is founded in the good, in the pure!"

"No, no, no," he said. He stepped back as if that would make it all the more emphatic. "You're talking rot!" he said. "Stupidity, rank superstition!"

"I don't believe you said those words!" I cried. "You are a monster!" I said. "She deserves her throne! So does the King, who sits beside her. They deserve their worshipers bringing flowers to them. Did you think you had the power to read minds for no good reason!" I came forward. "Do you remember when I first mocked you in the Temple? When I said you ought to station yourself at the courts and look into the minds of the accused? I had hit the mark in my ridicule!"

"No!" he roared. "This is absolutely not true," he said.

He turned his back on me, rushing into the house. I followed him.

He rushed down the stairway and into her sanctum, stopping short before her. She and her King sat as before. Not an eyelash moved. Only the flowers clung to life in the perfumed air.

I looked down at my hands, so white! Could I die now? Would I live centuries like the burnt one?

I studied their seemingly divine faces. They did not smile. They did not dream. They looked, and nothing more.

I fell down on my knees.

"Akasha," I whispered. "May I call you this name? Tell me what you want."

There was no change in her. None whatsoever.

"Well, speak, Mother!" declared Marius, his voice thick with sadness. "Speak! Is it what you've always wanted?"

Suddenly he dashed forward, mounted the two steps of her dais and pounded on her breasts with his fists.

I was horrified.

She didn't move, she didn't blink. His fist struck a hardness he could not budge. Only her hair, struck by his arm, gave a little sway.

I ran to him and tried to pull him away.

"Stop it, Marius, she'll destroy you!"

I was amazed at my strength. Surely it equalled his. But he allowed me to pull him back, his face flooded with tears.

"Oh, what have I done!" he said staring at her. "Oh, Pandora, Pandora! What have I done! I've made another blood drinker when I swore that there would never, never be another made, not so long as I survived!"

"Come upstairs," I said calmly. I glanced at the King and Queen. No sign of response or recognition. "It isn't proper, Marius, that we argue here in the Shrine. Come upstairs."

He nodded.

He let me lead him slowly out of the room. His head was bowed.

"Your long barbarian hair is most becoming," I said. "And I have eyes now to see you as never before. Our blood is intertwined as it might be in a child born to us."

He wiped at his nose, and didn't look at me.

We walked into the large library.

"Marius, is there nothing in me that fills your eye, nothing you find beautiful?"

"Oh, yes, my dear, there is everything!" he said. "But for the love of Heaven, bring your wits with you into this! Don't you see! Your life's been stolen not for a sacred truth but for a degraded mystery! Reading minds doesn't make me any wiser than the next man! I kill to live! As she once did, thousands and thousands of years ago. Oh, and she knew she had to do this. She knew the time had come."

"What time? What did she know?"

I stared at him. I was gradually realizing that I could no longer read his thoughts, and surely he couldn't read mine. But the hovering boys, they were just open books in their fear, thinking themselves the servants of kindhearted but very loud-voiced demons.

Marius sighed. "She did it because I had almost gained the courage to do what I had to do! To place them both and myself in the sun and finish forever what the Egyptian Elder had sought to do—rid the world of the King and Queen and all the fanged men and women who glut themselves on death! Oh, she is too clever."

"You really planned to do that?" I asked. "To immolate them and yourself?"

He made a small sarcastic sound. "Yes, of course, I planned it. Next week, next month, next year, next decade, after another hundred years, maybe in two hundred, maybe after I'd read all the books in the world and seen all the places, maybe in five hundred years, maybe . . . maybe soon in my loneliness."

I was at first too stunned to speak.

He smiled at me wisely and sadly. "Oh, but I cry like a child," he said softly.

"Where comes the confidence," I asked, "to put an end so swiftly to such bold and complex evidence of divine magic!"

"Magic!" he cursed.

"I'd rather if you did not do this," I said. "I don't mean the crying, I mean burning up the Mother and Father and . . ."

"I'm sure you would!" he answered. "And do you think I could bear to do it against your will, subject you to the fire? You innocent desperate idiot of a woman! Restore her altars! Oh! Restore her worship! Oh! You are out of your mind!"

"Idiot! You dare sling your insults at me! You think you've brought a slave into your household? You haven't even brought a wife."

Yes. Our minds were locked now to each other, and later I would find out that it was because of our heavy exchange of blood. But all I knew then was that we had to content ourselves with words like mortal men and women.

"I did not mean to use petty insults!" he said. He was stung.

"Well, then sharpen your great male reason and your lofty elegant patrician mode of expression!" I said.

We glowered at one another.

"Yes!" he said. "Reason," he said. He held up his finger. "You are the most clever woman I've ever known. And you listen to reason. I will explain and you will see. That is what must be done."

"Yes, and you are hotheaded and sentimental and give way to tears again and again—and you pound upon the Queen herself like a child throwing a tantrum!"

His face went red with immediate anger. It sealed his lips against his words.

He turned and went away.

"Do you cast me out?" I said. "Do you want me gone!" I shouted. "This is your house. Tell me now if you want me gone. I'll go now!"

He stopped. "No," he said.

He turned around and looked at me, shaken, and caught off guard. In a raw voice, he said, "Don't go, Pandora!" He blinked as if to clear his vision. "Don't go. Please, don't." And then he let fall a final whisper. "We have each other."

"And where do you go now, to get away from me?"

"Only to change her dress," he said with a sad bitter smile. "To clean and recostume 'such bold evidence of complex and divine magic.' "

He disappeared.

I turned to the violet outdoors. To the clouds stirred in a cauldron by the moon, to defy the darkness. To the big old trees that said, Mount our limbs, we will embrace you! To the scattered flowers everywhere that said, We are your bed. Lie down with us.

And so the two-hundred-year brawl began.

And it never really ended.

10

WITH my eyes still closed, I heard voices of the city, voices from nearby houses; I heard men talking as they passed on the road outside. I heard music coming from somewhere, and the laughter of women and children. When I concentrated I could understand what they said. I chose not to do this, and their voices melded with the breeze.

Suddenly, the state seemed unbearable. There seemed nothing to do but rush back to the chapel and kneel there and worship! These senses I had been given seemed fit for nothing else. If this was my destiny, then what was to become of me?

Through it all, I heard a soul weeping in agony; it was an echo of my own, a soul broken from a course of great hope, who could scarce believe that such fine beginnings should end in terror!

It was Flavius.

I leapt into the old gnarled olive tree. It was as simple as taking a step. I stood among the branches, and then leapt to the next, and then to the top of the wall, encrusted with vine. I walked along the wall towards the gate.

There he stood, his forehead pressed to the bars, both hands clutching at the iron. He bled from several slash marks on his cheek. He gnashed his teeth.

"Flavius!" I said.

He looked up with a start. "Lady Pandora!"

Surely by the light of the moon, he saw the miracle wrought in me, whatever its cause. For I saw the mortality in him, the deep wrinkles of his skin, the painful flutter of his gaze, a thin layer of soil clinging to him all over in the natural moisture of his mortal skin.

"You must go home," I said, climbing to sit on the wall, with legs on the outside. I bent down so he could hear me. He didn't back away but his eyes were huge with fascination. "Go see to the girls, and sleep, and get those marks attended to. The demon's dead, you needn't worry anymore about him. Come back here tomorrow night at sundown."

He shook his head. He tried to speak but he couldn't. He tried to gesture but he couldn't. His heart thundered in his chest. He glanced back down the road to the small far-flung lights of Antioch. He looked at me. I heard his heart galloping. I felt his shock, and his fear, and it was fear for me, not him. Fear that some awful fate had befallen me. He reached for the gate and clung to the bars, right arm hooked around and left hand clasping it as if he wouldn't be moved.

I saw myself as he saw me in his mind—in a boy's

sashed tunic, my hair wildly free, sitting atop the wall, as if my body were young and pliant. All lines of age had gone from me. He saw a face on me no one could have ever painted.

But the point was this. The man had reached his limit. He could go no further. And I knew most fully how I loved him.

"All right," I said. I stood up and leaned over with both my hands. "Come on, I'll lift you over the wall if I can."

He raised his arms, doubtful, eyes still drinking up every detail of my transformation.

He weighed nothing. I lifted him up and deposited him on his feet within the gate. I dropped down on the grass beside him and put my arm around him. How hot was his alarm. How strong his courage.

"Still your heart," I said. I led him towards the house, as he looked down at me, his chest heaving as though he were out of breath, but it was mere shock. "I'll take care of you."

"I had the thing," he said, "I had it by its arm!" How opaque his voice sounded, how filled with living fluid and effort. "I sank my dagger into it over and over, but it just slashed at my face and it was gone over the wall like a swarm of gnats, just darkness, immaterial darkness!"

"Flavius, it's dead, burnt to cinders!"

"Had I not heard your voice, oh, I was going mad! I heard the boys crying. I couldn't climb the wall with this damned leg. Then I heard your voice, and

I knew, knew you were alive!" He was filled with happiness. "You were with your Marius." The ease with which I could feel his love was sweet, and awe inspiring.

A sudden sense of the Shrine came back to me, of the Queen's nectar and the shower of flower petals. But I had to maintain my equilibrium in this new state. Flavius was also profoundly baffled.

I kissed him on the lips, warm, mortal lips, and then quickly like an artful cat I licked all the blood from the slash marks on his cheeks, feeling a shiver run through me.

I took him into the library, which in this house was the main room. The boys hovered somewhere about. They had been lighting lamps everywhere, and now they cowered. I could smell their blood and their young human flesh.

"You'll stay with me, Flavius. Boys, can you make a bedroom for my steward on this floor? You have fruit and bread, don't you? I can smell it. Have you enough furniture to make him a comfortable place to the far right, where he is out of the way?"

They came rushing out of their respective hiding places, and they too struck me as vividly human. I was distracted. The smallest natural things about them seemed precious, their thick black eyebrows, their round little mouths, their smooth cheeks.

"Yes, Madam, yes!" they said almost in one voice. They hurried forward.

"This is Flavius, my steward. He will stay with us.

For now, take him to the bath, heat the water and attend to him. Get him some wine."

They took Flavius in hand at once. But he paused.

"Don't abandon me, Madam," he said suddenly with the most serious and thoughtful expression. "I am loyal in all respects."

"I know," I said. "Oh, how clearly I understand. You cannot imagine."

Then it was off to the bath with the Babylonian boys, who seemed delighted to have something to do.

I found Marius's huge closets. He had enough clothes for the Kings of Parthia, Armenia, the Emperor's Mother, Livia, the dead Cleopatra, and an ostentatious patrician who paid no attention to Tiberius's stupid sumptuary laws.

I put on a much finer, long tunic, woven of silk and linen, and I chose a gold girdle. And with Marius's combs and brushes, I made a clean free mantle of my hair, free of all tangles, rippled and soft as it had been when I was a girl.

He had many mirrors, which, as you know, in those days were only polished metal. And I was rendered somber and mystified by the single fact that I was young again; my nipples were pink, as I had said; the lines of age no longer interrupted the intended endowments of my face or arms. Perhaps it is most accurate to say that I was timeless. Timeless in adulthood. And every solid object seemed there to serve in me my new strength.

I looked down at the blocks of marble tile which

made up the floor and saw in them a depth, a proof of process wondrous and barely understood.

I wanted to go out again, speak to the flowers, pick them up in handfuls. I wanted to talk urgently with the stars. I dared not seek the Shrine for fear of Marius, but if he had not been around I would have gone there and knelt at the Mother and merely looked at her, looked at her in silent contemplation, listening for the slightest articulation, though I knew, quite certainly after watching Marius's behavior, that there would be none.

She had moved her right arm without the seeming knowledge of the rest of her body. She had moved it to kill, and then to invite.

I went into the library, sat down at the desk, where lay all my pages, and I waited.

Finally, when Marius came, he too was freshly dressed, his hair parted in the middle and combed to his shoulders. He took a chair near me. It was ebony and curved and inlaid with gold, and I looked at him, realizing how very like the chair he was—a great preserved extension of all the raw materials which had gone into it. Nature did the carving and inlay, and then the whole had been lacquered.

I wanted to cry in his arms, but I swallowed my loneliness. The night would never desert me, and it was faithful in every open door with its intruding grass, and the veined olive branches rising to catch the light of the moon.

"Blessed is she who is made a blood drinker," I

said, "when the moon is full, and the clouds are rising like mountains in the transparent night."

"Probably so," he said.

He moved the lamp that stood on the desk between us, so that it didn't flicker in my eyes.

"I made my steward at home here," I said. "I offered him bath, bed and clothes. Do you forgive me? I love him and will not lose him. It's too late now for him to go back into the world."

"He's an extraordinary man," Marius said, "and most welcome here. Tomorrow perhaps he can bring your girls. Then the boys will have company and there will be some discipline by day. Flavius knows books, among other things."

"You're most gracious. I was afraid you would be angry. Why do you suffer so? I cannot read your mind; I did not obtain that gift." No, this wasn't correct. I could read Flavius's mind. I knew the boys at this very moment were very relieved by Flavius's presence as they helped him dress for bed.

"We are too closely linked by blood," he said. "I can never read your thoughts again either. We are thrown back on words like mortals, only our senses are infinitely keener, and the detachment we know at some times will be as cold as the ice in the North; and at other times feelings will enflame us, carry us on waves of burning sea."

"Hmmm," I said.

"You despise me," he said softly, contritely, "because I quenched your ecstasy, I took from you your joy, your convictions." He looked quite genuinely miserable. "I did this to you right at the happiest moment of your conversion."

"Don't be so sure you quenched it. I might still make her Temples, preach her worship. I'm an initiate. I have only begun."

"You will not revive her worship!" he said. "Of that I assure you! You will tell no one about her or what she is or where she is kept, and you will never make another blood drinker."

"My, if only Tiberius had such authority when he addressed the Senate!" I said.

"All Tiberius ever wanted was to study at the gymnasium at Rhodes, to go every day in a Greek cloak and sandals and talk philosophy. And so the propensity for action flowers in men of lesser mettle, who use him in his loveless loneliness."

"Is this a lecture for my improvement? Do you think I don't know this? What you don't know is that the Senate won't help Tiberius govern. Rome wants an Emperor now, to worship and to like. It was your generation, under Augustus, which accustomed us to forty years of autocratic rule. Don't talk to me of politics as though I were a fool."

"I should have realized that you understood it all," he said. "I remember you in your girlhood. Nobody could match your brilliance. Your fidelity to Ovid and his erotic writings was a rare sophistication, an understanding of satire and irony. A well-nourished Roman frame of mind."

I looked at him. His face too had been wiped clean of discernible age. I had time now to relish it, the squareness of his shoulders, the straightness and firmness of his neck, the distinct expression of his eyes and well-placed eyebrows. We had been made over into portraits of ourselves in marble by a master sculptor.

"You know," I said, "even under this crushing and annoying barrage of definition and declaration which you make to me, as if I were weeping for your ratification, I feel love for you, and know full well that we are alone in this, and married to one another, and I am not unhappy."

He appeared surprised, but said nothing.

"I am exalted, bruised in the heart," I said, "a hardened pilgrim. But I do wish you would not speak to me as if my full indoctrination and education were your primary concern!"

"I have to speak this way!" he said gently. His voice was all kindness in its heat. "It *is* my primary concern," he said. "If you can understand what happened with the end of the Roman Republic, if you can understand Lucretius and the Stoics, whole, then you can understand what we are. You have to do this!"

"I'll let that insult pass," I answered. "I'm not in the mood for listing for you every philosopher or poet I have read. Nor for recounting the level of talk around our nighttime table."

"Pandora, I don't mean any offense! But Akasha is not a goddess! Remember your dreams. She is a vial of precious strength. Your dreams told you she could be used, that any unscrupulous blood drinker could pass on the blood to another, that she is a form of demon, host to the power we share."

"She can hear you!" I whispered, outraged.

"Of course, she can. For fifteen years I've been her guardian. I've fought off those renegades from the East. And other connivers from the African hinterlands. She knows what she is."

No one could have guessed his age, save from the seriousness of his expression. A man in perfect form, that was what he seemed. I tried not to be dazzled by him, by the pulsing night behind him, and yet I wanted so to drift. "Some wedding feast," I said. "I have things to say to the trees."

"They will be there tomorrow night," he said.

The last image I had of her passed before my eyes, colored in ecstasy; she took the young Pharaoh from his chair and broke him into sticks. I saw her before that revelation, at the beginning of the swoon, running down the corridor laughing.

A slow fear crept over me.

"What is it?" Marius asked. "Confide in me."

"When I drank from her, I saw her like a girl, laughing." I recounted then the marriage, the flood of rose petals, and then her strange Egyptian Temple full of frenzied worshipers. At last I told him how she had entered the chamber of the little King, whose advisors warned him of her gods.

"She broke him up as if he were a boy of wood. She said, 'Little King, little Kingdom.' "

I picked up my pages, which earlier I had placed on this desk. I described the last dream I had had of her, when she threatened, screaming, to walk into the sun and destroy her disobedient children. I described all the things I had seen—the many migrations of my soul.

My heart hurt so much. Even as I explained, I saw her vulnerability, the danger that was embodied in her. I explained finally how I had written all this in Egyptian.

I was weary and wished truly that I had never opened eyes on this life! I felt the keen and total despair again of those nights of weeping in my little house in Antioch when I had pounded on walls, and driven my dagger into the dirt. If she had not run, laughing down that corridor! What did the image mean? And the little boy King, broken so helplessly?

I made a sum of it easily enough. I waited for Marius's belittling remarks. I hadn't much patience for him now.

"How do you interpret it?" he asked gently. He tried to take my hand but I withdrew it.

"It's bits and pieces of her recollection," I said. I was heartbroken. "It's what she remembers. There is but one suggestion of a future in it all," I said. "There is only one comprehensible image of a wish: our wedding, that we be together." My voice was full of sadness, yet I asked him.

"Why do you weep again, Marius?" I asked. "She must gather recollections like flowers picked at random from the garden of the world, like leaves falling into her hands, and from these recollections she fastened for me a garland! A wedding garland! A trap. I have no migrant soul. I think not. If I did have a migrant soul, then why would she alone, one so archaic, helpless, irrelevant to the world itself, so out of fashion and out of power, be the one to know this? To make it known to me? The only one to know?"

I looked at him. He was engaged yet crying. He showed no shame in it, and would obviously render no apology.

"What was it you said before?" I asked. " 'That I can read minds makes me no wiser than the next man'?" I smiled. "That is the key. How she laughed as she led me to you. How she wanted me to behold you in your loneliness."

He only nodded.

"I wonder how she knew to cast her net so far," I said, "to find me across the rolling sea."

"Lucius, that's how she knew. She hears voices from many lands. She sees what she wants to see. One night here I badly startled a Roman, who appeared to recognize me and then slunk away as if I were a danger to him. I went after him, thinking vaguely that there was something to this, his excessive fear.

"I soon realized a great weight distorted his conscience and twisted his every thought and movement. He was terrified to be recognized by someone from the capital. He wanted to leave.

"He went to the house of a Greek merchant, pounding on the door late, by torchlight, and demanded the payment of a debt owed to your Father.

The Greek told him what he had told him before, that the money would be repaid only to your Father himself.

"The next night I sought Lucius out again. This time the Greek had a surprise for him. A letter had just come from your Father by military ship. This was perhaps four days before your own arrival. The letter plainly stated that a favor was being asked of the Greek by your Father in the name of Hospitality and Honor. If the favor was granted, all debts were canceled. Everything would be explained by a letter accompanying a cargo destined for Antioch. The cargo would take some time, as the ship had many stops to make. The favor was of crucial importance.

"When your brother saw the date of this letter, he was stricken. The Greek, who was thoroughly sick of Lucius by this time, slammed the door in his face.

"I accosted Lucius only steps away. Of course he remembered me, the eccentric Marius of long ago. I pretended surprise to see him here and asked after you. He was in a panic and made up some story about your being married and living in Tuscany, and said that he was on his way out of town. He hurried off. But the moment's contact had been enough to see the testimony he'd given the Praetorian Guard against his family—all lies—and to imagine the deeds that had resulted from it.

"The next time, on waking, I couldn't find him. I kept watch on the house of the Greeks. I weighed in my mind a visit to the old man, the Greek merchant, some way to lay down a friendship with him. I thought of you. I pictured you. I remembered you. I made up poems in my head about you. I didn't hear or see anything of your brother. I presumed he'd left Antioch.

"Then one night I awoke and came upstairs and looked out to see the city full of random fires.

"Germanicus had died, never retracting his accusations that Piso had poisoned him.

"When I reached the house of the Greek merchant, it was nothing but burnt timbers. I caught no sight or sound of your brother anywhere. For all I knew they were all dead, your brother, and the Greek merchant family.

"All through the nights after, I searched for sight or sound of Lucius. I had no idea you were here, only an obsessive longing for you. I tried to remind myself that if I mourned for every mortal tie I had had when alive, I would go mad long before I had learnt anything about my gifts from our King and Queen.

"Then, I was in the bookseller's and it was early evening and the Priest slipped up to me. He pointed to you. There you stood in the Forum, and the philosopher and students were bidding you farewell. I was so close!

"I was so overcome with love I didn't even listen to the Priest until I realized he was speaking of strange dreams as he pointed to you. He was saying that only I could put it all together. It had to do with the blood drinker who had recently been in Antioch, not an uncommon occurrence. I have slain other blood drinkers before. I've vowed to catch this one.

"Then I saw Lucius. I saw you come together. His anger and guilt were nearly blinding to me with this blood drinker's vision. I heard your words effortlessly from a great distance, but would not move until you were safely away from him.

"I wanted to kill him then, but the wiser course seemed to stay right with you, to enter the Temple and stay by your side. I was not certain of my right to kill your brother for you, that it was what you wanted. I didn't know that until I'd told you of his guilt. Then I knew how much you wanted it done.

"Of course I had no idea how clever you had become, that all the talent for reason and words I'd loved in you when you were a girl was still there. Suddenly you were in the Temple, thinking three times faster than the other mortals present, weighing every aspect of what faced you, outwitting everyone. And then came the spectacular confrontation with your brother in which you caught him in the most clever net of truths, and thereby dispatched him, without ever touching him, but instead drawing three military witnesses into complicity with his death."

He broke off, then said, "In Rome, years ago, I followed you. You were sixteen. I remember your first marriage. Your Father took me aside, he was so gentle. 'Marius, you're destined to be a roaming historian,' he said. I didn't dare tell him my true estimation of your husband.

"And now you come to Antioch, and I think, in my self-centered manner, as you will promptly note—if ever a woman was created for me, it is this woman. And I know as soon as I leave you in the morning, that I must somehow get the Mother and Father out of Antioch, get them away, but then this blood drinker has to be destroyed, and then and only then can you be safely left."

"Safely abandoned," I said.

"Do you blame me?" he asked.

The question caught me off guard. I looked at him for a seemingly endless moment, allowing his beauty to fill my eyes, and sensing with intolerable keenness his sadness and desperation. Oh, how he needed me! How desperately he needed not just any mortal soul in which to confide, but me.

"You really did want to protect me, didn't you?" I asked. "And your explanation of all points is so completely rational; it has the elegance of mathematics. There is no need for reincarnation, or destiny, or any miraculous allowance for any part of what's happened."

"It's what I believe," he said sharply. His face grew blank, then stern. "I would never give you anything short of truth. Are you a woman who wants to be humored?"

"Don't be fanatical in your dedication to reason," I said.

These words both shocked and offended him.

"Don't cling to reason so desperately in a world of so many horrid contradictions!"

He was silenced.

"If you so cling to reason," I said, "then in the passage of time reason may fail you, and when it does you may find yourself taking refuge in madness."

"What on Earth do you mean?"

"You've made of reason and logic religion. It's obviously the only way you can endure what's happened to you, that you're a blood drinker and custodian, apparently, of these displaced and forgotten deities."

"They aren't deities!" He grew angry. "Thousands of years ago, they were made, through some mingling of spirit and flesh that rendered them immortal. They find their refuge obviously in oblivion. In your kindness you characterize it as a garden from which the Mother gathered flowers and leaves to make a garland for you, a trap, as you said. But this is your sweet girlish poetry. We do not know that they string very many words together."

"I am no sweet girl," I said. "Poetry belongs to everyone. Speak to me!" I said. "And put aside these words, 'girl' and 'woman.' Don't be so frightened of me."

"I am not," he said angrily.

"You are! Even as this new blood races through me still, eats at me and transforms me, I cling to neither reason nor superstition for my safety. I can walk through a myth and out of it! You fear me, because you don't know what I am. I look like a woman, I sound like a man, and your reason tells you the sum total is impossible!"

He rose from the table. His face took on a sheen like sweat but far more radiant.

"Let me tell you what happened to me!" he said resolutely.

"Good, do tell me," I said. "In straightforward manner."

He let this go by. I spoke against my heart. I wanted only to love him. I knew his cautions. But for all his wisdom, he displayed an enormous will, a man's will, and I had to know the source of it. I concealed my love.

"How did they lure you?"

"They didn't," he said calmly. "I was captured by the Keltoi in Gaul, in the city of Massilia. I was brought North, my hair allowed to grow long, then shut up amid barbarians in a great hollow tree in Gaul. A burnt blood drinker made me into a 'new god' and told me to escape the local Priests, go South to Egypt and find out why all the blood drinkers had been burnt, the young ones dying, the old one suffering. I went for my own reasons! I wanted to know what I was!"

"I can well understand," I said.

"But not before I saw blood worship at its most grisly and unspeakable—I was the god, mind you, Marius, who followed you adoringly all over Rome—and it was to me that these men were offered."

"I've read it in Caesar's history."

"You've read it but you haven't seen it. How dare you throw at me such a trivial boast!"

"Forgive me, I forgot your childish temper."

He sighed. "Forgive me, I forgot your practical and naturally impatient intellect."

"I'm sorry. I regret my words. I had to witness executions of Rome. It was my duty. And that was in the name of law. Who suffers more or less? Victims of sacrifice or the law?"

"Very well. I escaped these Keltoi and went to Egypt, and there I found the Elder, who was the keeper of the Mother and the Father, the Queen and the King, the first blood drinkers of all time, from which this enhancement of our blood flows. This Elder told me stories that were vague but compelling. The Royal Pair had once been human, no more. A spirit or demon had possessed one or both, lodging itself so firmly that no exorcism could oust it. The Royal Pair could transform others by giving the blood. They sought to make a religion. It was overthrown. Again and again it was overthrown. Anyone who possesses the blood can make another! Of course this Elder claimed ignorance of why so many had been burnt. But it was he who had dragged his sacred and royal charges into the sun after centuries of meaningless guardianship! Egypt was dead, he said to me. 'The granary of Rome,' he called it. He said the Royal Pair had not moved in a millennium."

This filled me with the most remarkable and poetic sense of horror.

"Well, one day's hot light was not enough anymore to destroy the ancient parents, but all over the world the children suffered. And this cowardly Elder, given only pain for his reward, a burned skin, lost the courage required to continue the exposure of the Royal Pair. He had no cause, one or another.

"Akasha spoke to me. She spoke as best she could. In images, pictures of what had happened since the beginning, how this tribe of gods and goddesses had sprung from her, and rebellions had occurred, and how much history was lost, and purpose was lost, and when it came to the forming of words, Akasha could make but only a few silent sentences: 'Marius, take us out of Egypt!' " He paused. " 'Take us out of Egypt, Marius. The Elder means to destroy us. Guard us or we perish here.' "

He took a breath; he was calmer now, not so angry, but very much shattered, and in my ever increasing vampiric vision, I knew more about him, how very courageous he was, how very determined to hold to principles in which he believed, in spite of the magic that had swallowed him whole before he had had time even to question it. His was an attempt at a noble life, in spite of all.

"My fate," he said, "was directly connected to hers, to them! If I left them, the Elder would sooner or later put them in the sun again, and I, lacking the blood of centuries, would burn up like wax! My life, already altered, would have been ended. But the Elder did not ask me to install a new priesthood. Akasha did not ask me to install a new religion! She did not speak of altars or worship. Only the old burnt-out god in the Northern grove among the barbarians had asked me to do such a thing when he sent me to the South, to Egypt, the motherland of all mysteries."

"How long have you kept them?"

"Over fifteen years. I lose count. They never move or speak. The wounded ones, those burnt so badly that time will take centuries to heal them, they learn that I am here. They come. I try to extinguish them before their minds can give forth a flash of a confirming image to other distant minds. She doesn't guide these burnt children to where she is, as she once guided me! If I am tricked or overwhelmed, she moves only as you saw, to crush the blood drinker. But she has called you, Pandora, reached out for you. And we know now to what exact purpose. And I've been cruel to you. Clumsy."

He turned to me. His voice grew tender. "Tell me, Pandora," he asked. "In the vision you saw, when we were married, were we young or old? Were you the girl of fifteen I sought too early perhaps, or the mature full blossom of a creature you are now? Are the families happy? Are we comely?"

I was hotly embraced by the sincerity of his words. The anguish and the pleading that lay behind them.

"We were as we are now," I said, cautiously answering his smile with my own. "You were a man fixed in the prime of life forever, and I? As I am at this hour."

"Believe me," he said with sweetness in his voice,

"I would not have spoken so harshly on this of all nights, but you have now so many other nights to come. Nothing can kill you now, but the sun or fire. Nothing in you will deteriorate. You have a thousand experiences to discover."

"And what of the ecstasy when I drank from her?" I asked. "What of her own beginnings and her suffering? Does she in no way connect herself to the sacred?"

"What is sacred?" he asked, shrugging his shoulder. "Tell me. What is sacred? Was it sanctity you saw in her dreams?"

I bowed my head. I couldn't answer.

"Certainly not the Roman Empire," he said, "Certainly not the temples of Augustus Caesar. Certainly not the worship of Cybele! Certainly not the cult of those who worship fire in Persia. Is the name Isis sacred anymore, or was it ever? The Elder in Egypt, my first and only instructor in all this, said that Akasha invented the stories of Isis and Osiris to suit her purposes, to give a poetry to her worship. I think rather she grafted herself upon old stories. The demon in those two grows with each new blood drinker made. It must."

"But to no purpose?"

"That it may know more?" he said. "That it may see more, feel more, through each of us which carries its blood? Perhaps it is such a creature as that and each of us is but a tiny part of it, carrying all its senses and capacities and returning our experiences to it. It reaches out through us to know the world!"

"I can tell you this," he said. He paused and put his hands on the desk. "What burns in me does not care if the victim is innocent or guilty of any crime. It thirsts. Not every night, but often! It says nothing! It does not talk of altars to me in my heart! It drives me as though I were the battle steed and it the mounted General! It is Marius who weeds the good from the bad, according to the old custom, for reasons you can well understand, but not this ravening thirst; this thirst knows nature but no morality."

"I love you, Marius," I said. "You and my Father are the only men I've ever really loved. But I must go out alone now."

"What did you say!" He was amazed. "It's just past midnight."

"You've been very patient, but I have to walk alone now."

"I'll come with you."

"You will not," I said.

"But you can't simply roam around Antioch on your own, alone."

"Why not? I can hear mortal thoughts now if I want to. A litter just passed. The slaves are so drunk it's a wonder they don't drop the thing and heave the Master into the road, and he himself is fast asleep. I want to walk alone, out there, in the city in the dark places and the dangerous places and the evil places and the places where even . . . where even a god would not go."

"This is your vengeance on me," he said. I walked

towards the gate and he followed. "Pandora, not alone."

"Marius, my love," I said, turning, taking his hand. "It is not vengeance. The words you spoke earlier, 'girl' and 'woman,' they have always circumscribed my life. I want only now to walk fearlessly with my arms bare and my hair down my back, into any cavern of danger I choose. I am drunk still from her blood, from yours! Things shimmer and flicker that should shine. I must be alone to ponder all you've said."

"But you have to be back before dawn, well before. You have to be with me in the crypt below. You can't merely lie in some room somewhere. The deadly light will penetrate—"

He was so protective, so lustrous, so infuriated.

"I will be back," I said, "and well before dawn, and for now, my heart will break if we are not, as of this moment, bound together."

"We are bound," he said. "Pandora, you could drive me mad."

He stopped at the bars of the gate.

"Don't come any farther," I said as I left.

I walked down towards Antioch. My legs had such strength and spring, and the dust and pebbles of the road were nothing to my feet, and my eyes penetrated the night to see the full conspiracy of owls and little rodents that hovered in the trees, eyeing me, then fleeing as if their natural senses warned them against me.

Soon I came into the city proper. I think the resolution with which I moved from little street to little street was enough to frighten anyone who would have contemplated molesting me. I heard only cowardice and erotic curses from the dark, those tangled ugly curses men heap on women they desire—half threat, half dismissal.

I could sense the people in their houses fast asleep, and hear the guards on watch, talking in their barracks behind the Forum.

I did all the things the new blood drinkers always do. I touched the surfaces of walls and stared, enchanted at a common torch and the moths that gave themselves up to it. I felt against my naked arms and fragile tunic the dreams of all Antioch surrounding me.

Rats fled up and down the gutters and the streets. The river gave off its own sound, and there came a hollow echoing from the ships at anchor, even from the faintest stirring of the water.

The Forum, resplendent with its ever burning lights, caught the moon as if it were a great human trap for it, the very reverse of an earthly crater, a man-made design that could be seen and blessed by the intransigent heavens.

When I came to my own house, I found I could climb to the very top easily, and there I sat on the tiled roof, so relaxed and secure and free, looking down into the courtyard, into the peristyle, where I had really learned—alone on those three nights—the truths that had prepared me for Akasha's blood.

In calmness and without pain, I thought it through

again—as if I owed this reconsideration to the woman I had been, the initiate, the woman who had sought refuge in the Temple. Marius was right. The Queen and King were possessed of some demon which spread through the blood, feeding upon it and growing, as I could feel it doing in me now.

The King and Queen did not invent justice! The Queen, who broke the little Pharaoh into sticks, did not invent law or righteousness!

And the Roman courts, bumbling awkwardly towards each decision, weighing all sides, refusing any magical or religious device, they did even in these terrible times strive for justice. It was a system based not upon the revelation of the gods, but upon reason.

But I could not regret the moment of intoxication when I'd drunk her blood and believed in her, and seen the flowers come down upon us. I could not regret that any mind could conceive of such perfect transcendence.

She had been my Mother, my Queen, my goddess, my all. I had known it as we were meant to know it when we drink the potions in the Temple, when we sing, when we are rocking in delirious song. And in her arms I had known it. In Marius's arms I'd known it as well, and in a safer measure, and I wanted only to be with him now.

How ghastly her worship seemed. Flawed and ignorant, being elevated to such power! And how revealing suddenly that at the core of mysteries there should lie such degrading explanations. Blood spilt on her golden gown!

All images and meaningful glimpses do but teach you deeper things, I thought again, as I had in the Temple, when I had settled for the consolation of a basalt statue.

It is I, and I alone, who must make of my new life a heroic tale.

I was very happy for Marius that he had such comfort in reason. But reason was only a created thing, imposed with faith upon the world, and the stars promise nothing to no one.

I had seen something deeper in those dark nights of hiding in this house in Antioch, in mourning for my Father. I had seen that at the very heart of Creation there very well might lie something as uncontrollable and incomprehensible as a raging volcano.

Its lava would destroy trees and poets alike.

So take this gift, Pandora, I told myself. Go home, thankful that you are again wed, for you have never made a better match or seen a more tantalizing future.

When I returned, and my return was very rapid, full of new lessons in how I might pass quickly over rooftops, scarce touching them, and over walls—when I returned, I found him as I had left him, only much sadder. He sat in the garden, just as he had in the vision shown to me by Akasha.

It must have been a place he loved, behind the villa with its many doors, a bench facing a thicket and a natural stream bubbling up and over the rocks and spilling down into a current through high grass.

He rose at once.

I took him in my arms.

"Marius, forgive me," I said.

"Don't say such a thing, I'm to blame for it all. And I didn't protect you from it."

We were in each other's arms. I wanted to press my teeth into him, drink his blood, and then I did, and felt him taking the blood from me. This was a union more powerful than any I had ever known in a marriage bed, and I yielded to it as I never yielded in life to anyone.

I felt an exhaustion sweep me suddenly. I withdrew my kiss with its teeth.

"Come on, now," he said. "Your slave is asleep. And during the day, while we must sleep, he will bring all your possessions here, and those girls of yours, should you want to keep them."

We walked down the stairs, we entered another room. It took all Marius's strength to pull back the door, which meant simply that no mortal man could do it.

There lay a sarcophagus, plain, of granite.

"Can you lift the lid of the sarcophagus?" Marius asked.

"I am feeling weak!"

"It's the sun rising, try to lift the lid. Slide it to one side."

I did, and inside I found a bed of crushed lilies and

rose petals, of silken pillows, and bits of dried flower kept for scent.

I stepped in, turned around, sat and stretched out in this stone prison. At once he took his place in the tomb beside me, and pushed the lid back to its place, and all the world's light in any form was shut out, as if the dead would have it so.

"I'm drowsy. I can hardly form words."

"What a blessing," he said.

"There is no need for such an insult," I murmured. "But I forgive you."

"Pandora, I love you!" he said helplessly.

"Put it inside me," I said, reaching between his legs. "Fill me and hold me."

"This is stupid and superstitious!"

"It is neither," I said. "It is symbolic and comforting."

He obeyed. Our bodies were one, connected by this sterile organ which was no more to him now than his arm, but how I loved the arm he threw over me and the lips he pressed to my forehead.

"I love you, Marius, my strange, tall and beautiful Marius."

"I don't believe you," he said, his voice barely a whisper.

"What do you mean?"

"You'll despise me soon enough for what I've done to you."

"Not so, oh, rational one. I am not as eager to grow old, wither and die, as you might think. I should like a chance to know more, to see more . . ."

I felt his lips against my forehead.

"Did you really try to marry me when I was fifteen?"

"Oh, agonizing memories! Your Father's insults still sting my ears! He had me all but thrown out of your house!"

"I love you with my whole heart," I whispered. "And you have won. You have me now as your wife."

"I have you as something, but I do not think that 'wife' is the word for it. I wonder that you've already forgotten your earlier strenuous objection to the term."

"Together," I said, scarce able to talk on account of his kisses. I was drowsy, and loved the feel of his lips, their sudden eagerness for pure affection. "We'll think of another word more exalted than 'wife.' "

Suddenly I moved back. I could not see him in the dark.

"Are you kissing me so that I will not talk?"

"Yes, that's exactly what I was doing," he said.

I turned away from him.

"Turn back, please," he said.

"No," I said.

I lay still, realizing dimly that his body felt quite normal to me now, because mine was as hard as his was, as strong perhaps. What a sublime advantage. Oh, but I loved him. I loved him! So let him kiss the back of the neck! He could not force me to turn towards him!

The sun must have risen.

For a silence fell on me which was as if the universe with all its volcanoes and raging tides—and all its Emperors, Kings, judges, Senators, philosophers and Priests—had been erased from existence.

11

WELL, David, there you have it.

I could continue the Plautus-Terence style comedy for pages. I could vie with Shakespeare's *Much Ado About Nothing*.

But that is the basic story. That is what lies behind the flippant capsule version in *The Vampire Lestat*, fashioned into its final trivial form by Marius or Lestat, who knows.

Let me lead you through those points which are sacred and burn still in my heart, no matter how easily they have been dismissed by another.

And the tale of our parting is not mere dissonance but may contain some lesson.

Marius taught me to hunt, to catch the evildoer only, and to kill without pain, enwrapping the soul of my victim in sweet visions or allowing the soul to illuminate its own death with a cascade of fantasies which I must not judge, but merely devour, like the blood. All that does not require detailed documentation.

We were matched in strength. When some burnt

and ruthlessly ambitious blood drinker did find his way to Antioch, which happened only a few times and then not at all, we executed the suppli-cant together. These were monstrous mentalities, forged in ages we could hardly understand, and they sought the Queen like jackals seek the bodies of the human dead.

There was no argument between us over any of them.

We often read aloud to each other, and we laughed together at Petronius's *Satyricon*, and we shared both tears and laughter later as we read the bitter satires of Juvenal. There was no end of new satire and history coming from Rome and from Alexandria.

But something forever divided Marius from me.

Love grew but so did constant argument, and argument became more and more the dangerous cement of the bond.

Over the years, Marius guarded his delicate ratio-nality as a Vestal Virgin guards a sacred flame. If ever any ecstatic emotion took hold of me, he was there to grab me by the shoulders and tell me in no uncertain terms that it was irrational. Irrational, ir-rational, irrational!

When the terrible earthquake of the second cen-tury struck Antioch, and we were unharmed, I dared speak of it as a Divine Blessing. This set Marius into a rage, and he was quick to point that the same Divine Intervention had also protected the Roman Emperor Trajan, who was in the city at the time. What was I to make of that?

For the record, Antioch quickly rebuilt itself, the markets flourished, more slaves poured in, nothing stopped the caravans headed for the ships, and the ships headed for the caravans.

But long before that earthquake we had all but come to blows night after night.

If I lingered for hours in the room of the Mother and the Father, Marius invariably came to collect me and bring me back to my senses. He could not read in peace with me in such a state, he declared. He could not think because he knew I was downstairs deliberately inviting madness.

Why, I demanded, must his domination extend to every corner of our entire house and garden? And how was it that I was his match in strength when an old burnt blood drinker found his way to Antioch and we picked up the word of his killing and had to do away with him?

"We are not matched in minds?" I demanded.

"Only you could ask that question!" came his reply.

Of course the Mother and Father never moved or spoke again. No blood dreams, no divine directive ever reached me. Only now and then did Marius remind me of this. And after a long while, he allowed me to tend the Shrine with him, to see full well the extent of their silent and seemingly mindless compliance. They appeared utterly beyond reach; their cooperation was sluggish and frightening to witness.

When Flavius fell ill in his fortieth year, Marius

and I had the first of our truly terrible battles. This came early on, well before the earthquake.

It was, by the way, a wondrous time because the wicked old Tiberius was filling Antioch with new and wonderful buildings. She was the rival of Rome. But Flavius was ill.

Marius could scarce bear it. He had become more than fond of Flavius—they talked about Aristotle all the time, and Flavius proved one of those men who can do anything for you, from managing a household to copying the most esoteric and crumbling text with complete accuracy.

Flavius had never put a single question to us as to what we were. In his mind, I found, devotion and acceptance far superseded curiosity or fear.

We hoped Flavius had only a minor illness. But finally, as Flavius's fever grew worse, Flavius turned his head away from Marius whenever Marius came to him. But he held on to my hand always when I offered it. Frequently I lay beside him for hours, as he had once lain beside me.

Then one night Marius took me to the gate and said, "He'll be dead by the time I come back. Can you bear this alone?"

"Do you run from it?" I asked.

"No," he said. "But he doesn't want me to see him die; he doesn't want me to see him groan in pain."

I nodded.

Marius left.

Marius had long ago laid down the rule that no

other blood drinker was ever to be made. I didn't bother to question him on this.

As soon as he was gone, I made Flavius into a vampire. I did it just the way the burnt one, Marius and Akasha had done it to me, for Marius and I had long discussed the methods—withdraw as much blood as you can, then give it back until you are near to fainting.

I did faint and wake to see this splendid Greek standing over me, smiling faintly, all disease gone from him. He reached down to take my hand and help me to my feet.

Marius walked in, stared at the reborn Flavius in amazement and said, "Get out, out of this house, out of this city, out of this province, out of this Empire."

Flavius's last words to me were:

"Thank you for this Dark Gift." That is the first I ever heard that particular phrase, which appears so often in Lestat's writings. How well this learned Athenian understood it.

For hours I avoided Marius. I would never be forgiven! Then I went out into the garden. I discovered Marius was grieving, and when he looked up, I realized that he had been utterly convinced that I meant to go off with Flavius. When I saw this, I took him in my arms. He was full of quiet relief and love; he forgave me at once for my "absolute rashness."

"Don't you see," I said, taking him in hand, "that I adore you? But you cannot rule over me! Can you not consider in your reasonable fashion that the greatest part of our gift eludes you—it's the freedom from the confines of male, female!"

"You can't convince me," he said, "for one moment that you don't feel, reason and act in the manner of a woman. We both loved Flavius. But why another blood drinker?"

"I don't know except that Flavius wanted it, Flavius knew all about our secrets, there was a . . . an understanding between me and Flavius! He had been loyal in the darkest hours of my mortal life. Oh, I can't explain it."

"A woman's sentiments, exactly. And you have launched this creature into eternity."

"He joins our search," I replied.

About the middle of the century, when the city was very rich and the Empire was about as peaceful as it was ever going to be for the next two hundred years, the Christian Paul came to Antioch.

I went to hear him speak one night and came home, saying casually that the man could convert the very stones to this faith, such was his personal power.

"How can you spend your time on such things!" Marius demanded. "Christians. They aren't even a cult! Some worship John, some worship Jesus. They fight amongst one another! Don't you see what this man Paul has done?"

"No, what?" I said. "I didn't say I was going to join the sect. I only said I stopped to hear him. Who is hurt by that?"

"You, your mind, your equilibrium, your common sense. It's compromised by the foolish things in which you take an interest, and frankly the principle of truth is hurt!" He had only just begun.

"Let me tell you about this man Paul," Marius said. "He never knew either the Baptizer John or the Galilean Jesus. The Hebrews have thrown him out of the group. Jesus and John were both Hebrews! And so Paul has now turned to everyone. Jew and Christian alike, and Roman and Greek, and said, 'You needn't follow the Hebrew observance. Forget the Feasts in Jerusalem. Forget Circumcision. Become a Christian.' "

"Yes, that is true," I said with a sigh.

"It's a very easy religion to take up," he said. "It's nothing. You have to believe that this man rose from the Dead. And by the way, I've combed the available texts which are floating all over the marketplaces. Have you?"

"No. I'm surprised you've found this search worthy of your time."

"I don't see anywhere in the writings of those who knew John and Jesus where these two are quoted as saying either one of them will rise from the Dead, or that all who believe in them will have life after death. Paul added all that. What an enticing promise! And you should hear your friend, Paul, on the subject of Hell! What a cruel vision—that flawed mortals could sin in this life so grievously that they would burn for all eternity."

"He's not my friend. You make so much of my passing remarks. Why do you feel so strongly?"

"I told you, I care about what is true, what is reasonable!"

"Well, there's something you're missing about this group of Christians, some way in which when they come together they share a euphoric love and and they believe in great generosity—"

"Oh, not again! And are you to tell me this is good?"

I didn't answer.

He was returning to his work when I spoke.

"You fear me," I said to him. "You fear that I'll be swept off my feet by somebody of belief and abandon you. No. No, that's not right. You fear that you will be swept up. That the world will somehow entice you back into it, so that you won't live here with me, the superior Roman observer recluse, anymore, but go back, seeking mortal comforts of companionship and proximity to others, friendship with mortals, their recognition of you as one of them when you are not one of them!"

"Pandora, you talk gibberish."

"Keep your proud secrets," I said. "But I do fear for you, that I will admit."

"Fear for me? And why?" he demanded.

"Because you don't realize everything perishes, everything is artifice! That even logic and mathematics and justice have no ultimate meaning!"

"That's not true," he said.

"Oh, yes it is. Some night will come when you will see what I saw, when I first came to Antioch, before you'd found me, before this transformation which should have swept away everything in its path.

"You will see a darkness," I went on, "a darkness so total that Nature never knows it anywhere on Earth at any time, in any place! Only the human soul can know it. And it goes on forever. And I pray that when you finally can no longer escape from it, when you realize it is all around you, that your logic and your reason give you some strength against it."

He gave me the most respectful look. But he didn't speak. I continued:

"Resignation will do you no good," I said, "when such a time comes. Resignation requires will, and will requires decision, and decision requires belief, and belief requires that there is something to believe in! And all action or acceptance requires a concept of a witness! Well, there is nothing, and there are no witnesses! You don't know that yet, but I do. I hope, when you find it out, someone can comfort you as you dress and groom those monstrous relics below the stairs! As you bring their flowers!" I was so angry. I went on:

"Look back on me when this moment comes—if not for forgiveness, look back on me as a model. For I have seen this, and I have survived. And it matters not that I stopped to listen to Paul preach of Christ, or that I weave flowers into crowns for the Queen, or that I dance like a fool under the moon in the garden before dawn, or that I . . . that I love you. It matters not. Because there is nothing. And no one to see. No one!" I sighed. It was time to finish.

"Go back to your history, this stack of lies that tries to link event to event with cause and effect, this preposterous faith that postulates that one thing follows from another. I tell you, it's not so. But it is very Roman of you to think so."

He sat silent looking up at me. I couldn't tell what his thoughts were or what his heart felt. Then he asked:

"What would you have me do?" He had never looked more innocent.

Bitterly, I laughed. Did we not speak the same language? He heard not one word I had uttered. Yet he presented me not with a reply, but only with this simple question.

"All right," I said. "I'll tell you what I want. Love me, Marius, love me, but leave me alone!" I cried out. I had not even thought. The words just came. "Leave me alone, so that I may seek my own comforts, my own means to remain alive, no matter how foolish or pointless these comforts appear to you. Leave me alone!"

He was wounded, so uncomprehending, looking so innocent still.

We had many similar arguments as the decades passed.

Sometimes he would come to me after; he would fall into long thoughtful talks about what he felt was happening with the Empire, how the Emperors were going mad and the Senate had no power, how the very progress of man was unique in Nature and something to be watched. How he would crave life, he thought, until there was no more life.

"Even if there is nothing left but desert waste," he said, "I should want to be there, to see dune folding upon dune," he went on. "If there was but one lamp left in all the world, I'd want to watch its flame. And so would you."

But the terms of the battle, and its heat, never really changed.

At heart he thought I hated him for having been so unkind on the night I was given the Dark Blood. I told him this was childish. I could not convince him that my soul and my intelligence were infinitely too large for such a simple grudge, and that I owed him no explanation for my thoughts, words and deeds.

For two hundred years, we lived and loved together. He became ever more beautiful to me.

As more and more barbarians from the North and from the East poured into the city, he felt no necessity to dress like a Roman anymore, and frequently wore the jeweled clothes of the Easterners. His hair seemed to be growing finer, lighter. He seldom cut it, which of course he would have had to do every night had he wanted it short. It was a splendor on his shoulders.

As his face grew ever more smooth, away went the few lines that could so easily design anger in his expression. As I've told you before, he greatly resembles Lestat. Only he is more compact of build, and jaw and chin had hardened just a little more with age before the Dark Gift. But the unwanted folds were receding from his eyes.

Sometimes for nights on end, in fear of a fight, we didn't speak. There was between us always a continuous physical affection—embraces, kisses, sometimes the mere silent lock of our hands.

But we knew we had now lived far beyond a normal human life span.

You need from me no detailed history of that remarkable time. It is too well known. Only let me place here a few reminders. Only let me describe for you my perspective on the changes happening all over the Empire.

Antioch as a thriving city proved indestructible. The Emperors began to favor it and visit it. More Temples went up to the Eastern cults. And then Christians of all kinds poured into Antioch.

Indeed, the Christians of Antioch comprised at last an immense and fascinating bunch of people arguing with each other.

Rome went to war on the Jews, crushing Jerusalem completely and destroying the sacred Hebrew Temple. Many brilliant Jewish thinkers came to Antioch as well as Alexandria.

Twice or perhaps even three times, Roman legions pushed past us, North of us, into Parthia; once we even had a little rebellion of our own, but Rome always resecured the city of Antioch. So the market closed for a day! On went the trade, the great lust of the caravans for the ships, and of the ships for the caravans, and Antioch was the bed in which they must wed each other.

There was little new poetry. Satire. Satire seemed the only safe or honest expression of the Roman mind now, and so we had the riotously funny story *The Golden Ass*, by Apuleius, which seemed to make fun of every religion. But there was a bitterness to the poet Martial. And those letters of Pliny which reached me were full of dire judgments on the moral chaos of Rome.

I began as a vampire to feed exclusively on soldiers. I liked them, their look, their strength. I fed so much so on them, that in my carelessness, I became a legend amongst them, "The Greek Lady Death," this on account of my clothes which to them appeared archaic. I struck at random in the dark streets. There wasn't a chance of their ever surrounding me or stopping me, so great was my skill, my strength and my thirst.

But I saw things in their rebellious deaths, the blaze of a pitched battle in a march, a hand-to-hand struggle on a steep mountain. I took them down gently into the finish, filling myself to the brim with their blood, and sometimes, through a veil it seemed, I saw the souls of those whom they themselves had slain.

When I told Marius this, he said it was just the kind of mystical nonsense he would expect of me.

I didn't press the point.

He watched with keen interest the developments of Rome. To me they seemed merely surprising.

He pored over the histories of Dio Cassius and Plutarch and Tacitus, and pounded his fist when he heard of the endless skirmishes on the Rhine River, and the push Northward into Britannia and the building of Hadrian's wall to forever keep away the Scots, who like the Germans would yield to no one.

"They are not patrolling, preserving, containing an Empire any longer," he said. "Conserving a way of life! It's just war, and trade!"

I couldn't disagree.

It was really even worse than he knew. If he had gone as often as I did to listen to the philosophers he would have been appalled.

Magicians were appearing everywhere, claiming to be able to fly, to see visions, to heal with the laying on of hands! They got into battles with the Christians and the Jews. I don't think the Roman army paid them any attention.

Medicine as I had known it in my mortal life had been flooded with a river of Eastern secret formulae, amulets, rituals, and little statues to clutch.

Well over half the Senate was no longer Italian by birth. This meant that our Rome was no longer our Rome. And the title of Emperor had become a joke. There were so many assassinations, plots, squabbles, false emperors and palace coups that it soon became perfectly clear that the Army ruled. The Army chose the Emperor. The Army sustained him.

The Christians were divided into warring sects. It was positively astonishing. The religion didn't burn itself out in dispute. It gained strength in division. Occasional furious persecutions—in which people were executed for not worshiping at Roman altars—only seemed to deepen the sympathy of the populace with this new cult.

And the new cult was rampant with debate on every principle with regard to the Jews, God and Jesus.

The most amazing thing had happened to this religion. Spreading wildly on fast ships, good roads and well-maintained trade routes, it suddenly found itself in a peculiar position. The world had not come to an end, as Jesus and Paul had predicted.

And everybody who had ever known or seen Jesus was dead. Finally everyone who had ever known Paul was dead.

Christian philosophers arose, picking and choosing from old Greek ideas and old Hebrew traditions.

Justin of Athens wrote that Christ was the Logos; you could be an atheist and still be saved in Christ if you upheld reason.

I had to tell this to Marius.

I thought sure it would set him off, and the night was dull, but he merely countered with more outlandish talk of the Gnostics.

"A man named Saturninus popped up in the Forum today," he said. "Perhaps you heard talk of him. He preaches a wild variant of this Christian creed you find so amusing, in which the God of the Hebrews is actually the Devil and Jesus the new God. This was not the man's first appearance. He and his followers, thanks to the local Christian Bishop Ignatius, are headed for Alexandria."

"There are books with those ideas already here," I said, "having come from Alexandria. They are impenetrable to me. Perhaps not to you. They speak of Sophia, a female principle of Wisdom, which preceded the Creation. Jews and Christians alike want somehow to include this concept of Sophia in their faith. It so reminds me of our beloved Isis."

"Your beloved Isis!" he said.

"It seems that there are minds who would weave it all together, every myth, or its essence, to make a glorious tapestry."

"Pandora, you are making me ill again," he warned. "Let me tell you what your Christians are doing. They are tightly organizing. This Bishop Ignatius will be followed by another, and the Bishops want to lay down now that the age of private revelation had ended; they want to weed through all the mad scrolls on the market and make a canon which all Christians believe."

"I never thought such could happen," I said. "I agreed with you more than you knew when you condemned them."

"They are succeeding because they are moving away from emotional morality," he said. "They are organizing like Romans. This Bishop Ignatius is very strict. He delegates power. He pronounced on the accuracy of manuscripts. Notice the prophets are getting thrown out of Antioch."

"Yes, you're right," I said. "What do you think? Is it good or bad?"

"I want the world to be better," he said. "Better for men and women. Better. Only one thing is clear: the old blood drinkers have by now died out, and there is nothing you or I, or the Queen and the King can do to interfere in the flow of human events. I believe men and women must try harder. I try to understand evil ever more deeply with any victim I take.

"Any religion that makes fanatical claims and demands on the basis of a god's will frightens me."

"You are a true Augustan," I said. "I agree with you, but it is fun to read these mad Gnostics. This Marcion and this Valentinus."

"Fun for you perhaps. I see danger everywhere. This new Christianity, it isn't merely spreading, it's changing in each place as it spreads; it's like an animal which devours the local flora and fauna and then takes on some specific power from the food."

I didn't argue with him.

By the end of the second century, Antioch was a heavily Christian city. And it seemed to me as I read the works of new Bishops and philosophers that worse things than Christianity could come upon us.

Realize, however, David, that Antioch did not lie under a cloud of decay; there was no sense in the air of the end of the Empire. If anything there was bustling energy everywhere. Commerce gives one this feel, that false sense that there is growth and creativity, perhaps, when there is none. Things are exchanged, not necessarily improved.

Then came the dark time for us. Two forces came together which bore down on Marius, straining all his courage. Antioch was more interesting than it had ever been.

The Mother and the Father had never stirred since the first night of my coming!

Let me describe the first disaster, because for me it was not so hard to bear, and I had only sympathy for Marius.

As I've told you, the question of who was Emperor had become a joke. But it really became a howl with the events of the early 200s.

The Emperor of the moment was Caracalla, a regular murderer. On a pilgrimage to Alexandria to see the remains of Alexander the Great, he had—for reasons no one knows even now—rounded up thousands of young Alexandrians and slaughtered them. Alexandria had never seen such a massacre.

Marius was distraught. All the world was distraught.

Marius spoke of leaving Antioch, of getting far far away from the ruin of the Empire. I began to agree with him.

Then this revolting Emperor Caracalla marched in our direction, intending to make a war on the Parthians North of us and to the East of us. Nothing out of the ordinary for Antioch!

His Mother—and you need not remember these names—Julia Domna, took up residence in Antioch. She was dying from cancer of her breast. And let me add here that this woman had, with her son Caracalla, helped murder her other son, Geta, because the two brothers had been sharing Imperial power and threatening to make a Civil War.

Let me continue, and again you need not remember the names.

Troops were massed for this Eastern war against two Kings to the East, Vologases the Fifth and Artabanus the Fifth. Caracalla did make war, achieve victory and return in triumph. Then, only miles from Antioch, he was assassinated by his own soldiers while trying to relieve himself!

All this cast Marius in a hopeless frame of mind. For hours he sat in the Shrine staring at the Mother and the Father. I felt I knew what he was thinking, that we should immolate ourselves and them, but I couldn't bear the thought of it. I didn't want to die. I didn't want to lose life. I didn't want to lose Marius.

I did not care so much about the fate of Rome. Life still stretched before me, extending the promise of wonders.

Back to the Comedy. The Army promptly made an Emperor out of a man from the Provinces named Macrinus, who was a Moor and wore an earring in his ear.

He at once had a fight with the dead Emperor's Mother, Julia Domna, because he wouldn't allow her to leave Antioch to die elsewhere. She starved herself to death.

This was all too close to home! These lunatics were in our city, not far away in a capital which we mourned.

Then war broke out again, because the Eastern Kings, who were caught off guard before by Caracalla, were now ready, and Macrinus had to lead the Legions into battle.

As I told you, the Legions now controlled everything. Somebody should have told Macrinus. Instead of fighting he bought off the enemy. The troops were hardly proud of this. And then he cracked down on them, taking away some of their benefits.

He didn't seem to grasp that he had to maintain their approval to survive. Though of course what good had this done for Caracalla, whom they loved?

Whatever, the sister of Julia Domna, named Julia Maesa, who was a Syrian and of a family dedicated to the Syrian sun god, seized this dreary moment in the life of the lusty legions to put her grandson, born of Julia Soemis, in power as Emperor! It was an outrageous plan actually, for any number of reasons. First and foremost, all three Julias were Syrian. The boy himself was fourteen years old, and also he was a hereditary Priest of the Syrian sun god.

But somehow or other Julia Maesa and her daughter's lover, Gannys, managed to convince a bunch of soldiers in a tent that this fourteen-year-old Syrian boy should become the Emperor of Rome.

The Army deserted the Imperial Macrinus, and he and his son were hunted down and murdered.

So, high on the shoulders of proud soldiers rode this fourteen-year-old boy! But he didn't want to be called by his Roman name. He wanted to be called by the name of the god he worshiped in Syria, Elagabalus. The very presence of him in Antioch shook the nerves of all citizens. At last, he and three remaining Julias—his aunt, his Mother and his grandmother, all of them Syrian Priestesses—left Antioch.

In Nicomedia, which was very near to us, Elagabalus murdered his Mother's lover. So who was left? He also picked up an enormous sacred black stone and brought it back to Rome, saying that this stone was sacred to the Syrian sun god, whom all must now worship.

He was gone, across the sea, but it took sometimes no more than eleven days for a letter to reach Antioch from Rome, and soon there were rampant rumors. Who will ever know the truth about him?

Elagabalus. He built a Temple for the stone on the Palatine Hill. He made Romans stand around in Phoenician gowns while he slaughtered cattle and sheep in sacrifice.

He begged the physicians to try to transform him into a woman by creating a proper opening between his legs. Romans were horrified by this. At night he dressed as a woman, complete with a wig, and went prowling taverns.

All over the Empire the soldiers started to riot.

Even the three Julias, grandmother Julia Maesa,

his aunt Julia Domna, and his own Mother, Julia Soemis, started to get sick of him. After four years, four years, mind you, of this maniac's rule, the soldiers killed him and threw his body in the Tiber.

It did not seem to Marius that there was anything left of the world we had once called Rome. And he was thoroughly sick of all the Christians in Antioch, their fights over doctrine. He found all mystery religions dangerous now. He served up this lunatic Emperor as a perfect example of the fanaticism gaining ground in the times.

And he was right. He was right.

It was all I could do to keep him from despair. In truth he had not yet confronted that terrible darkness I had once spoken of; he was far too agitated, far too irritated and quarrelsome. But I was very frightened for him, and hurt for him, and didn't want him to see more darkly, as I did, to be more aloof, expecting nothing and almost smiling at the collapse of our Empire.

Then the very worst thing happened, something we had both feared in one form or another. But it came upon us in the worst possible form.

One night there appeared at our eternally open doors five blood drinkers.

Neither of us had caught the sound of their approach. Lounging about with our books, we looked up to see these five, three women and a man and a boy, and to realize that all wore black garments. They were dressed like Christian hermits and ascetics who deny the flesh and starve themselves. Antioch had a whole passel of these men in the desert roundabouts.

But these were blood drinkers.

Dark of hair and eye, and dark of skin, they stood before us, their arms folded.

Dark of skin, I thought quickly. They are young. They were made after the great burning. So what if there are five?

They had in general rather attractive faces, well-shaped features and groomed eyebrows, and deep dark eyes, and all over them I saw the marks of their living bodies—tiny wrinkles next to their eyes, wrinkled around their knuckles.

They seemed as shocked to see us as we were to see them. They stared at the brightly lighted library; they stared at our finery, which was in such contrast to their ascetic robes.

"Well," said Marius, "who are you?"

Cloaking my thoughts, I tried to probe theirs. Their minds were locked. They were dedicated to something. It had the very scent of fanaticism. I felt a horrid foreboding.

They started timidly to enter the open door.

"No, stop, please," said Marius in Greek. "This is my house. Tell me who you are, and then I perhaps shall invite you over my threshold."

"You're Christians, aren't you?" I said. "You have the zeal."

"We are!" said one in Greek. It was the man. "We

are the scourge of humanity in the name of God and his son, Christ. We are the Children of Darkness."

"Who made you?" asked Marius.

"We were made in a sacred cave and in our Temple," said another, a woman, speaking in Greek also. "We know the truth of the Serpent, and his fangs are our fangs."

I climbed to my feet and moved towards Marius.

"We thought you would be in Rome," said the young man. He had short black hair, and very round innocent eyes. "Because the Christian Bishop of Rome is now supreme among Christians and the theology of Antioch is no longer of great matter."

"Why would we be in Rome?" asked Marius. "What is the Roman Bishop to us?"

The woman took the fore. Her hair was severely parted in the middle but her face was very regal and regular. She had in particular beautifully defined lips.

"Why do you hide from us? We have heard of you for years! We know that you know things—about us and where the Dark Gift came from, that you know how God put it into the world, and that you saved our kind from extinction."

Marius was plainly horrified, but gave little sign of it.

"I have nothing to tell you," he said, perhaps too hastily. "Except I do not believe in your God or your Christ and I do not believe God put the Dark Gift, as you call it, into the world. You have made a terrible mistake."

They were highly skeptical and utterly dedicated.

"You have almost reached salvation," said another, the boy at the far end of the line, whose hair was unshorn and hung to his shoulders. He had a manly voice, but his limbs were small. "You have almost reached the point where you are so strong and white and pure that you need not drink!"

"Would that that were true, it's not," said Marius.

"Why don't you welcome us?" asked the boy. "Why don't you guide us and teach us that we may better spread the Dark Blood, and punish mortals for their sins! We are pure of heart. We were chosen. Each of us went into the cave bravely and there the dying devil, a crushed creature of blood and bone, cast out of Heaven in a blaze of fire, passed on to us his teachings."

"Which were what?" asked Marius.

"Make them suffer," the woman said. "Bring death. Eschew all things of the world, as do the Stoics and the hermits of Egypt, but bring death. Punish them."

The woman had become hostile. "This man won't help us," she said under her breath. "This man is profane. This man is a heretic."

"But you must receive us," said the young man who had spoken first. "We have searched so long and so far, and we come to you in humility. If you wish to live in a palace, then perhaps that is your right, you have earned it, but we have not. We live in darkness, we enjoy no pleasure but the blood, we feast on the weak and the diseased and the innocent alike. We do the will of Christ as the Serpent did the will of God in Eden when he tempted Eve."

"Come to our Temple," said one of the others, "and see the tree of life with the sacred Serpent wound around it. We have his fangs. We have his power. God made him, just as God made Judas Iscariot, or Cain, or the evil Emperors of Rome."

"Ah," I said, "I see. Before you happened on the god in the cave, you were worshipers of the snake. You're Ophites, Sethians, Nassenians."

"That was our first calling," said the boy. "But now we are of the Children of Darkness, committed to sacrifice and killing, dedicated to inflicting suffering."

"Oh, Marcion and Valentinus," Marius whispered. "You don't know the names, do you? They're the poetic Gnostics who invented the morass of your philosophy a hundred years ago. Duality—that, in a Christian world, evil could be as powerful as good."

"Yes, we know this." Several spoke at once. "We don't know those profane names. But we know the Serpent and what God wants of us."

"Moses lifted the Serpent in the desert, up over his head," said the boy. "Even the Queen of Egypt knew the Serpent and wore him in her crown."

"The story of the great Leviathan has been eradicated in Rome," said the woman. "They took it out of the sacred books. But we know it!"

"So you learned all this from Armenian Christians," said Marius. "Or was it Syrians."

A man, short of stature, with gray eyes, had not

spoken all this while, but he stepped forward now and addressed Marius with considerable authority.

"You hold ancient truths," he said, "and you use them profanely. All know of you. The blond Children of Darkness in the Northern woods know of you, and that you stole some important secret out of Egypt before the Birth of Christ. Many have come here, glimpsed you and the woman, and gone away in fear."

"Very wise," said Marius.

"What did you find in Egypt?" asked the woman. "Christian monks live now in those old rooms that once belonged to a race of blood drinkers. The monks don't know about us, but we know all about them and you. There was writing there, there were secrets, there was something that by Divine Will belongs now in our hands."

"No, there was nothing," said Marius.

The woman spoke up again, "When the Hebrews left Egypt, when Moses parted the Red Sea, did the Hebrews leave something behind? Why did Moses raise the snake in the desert? Do you know how many we are? Nearly a hundred. We travel to the far North, to the South, and even to the East to lands you would not believe."

I could see Marius was distraught.

"Very well," I said, "we understand what you want and why you have been led to believe that we can satisfy you. I ask you, please, to go out in the Garden and let us speak. Respect our house. Don't harm our slaves."

"We wouldn't dream of it."

"And we'll be back shortly."

I snatched Marius's hand and pulled him down the stairs.

"Where are you going?" he whispered. "Block all images from your mind! They must glimpse nothing."

"They won't glimpse," I said, "and from where I will stand as I talk to you, they won't hear either."

He seemed to catch my meaning. I led him into the sanctuary of the unchanged Mother and Father, closing the stone doors behind me.

I drew Marius behind the seated King and Queen.

"They can probably hear the hearts of the Pair," I whispered in the softest manner audible. "But maybe they won't hear us over that sound. Now, we have to kill them, destroy them completely."

Marius was amazed.

"Look, you know we have to do this!" I said. "You have to kill them and anybody like them who ever comes near us. Why are you so shocked? Get ready. The simplest way is cut them to pieces first, and then burn them."

"Oh, Pandora," he sighed.

"Marius, why do you cringe?"

"I don't cringe, Pandora," he said. "I see myself irrevocably changed by such an act. To kill when I thirst, to keep to myself and keep these here who must be kept by somebody, that I have done for so long. But to become an executioner? To become like the Emperors burning Christians! To commence a war against this race, this order, this cult, whatever it is, to take such a stand."

"No choice, come on. There are many decorative swords in the room where we sleep. We should take the big curved swords. And the torch. We should go to them and tell them how sorry we are for what we must impart to them, then do it!"

He didn't answer.

"Marius, are you going to let them go so that others will come after us? The only security lies in destroying every blood drinker who ever discovers us and the King and Queen."

He walked away from me and stood before the Mother. He looked into her eyes. I knew that he was silently talking to her. And I knew that she was not answering.

"There is one other possibility," I said, "and it's quite real." I beckoned for him to come back, behind them, where I felt safest to plot.

"What is it?" he asked.

"Give the King and the Queen over to them. And you and I are free. They will care for the King and Queen with religious fervor! Maybe the King and Queen will even allow them to drink—"

"That's unspeakable!" he said.

"Exactly my feelings. We shall never know if we are safe. And they shall run rampant through the world like supernatural rodents. So do you have a third plan?"

"No, but I'm ready. We use the fire and the swords

together. Can you tell the lies that will charm them as we approach, armed and carrying torches?"

"Oh, yes, of course," I said.

We went into the chamber and took up the big curved swords that were keenly sharp and came from the desert world of the Arabs. We lighted another torch from that at the foot of the stairs and we went up together.

"Come to me, Children," I said as I entered the room, loudly, "come, for what I have to reveal requires the light of this torch, and you will soon know the sacred purpose of this sword. How devout you are."

We stood before them.

"How young you are!" I said.

Suddenly, the panic swept them together. They made it so simple for us by clustering in this manner that we had the task done in moments, lighting their garments, hacking their limbs, ignoring their piteous cries.

Never had I used my full strength and speed, never my full will, as I did against them. It was exhilarating to slash them, to force the torch upon them, to slash them until they fell, until they lost all life. Also, I did not want them to suffer.

Because they were so young, so very young as blood drinkers, it took quite some time to burn the bones, to see that all was ashes.

But it was finally done, and we stood together—Marius and I—in the garden, our garments smeared with soot, staring down at blowing grass, making certain with our eyes that the ashes were blown in all directions.

Marius turned suddenly and walked fast away from me, and down the stairs and into the Mother's Sanctuary.

I rushed after him in panic. He stood holding the torch and the bloody sword—oh, how they had bled—and he looked into Akasha's eyes.

"Oh, loveless Mother!" he whispered. His face was soiled with blood and grime. He looked at the flaming torch and looked up at the Queen.

Akasha and Enkil showed no sign of any knowledge of the massacre above. They showed neither approval, nor gratitude, nor any form of consciousness. They showed no awareness of the torch in his hand, or his thoughts, whatever they might be.

It was a finish for Marius, a finish to the Marius I had known and loved at that time.

He chose not to leave Antioch. I was for getting away and taking them away, for wild adventures, and seeing the wonders of the world.

But he said no. He had but one obligation. And that was to lay in wait for others until he had killed every one of them.

For weeks he wouldn't speak or move, unless I shook him and then he pleaded with me to leave him alone. He rose from the grave only to sit with the sword and the torch waiting.

It became unbearable to me. Months passed. I

said, "You are going mad. We should take them away!"

Then one night, very angry and alone, I cried out foolishly, "I would I were free of them and you!" And leaving the house, I did not return for three nights.

I slept in dark safe places I made for myself with ease. Every time I thought of him, I thought of his sitting motionless there, so very like them, and I was afraid.

If only he did know true despair; if only he had confronted what we now call "the absurd." If only he had faced the nothingness! Then this massacre would not have demoralized him.

Finally one morning just before sunrise, when I was safely hidden, a strange silence fell over Antioch. A rhythm I had heard there all my days was gone. I was trying to think, What could this mean? But there was time to find out.

I had made a fatal miscalculation. The villa was empty. He had arranged for the transport by day. I had no clue as to where he had gone! Everything belonging to him had been taken, and all that I possessed scrupulously left behind.

I had failed him when he most needed me. I walked in circles around the empty Shrine. I screamed and let the cry echo off the walls.

He never returned to Antioch. No letter ever came.

After six months or more, I gave up and left.

Of course you know the dedicated, religious Christian vampires never died out, not until Lestat came dressed in red velvet and fur to dazzle them and make a mockery of their beliefs. That was in the Age of Reason. That is when Marius received Lestat. Who knows what other vampire cults exist?

As for me, I had lost Marius again by then.

I had seen him for only a single precious night one hundred years earlier, and of course thousands of years after the collapse of what we call "the ancient world."

I saw him! It was in the fancy fragile times of Louis XIV, the Sun King. We were at a court ball in Dresden. Music played—the tentative blend of clavichord, lute, violin—making the artful dances which seemed no more than bows and circles.

Across a room, I suddenly saw Marius!

He had been looking at me for a great while, and gave me now the most tragic and loving smile. He wore a big full-bottomed curly wig, dyed to the very color of his true hair, and a flared velvet coat, and layers of lace, so favored by the French. His skin was golden. That meant fire. I knew suddenly he had suffered something terrible. A jubilant love filled his blue eyes, and without forsaking his casual posture—he was leaning his elbow on the edge of the clavichord—he blew a kiss to me with his fingers.

I truly could not trust my eyes. Was he really there? Was I, myself, sitting here, in boned and low-necked bodice, and these huge skirts, one pulled back in artful folds to reveal the other? My skin in this age seemed an artificial contrivance. My hair had been professionally gathered and lifted into an ornate shape.

I had paid no mind to the mortal hands which had so bound me. During this age I let myself be led through the world by a fierce Asian vampire, about whom I cared nothing. I had fallen into an ever existing trap for a woman: I had become the noncommittal and ostentatious ornament of a male personality who for all his tiresome verbal cruelty possessed sufficient force to carry us both through time.

The Asian was off slowly taking his carefully chosen victim in a bedroom above.

Marius came towards me and kissed me and took me in his arms. I shut my eyes. "This is Marius!" I whispered. "Truly Marius."

"Pandora!" he said, drawing back to look at me. "My Pandora!"

His skin had been burned. Faint scars. But it was almost healed.

He led me out on the dance floor! He was the perfect impersonation of a human being. He guided me in the steps of the dance. I could scarce breathe. Following his lead, shocked at each new artful turn by the rapture of his face, I could not measure centuries or even millennia. I wanted suddenly to know everything—where he had been, what had befallen him. Pride and shame in me held no sway. Could he see that I was no more than a ghost of the woman he'd known? "You are the hope of my soul!" I whispered.

Quickly he took me away. We went in a carriage to his palace. He deluged me with kisses. I clung to him.

"You," he said, "my dream, a treasure so foolishly thrown away, you are here, you have persevered."

"Because you see me, I am here," I said bitterly. "Because you lift the candle, I can almost see my strength in the looking glass."

Suddenly I heard a sound, an ancient and terrible sound. It was the heartbeat of Akasha, the heartbeat of Enkil.

The carriage had come to a halt. Iron gates. Servants.

The palace was spacious, fancy, the ostentatious residence of a rich noble.

"They are in there, the Mother and the Father?" I asked.

"Oh, yes, unchanged. Utterly reliable in their eternal silence." His voice seemed to defy the horror of it.

I couldn't bear it. I had to escape the sound of her heart. An image of the petrified King and Queen rose before my eyes.

"No! Get me away from here. I can't go in. Marius, I cannot look on them!"

"Pandora, they are hidden below the palace. There is no need to look on them. They won't know. Pandora, they are the same."

Ah! The same! My mind sped back, over perilous terrain, to my very first nights, alone and mortal, in

Antioch, to the later victories and defeats of that time. Ah! Akasha was the same! I feared I would begin to scream and be unable to control it.

"Very well," said Marius, "we'll go where you want."

I gave the coachman the location of my hiding place.

I couldn't look at Marius. Valiantly, he kept the pretense of happy reunion. He talked of science and literature, Shakespeare, Dryden, the New World full of jungles and rivers. But behind his voice I heard the joy drained from him.

I buried my face against him. When the carriage stopped I leapt out and fled to the door of my little house. I looked back. He stood in the street.

He was sad and weary, and slowly he nodded and made a gesture of acceptance. "May I wait it out?" he asked. "Is there hope you'll change your mind? I'll wait here forever!"

"It's not my mind!" I said. "I leave this city tonight. Forget me. Forget you ever saw me!"

"My love," he said softly. "My only love."

I ran inside, shutting the door. I heard the carriage pull away. I went wild, as I had not since mortal life, beating the walls with my fists, trying to restrain my immense strength and trying not to let loose the howls and cries that wanted to break from me.

Finally I looked at the clock. Three hours left until dawn.

I sat down at the desk and wrote to him:

Marius,

At dawn we will be taken to Moscow. The very coffin in which I rest is to carry me many miles the first day. Marius, I am dazed. I can't seek shelter in your house, beneath the same roof as the ancient ones. Please, Marius, come to Moscow. Help me to free myself of this predicament. Later you can judge me and condemn me. I need you. Marius, I shall haunt the vicinity of the Czar's palace and the Great Cathedral until you come. Marius, I know I ask of you that *you* make a great journey, but please come. I am a slave to this blood drinker's will.

I love you,
Pandora

Running back out in the street, I hurried in the direction of his house, trying to retrace the path which I had so stupidly ignored.

But what about the heartbeat? I would hear it, that ghastly sound! I had to run past it, run through it, long enough to give Marius this letter, perhaps to let him grasp me by the wrist and force me to some safe place, and drive away before dawn the Asian vampire who kept me.

Then the very carriage appeared, carrying in it my fellow blood drinker from the ball.

He stopped for me at once.

I took the driver aside. "The man who brought

me home," I said. "We went to his house, a huge palace."

"Yes, Count Marius," said the driver. "I just took him back to his own home."

"You must take this letter to him. Hurry! You must go to his house and put it in his hands! Tell him I had no money to give you, that he must pay you, I demand that you tell him. He will pay you. Tell him the letter is from Pandora. You must find him!"

"Who are you speaking of?" demanded my Asian companion.

I motioned to the driver to leave! "Go!" Of course my consort was outraged. But the carriage was already on its way.

Two hundred years passed before I learned the very simple truth: Marius never received that letter!

He had gone back to his house, packed up his belongings and, the following night, left Dresden in sorrow, only finding the letter long after, as he related it to the Vampire Lestat, "a fragile piece of writing," as he called it, "that had fallen to the bottom of a cluttered traveling case."

When did I see him again?

In this modern world. When the ancient Queen rose from her throne and demonstrated the limits of her wisdom, her will and her power.

Two thousand years after, in our Twentieth Century still full of Roman columns and statues and pediments and peristyles, buzzing with computers and warmth-giving television, with Cicero and Ovid in every public library, our Queen, Akasha, was wakened by the image of Lestat on a television screen, in the most modern and secure of shrines, and sought to reign as a goddess, not only over us, but over humankind.

In the most dangerous hour, when she threatened to destroy us all if we did not follow her lead—and she had already slaughtered many—it was Marius with his reasoning, his optimism, his philosophy who talked to her, tried to calm her and divert her, who stalled her destructive intent until an ancient enemy came to fulfill an ancient curse, and struck her down with ancient simplicity.

David, what have you done to me in prodding me to write this narrative?

You have made me ashamed of the wasted years. You have made me acknowledge that no darkness has been ever deep enough to extinguish my personal knowledge of love, love from mortals who brought me into the world, love for goddesses of stone, love for Marius.

Above all, I cannot deny the resurgence of this love for Marius.

And all around me in this world I see evidence of love. Behind the image of the Blessed Virgin and her Infant Jesus, behind the image of the Crucified Christ, behind the remembered basalt image of Isis. I see love. I see it in the human struggle. I see its undeniable penetration in all that humans have accomplished in their poetry, their painting, their music, their love of one another and refusal to accept suffering as their lot.

Above all, however, I see it in the very fashioning of the world which outshines all art, and cannot by sheer randomness have accumulated such beauty.

Love. But whence comes this love? Why is it so secretive about its source, this love that makes rain and trees and has scattered the stars over us as the gods and goddesses once claimed to do?

So Lestat, the brat Prince, woke the Queen; and we survived her destruction. So Lestat, the brat Prince, had gone to Heaven and Hell and brought back disbelief, horror and the Veil of Veronica! Veronica, an invented Christian name which means *vera ikon*, or true icon. He found himself plunged into Palestine during the very years that I lived, and there saw something that has shattered the faculties in humans which we cherish so much: faith, reason.

I have to go to Lestat, look into his eyes. I have to see what he saw!

Let the young sing songs of death. They are stupid.

The finest thing under the sun and the moon is the human soul. I marvel at the small miracles of kindness that pass between humans, I marvel at the growth of conscience, at the persistence of reason in the face of all superstition or despair. I marvel at human endurance.

I have one more story to tell you. I don't know why I want to record it here. But I do. Perhaps it's because I feel you—a vampire who sees spirits—will understand this, and understand perhaps why I remained so unmoved by it.

Once in the Sixth Century—that is, five hundred years after the birth of Christ and three hundred years since I had left Marius—I went wandering in barbarian Italy. The Ostrogoths had long ago overrun the peninsula.

Then other tribes swept down on them, looting, burning, carrying off stones from old Temples.

It was like walking on burning coals for me to go there.

But Rome did struggle with some conception of itself, its principles, trying to blend the pagan with the Christian, and find some respite from the barbarian raids.

The Roman Senate still existed. Of all institutions it had survived.

And a scholar, sprung from the same stock as myself, Boethius, a very learned man who studied the ancients and the saints, had recently been put to death, but not before he had given us a great book. You can find it in any library today. It is, of course, *The Consolation of Philosophy*.

I had to see the ruined Forum for myself, the burnt and barren hills of Rome, the pigs and goats roaming where once Cicero had spoken to the crowds. I had to see the forsaken poor living desperately along the banks of the Tiber.

I had to see the fallen classical world. I had to see the Christian churches and shrines.

I had to see one scholar in particular. Like Boethius he had come from old Roman stock, and like Boethius he had read the classics and the saints. He was a man who wrote letters that went all over the world, even as far as to the scholar Bede in England.

And he had built a monastery there, some great flare of creativity and optimism, in spite of ruin and war.

This man was of course the scholar Cassiodorus, and his monastery lay at the very tip of the boot of Italy, in the paradisal land of green Calabria.

I came upon it in early evening, as I planned, when it looked like a great and splendid lighted little city.

Its monks were copying away ferociously in the Scriptorium.

And there in his cell, wide open to the night, sat Cassiodorus himself, at his writing, a man past ninety years of age.

He had survived the barbarian politics that doomed his friend Boethius, having served the Aryan Ostrogoth Emperor Theodoric, having lived to retire from Civil Service—he had survived to build this monastery, his dream, and to write to monks all over the world, to share what he knew with them of the ancients, to conserve the wisdom of the Greeks and the Romans.

Was he truly the last man of the ancient world, as some have said? The last man who could read both Latin and Greek? The last man who could treasure both Aristotle and the dogma of the Roman Pope? Plato and Saint Paul?

I didn't know then that he would be so well remembered. And I didn't know how soon he'd be forgotten!

Vivarium, on its mountain slopes, was an architectural triumph. It had its sparkling ponds to catch and hold fish—the characteristic which gave it its name. It had its Christian church with the inevitable cross, its dormitories, its rooms for the weary guest traveler. Its library was rich in the classics of my time, as well as gospels which have now been lost. The monastery was rich in all the fruits of the field, all crops needed for food, trees laden with fruit, fields of wheat.

The monks cared for all of this, and they dedicated themselves to copying books day and night in their long Scriptorium.

There were beehives there, on this gentle moonlighted coast, hundreds of beehives from which the monks harvested honey to eat, and wax for sacred candles, and royal jelly for an ointment. The beehives covered a hill as big as the orchard or the farmland of Vivarium.

I spied on Cassiodorus. I walked among the beehives, and marveled as I always do at the inexplicable organization of bees, for the mysteries of the bees and their dance and their hunting for pollen and their breeding was all known to my eye long before it was understood by the human world.

As I left the hives, as I moved away towards the distant beacon of Cassiodorus's lamp, I looked back. I beheld something.

Something collected itself from the hives, something immense and invisible and forceful that I could both feel and hear. I was not gripped by fear, merely sparked by a temporary hope that some New Thing had come into the world. For I am not a seer of ghosts and never was.

This force rose out of the very bees themselves, out of their intricate knowledge and their countless sublime patterns, as though they had somehow accidentally evolved it, or empowered it with consciousness through the means of their endless creativity, meticulousness and endurance.

It was like an old Roman woodland spirit of the forest.

I saw this force fly loosely over the fields. I saw it enter the body of a straw man who stood in the fields, a scarecrow which the monks had made with a fine round wooden head, painted eyes, crude nose and smiling mouth—a creature whole and entire who could be moved from time to time, intact in his monk's hood and robe.

I saw this scarecrow, this man of straw and wood hurry whirling and dancing through the fields and the vineyards until he had reached Cassiodorus's cell.

I followed!

Then I heard a silent wail rise from the being. I heard it and I saw the scarecrow in a bending, bowing dance of sorrow, its bundled straw hands over ears it didn't have. It writhed with grief.

Cassiodorus was dead. He had died quietly within his lamp-lighted cell, his door open, at his writing table. He lay, gray-haired, ancient, quiet against his manuscript. He had lived over ninety years. And he was dead.

This creature, this scarecrow, was wild with suffering and grief, rocking and moaning, though it was a sound no human could have heard.

I who have never seen spirits stared at it in wonder. Then it perceived that I was there. It turned. He—for so it seemed in this ragged attire and body of straw—reached out to me. He flung out his straw arms. The straw fell from his sleeves. His wooden head wobbled on the pole that was his spine. He—It—implored me: he begged me for the answer to the greatest questions humans and immortal have ever posed. He looked to me for answers!

Then glancing back again at the dead Cassiodorus, he ran to me, across the sloping grass, and the need came out of him, poured from him, his arms out as it beheld me. Could I not explain? Could I not contain in some Divine Design the mystery of the loss of Cassiodorus! Cassiodorus who had with his Vivarium rivaled the hive of bees in elegance and glory! It was Vivarium which had drawn this consciousness together from the hives! Could I not ease this creature's pain!

"There are horrors in this world," I whispered. "It is made up of mystery and dependent upon mystery. If you would have peace, go back to the hives; lose your human shape, and descend again, fragmented into the mindless life of the contented bees from which you rose."

He was fixed, and he listened to me.

"If you would have fleshly life, human life, hard life which can move through time and space, then fight for it. If you would have human philosophy then struggle and make yourself wise, so that nothing can hurt you ever. Wisdom is strength. Collect yourself, whatever you are, into something with a purpose.

"But know this. All is speculation under the sky. All myth, all religion, all philosophy, all history—is lies."

The thing, whether it be male or female, drew up its bundled straw hands, as if to cover its mouth. I turned my back on it.

I walked away silently through the vineyards. In a little while the monks would discover that their Father Superior, their genius, their saint, had died at his work.

I looked back in amazement to discover that the figure of straw remained, organized, assuming the posture of an upright being, watching me.

"I will not believe in you!" I shouted back to this man of straw. "I will not search with you for any answer! But know this: if you would become an organized being as you see in me, love all mankind and womankind and all their children. Do not take your strength from blood! Do not feed on suffering. Do not rise like a god above crowds chanting in adoration. Do not lie!"

It listened. It heard. It remained still.

I ran. I ran and ran up the rocky slopes and

through the forests of Calabria until I was far far away from it. Under the moon, I saw the sprawling majesty of Vivarium with its cloisters and sloped roofs as it surrounded the shores of its shimmering inlet from the sea.

I never saw the straw creature again. I don't know what it was. I don't want you to ask me any question about it.

You tell me spirits and ghosts walk. We know such beings exist. But that was the last I saw of that being.

And when next I drifted through Italy, Vivarium had been long destroyed. The earthquakes had shaken loose the last of its walls. Had it been sacked first by the next wave of ignorant tall men of Northern Europe, the Vandals? Was it an earthquake that brought about its ruin?

No one knows. What survives of it are the letters that Cassiodorus sent to others.

Soon the classics were declared profane. Pope Gregory wrote tales of magic and miracles, because it was the only way to convert thousands of superstitious uncatechized Northern tribes to Christianity in great en masse baptisms.

He conquered the warriors Rome could never conquer.

The history of Italy for one hundred years falls into absolute darkness after Cassiodorus. How do the books put it? For a century, nothing is heard from Italy.

Ah, what a silence!

Now David, as you come to these final pages, I

must confess, I have left you. The smiles with which I gave you these notebooks were deceptive. Feminine wiles, Marius would call them. My promise to meet with you tomorrow night here in Paris was a lie. I will have left Paris by the time you come to these lines. I go to New Orleans.

It's your doing, David. You have transformed me. You have given me a desperate faith that in narrative there is a shadow of meaning. I now know a new strident energy. You have trained me through your demand upon my language and my memory to live again, to believe again that some good exists in this world.

I want to find Marius. Thoughts of other immortals fill the air. Cries, pleas, strange messages . . .

One who was believed gone from us is now apparently known to have survived.

I have strong reason to believe that Marius has gone to New Orleans, and I must be reunited with him. I must seek out Lestat, to see this fallen brat Prince lying on the chapel floor unable to speak or move.

Come join me, David. Don't fear Marius! I know he will come to help Lestat. I do the same.

Come back to New Orleans.

Even if Marius is not there, I want to see Lestat. I want to see the others again. What have you done, David? I now contain—with this new curiosity, with this flaming capacity to care once more, with reborn capacity to sing—I now contain the awful capacity to want and to love.

For that, if for nothing else, and there is indeed much more, I shall always thank you. No matter what suffering is to come, you have quickened me. And nothing you do or say will ever cause the death of my love for you.

THE END

Final: July 5, 1997

VITTORIO,
THE VAMPIRE

This novel is dedicated to
Stan, Christopher, Michele and Howard;
to Rosario and Patrice;
to Pamela and Elaine;
and to Niccolo.

This novel is
dedicated
by
Vittorio
to the people of
Florence, Italy.

1

WHO I AM, WHY I WRITE, WHAT IS TO COME

WHEN I was a small boy I had a terrible dream. I dreamt I held in my arms the severed heads of my younger brother and sister. They were quick still, and mute, with big fluttering eyes, and reddened cheeks, and so horrified was I that I could make no more of a sound than they could.

The dream came true.

But no one will weep for me or for them. They have been buried, nameless, beneath five centuries of time.

I am a vampire.

My name is Vittorio, and I write this now in the tallest tower of the ruined mountaintop castle in which I was born, in the northernmost part of Tuscany, that most beautiful of lands in the very center of Italy.

By anyone's standards, I am a remarkable vampire, most powerful, having lived five hundred years from the great days of Cosimo de' Medici, and even the angels will attest to my powers, if you can get them to speak to you. Be cautious on that point.

I have, however, nothing whatsoever to do with the "Coven of the Articulate," that band of strange romantic vampires in and from the Southern New World city of New Orleans who have regaled you already with so many chronicles and tales.

I know nothing of those heroes of macabre fact masquerading as fiction. I know nothing of their enticing paradise in the swamplands of Louisiana. You will find no new knowledge of them in these pages, not even, hereafter, a mention.

I have been challenged by them, nevertheless, to write the story of my own beginnings—the fable of my making—and to cast this fragment of my life in book form into the wide world, so to speak, where it may come into some random or destined contact with their well-published volumes.

I have spent my centuries of vampiric existence in clever, observant roaming and study, never provoking the slightest danger from my own kind, and never arousing their knowledge or suspicions.

But this is not to be the unfolding of my adventures.

It is, as I have said, to be the tale of my beginnings. For I believe I have revelations within me which will be wholly original to you. Perhaps when my book is finished and gone from my hands, I may take steps to become somehow a character in that grand *roman-fleuve* begun by other vampires in San Francisco or New Orleans. For now, I cannot know or care about it.

As I spend my tranquil nights, here, among the overgrown stones of the place where I was so happy as a child, our walls now broken and misshapen among the thorny blackberry vines and fragrant smothering forests of oak and chestnut trees, I am compelled to record what befell me, for it seems that I may have suffered a fate very unlike that of any other vampire.

I do not always hang about this place.

On the contrary, I spend most of my time in that city which for me is the queen of all cities—Florence—which I loved from the very first moment I saw it with a child's eyes in the years when Cosimo the Elder ran his powerful Medici bank with his own hand, even though he was the richest man in Europe.

In the house of Cosimo de' Medici lived the great sculptor Donatello making sculptures of marble and bronze, as well as painters and poets galore, writers on magic and makers of music. The great Brunelleschi, who had made the very dome of Florence's greatest church, was building yet another Cathedral for Cosimo in those days, and Michelozzo was rebuilding not only the monastery of San Marco but commencing the palazzo for Cosimo which would one day be known to all the world as the Palazzo Vecchio. For Cosimo, men went all over Europe seeking in dusty libraries long forgotten the classics of Greece and Rome, which Cosimo's scholars would translate into our native Italian, the language which Dante had boldly chosen many years before for his *Divine Comedy*.

And it was under Cosimo's roof that I saw, as a mortal boy of destiny and promise—yes, I myself saw—the great guests of the Council of Trent who had come from far Byzantium to heal the breach between the Eastern and Western church: Pope Eugenius IV of Rome, the Patriarch of Constantinople and the Emperor of the East himself, John VIII Paleologus. These great men I saw enter the city in a terrible storm of bitter rain, but nevertheless with indescribable glory, and these men I saw eat from Cosimo's table.

Enough, you might say. I agree with you. This is no history of the Medici. But let me only say that anyone who tells you that they were scoundrels, these great men, is a perfect idiot. It was the descendants of Cosimo who took care of Leonardo da Vinci, Michelangelo and artists without count. And it was all because a banker, a moneylender if you will, thought it splendid and good to give beauty and magnificence to the city of Florence.

I'll come back to Cosimo at the right point, and only for a few brief words, though I must confess I am having trouble being brief here on any score, but for now let me say that Cosimo belongs to the living.

I have been in bed with the dead since 1450.

Now to tell how it began, but allow me one more preface.

Don't look here, please, for antique language. You will not find a rigid fabricated English meant to conjure castle walls by stilted diction and constricted vocabulary.

I shall tell my tale naturally and effectively, wallowing in words, for I love them. And, being an immortal, I have devoured over four centuries of

English, from the plays of Christopher Marlowe and Ben Jonson to the abrupt and harshly evocative words of a Sylvester Stallone movie.

You'll find me flexible, daring, and now and then a shock. But what can I do but draw upon the fullest descriptive power I can command, and mark that English now is no more the language of one land, or even two or three or four, but has become the language of all the modern world from the backwoods of Tennessee to the most remote Celtic isles and down under to the teeming cities of Australia and New Zealand.

I am Renaissance-born. Therefore I delve in all, and blend without prejudice, and that some higher good pertains to what I do, I cannot doubt.

As for my native Italian, hear it softly when you say my name, Vittorio, and breathe it like perfume from the other names which are sprinkled throughout this text. It is, beneath all, a language so sweet as to make of the English word "stone" three syllables: *pi-ea-tra.* There has never been a gentler language on earth. I speak all other tongues with the Italian accent you'll hear in the streets of Florence today.

And that my English-speaking victims find my blandishments so pretty, accented as they are, and yield to my soft lustrous Italian pronunciations, is a constant source of bliss for me.

But I am not happy.

Don't think so.

I wouldn't write a book to tell you that a vampire was happy.

I have a brain as well as a heart, and there hovers

about me an etheric visage of myself, created most definitely by some Higher Power, and entangled completely within the intangible weave of that etheric visage is what men call a soul. I have such. No amount of blood can drown away its life and leave me but a thriving revenant.

Okay. No problem. Yes, yes. Thank you!—as everybody in the entire world can say in English. We're ready to begin.

Except I want to give you a quote from an obscure but wonderful writer, Sheridan Le Fanu, a paragraph spoken in extreme angst by a haunted character in one of his many exquisitely written ghost stories. This author, a native of Dublin, died in 1873, but mark how fresh is this language, and how horrifying the expression of the character Captain Barton in the story called "The Familiar":

> Whatever may be my uncertainty as to the authenticity of what we are taught to call revelation, of one fact I am deeply and horribly convinced, that there does exist beyond this a spiritual world—a system whose workings are generally in mercy hidden from us—a system which may be, and which is sometimes, partially and terribly revealed. I am sure—I *know* . . . that there is a God—a dreadful God—and that retribution follows guilt, in ways the most mysterious and stupendous—by agencies the most inexplicable and terrific;—there is a spiritual system—great God, how I have been convinced!—a system malignant, and implacable, and omnipotent, under whose

persecutions I am, and have been, suffering the torments of the damned!

What do you think of that?

I am myself rather mortally struck by it. I don't think I am prepared to speak of our God as "dreadful" or our system as "malignant," but there seems an eerie inescapable ring of truth to these words, written in fiction but obviously with much emotion.

It matters to me because I suffer under a terrible curse, quite unique to me, I think, as a vampire. That is, the others don't share it. But I think we all—human, vampire, all of us who are sentient and can weep—we all suffer under a curse, the curse that we know more than we can endure, and there is nothing, absolutely nothing, we can do about the force and the lure of this knowledge.

At the end, we can take this up again. See what you make of my story.

It's early evening here. The brave remnant of my father's highest tower still rises boldly enough against the sweetly star-filled heavens for me to see from the window the moonlighted hills and valleys of Tuscany, aye, even as far as the twinkling sea below the mines of Carrara. I smell the flowering green of the steep undiscovered country round where the irises of Tuscany still break out in violent red or white in sunny beds, to be found by me in the silky night.

And so embraced and protected, I write, ready for the moment when the full yet ever obscure moon leaves me for the hideaway of clouds, to light the candles that stand ready, some six, ensconced within the thick ruggedly worked silver of the candelabra which once stood on my father's desk, in those days when he was the old-style feudal lord of this mountain and all its villages, and the firm ally in peace and war of the great city of Florence and its unofficial ruler, when we were rich, fearless, curious and wondrously contented.

Let me speak now of what has vanished.

2

MY SMALL MORTAL LIFE, THE BEAUTY OF FLORENCE, THE GLORY OF OUR SMALL COURT— WHAT IS VANISHED

I WAS sixteen years old when I died. I have good height, thick brown hair down to the shoulders, hazel eyes that are far too vulnerable to behold, giving me the appearance of an androgyne in a way, and a desirable narrow nose with unremarkable nostrils, and a medium-sized mouth which is neither voluptuous nor stingy. A beautiful boy for the time. I wouldn't be alive now if I hadn't been.

That's the case with most vampires, no matter who says otherwise. Beauty carries us to our doom. Or, to put it more accurately, we are made immortal by those who cannot sever themselves from our charms.

I don't have a childish face, but I have an almost angelic one. My eyebrows are strong, dark, high enough over my eyes to allow them entirely too much luster. My forehead would be a little too high if it wasn't so straight, and if I didn't have so much thick brown hair, making as it does a curly, wavy frame for the whole picture. My chin is slightly too strong, too squared off for the rest. I have a dimple in it.

My body is overmuscular, strong, broad-chested, my arms powerful, giving an impression of manly power. This rather rescues my obdurate-looking jaw and allows me to pass for a full-fledged man, at least from a distance.

This well-developed physique I owe to tremendous practice with a heavy battle sword in the last years of my life, and ferocious hunting with my falcons in the mountains, up and down which I ran often on foot, though I had already four horses of my own by that age, including one of that special majestic breed made to support my weight when I wore my full suit of armor.

My armor is still buried beneath this tower. I never used it in battle. Italy was seething with war in my time, but all of the battles of the Florentines were being fought by mercenaries.

All my father had to do was declare his absolute loyalty to Cosimo, and let no one representing the Holy Roman Empire, the Duke of Milan or the Pope in Rome move troops through our mountain passes or stop in our villages.

We were out of the way. It was no problem. Enterprising ancestors had built our castle three hundred years before. We went back to the time of the Lombards, or those barbarians who had come down from the North into Italy, and I think we had their blood in us. But who knows? Since the Fall of ancient Rome, so many tribes had invaded Italy.

We had interesting pagan relics lying about; alien tombstones most ancient were sometimes found in the fields, and funny little stone goddesses which the peasants still cherished if we didn't confiscate them. Beneath our towers were vaults that some said went back to the days even before the Birth of Christ, and I know now that is true. These places belonged to the people known to history as the Etruscans.

Our household, being of the old feudal style, scorning trade and requiring of its men that they be bold and brave, was full of treasure acquired through wars without count or record—that is, old silver and gold candelabra and sconces, heavy chests of wood with Byzantine designs encrusted on them, the usual Flemish tapestries, and tons of lace, and bed hangings hand-trimmed with gilt and gems, and all of the most desirable finery.

My father, admiring the Medici as he did, bought up all kinds of luxury items on his trips to Florence. There was little bare stone in any important room, because flowered wool carpets covered all, and every hallway or alcove had its own towering armoire filled with rattling, rusting battle dress of heroes whose names nobody even remembered.

We were incalculably rich: this I had more or less overheard as a child, and there was some hint that it had to do as much with valor in war as with secret pagan treasure.

There had been centuries of course when our family had warred with other hill towns and forts, when castle besieged castle and walls were ripped down as soon as they were built, and out of the city of Florence had gone the ever quarreling and murderous Guelfs and Ghibellines.

The old Commune of Florence had sent armies to

tear down castles like ours and reduce any threatening Lord to nothingness.

But that time was long over.

We had survived due to cleverness and good choices, and also because we were much off to ourselves, in high craggy uninviting country, crowning a true mountain, as this is where the Alps come down into Tuscany, and those castles most near to us were abandoned ruins.

Our nearest neighbor did rule his own mountain enclave of villages in loyalty to the Duke of Milan.

But he didn't bother with us or we him. It was a remote political matter.

Our walls were thirty feet high, immensely thick, older than the castle and keeps, old indeed beyond anyone's most romantic tales and constantly being thickened and repaired, and inside the compound there existed three little villages busy with good vineyards that yielded marvelous red wine; prosperous beehives; blackberries; and wheat and the like; with plenty of chickens and cows; and enormous stables for our horses.

I never knew how many people labored in our little world. The house was full of clerks who took care of such things, and very seldom did my father sit in judgment on any sort of case himself or was there cause to go to the courts of Florence.

Our church was the designated church for all the country round, so that those few who lived in less protected little hamlets down the mountain—and there were plenty—came to us for their baptisms, and marriages, and such, and we had for long periods of time within our walls a Dominican priest who said Mass for us every morning.

In olden times, the forest had been severely cut down on our mountain so that no invading enemy could make his way up the slopes, but by my time no such protection was necessary.

The woods had grown back full and sweet in some gullies and over old paths, even as wild as it is now, and almost up to the walls. One could make out clearly from our towers a dozen or so small towns descending to the valleys, with their little quilts of tilled fields, orchards of olive trees and vineyards. They were all under our governance and loyal to us. If there had been any war they would have come running to our gates as their ancestors had done, and rightly so.

There were market days, village festivals, saints' days, and a little alchemy now and then, and occasionally even a local miracle. It was a good land, ours.

Visiting clerics always stayed a long time. It wasn't uncommon to have two or three priests in various towers of the castle or in the lower, newer, more modern stone buildings.

I had been taken to Florence to be educated when I was very small, living in deluxe and invigorating style in the palazzo of my mother's uncle, who died before I was thirteen, and it was then—when the house was closed—that I was brought home, with two elderly aunts, and after that only visited Florence on occasion.

My father was still at heart an old-fashioned man, instinctively an indomitable Lord, though he was content to keep his distance from the power struggles of the capital, to have huge accounts in the Medici banks and to live an old-style courtly life in his own domain, visiting Cosimo de' Medici himself when he did journey into Florence on business.

But when it came to his son, my father wanted that I should be reared as a prince, a padrone, a knight, and I had to learn all the skills and values of a knight, and at thirteen, I could ride in full battle dress, my helmeted head bowed, at full speed with my spear thrust towards the straw-filled target. I had no difficulty with it. It was as much fun as hunting, or swimming in mountain streams, or having horse races with the village boys. I took to it without rebellion.

I was, however, a divided being. The mental part of me had been nourished in Florence by excellent teachers of Latin, Greek, philosophy and theology, and I had been deep into the boys' pageants and plays of the city, often taking the leading parts in the dramas presented by my own Confraternity in my uncle's house, and I knew how to solemnly portray the Biblical Isaac about to be sacrificed by the obedient Abraham, as well as the charming Angel Gabriel discovered by a suspicious St. Joseph with his Virgin Mary.

I pined for all that now and then, the books, the lectures in the Cathedrals to which I'd listened with precocious interest, and the lovely nights in my uncle's Florentine house when I'd fallen asleep to the sounds of spectacular opera extravaganzas, my mind brim full of the dazzle of miraculous figures swooping down on wires, lutes and drums playing wildly, dancers frolicking almost like acrobats and voices soaring beautifully in unison.

It had been an easy childhood. And in the boys' Confraternity to which I belonged, I'd met the poorer children of Florence, the sons of the merchants, orphans and boys from the monasteries and schools, because that is the way it was in my time for a landed Lord. You had to mix with the people.

I think I crept out of the house a lot as a small child, easily as much as I slipped out of the castle later. I remember too much of the festivals and saints' days and processions of Florence for a disciplined child to have seen. I was too often slipping in and out of the crowd, looking at the spectacularly decorated floats in honor of the saints, and marveling at the solemnity of those in silent ranks who carried candles and walked very slowly as if they were in a trance of devotion.

Yes, I must have been a scamp. I know I was. I went out by the kitchen. I bribed the servants. I had too many friends who were out-and-out routies or beasties. I got into mayhem and then ran home. We played ball games and had battles in the piazzas, and the priests ran us off with switches and threats. I was good and bad, but not ever really wicked.

When I died to this world, at the age of sixteen, I never looked on a daylighted street again, not in Florence or anywhere. Well, I saw the best of it, that I can say. I can envisage with no difficulty the spectacle of the Feast of St. John, when every single solitary shop in Florence had to put out front all of its costly wares, and monks and friars sang the sweetest hymns on their way to the Cathedral to give thanks to God for the blessed prosperity of the city.

I could go on. There is no end to the praise one can heap upon the Florence of those times, for she was a city of men who worked at trades and business yet made the greatest art, of sharp politicians and true raving saints, of deep-souled poets and the most audacious scoundrels. I think Florence knew many things by that time that would only much later be learnt in France and England, and which are not known in some countries to this day. Two things were true. Cosimo was the most powerful man in all the world. And the people, and only the people, ruled Florence then and forever.

But back to the castle. I kept up my reading and studies at home, switching from knight to scholar in a twinkling. If there was any shadow on my life, it was that at sixteen I was old enough to go to a real university, and I knew it, and I sort of wanted to do it, but then again, I was raising new hawks, training them myself and hunting with them, and the country round was irresistible.

By this age of sixteen, I was considered bookish by the clan of elder kinsmen who gathered at the table every night, my parents' uncles mostly, and all very much of a former time when "bankers had not run the world," who had marvelous tales to tell of the Crusades, to which they had gone when they were young, and of what they had seen at the fierce battle of Acre, or fighting on the island of Cyprus or Rhodes, and what life had been like at sea, and in many exotic ports where they had been the terror of the taverns and the women.

My mother was spirited and beautiful, with brown hair and very green eyes, and she adored country life, but she'd never known Florence except from the inside of a convent. She thought there was something seriously wrong with me that I wanted to read Dante's poetry and write so much of my own.

She lived for nothing but receiving guests in gracious style, seeing to it that the floors were strewn with lavender and sweet-smelling herbs, and that the wine was properly spiced, and she led the dance herself with a great-uncle who was very good at it, because my father would have nothing to do with dancing.

All this to me, after Florence, was rather tame and slow. Bring on the war stories.

She must have been very young when she was married off to my father, because she was with child on the night she died. And the child died with her. I'll come to that quickly. Well, as quickly as I can. I'm not so good at being quick.

My brother, Matteo, was four years younger than me, and an excellent student, though he had not been sent off anywhere as yet (would that he had), and my sister, Bartola, was born less than a year after me, so close in fact that I think my father was rather ashamed of it.

I thought them both—Matteo and Bartola—the most lovely and interesting people in the world. We had country fun and country freedom, running in the woods, picking blackberries, sitting at the feet of gypsy storytellers before they got caught and sent away. We loved one another. Matteo worshipped me too much because I could outtalk our father. He didn't see our father's quiet strength, or well-fashioned old manners. I was Matteo's real teacher in all things, I suppose. As for Bartola, she was far too wild for my mother, who was in an eternal state of shock over the state of Bartola's long hair, the hair being all full of twigs and petals and leaves and dirt from the woods where we'd been running.

Bartola was forced into plenty of embroidering, however; she knew her songs, her poetry and prayers. She was too exquisite and too rich to be rushed into anything she didn't want. My father adored her, and more than once in very few words assured himself that I kept constant watch over her in all our woodland wanderings. I did. I would have killed anyone who touched her!

Ah. This is too much for me! I didn't know how hard this was going to be! Bartola. Kill anyone who touched her! And now nightmares descend, as if they were winged spirits themselves, and threaten to shut out the tiny silent and ever drifting lights of Heaven.

Let me return to my train of thought.

My mother I never really understood, and probably misjudged, because everything seemed a matter of style and manners with her, and my father I found to be hysterically self-satirical and always funny.

He was, beneath all his jokes and snide stories, actually rather cynical, but at the same time kind; he saw through the pomp of others, and even his own pretensions. He looked upon the human situation as hopeless. War was comic to him, devoid of heroes and full of buffoons, and he would burst out laughing in the middle of his uncles' harangues, or even in the middle of my poems when I went on too long, and I don't think he ever deliberately spoke a civil word to my mother.

He was a big man, clean shaven and long-haired, and he had beautiful long tapering fingers, very unusual for his size, because all his elders had thicker hands. I have the same hands myself. All the beautiful rings he wore had belonged to his mother.

He dressed more sumptuously than he would have dared to do in Florence, in regal velvet stitched with pearls, and wore massive cloaks lined in ermine. His gloves were true gauntlets trimmed in fox, and he had large grave eyes, more deep-set than mine, and full of mockery, disbelief and sarcasm.

He was never mean, however, to anyone.

His only modern affectation was that he liked to drink from fine goblets of glass, rather than old cups of hardwood or gold or silver. And we had plenty of sparkling glass always on our long supper table.

My mother always smiled when she said such things to him as "My Lord, please get your feet off the table," or "I'll thank you not to touch me until you've washed your greasy hands," or "Are you really coming into the house like that?" But beneath her charming exterior, I think she hated him.

The one time I ever heard her raise her voice in anger, it was to declare in no uncertain terms that half the children in our villages round had been sired by him, and that she herself had buried some eight tiny infants who had never lived to see the light, because he couldn't restrain himself any better than a rampant stallion.

He was so amazed at this outburst—it was behind closed doors—that he emerged from the bedchamber looking pale and shocked, and said to me, "You know, Vittorio, your mother is nothing as stupid as I always thought. No, not at all. As a matter of fact, she's just boring."

He would never under normal circumstances have said anything so unkind about her. He was trembling.

As for her, when I tried to go in to her, she threw a silver pitcher at me. I said, "But Mother, it's Vittorio!" and she threw herself into my arms. She cried bitterly for fifteen minutes.

We said nothing during this time. We sat together in her small stone bedroom, rather high up in the oldest tower of our house, with many pieces of gilded furniture, both ancient and new, and then she wiped her eyes and said, "He takes care of everyone, you know. He takes care of my aunts and my uncles, you know. And where would they be if it weren't for him? And he's never denied me anything."

She went rambling on in her smooth convent-modulated voice. "Look at this house. It's filled with elders whose wisdom has been so good for you children, and all this on account of your father, who is rich enough to have gone anywhere, I suppose, but he is too kind. Only, Vittorio! Vittorio, don't . . . I mean . . . with the girls in the village."

I almost said, in a spasm of desire to comfort her,

that I had only fathered one bastard to my knowledge, and he was just fine, when I realized this would have been a perfect disaster. I said nothing.

That might have been the only conversation I ever had with my mother. But it's not really a conversation because I didn't say anything.

She was right, however. Three of her aunts and two of her uncles lived with us in our great high-walled compound, and these old people lived well, always sumptuously dressed in the latest fabrics from the city, and enjoying the purest courtly life imaginable. I couldn't help but benefit from listening to them all the time, which I did, and they knew plenty of all the world.

It was the same with my father's uncles, but of course it was their land, this, their family's, and so they felt more entitled, I assume, as they had done most of the heroic fighting in the Holy Land, or so it seemed, and they quarreled with my father over anything and everything, from the taste of the meat tarts served at supper to the distractingly modern style of the painters he hired from Florence to decorate our little chapel.

That was another sort of modern thing he did, the matter of the painters, maybe the only modern thing other than liking things made of glass.

Our little chapel had for centuries been bare. It was, like the four towers of our castle and all the walls around, built of a blond stone which is common in Northern Tuscany. This is not the dark stone you see so much in Florence, which is gray and looks perpetually unclean. This northern stone is almost the color of the palest pink roses.

But my father had brought pupils up from Florence when I was very young, good painters who had studied with Piero della Francesca and other such, to cover these chapel walls with murals taken from the lovely stories of saints and Biblical giants in the books known as *The Golden Legend*.

Not being himself a terribly imaginative man, my father followed what he had seen in the churches of Florence in his design and instructed these men to tell the tales of John the Baptist, patron saint of the city and cousin of Our Lord, and so it was that during the last years of my life on earth, our chapel was enfolded with representations of St. Elizabeth, St. John, St. Anne, the Blessed Mother, Zachary and angels galore, all dressed—as was the way of the time—in their Florentine finest.

It was to this "modern" painting, so unlike the stiffer work of Giotto or Cimabue, that my elderly uncles and aunts objected. As for the villagers, I don't think they exactly understood it all either, except they were so overawed in the main by the chapel at a wedding or baptism that it didn't matter.

I myself of course was terrifically happy to see these paintings made, and to spend time with the artists, who were all gone by the time that my life was brought to a halt by demonic slaughter.

I'd seen plenty of the greatest painting in Florence and had a weakness for drifting about, looking at splendid visions of angels and saints in the rich dedicated chapels of the Cathedrals, and had even—on one of my trips to Florence with my father—in Cosimo's house, glimpsed the tempestuous painter Filippo Lippi, who was at that time actually under lock and key there to make him finish a painting.

I was much taken with the plain yet compelling man, the way that he argued and schemed and did everything but throw a tantrum to get permission to leave the palazzo while lean, solemn and low-voiced Cosimo just smiled and talked him down more or less out of his hysteria, telling him to get back to work and that he would be happy when he was finished.

Filippo Lippi was a monk, but he was mad for women and everybody knew it. You could say that he was a favorite bad guy. It was for women that he wanted out of the palazzo, and it was even suggested later at the supper table of our hosts in Florence on that visit that Cosimo ought to lock a few women in the room with Filippo, and that maybe that would keep Filippo happy. I don't think Cosimo did any such thing. If he had, his enemies would have made it the grand news of Florence.

Let me make note, for it is very important. I never forgot that glimpse of the genius Filippo, for that is what he was—and is—to me.

"So what did you so like about him?" my father asked me.

"He's bad and good," I said, "not just one or the other. I see a war going on inside of him! And I saw some of his work once, work he did with Fra Giovanni"—this was the man later called Fra Angelico by all the world—"and I tell you, I think he is brilliant. Why else would Cosimo put up with such a scene? Did you hear him!"

"And Fra Giovanni is a saint?" asked my father.

"Hmmmmm, yes. And that's fine, you know, but did you see the torment in Fra Filippo? Hmmm, I liked it."

My father raised his eyebrows.

On our next and very last trip to Florence, he took me to see all of Filippo's paintings. I was amazed that he had remembered my interest in this man. We went from house to house to look at the loveliest works, and then to Filippo's workshop.

There an altarpiece commissioned by Francesco Maringhi for a Florentine church—*The Coronation of the Virgin*—was well under way, and when I saw this work, I nearly fainted dead from shock and love of it.

I couldn't leave it alone. I sighed and wept.

I had never seen anything as beautiful as this painting, with its immense crowd of still attentive faces, its splendid collection of angels and saints, its lithe and graceful feline women and willowy celestial men. I went crazy for it.

My father took me to see two more of his works, which were both paintings of the Annunciation.

Now, I have mentioned that as a child, I had played the Angel Gabriel coming to the Virgin to announce the Conception of Christ in her womb, and the way we played, he was supposed to be a pretty beguiling and virile angel, and Joseph would come in and, lo, find this overwhelming male with his pure ward, the Blessed Mary.

We were a worldly bunch, but you know, we gave the play a little spice. I mean we cooked it up a bit. I don't think it says anything in scripture about St. Joseph happening on a tryst.

But that had been my favorite role, and I had particularly enjoyed paintings of the Annunciation.

Well, this last one I saw before I left Florence, done by Filippo sometime in the 1440s, was beyond anything I had beheld before.

The angel was truly unearthly yet physically perfect. Its wings were made of peacock feathers.

I was sick with devotion and covetousness. I wished we could buy this thing and take it back home. That wasn't possible. No works of Filippo were on the market then. So my father finally dragged me away from this painting, and off we went home the next day or so.

Only later did I realize how quietly he listened to what I said as I ranted on and on about Fra Filippo:

"It's delicate, it's original, and yet it is commendable according to everybody's rules, that's the genius of it, to change, but not so much, to be inimitable, yet not beyond the common grasp, and that's what he's done, Father, I tell you."

I was unstoppable.

"This is what I think about that man," I said. "The carnality in him, the passion for women, the near beastly refusal to keep his vows is at war always with the priest, for look, he wears his robes, he is Fra Filippo. And out of that war, there comes into the faces he paints a look of utter surrender."

My father listened.

"That's it," I said. "Those characters reflect his own continued compromise with the forces he cannot reconcile, and they are sad, and wise, and never innocent, and always soft, reflective of mute torment."

On the way back home, as we were riding together through the forest, up a rather steep road, very casually my father asked me if the painters who had done our chapel were good.

"Father, you're joking," I said. "They were excellent."

He smiled. "I didn't know, you know," he said. "I just hired the best." He shrugged.

I smiled.

Then he laughed with good nature. I never asked him when and if I could leave home again to study. I think I figured I could make both of us happy.

We must have made twenty-five stops on that last journey home from Florence. We were wined and dined at one castle after another, and wandered in and out of the new villas, lavish and full of light, and given over to their abundant gardens. I clung to nothing in particular because I thought it was my life, all those arbors covered with purple wisteria, and the vineyards on the green slopes, and the sweet-cheeked girls beckoning to me in the loggias.

Florence was actually at war the year we made this journey. She had sided with the great and famous Francesco Sforza, to take over the city of Milan. The cities of Naples and Venice were on the side of Milan. It was a terrible war. But it didn't touch us.

It was fought in other places and by hired men, and the rancor caused by it was heard in city streets, not on our mountain.

What I recall from it were two remarkable characters involved in the fray. The first of these was the Duke of Milan, Filippo Maria Visconti, a man who had been our enemy whether we liked it or not because he was the enemy of Florence.

But listen to what this man was like: he was hideously fat, it was said, and very dirty by nature, and sometimes would take off all his clothes and roll around naked in the dirt of his garden! He was terrified of the sight of a sword and would scream if he saw it unsheathed, and he was terrified too to have his portrait painted because he thought he was so ugly, which he was. But that was not all. This man's weak little legs wouldn't carry him, so his pages had to heft him about. Yet he had a sense of humor. To scare people, he would suddenly draw a snake out of his sleeve! Lovely, don't you think?

Yet he ruled the Duchy of Milan for thirty-five years somehow, this man, and it was against Milan that his own mercenary, Francesco Sforza, turned in this war.

And that man I want to describe only briefly because he was colorful in an entirely different way, being the handsome strong brave son of a peasant—a peasant who, kidnapped as a child, had managed to become the commander of his band of kidnappers—and this Francesco became commander of the troop only when the peasant hero drowned in a stream trying to save a page boy. Such valor. Such purity! Such gifts.

I never laid eyes on Francesco Sforza until I was already dead to the world and a prowling vampire, but he was true to his descriptions, a man of heroic proportions and style, and believe it or not, it was to this bastard of a peasant and natural soldier that the weak-legged crazy Duke of Milan gave his own daughter in marriage, and this daughter, by the way, was not by the Duke's wife, poor thing, for she was locked up, but by his mistress.

It was this marriage which led eventually to the war. First Francesco was fighting bravely for Duke Filippo Maria, and then when the weird unpredictable little Duke finally croaked, naturally his son-in-law, handsome Francesco, who had charmed everybody in Italy from the Pope to Cosimo, wanted to become the Duke of Milan!

It's all true. Don't you think it's interesting? Look it up. I left out that the Duke Filippo Maria was also so scared of thunder that he was supposed to have built a soundproof room in his palace.

And there is more to it than that. Sforza more or less had to save Milan from other people who wanted to take it over, and Cosimo had to back him, or France would have come down on us, or worse.

It was all rather amusing, and as I have said, I was well prepared already at a young age to go into war or to court if it was ever required of me, but these wars and these two characters existed for me in dinner table talk, and every time someone railed about the crazy Duke Filippo Maria, and one of his insane tricks with a snake out of his sleeve, my father would wink at me and whisper in my ear, "Nothing like pure lordly blood, my son." And then laugh.

As for the romantic and brave Francesco Sforza, my father had wisely nothing to say as long as the man was fighting for our enemy, the Duke, but once we had all turned together against Milan, then my father commended the bold self-made Francesco and his courageous peasant father.

There had been another great lunatic running around Italy during earlier times, a freebooter and ruffian named Sir John Hawkwood, who would lead his mercenaries against anybody, including the Florentines.

But he had ended up loyal to Florence, even became a citizen, and when he departed this earth, they gave him a splendid monument in the Cathedral! Ah, such an age!

I think it was a really good time to be a soldier, you know, to sort of pick and choose where you would fight, and get as carried away with it all as you wanted to.

But it was also a very good time for reading poetry, and for looking at paintings and for living in utter comfort and security behind ancestral walls, or wandering the thriving streets of prosperous cities. If you had any education at all, you could choose what you wanted to do.

And it was also a time to be very careful. Lords such as my father did go down to destruction in these wars. Mountainous regions that had been free and pretty much left alone could be invaded and destroyed. It happened now and then that someone who had pretty much stayed out of things got himself worked up against Florence and in came the clattering and clanking mercenaries to level everything.

By the way, Sforza won the war with Milan, and part of the reason was that Cosimo lent him the required money. What happened after that was absolute mayhem.

Well, I could go on describing this wonderland of Tuscany forever.

It is chilling and saddening for me to try to imagine what might have become of my family had evil not befallen us. I cannot see my father old, or imagine myself struggling as an elderly man, or envision my sister married, as I hoped, to a city aristocrat rather than a country baron.

It is a horror and a joy to me that there are villages and hamlets in these very mountains which have from that time never died out—never—surviving through the worst of even modern war, to thrive still with tiny cobbled market streets and pots of red geraniums in their windows. There are castles which survive everywhere, enlivened by generation after generation.

Here there is darkness.

Here is Vittorio writing by the light of the stars.

Brambles and wild scratching things inhabit the chapel below, where the paintings are still visible to no one and the sacred relics of the consecrated altar stone are beneath heaps of dust.

Ah, but those thorns protect what remains of my home. I have let them grow. I have allowed the roads to vanish in the forest or broken them myself. I must have something of what there was! I must.

But I accuse myself again of going on and on, and I do, there is no doubt.

This chapter ought to be over.

But it's very like the little plays we used to do in my uncle's house, or those I saw before the Duomo in Cosimo's Florence. There must be painted backdrops, props of fine detail, wires rigged for flight and costumes cut out and sewn before I can put my players on the boards and tell the fable of my making.

I can't help it. Let me close my essay on the glories of the 1400s by saying what the great alchemist Ficino would say of it some years later on: It was "an age of gold."

I go now to the tragic moment.

3

IN WHICH THE HORROR DESCENDS UPON US

THE beginning of the end came the following spring. I had passed my sixteenth birthday, which had fallen that year on the very Tuesday before Lent, when we and all the villages were celebrating Carnival. It had come rather early that year, so it was a bit cold, but it was a gay time.

It was on that night before Ash Wednesday that I had the terrible dream in which I saw myself holding the severed heads of my brother and my sister. I woke up in a sweat, horrified by this dream. I wrote it down in my book of dreams. And then actually I forgot about it. That was common with me, only it had been truly the most horrid nightmare I'd ever had. But when I mentioned my occasional nightmares to my mother or father or anyone else, they always said:

"Vittorio, it's your own fault for reading the books you read. You bring it on yourself."

To repeat, the dream was forgotten.

The country was by Easter in great flower, and the first warnings of horror to come, though I knew them not to be, were that the lower hamlets on our mountain were quite suddenly abandoned.

My father and I and two of the huntsmen and a gamekeeper and a soldier rode down to see for ourselves that the peasants in those parts had departed, some time before in fact, and taken the livestock with them.

It was eerie to see those deserted towns, small as they were and as insignificant.

We rode back up the mountain as a warm embracing darkness surrounded us, yet we found all the other villages we passed battened down with hardly a seam of light showing through the chinks of a shutter, or a tiny stem of reddened smoke rising from a chimney.

Of course my father's old clerk went into a rant that the vassals should be found, beaten, made to work the land.

My father, benevolent as always and completely calm, sat at his desk in the candlelight, leaning on his elbow, and said that these had all been free men; they were not bound to him, if they did not choose to live on his mountain. This was the way of the modern world, only he wished he knew what was afoot in our land.

Quite suddenly, he took notice of me standing and observing him, as if he hadn't seen me before, and he broke off the conference, dismissing the whole affair.

I thought nothing much about it.

But in the days that followed, some of the villagers from the lower slopes came up to live within the walls. There were conferences in my father's chambers. I heard arguments behind closed doors, and one night, at supper, all sat entirely too somber for our family, and finally my father rose from his massive chair, the Lord in the center of the table as always, and declared, as if he'd been silently accused:

"I will not persecute some old women because they have stuck pins in wax dolls and burnt incense and read foolish incantations that mean nothing. These old witches have been on our mountain forever."

My mother looked truly alarmed, and then gathering us all up—I was most unwilling—she took us away, Bartola, Matteo and me, and told us to go to bed early.

"Don't stay up reading, Vittorio!" she said.

"But what did Father mean?" asked Bartola.

"Oh, it's the old village witches," I said. I used the Italian word *strega*. "Every now and then, one goes too far, there's a fight, but mostly it's just charms to cure a fever and such."

I thought my mother would hush me up, but she stood in the narrow stone stairs of the tower looking up at me with marked relief on her face, and she said:

"Yes, yes, Vittorio, you are so right. In Florence, people laugh at those old women. You know Gattena yourself; she never really did more then sell love potions to the girls."

"Surely we're not to drag her before a court!" I said, very happy that she was paying attention.

Bartola and Matteo were rapt.

"No, no, not Gattena, certainly not. Gattena's vanished. Run off."

"Gattena?" I asked, and then as my mother

turned away, refusing, it seemed, to say another word, gesturing for me to escort my sister and brother safely to bed, I realized the gravity of this.

Gattena was the most feared and comical of the old witches, and if she had run off, if she was afraid of something, well, that was news, because she thought herself the one to be feared.

The following days were fresh and lovely and undisturbed by anything for me and my Bartola and Matteo, but when I looked back later, I recalled there was much going on.

One afternoon, I went up to the highest lookout window of the old tower where one guardsman, Tori, we called him, was falling asleep, and I looked down over all our land for as far as I could see.

"Well, you won't find it," he said.

"What's that?" I remarked.

"Smoke from a single hearth. There is no more." He yawned and leaned against the wall, heavily weighed down by his old boiled-leather jerkin, and sword. "All's well," he said, and yawned again. "So they like city life, or to fight for Francesco Sforza over the Duchy of Milan, so let them go. They didn't know how good they had it."

I turned away from him and looked over the woods again, and down into the valleys that I could see, and beyond to the slightly misty blue sky. It was true, the little hamlets seemed frozen in time down there, but how could one be so sure? It was not such a clear day. And besides, everything was fine within the household.

My father drew olive oil, vegetables, milk, butter and many such goods from these villages, but he didn't need them. If it was time for them to pass away, so be it.

Two nights later, however, it was undeniably obvious to me that everyone at supper was perpetually under a strain of sorts, which went entirely unvoiced, and that an agitation had gripped my mother, so that she was no longer engaging in her endless courtly chatter. Conversation was not impossible, but it had changed.

But for all the elders who seemed deeply and secretly conflicted, there were others who seemed relatively oblivious to such things, and the pages went about serving gaily, and a little group of musicians, who'd come up the preceding day, gave us a lovely series of songs with the viol and the lute.

My mother couldn't be persuaded to do her old slow dances, however.

It must have been very late when an unexpected visitor was announced. No one had left the main hall, except Bartola and Matteo, who had been taken off to bed by me earlier and left in the care of our old nurse, Simonetta.

The Captain of my father's Guard came into the hall, clicked his heels and bowed to my father and said:

"My Lord, it seems there is a man of great rank come to the house, and he will not be received in the light, or so he says, and demands that you come out to him."

Everyone at the table was at once alert, and my mother went white with anger and umbrage.

No one ever used the word "demand" to my father.

Also it was plain to me that our Captain of the Guard, a rather prepossessing old soldier who'd seen many battles with the wandering mercenaries, was himself overvigilant and a little shaken.

My father rose to his feet. He did not speak or move, however.

"Would you do that, my Lord, or should I send this Signore away?" the Captain asked.

"Tell him that he is most welcome to come into my house as my guest," said my father, "that we extend to him in the name of Christ Our Lord our full hospitality."

His very voice seemed to have a calming effect on the whole table, except perhaps for my mother, who seemed not to know what to do.

The Captain looked almost slyly at my father, as if to convey the secret message that this would never do, but he went off to deliver the invitation.

My father did not sit down. He stood staring off, and then he cocked his head, as though listening. He turned and snapped his fingers, drawing to attention the two guards slumbering at the ends of the hall.

"Go through the house, see to everything," he said in a soft voice. "I think I hear birds which have entered the house. It's the warm air, and there are many open windows."

These two went off, and immediately two other soldiers appeared to take their place. That in itself was not usual, for it meant that there were many men on duty.

The Captain came back alone, and once more bowed.

"My Lord, he will not come into the light, he says, but that you must come out to him, and he has little time to wait on you."

This was the first time I had ever seen my father really angry. Even when he whipped me or a peasant boy, he was rather lazy about it. Now the fine lineaments of his face, so given to reassurance by their very proportions, became absolutely wrathful.

"How dare he?" he whispered.

Yet he strode around the table, came in front of it and marched off with the Captain of the Guard hastening behind him.

I was out of my chair at once and after him. I heard my mother cry out softly, "Vittorio, come back."

But I stole down the stairs after my father, and into the courtyard, and only when he himself turned around and pressed my chest hard with his hand did I halt.

"Stay there, my son," he said with his old kindly warmth. "I shall see to it."

I had a good vantage point, right at the door of the tower, and there across the courtyard, at the gates in the full light of the torches, I saw this strange Signore who would not come into the light of the hall, for he did not seem to mind this outdoor illumination.

The huge gates of the arched entrance were locked and bolted for the night. Only the small man-sized gate was opened, and it was there that he stood, with the blazing crackling fire on either side of him, glorying in it, it seemed to me, in his splendid raiment of dark, wine-red velvet.

From head to toe he was dressed in this rich color, hardly the current style, but every detail of him, from his bejeweled doublet and blown-up sleeves of satin and velvet stripes, was this same hue, as though carefully dyed in the best fullers in Florence.

Even the gems sewn into his collar and hanging about his neck on a heavy golden chain were wine red—most likely rubies or even sapphires.

His hair was thick and black, hanging sleekly onto his shoulders, but I couldn't see his face, no, not at all, for the velvet hat he wore overshadowed it, and I caught but a glimpse of very white skin, the line of his jaw and a bit of his neck, for nothing else was visible. He wore a broadsword of immense size, with an antique scabbard, and casually over one shoulder was a cloak of the same wine-dark velvet trimmed in what seemed to my distant eyes to be ornate gilt symbols.

I strained, trying to make them out, this border of signs, and I thought I could see a star and crescent moon worked into his fancy adornments, but I was really too far away.

The man's height was impressive.

My father stopped quite far short of him, yet when he spoke his voice was soft and I couldn't hear it, and out of the mysterious man, who still revealed nothing now of his face but his smiling mouth and white teeth, there came a silky utterance that seemed both surly and charming.

"Get away from my house in the name of God and Our Holy Redeemer!" my father cried out suddenly. And with a quick gesture, he stepped forward and powerfully thrust this splendid figure right out of the gate.

I was amazed.

But from the hollow mouth of darkness beyond the opening there came only a low satin laughter, a mocking laughter, and this it seemed was echoed by others, and I heard a powerful thundering of hooves, as though several horsemen had commenced at once to ride off.

My father himself slammed the gate. And turned and made the Sign of the Cross, and pressed his hands together in prayer.

"Dear Lord God, how dare they!" he said, looking up.

It was only now, as he stormed back towards me and towards the tower itself, that I realized the Captain of the Guard was paralyzed with seeming terror.

My father's eye caught mine as soon as he came into the light from the stairs, and I gestured to the Captain. My father spun round.

"Batten down my house," my father called out. "Search it from top to bottom and batten it down and call out the soldiery and fill the night with torches, do you hear? I will have men in every tower and on the walls. Do it at once. It will give peace and calm to my people!"

We had not yet reached the supper room when an old priest living with us then, a learned Dominican named Fra Diamonte, came down with his white hair all mussed, and his cassock half unbuttoned, and his prayer book in his hand.

"What is it, my Lord?" he asked. "What in the name of God has happened?"

"Father, trust in God and come and pray with me in the chapel," said my father to him. He then pointed to another guard who was fast approaching. "Light up the chapel, all its candles, for I want to pray. Do it now, and have the boys come down and play for me some sacred music."

He then took my hand and that of the priest. "It's nothing, really, you must both of you know that. It's all superstitious foolishness, but any excuse which makes a worldly man like me turn to his God is a good one. Come on, Vittorio, you and Fra Diamonte and I will pray, but for your mother put on a good face."

I was much calmer, but the prospect of being up all night in the lighted chapel was both welcome and alarming.

I went off to get my prayer books, my Mass books and books of other devotions, fine vellum books from Florence, with gilt print and beautifully edged illustrations.

I was just coming out of my room when I saw my father there with my mother, saying to her, "And do not leave the children alone for a moment, and you, you in this state, I will not tolerate this distress."

She touched her belly.

I realized she was with child again. And I realized, too, that my father was really alarmed about something. What could it mean, "Do not leave the children alone for a moment"? What could this mean?

The chapel was comfortable enough. My father had long ago provided some decent wooden and velvet-padded prie-dieux, though on feast days everyone stood. Pews didn't exist in those times.

But he also spent some of the night showing me the vault beneath the church, which opened by means of a ring handle on a trapdoor, faced in stone, the ring itself fitted down flat beneath what appeared to be only one of many marble inlaid ornaments in the floor tiles.

I knew of these crypts but had been whipped for sneaking into them when I was a child, and my father had told me back then how disappointed in me he'd been that I couldn't keep a family secret.

That admonition had hurt far more than the whipping. And I'd never asked to go with him into the crypts, which I knew he had done over the years now and then. I thought treasure was down there, and secrets of the pagans.

Well, I saw now there was a cavernous room, carved high and deep out of the earth, and faced with stone, and that it was full of varied treasure. There were old chests and even old books in heaps. And two bolted doorways.

"Those lead to old burial places that you don't need to go to," he said, "but you need to know of this place now. And remember it."

When we came back up into the chapel, he put the trapdoor right, laid down the ring, relaid the marble tile, and the whole was quite invisible.

Fra Diamonte pretended not to have seen. My mother was asleep and so were the children.

We all fell asleep before dawn in the chapel.

My father walked out in the courtyard at sunup, when the cocks were crowing all over the villages inside the walls, and he stretched and looked up at the sky and then shrugged his shoulders.

Two of my uncles ran at him, demanding to know what Signore from where dared to propose a siege against us and when we were supposed to have this battle.

"No, no, no, you've got it all wrong," my father said. "We're not going to war. You go back to bed."

But he had no sooner spoken these words than a ripping scream brought us all around, and through the opening courtyard gates there came one of the village girls, one of our near and dear girls, shrieking the terrible words:

"He's gone, the baby's gone, they've taken him."

The rest of the day was a relentless search for this missing child. But no one could find him. And it was soon discovered that one other child had also vanished without a trace. He had been a half-wit, rather beloved because he caused no harm, but so addle-brained he couldn't even much walk. And everyone was ashamed to say that they did not even know how long that half-wit had been missing.

By dusk, I thought I would go mad if I didn't get to see my father alone, if I couldn't push my way into the locked chambers where he sat with his uncles and the priests arguing and fighting. Finally, I hammered so loudly on the door and kicked so much that he let me in.

The meeting was about to break up and he drew me down by himself, and he said with wild eyes:

"Do you see what they've done? They took the very tribute they demanded of me. They took it! I refused it and they took it."

"But what tribute? You mean the children?"

He was wild-eyed. He rubbed his unshaven face, and he crashed his fist down on his desk, and then he pushed over all his writing things.

"Who do they think they are that they come to me by night and demand that I tender to them those infants unwanted by anyone?"

"Father, what is this? You must tell me."

"Vittorio, you will tomorrow be off to Florence, at the first light, and with the letters I mean to write tonight. I need more than country priests to fight this. Now get ready for the journey."

He looked up quite suddenly. He appeared to listen, and then to look about. I could see the light was gone from the windows. We ourselves were just dim figures, and he had thrown the candelabra down. I picked it up.

I watched him sidelong as I took one of the candles and lighted it by the torch at the door and brought it back, and then lighted the other candles.

He listened, still and alert, and then without making a sound he rose to his feet, his fists on the desk, seemingly uncaring of the light that the candles threw on his shocked and wary face.

"What do you hear, my Lord?" I said, using the formal address for him without so much as realizing it.

"Evil," he whispered. "Malignant things such as God only suffers to live because of our sins. Arm yourself well. Bring your mother, your brother and your sister to the chapel, and hurry. The soldiers have their orders."

"Shall I have some supper brought there as well, just bread and beer, perhaps?" I asked.

He nodded as though that were scarcely a concern.

Within less than an hour we were all gathered inside the chapel, the entire family, which included then five uncles and four aunts, and with us were two nurses and Fra Diamonte.

The little altar was decked out as if for Mass, with the finest embroidered altar cloth and the thickest golden candlesticks with blazing candles. The Image of Our Crucified Christ shone in the light, an ancient colorless and thin wooden carving that had hung on the wall there since the time of St. Francis, when the great saint was supposed to have stopped at our castle two centuries ago.

It was a naked Christ, common in those times, and a figure of tortured sacrifice, nothing as robust and sensual as those crucifixes made these days, and it stood out powerfully in contrast to the parade of freshly painted saints on the walls in their brilliant scarlet and gold finery.

We sat on plain brown benches brought in for us, nobody speaking a word, for Fra Diamonte had that morning said Mass and bestowed into the Tabernacle the Body and Blood of Our Lord in the form of the Sacred Host, and the chapel was now, as it were, put to its full purpose as the House of God.

We did eat the bread, and drink a little bit of the beer near the front doors, but we kept quiet.

Only my father repeatedly went out, walking boldly into the torch-lighted courtyard and calling up to his soldiers in the towers and on the walls, and even sometimes being gone to climb up and see for himself that all was well under his protection.

My uncles were all armed. My aunts said their rosaries fervently. Fra Diamonte was confused, and my mother seemed pale to death and sick, perhaps from the baby in her womb, and she clung to my sister and brother, who were by this time pretty frankly frightened.

It seemed we would pass the night without incident.

It couldn't have been two hours before dawn when I was awakened from a shallow slumber by a horrid scream.

At once my father was on his feet, and so were my uncles, drawing out their swords as best they could with their knotted old fingers.

Screams rose all around in the night, and there came the alarms from the soldiers and the loud riotous clanging of old bells from every tower.

My father grabbed me by the arm. "Vittorio, come," he said, and at once, pulling up the handle of the trapdoor, he threw it back and thrust into my hand a great candle from the altar.

"Take your mother, your aunts, your sister and your brother down, now, and do not come out, no matter what you hear! Do not come out. Lock the trapdoor above you and stay there! Do as I tell you!"

At once I obeyed, snatching up Matteo and Bartola and forcing them down the stone steps in front of me.

My uncles had rushed through the doors into the courtyard, shouting their ancient war cries, and my aunts stumbled and fainted and clutched to the altar and would not be moved, and my mother clung to my father.

My father was in a very paroxysm. I reached out for my eldest aunt, but she was in a dead faint before the altar, and my father thundered back to me, forced me into the crypt and shut the door.

I had no choice but to latch the trapdoor as he had shown me how to do, and to turn with the flickering candle in my hand and face the terrified Bartola and Matteo.

"Go down all the way," I cried, "all the way."

They nearly fell, trying to move backward down the steep narrow steps that were by no means easy to descend, their faces turned towards me.

"What is it, Vittorio, why do they want to hurt us?" Bartola asked.

"I want to fight them," Matteo said. "Vittorio, give me your dagger. You have a sword. It's not fair."

"Shhh, be quiet, do as our father said. Do you think it pleases me that I can't be out there with the men? Quiet!"

I choked back my tears. My mother was up there! My aunts!

The air was cold and damp, but it felt good. I broke out in a sweat, and my arm ached from holding the big golden candlestick. Finally we sank down in a huddle, the three of us at the far end of the chamber, and it felt soothing to me to touch the cold stone.

But in the interval of our collective silence I could hear through the heavy floor howls from above, terrible cries of fear and panic, and rushing feet, and even the high chilling whinnies of the horses. It sounded as if horses had come crashing into the chapel itself over our heads, which was not at all impossible.

I rose to my feet and rushed to the two other doors of the crypt, those which led to the burial chambers or whatever they were, I didn't care! I moved the latch on one, and could see nothing but a low passage, not even tall enough for me, and barely wide enough for my shoulders.

I turned back, holding the only light, and saw the children rigid with fear, gazing up at the ceiling as the murderous cries continued.

"I smell fire," Bartola whispered suddenly, her face wet at once with tears. "Do you smell it, Vittorio? I hear it."

I did hear it and I did smell it.

"Both of you make the Sign of the Cross; pray now," I said, "and trust in me. We will get out of here."

But the clamor of the battle went on, the cries did not die out, and then suddenly, so suddenly it was as wondrous and frightful as the noise itself, there fell a silence.

A silence fell over all, and it was too complete to spell victory.

Bartola and Matteo clung to me, on either side.

Above, there was a clatter. The chapel doors were being thrown back, and then quite suddenly the trapdoor was yanked up and open, and in the glimmer of firelight beyond I saw a dark slender long-haired figure.

In the gust my candle went out.

Except for the infernal flicker above and beyond, we were committed unmercifully to total darkness.

Once again distinctly, I saw the outline of this figure, a tall, stately female with great long locks and a waist small enough for both my hands as she appeared to fly down the stairs soundlessly towards me.

How in the name of Heaven could this be, this woman?

Before I could think to pull my sword on a female assailant or make sense of anything at all, I felt her tender breasts brushed against my chest, and the cool of her skin as she seemed to be throwing her arms about me.

There was a moment of inexplicable and strangely sensuous confusion when the perfume of her tresses and her gown rose in my nostrils, and I fancied I saw the glistening whites of her eyes as she looked at me.

I heard Bartola scream, and then Matteo also.

I was knocked to the floor.

The fire blazed bright above.

The figure had them both, both struggling screaming children in one seemingly fragile arm, and stopping, apparently to look at me, a raised sword in her other hand, she raced up the stairway into the firelight.

I pulled my sword with both hands, rushed after her, up and out into the chapel, and saw that she had somehow by the most evil power all but reached the door, an impossible feat, her charges wailing and crying out for me, "Vittorio, Vittorio!"

All the upper windows of the chapels were full of fire, and so was the rose window above the crucifix.

I could not believe what I beheld, this young woman, who was stealing from me my sister and brother.

"Stop in the name of God!" I shouted at her. "Coward, thief in the night."

I ran after her, but to my utter astonishment she did stop, still, and turned to look at me again, and this time I saw her full in all her refined beauty. Her face was a perfect oval with great benign gray eyes, her skin like the finest Chinese white enamel. She had red lips, too perfect even for a painter to make by choice, and her long ashen blond hair was gray like her eyes in the light of the fire, sweeping down her back in a pampered swaying mass. Her gown, though stained dark with what must have been blood, was the same wine-red color I had seen in the apparel of the evil visitor of the night before.

With the most curious and then poignant face, she merely stared at me. Her right hand held her sword upraised, but she didn't move, and then she released from the powerful grip of her left arm my struggling brother and sister.

Both tumbled sobbing to the floor.

"Demon. Strega!" I roared. I leapt over them and advanced on her, swinging the sword.

But she dodged so swiftly that I didn't even see it. I couldn't believe that she was so far from me, standing now with the sword down, staring at me still and at the sobbing children.

Suddenly her head turned. There was a whistling cry, and then another and another. Through the door of the chapel, seeming to leap from the fires of Hell itself, there came another red-clad figure, hooded in velvet and wearing gold-trimmed boots, and as I swung my sword at him, he threw me aside and, in one instant, cut off the head of Bartola and then severed the head of the screaming Matteo.

I went mad. I howled. He turned on me. But from the female there came a sudden firm negation.

"Leave him alone," she cried in a voice that was both sweet and clear, and then off he went, this murderer, this hooded fiend in his gold-trimmed boots, calling back to her.

"Come on, now, have you lost your wits? Look at the sky. Come, Ursula."

She didn't move. She stared at me as before.

I sobbed and cursed and, grabbing my sword, ran at her again, and this time saw my blade descend to cut off her right arm, right below the elbow. The white limb, small and seemingly fragile like all of her parts, fell to the paved floor with her heavy sword. Blood spurted from her.

She did no more than look at it. And then at me with the same poignant, disconsolate and near heartbroken face.

I lifted my sword again. "Strega!" I cried, clenching my teeth, trying to see through my tears. "Strega!"

But in another feat of evil, she had moved back, far away from me, as if pulled by an invisible force, and in her left hand she now held her right, which still clutched her sword as if it were not severed. She replaced the limb I had cut off. I watched her. I watched her put the limb in place and turn it and adjust it until it was as it should be, and then before my astonished eyes, I saw the wound I had made utterly seal up in her white skin.

Then the loose bell sleeve of her rich velvet gown fell down again around her wrist.

In a twinkling she was outside the chapel, only a silhouette now against the distant fires burning in the tower windows. I heard her whisper:

"Vittorio."

Then she vanished.

I knew it was vain to go after her! Yet still I ran out and swung my sword around in a great circle, crying out in rage and bitterness and mad menace at all the world, my eyes now blinded with tears, and my throat full to choking.

Everything was still. Everyone was dead. Dead. I knew it. The courtyard was strewn with bodies.

I ran back into the chapel. I grabbed up the head of Bartola and the head of Matteo into my arms. I sat down and held them in my lap, and I sobbed.

They seemed still alive, these severed heads, their eyes flashing, and their lips even moving with hopeless attempts to speak. Oh, God! It was beyond all human endurance. I sobbed.

I cursed.

I laid them side by side, these two heads in my lap, and I stroked their hair and stroked their cheeks and whispered comforting words to them, that God was close, God was with us, God would take care of us forever, that we were in Heaven. Oh, please, I beg you, God, I prayed in my soul, don't let them have the feeling and the consciousness which they still seem to possess. Oh, no, not such. I can't bear it. I cannot. No. Please.

At dawn, finally, when the sun poured arrogantly through the door of the chapel, when the fires had died away, when the birds sang as if nothing had happened, the innocent little heads of Bartola and Matteo were lifeless and still, and very obviously dead, and their immortal souls were gone from them, if they had not flown at the moment when the sword had severed these heads from the bodies.

I found my mother murdered in the courtyard. My father, covered with wounds on his hands and arms, as if he had grabbed at the very swords that struck him, lay dead on the stairs of the tower.

The work all around had been swift. Throats cut, and only here and there the evidence, as with my father, of a great struggle.

Nothing was stolen. My aunts, two dead in the far corner of the chapel, and two others in the yard, wore still all their rings and necklets and circlets about their hair.

Not a jeweled button had been ripped away.

It was the same throughout the entire compound.

The horses were gone, the cattle had roamed into the woods, the fowl flown. I opened the little house full of my hunting falcons, took off their hoods and let them all go into the trees.

There was no one to help me bury the dead.

By noon, I had dragged my family, one by one, to the crypt and tumbled them unceremoniously down the steps, and then laid them all out, side by side in the room, as best I could.

It had been a backbreaking task. I was near to

fainting as I composed the limbs of each person, and last of all my father.

I knew that I could not do it for everyone else here in our compound. It was simply impossible. Besides, whatever had come might well come again, as I had been left alive, and there was a hooded demon man who had witnessed it, a vicious hooded assassin who had slaughtered two children piteously.

And whatever was the nature of this angel of death, this exquisite Ursula, with her barely tinted white cheeks and her long neck and sloping shoulders, I didn't know. She herself might come back to avenge the insult I had done her.

I had to leave the mountain.

That these creatures were not anywhere around now I felt instinctively, both in my heart and from the wholesomeness of the warm and loving sun, but also because I had witnessed their flight, heard their whistles to one another and heard the ominous words of the demon man to the woman, Ursula, that she must hurry.

No, these were things of the night.

So I had time to climb the highest tower and look at the country round.

I did. I confirmed that there was no one who could have seen the smoke of our few burning wooden floors and torched furniture. The nearest castle was a ruin, as I have said. The lower hamlets were long abandoned.

The nearest village of any size was a full day's walk, and I had to be off if I meant to get to any kind of hiding place by nightfall.

A thousand thoughts tormented me. I knew too

many things. I was a boy; I could not even pass for a man! I had wealth in the Florentine banks but it was a week's ride from where I was! These were demons. Yet they had come into a church. Fra Diamonte had been struck dead.

Only one thought finally was possible for me.

Vendetta. I was going to get them. I was going to find them and get them. And if they couldn't come out by the light of day, then it would be by that means that I would get them! I would do it. For Bartola, for Matteo, for my father and mother, for the humblest child who had been taken from my mountain.

And they had taken the children. Yes, that they had done. I confirmed it before I left, for it was slow to dawn on me with all my concerns, but they had. There was not a corpse of a child on the place, only those boys of my age had been killed, but anything younger had been stolen away.

For what! For what horrors! I was beside myself.

I might have stood in the tower window, with clenched fist, consumed with anger and the vow for vendetta, if a welcome sight hadn't distracted me. Down in the closest valley, I saw three of my horses wandering about, aimlessly, as though wanting to be called home.

At least I should have one of my finest to ride, but I had to get moving. With a horse I might just reach a town by nightfall. I didn't know the land to the north. It was mountain country, but I had heard of a fair-sized town not too far away. I had to get there, for refuge, to think and to consult with a priest who had a brain in his head and knew demons.

My last task was ignominious and revolting to me, but I did it. I gathered up all the wealth I could carry.

This meant that I retired first to my own room, as if this were an ordinary day, dressed myself in my best dark hunter's green silk and velvet, put on my high boots and took up my gloves, and then taking the leather bags which I could affix to my horse's saddle, I went down into the crypt and took from my parents and my aunts and uncles their very most treasured rings, necklaces and brooches, the buckles of gold and silver which had come from the Holy Land. God help me.

Then I filled my purse with all the gold ducats and florins I could find in my father's coffers, as if I were a thief, a very thief of the dead it seemed to me, and hefting these heavy leather bags, I went to get my mount, saddle him and bridle him and start off, a man of rank, with his weaponry, and his mink-edged cape, and a Florentine cap of green velvet, off into the forest.

4

IN WHICH I COME UPON FURTHER MYSTERIES, SUFFER SEDUCTION AND CONDEMN MY SOUL TO BITTER VALOR

OW, I was too full of rancor to be thinking straight, as I've already described, and surely you will understand this. But it wasn't smart of me to go riding through the woods of Tuscany dressed so richly, and by myself, because any woods in Italy was bound to have its bandits.

On the other hand, playing the poor scholar wouldn't have been the best choice either, it seemed to me.

I can't claim to have made a real decision. The desire for vengeance upon the demons that had destroyed us was the only central passion I could abide.

So there I was, riding steadily by mid-afternoon, trying to keep to the valley roads as I lost sight of our towers, trying not to cry anymore like a child, but being drawn off into the mountainous land over and over again.

My head was swimming. And the landscape gave me little time to think.

Nothing could have been more forlorn.

I came within sight of two huge ruined castles

very soon after my departure, copings and ramparts lost in the greedy forest, which made me mindful that these had been the holdings of old Lords who had been fool enough to resist the power of Milan or Florence. It was enough to make me doubt my sanity, enough to make me think that we had not been annihilated by demons but that common enemies had made the assault.

It was utterly grim to see their broken battlements looming against the otherwise cheerful and brilliant sky, and to come upon the overgrown fragments of villages with their tumbledown hovels and forgotten crossroads shrines in which stone Virgins or saints had sunk into spiderwebs and shadows.

When I did spy a high distant well-fortified town, I knew well it was Milanese and had no intention of going up there. I was lost!

As for the bandits, I only ran into one little ragged band, which I took on immediately with a deluge of chatter.

If anything, the little pack of idiots gave me some distraction. My blood ran as fast as my tongue:

"I'm riding in advance of a hundred men," I declared. "We search for a band of outlaws claiming to be fighting for Sforza when they're nothing but rapists and thieves; you seen any of them? I have a florin for each of you if you can tell me anything. We mean to cut them down on sight. I'm tired. I'm sick of this."

I tossed them some coins.

They were off immediately.

But not before they let slip in talk of the country round that the nearest Florentine town was Santa

Maddalana, which was two hours up ahead, and that it would close its gates at night, and nobody could talk his way into it.

I pretended to know all about that and to be on the way to a famous monastery that I knew lay farther north, which I couldn't possibly have reached, and then threw more money over my shoulder as I raced off, hollering out that they ought to ride on to meet the band coming behind who would pay them for their service.

I know they were debating all the time whether to kill me and take everything I had or not. It was a matter of stares and bluffs and fast talking and standing one's ground, and they were just utter ruffians, and somehow I got out of it.

I rode off as quickly as I could, left the main road and cut towards the slopes from which I could see in the far distance the vague outline of Santa Maddalana. A big town. I could see four massive towers all gathered near the obvious front gates, and several distinct church steeples.

I had hoped for something before this Santa Maddalana, something small, less fortified. But I couldn't remember names or was too lost now to go looking further.

The afternoon sunshine was brilliant but now at a slant. I had to make for Santa Maddalana.

When I reached the mountain proper on which this town was built, I went up sharply on the small paths used by the shepherds.

The light was fading fast. The forest was too thick to be safe so near a walled town. I cursed them that they didn't keep the mountain cleared, but then I had the safety of cover.

There were moments amid the deepening darkness when it seemed virtually impossible to reach the summit; the stars now lighted a glowing sapphirine sky, but that only made the venerable town in all its majesty seem ever more unattainable.

Finally the heedless night did plunge down amongst the thick trunks of the trees, and I was picking my way, counting on the instincts of my horse more than my own failing vision. The pale half-moon seemed in love with the clouds. The sky itself was nothing but bits and pieces thanks to the canopy of foliage above me.

I found myself praying to my father, as if he were safely with my guardian angels about me, and I think I believed in him and his presence more surely than I had ever believed in angels, saying, "Please, Father, help me get there. Help me get to safety, lest those demons render my vengeance impossible."

I gripped my sword hard. I reminded myself of the daggers I wore in my boots, in my sleeve, in my jacket and in my belt. I strained to see by the light of the sky, and had to trust my horse to pick his way through the thick tree trunks.

At moments I stopped very still. I heard no unusual sound. Who else would be fool enough to be out in the night of this forest? At some point very near the end of the journey, I found the main road, the forest thinned and then gave way to smooth fields and meadows, and I took the twists and turns at a gallop.

At last the town rose right up in front of us, as it

happens when you reach the gates by a final turn, you seem to have been thrown up on the ground at the foot of a magic fortress—and I took a deep breath of thanks, no matter that the giant gates were firmly shut as if a hostile army were camped beneath it.

This had to be my haven.

Of course the Watch, a sleepy soldier hollering down from above, wanted to know who I was.

Once again the effort of making up something good distracted me from wayward, near uncontrollable, images of the fiend Ursula and her severed arm, and the decapitated bodies of my brother and sister fallen on the chapel floor in mid-gesture.

I cried out, in a humble tone but with pretentious vocabulary, that I was a scholar in the employ of Cosimo de' Medici come on a search for books in Santa Maddalana, in particular old prayer books pertaining to the saints and appearances of the Blessed Virgin Mary in this district.

What nonsense.

I had come, I declared, to visit the churches and schools and whatever old teachers the town might shelter, and to take back what I could purchase with good gold Florentine coin to my master in Florence.

"Yes, but your name, your name!" the soldier insisted as he opened the small lower gate only a crack, his lantern held high to inspect me.

I knew I made a good picture on my horse.

"De' Bardi," I declared. "Antonio De' Bardi, kinsman of Cosimo," I said with fierce nerve, naming the family of Cosimo's wife because it was the only name that came into my head. "Look, kindly man, take this payment for me, have a good supper with your wife as my guests, here, I know it's late, I'm so tired!"

The gate was opened. I had to dismount to lead my horse with lowered head through it and into the echoing stone piazza right inside.

"What in the name of God," asked the Watchman, "were you doing in these woods after dark alone? Do you know the dangers? And so young? What is the Bardi these days that they let their secretaries go riding all over unescorted?" He pocketed the money. "Look at you, a mere child! Somebody could murder you for your buttons. What's the matter with you?"

This was an immense piazza, and I could see more than one street leading off. Good luck. But what if the demons were here too? I had no clue as to where such things might roost or hide! But I went on talking.

"It's all my fault. I got lost. Tell on me and you'll get me in trouble," I said. "Show me to the Albergo. I'm so tired. Here, take this, no, you must." I gave him more money. "I got lost. I didn't listen. I'm about to faint. I need wine and supper and a bed. Here, good man, no, no, no, take more, I insist. The Bardi would not have it otherwise."

He ran out of pockets for the money, but managed somehow to stuff it in his shirt and then led me by torchlight to the Inn, banging on the door, and a sweet-faced old woman came down, grateful for the coins I thrust into her hand at once, to show me to a room.

"High up and looking out over the valley," I said,

"if you please, and some supper, it can be stone cold, I don't care."

"You're not going to find any books in this town," said the Watchman, standing about as I beat it up the stairs after the woman. "All the young people go off; it's a peaceable place, just happy little shopkeepers. Young men today run off to universities. But this is a beautiful place to live, simply beautiful."

"How many churches do you have?" I asked the old woman when we'd reached the room. I told her that I must keep the lighted candle for the night.

"Two Dominican, one Carmelite," said the Watchman, slouching in the little door, "and the beautiful old Franciscan church, which is where I go. Nothing bad ever happens here."

The old woman shook her head and told him to be quiet. She set the candle down and gestured that it could stay.

The Watchman went on chattering as I sat on the bed, staring at nothing, until she'd brought a plate of cold mutton and bread, and a pitcher of wine.

"Our schools are strict," the man went on.

Again the old woman told him to hush up.

"Nobody dares to make trouble in this place," he said, and then both of them were gone.

I fell on my plate like an animal. All I wanted was strength. In my grief I couldn't even think of pleasure. I looked out on a tiny bit of high star-sprinkled sky for a little while, praying desperately to every saint and angel whose name I knew for help, and then I locked up the window tight.

I bolted the door.

And making sure that the candle was well sheltered in the corner, and plenty big enough to last until dawn, I fell into the lumpy little bed, too exhausted to remove boots or sword or daggers or anything else. I thought I'd fall into a deep sleep, but I lay rigid, full of hatred, and hurt, and swollen broken soul, staring into the dark, my mouth full of death as if I'd eaten it.

I could hear distantly the sounds of my horse being tended to downstairs, and some lonely steps on the deserted stone street. I was safe, at least that much was so.

Finally sleep came. It came totally and completely and sweetly; the net of nerves which had held me suspended and maddened simply dissolved, and I sank down into a dreamless darkness.

I was conscious of that sweet point where nothing for the moment matters except to sleep, to replenish and to fear yet no dreams, and then nothing.

A noise brought me around. I was immediately awake. The candle had gone out. I had my hand on my sword before my eyes opened. I lay on the narrow bed, back to the wall, facing the room and in a seemingly sourceless light. I could just make out the bolted door, but I couldn't see the window above me unless I turned my head to look up, and I knew, positively knew, that this window, heavily barred, had been broken open. The little light which fell on the wall came from the sky outside. It was a fragile, weak light, slipping down against the wall of the town and giving my little chamber the attitude of a prison cell.

I felt the cool fresh air come down around my

neck and felt it on my cheek. I clutched the sword tight, listening, waiting. There were small creaking sounds. The bed had moved ever so slightly, as if from a pressure.

I couldn't focus my eyes. Darkness suddenly obscured everything, and out of this darkness there rose a shape before me, a figure bending over me, a woman looking right into my face as her hair fell down on me.

It was Ursula.

Her face was not an inch from mine. Her hand, very cool and smooth, closed over my own, on the hilt of my sword, with a deadly force, and she let her eyelashes stroke my cheek and then kissed my forehead.

I was enveloped in sweetness, no matter how hot my rebellion. A sordid flood of sensation penetrated to my very entrails.

"Strega!" I cursed her.

"I didn't kill them, Vittorio." Her voice was imploring but with dignity and a curious sonorous strength, though it was only a small voice, very young in tone and feminine in timbre.

"You were taking them," I said to her. I tried in a violent spasm to free myself. But her hand held me powerfully fast, and when I tried to free my left arm from under me, she caught my wrist and held me there too, and then she kissed me.

There came that magnificent perfume from her which I had breathed in before, and the stroking of her hair on my face and neck sent shameless chills through me.

I tried to turn my head, and she let her lips touch my cheek gently, almost respectfully.

I felt the length of her body against me, the definite swell of her breasts beneath costly fabric, and the smooth length of her thigh beside me in the bed, and her tongue touched my lips. She licked at my lips.

I was immobilized by the chills that went through me, humiliating me and kindling the passion inside me.

"Get away, strega," I whispered.

Filled with rage, I couldn't stop the slow smolder that had caught hold in my loins; I couldn't stop the rapturous sensations that were passing over my shoulders and down my back, and even through my legs.

Her eyes glowed above me, the flicker of her lids more a sensation than a spectacle I could see with my own eyes, and again her lips closed over mine, sucking at my mouth, teasing it, and then she drew back and pressed her cheek against me.

Her skin, which had looked so like porcelain, felt softer than a down feather against me, ah, all of her seemed a soft doll, made of luscious and magical materials far more yielding than flesh and blood yet utterly on fire with both, for a heat came out of her in a rhythmic throb, emanating right from the coolness of her fingers stroking my wrists as they held them, and then the heat of her tongue shot into my lips, against my will, with a wet, delicious and vehement force against which I could do nothing.

There formed in my crazed mind some realization that she had used my own hot desire to render me helpless, that carnal madness had made of me a body constructed about metal wires that could not help but conduct the fire she poured into my mouth.

She drew her tongue back and sucked with her lips again. My entire face was tingling. All my limbs were struggling both against her and to touch her, yes, embrace her yet fight her.

She lay against the very evidence of my desire. I couldn't have hidden it. I hated her.

"Why? What for!" I said, tearing my mouth loose. Her hair descended on both sides as she lifted her head. I could scarcely breathe for the unearthly pleasure.

"Get off me," I said, "and go back into Hell. What is this mercy to me! Why do this to me?"

"I don't know," she answered in her clever, tremulous voice. "Maybe it's only that I don't want you to die," she said, breathing against my chest. Her words were rapid, like her heated pulse. "Maybe more," she said, "I want you to go away, go south to Florence, go away and forget all that's happened, as if it were nightmares or witches' spells, as if none of it took place; leave this town, go, you must."

"Stop your foul lies," I said before I could stop myself. "You think I'll do that? You murdered my family, you, you and yours, whatever you are!"

Her head dipped, her hair ensnaring me. I fought vainly to get loose. It was out of the question. I couldn't budge her grip.

All was blackness, and indescribable softness. I felt a sudden tiny pain in my throat, no more than the prick of pins, and my mind was suddenly flooded with the most tranquil happiness.

It seemed I'd stumbled into a blowing meadow of flowers, quite far away from this place and from all woes, and she lay with me, fallen against silently crushed stems and uncomplaining irises, Ursula, with her undone ashen hair, and she smiled with the most engaging and demanding eyes, fervent, perhaps even brilliant, as if ours were a sudden and total infatuation of mind as well as body. On my chest she climbed, and though she rode me, looking down at me with exquisite smiling lips, she parted her legs gently for me to enter her.

It seemed a delirious blending of elements, the wet contracting secretive pocket between her legs and this great abundance of silent eloquence pouring from her gaze as she looked lovingly down at me.

Abruptly it stopped. I was dizzy. Her lips were against my neck.

I tried with all my might to throw her off.

"I will destroy you," I said. "I will. I vow it. If I have to chase you into the mouth of Hell," I whispered. I strained against her grasp so hard that my own flesh burned against hers. But she wouldn't relent. I tried to clear my mind. No, no dreams of sweetness, no.

"Get away from me, witch."

"Hush, be quiet," she said sorrowfully. "You are so young and so stubborn, and so brave. I was young like you. Oh, yes, and so determined and such a fearless paragon."

"Don't talk your filth to me," I said.

"Hush," she said again. "You'll wake the house. What good will that do?" How painful, earnest and enticing she sounded. Her voice itself could have seduced me from behind a curtain. "I cannot make you safe forever," she said, "or even for very long. Vittorio, go."

She drew back so that I could see her sincere and large yielding eyes all the better. She was a masterpiece. And such beauty, the perfect simulacrum of the fiend I'd seen in the firelight of my chapel, needed no potions or spells to advance her cause. She was flawless and intimately magnificent.

"Oh, yes," she confessed, her half-visible eyes searching my face, "and I do find such beauty in you it pulls on my heart," she said. "Unfairly, unjustly. How am I to suffer this as well as all else?"

I struggled. I wouldn't answer. I wouldn't feed this enigmatic and infernal blaze.

"Vittorio, get out of here," she said, lowering her voice ever more delicately and ominously. "You have a few nights, maybe not even that. If I come to you again, I may lead them to you. Vittorio—. Don't tell anyone in Florence. They'll laugh at you."

She was gone.

The bed creaked and rocked. I was on my back, and my wrists ached from the pressure of her hands, and above me the window gaped on the gray featureless light, the wall beside the Inn rising up towards a sky I couldn't quite see from this helpless vantage point.

I was alone in the room. She was nowhere.

All of a sudden, I willed my limbs to action, but before I could so much as move, she appeared again, above in the window, visible from the waist to the top of her bowed head, peering down at me, and with her hands she tore loose the low embroidered border of her gown and bared her naked white breasts before me—tiny, rounded, very close together and with piquant nipples visible only in their darkness. With her right hand she scratched her left breast, just above the little nipple, made it bleed.

"Witch!"

I rose up to grab hold of her, to kill her, and instead felt her hand grasp my head, and there came the pressure of her left breast into my very mouth, irresistibly frail yet firm. Once again, all that was real melted and was swept away like so much idle smoke rising from a fire, and we were together in the meadow which belonged only to us, only to our diligent and indissoluble embraces. I sucked the milk from her, as if she was maiden and mother, virgin and queen, all the while I broke with my thrusts whatever flower remained inside of her to be torn open.

I was let go. I fell. Helpless, unable even to raise a hand to keep her from flying, I fell down, weak and stupid onto the bed, my face wet and my limbs trembling.

I couldn't sit up. I could do nothing. I saw in flashes our field of tender white irises and red irises, the loveliest flowers of Tuscany, the wild irises of our land, blowing in the greenest grass, and I saw her running away from me. Yet all this was transparent, half-tinted, and could not mask the tiny cell of a room as it had done before, only linger, like a veil drawn across my face, to torment me with its tickling weightless silkiness.

"Spells!" I whispered. "My God, if you have ever committed me to guardian angels, will you spur them on now to cover me with their wings!" I sighed. "I need them."

Finally, shakily and with dim vision, I sat up. I rubbed at my neck. Chills ran up and down my spine, and the backs of my arms. My body was still full of desire.

I squeezed my eyes shut, refusing to think of her yet wanting anything, any source of stimulation, that would soothe this awful need.

I lay back again, and was very still until this carnal madness had left me.

I was a man again then, for not having been, at random, a man.

I got up, ready for tears, and I took my candle down to the main room of the Inn, trying not to make a sound on the crooked winding stone stairs, and I got a light from a candle there on a hook on the wall, at the mouth of the passage, and I went back up, clinging to this comforting little light, shielding the shuddering flame with my cupped hand and praying still, and then I set down the candle.

I climbed up and tried to see what I could from the window.

Nothing, nothing but an impossible drop beneath me, a sloping wall up which a flesh-and-blood maiden could never have climbed, and higher, the mute, passive sky, in which the few stars had been covered by fleecy clouds as if not to acknowledge my prayers or my predicament.

It seemed absolutely certain I was going to die.

I was going to fall victim to these demons. She was right. How could I possibly exact the revenge they deserved? How in Hell could I do it! Yet I believed in my purpose utterly. I believed in my revenge as completely as I believed in her, this witch whom I had touched with my very own fingers, who had dared to kindle a wanton conflict in my soul, who had come with her comrades of the night to slaughter my family.

I couldn't overmaster the images of the night before, of her standing bewildered in the chapel door. I couldn't get the taste of her off my lips. All I had to do was think of her breasts, and my body would weaken as if she were feeding my desire from her nipple.

Make this subside, I prayed. You cannot run. You cannot go off to Florence, you cannot live forever with nothing but the memory of the slaughter you saw, that is impossible, unthinkable. You cannot.

I wept when I realized that I wouldn't be alive now if it had not been for her.

It was she, the ashen-haired one I was cursing with every breath, who had stopped her hooded companion from killing me. It would have been a complete victory!

A calm came over me. Well, if I was going to die, there was no choice, really. I would get them first. I would somehow do it.

As soon as the sun was up, so was I, and walking

around the town, my saddlebags over my shoulder casually, as if they didn't contain a fortune, I sized up quite a portion of Santa Maddalana, with its treeless, narrow-stoned streets, built centuries before, perhaps some of its buildings with their wild patternless mortared stones going back even to Roman times.

It was a marvelously peaceful and prosperous town.

The forges were already at work, and so were the cabinetmakers and also the saddlemakers; there were several shoemakers dealing in some fine slippers as well as the workaday boots, and quite a cluster of jewelers and men who worked in a great variety of precious metals, as well as the usual swordmakers, men who made keys and the like and those who dealt in hides and furs.

I passed more fancy shops than I could count. One could buy fancy fabrics here, right from Florence, I supposed, and lace from north and south it seemed, and Oriental spices. The butchers were having a time of it with the abundance of fresh meat. And there were many wine shops, and I passed at least a couple of busy notaries, letter writers and the like, and several doctors or, rather, apothecaries.

Carts were rolling through the front gates, and there was even a little crush in the streets now and then before the sun was even high enough to come fiercely down over the close-tiled roofs and hit the bare stones on which I plodded uphill.

The churches rang their bells for Mass, and I saw plenty of schoolchildren rushing past me, all rather clean and neatly dressed, and then two little crews being paraded by monks into the churches, both of which were quite antique and had no ornament on the front at all, save for statues deep in niches—saints who scarcely had any features left to them at all—the heavily patched stones of the facades obviously having weathered the frequent earthquakes of this region.

There were two rather ordinary bookshops that had almost nothing much, except the prayer books one would expect to find, and these at very high prices. Two merchants sold really fine wares from the East. And there was a cluster of carpet sellers, too, who dealt in an impressive variety of country-made goods and intricate carpets from Byzantium.

Lots of money was changing hands. There were well-dressed people showing off their fine clothes. It seemed a self-sufficient place, though there were travelers coming uphill with the clop of horses' hooves echoing on the barren walls. And I think I spied one neglected and very much fortified convent.

I passed at least two more inns, and as I crisscrossed through the barely passable alleyways here and there, I ascertained that there were actually three basic streets to the town, all running parallel up and down the hill.

At the far deep end were the gates by which I had entered, and the huge farmers' markets opened now in the piazza.

At the high end was the ruined fortress or castle where once the Lord had lived—a great cumbersome mass of old stones, of which only a part was visible from the street, and in the lower floors of this complex there were the town's governing offices.

There were several small grottoes or piazzas, and old fountains almost crumbled away but still giving forth their gurgling water. Old women were busy, shuffling along with their market baskets and their shawls in spite of the warmth; and I saw beautiful young girls about giving me the eye, all of them very young.

I didn't want any part of them.

As soon as Mass was over and school had begun, I went to the Dominican church—the largest and most impressive of the three I could readily see—and asked at the rectory for a priest. I had to go to Confession.

There came out a young priest, very handsome with well-formed limbs and a healthy look to his complexion and a truly devout manner to him, his black and white robes very clean-looking. He looked at my attire, and my sword, indeed he took me in very respectfully but quite comprehensively, and obviously presuming me to be a person of importance, invited me into a small room for the Confession.

He was gracious more than servile. He had no more than a crown of golden hair clipped very short around the top of his bald head, and large almost shy eyes.

He sat down, and I knelt close to him on the bare floor, and then out of me came the whole lurid tale.

With bowed head, I went on and on with it, rushing from one thing to another, from the first hideous happenings that had so stirred my curiosity and alarm, to my father's fragmented and mysterious words and at last to the raid itself and the dreadful assassination of everyone in our compound. By the time I came to the death of my brother and sister, I was gesticulating madly, and all but shaping my brother's head with my hands in the empty air, and gasping and unable to catch my breath.

Only when I was utterly finished with every last word did I look up and realize that the young priest was staring down at me in perfect distress and horror.

I didn't know what to make of his expression. You could have seen the very same face on a man startled by an insect or an approaching battalion of bloody murderers.

What had I expected, for the love of God?

"Look, Father," I said. "All you have to do is send someone up that mountain and see for yourself!" I shrugged, and implored him with my open hands. "That's all! Send someone to look. Nothing's stolen, Father, nothing's taken, but what I took! Go look! I'll wager nothing has been disturbed except by ravens and buzzards if such are like to go up there."

He said nothing. The blood was palpitating in his young face, and his mouth was open and his eyes had a dazed, miserable look.

Oh, this was too marvelous. A silky boy of a priest, probably fresh out of the seminary, used to hearing nuns tell of evil thoughts, and men once a year muttering resentfully about vices of the flesh because their wives had dragged them to their duty.

I became incensed.

"You are under the Seal of the Confessional," I said, trying to be patient with him, and not to play the Lord too much, because I could do that with priests if I wasn't careful; they made me so mad when they were stupid. "But I will give you permission, under the Seal, to send a messenger up that mountain to see with your own eyes . . ."

"But son, don't you see," he said, speaking with surprising resolve and firmness in his low voice. "The Medici themselves may have sent this band of assassins."

"No, no, no, Father," I pleaded, shaking my head. "I saw her hand fall. I cut off the creature's hand, I tell you. I saw her put it back. They were demons. Listen to me. These are witches, these are from Hell, these beings, and there's too many of them for me to fight alone. I need help. There's no time for disbelief. There's no time for rational reservations. I need the Dominicans!"

He shook his head. He didn't even hesitate.

"You are losing your mind, son," he said. "Something dreadful has happened to you, there's no doubt of that, and you believe all this, but it didn't happen. You are imagining things. Look, there are old women around who claim they make charms . . ."

"I know all that," I said. "I know an ordinary alchemist or witch when I see one. This was no side-street magic, Father, no country bunch of curses. I'm telling you, these demons slaughtered everyone in the castle, in the villages. Don't you see?"

I went into the lurid particulars again. I told how she had come into the window of my room, but then when I was halfway through it, I realized how utterly worse I was making it by going on about Ursula.

Why, this man thought I'd woken in a hot dream, imagining a damned succubus. This was futile, this entire enterprise.

My heart was hurting me in my chest. I was sweating all over. This was a waste of time.

"Give me absolution, then," I said.

"I want to ask something of you," he said. He touched my hand. He was trembling. He looked more dazed and perplexed than even before, and very concerned, for my state of mind, I assumed.

"What is that?" I said coldly. I wanted to get away. I had to find a monastery! Or a damned alchemist. There were alchemists in this town. I could find someone, someone who had read the old works, the works of Hermes Trismegistus or Lactantius or St. Augustine, somebody who knew about demons.

"Have you read St. Thomas Aquinas?" I asked, choosing the most obvious demonologist of whom I could think. "Father, he talks all about demons. Look, you think I would have believed all this myself last year at this time? I thought all sorcery was for backdoor swindlers. These were demons!" I could not be deterred. I went at him.

"Father, in the *Summa Theologica*, the first book, St. Thomas talks of the fallen angels, that some of them are allowed to be here on earth, so that all of these fallen angels don't just fall out of the natural scheme of things. They are here, allowed to be useful, to tempt men, and Father, they carry the fire of Hell about with them! It's in St. Thomas. They are here. They have . . . have . . . bodies we can't understand. The *Summa* says so. It says that angels have bodies which are beyond our understanding! That's what this woman possesses." I struggled to remember the actual argument. I struggled in Latin. "This is what she does, this being! It's a form, it's a limited form, but one that I can't understand, but she was there, and I know it on account of her actions."

He put up his hand for my patience.

"Son, please," he said. "Allow me to confide what you have confessed to me to the Pastor," he asked me. "You understand, if I do this, he too will be bound by the same Seal of Confession as I am bound. But let me ask him to come in and let me tell him what you have said, and let me ask that he speak to you. You understand, I cannot do any of this without your solemn permission."

"Yes, I know all that," I said. "What good will this do? Let me see this Pastor."

Now I was being too haughty entirely, too impertinent. I was exhausted. I was doing the old Signore trick of treating a country priest like he was a servant. This was a man of God, and I had to get a grip on myself. Maybe the Pastor had read more, understood more. Oh, but who would understand who had not seen?

There came back to me a fleeting yet vivid and searing memory of my father's anxious face on the night before the demons had struck. The pain was inexpressible.

"I'm sorry, Father," I said to the priest. I winced,

trying to contain this memory, this awful drench of misery and hopelessness. I wondered why any of us were alive, ever, for any reason!

And then the words of my exquisite tormentor came back, her own tortured voice of the last night saying that she had been young too, and such a paragon. What had she meant, speaking of herself with such sorrow?

My study of Aquinas came back to haunt me. Were not demons supposed to remain absolutely confirmed in their hatred of us? In the pride which had made them sin?

That was not the sinuous luscious creature who had come to me. But this was folly. I was feeling for her, which is what she had wanted me to do. I had only so many hours of daylight to plan her destruction and must be on with it.

"Please, yes, Father, as you wish," I said. "But bless me first."

This drew him out of his troubled ruminations. He looked at me as if I'd startled him.

At once he gave his blessing and his absolution.

"You can do what you wish with the Pastor," I said. "Yes, please, ask the Pastor if he will see me. And here, for the church." I gave him several ducats.

He stared at the money. But he didn't touch it. He stared at this gold as if it were hot coals.

"Father, take it. This is a tidy little fortune. Take it."

"No, you wait here—or I tell you what, you come out into the garden."

The garden was lovely, a little old grotto, from

which you could see the town sneaking up on the right all the way to the castle, and then you could see over the walls far out over the mountains. There was an antique statue of St. Dominic there, a fountain and a bench, and some old words carved into the stone about a miracle.

I sat down on the bench. I looked up at the healthy blue sky and the virgin white clouds, and I tried to catch my breath inside of myself. Could I be mad? I wondered. That was ridiculous.

The Pastor startled me. He came plunging out of the low arched doorway of the rectory, an elderly man with almost no hair at all, and a small bulging nose and ferocious large eyes. The younger priest was running to keep up with him.

"Get out of here," the Pastor said to me in a whisper. "Get out of our town. Get clear away from it, and don't tell your stories to anybody in it, you hear me?"

"What?" I asked. "What sort of solace is this!"

He was steaming. "I'm warning you."

"Warning me of what?" I demanded. I didn't bother to get up from the bench. He glowered over me. "You're under the Seal of Confession. What are you going to do if I don't leave?" I asked.

"I don't have to do anything, that's just it!" he said. "Go away and take your misery with you." He stopped, clearly at a loss, embarrassed perhaps, as if he'd said something he regretted. He ground his teeth and looked off and then back at me.

"For your own sake, leave," he said in a whisper. He looked at the other priest. "You go," he said, "and let me talk to him."

The young priest was in a total fright. He left immediately.

I looked up at the Pastor.

"Leave," he said to me in his low, mean voice, his lower lip drawing back to reveal his lower teeth. "Get out of our town. Get out of Santa Maddalana."

I looked at him with cold contempt. "You know about them, don't you?" I said in a low voice.

"You're mad. Mad!" he said. "If you speak of demons to people here you'll end up burnt at the stake yourself for a sorcerer. You think it can't happen?"

It was hatred in his eyes, shameless hatred.

"Oh, poor damned priest," I said, "you're in league with the Devil."

"Get out!" he growled.

I got up and looked down into his swelling eyes, his pouting, overworked mouth.

"Don't you dare break the Seal of my Confession, Father," I said. "If you do, I'll kill you."

He stood stock-still, staring at me.

I smiled very coldly and went to pass on through the rectory and away.

He ran after me, whispering like a steaming kettle. "You misunderstand everything. You're crazy, you're imagining things. I'm trying to save you from persecution and villainization."

I turned around at the door to the church and glared him into utter silence.

"You've tipped your hand," I said. "You're too merciless. Remember what I said. Break the Seal and I'll kill you."

He was as frightened now as the young priest had been.

I stood looking at the altar for a long while, ignoring him, forgetting him utterly, my mind pretending to have thoughts in it, to be construing and planning when all I could do was endure. Then I made the Sign of the Cross and I left the church.

I was in utter despair.

For a while I walked around. Once again, it was only the most pleasant town I had ever seen, with everyone happily at work, with best-swept cobbled streets, and pretty flower boxes under all the windows, and prettily dressed people going about their affairs.

It was the cleanest place I'd ever seen in my life, and the most contented. And the people, they were all eager to sell me their wares, but they didn't press it terribly much. But it was an awfully dull town in a way. There were no people my age, none at all that I saw. In fact, there weren't all that many children.

What should I do? Where should I go? What was I looking for?

I didn't quite know how to answer my own questions, but I was certainly on my guard for the slightest evidence that this town somehow harbored the demons, that Ursula had not found me here, but that I had found her.

The mere thought of her overcame me with a cool, inviting shock of desire. I saw her breasts, felt the taste of her, saw in a blurred flash the flowered meadow. No!

Think. Make some plan. As for this town, no matter what the priest knew, these people were too wholesome for harboring demons.

5

THE PRICE OF PEACE AND THE PRICE OF VENGEANCE

S the heat of the day started to really rise, I went into the arbor of the Inn for the heavy noon meal and sat down by myself under the wisteria, which was blooming magnificently over the latticework. This place was on the same side of the town as the Dominican church, and it too had a lovely view of the town to the left and a view out over the mountains.

I closed my eyes, and putting my elbows on the table, I clasped my hands and I prayed. "God, tell me what to do. Show me what is to be done." And then I was quiet in my heart, waiting, thinking.

What were my choices?

Take this tale to Florence? Who would believe it? Go to Cosimo himself and tell him this story? Much as I admired and trusted the Medici, I had to realize something. Nobody of my family was living but me. I alone could lay claim to our fortunes in the Medici bank. I didn't think Cosimo would deny my signature or my face. He'd give over to me what was mine, whether I had kinsmen or not, but a story of demons? I'd wind up locked up somewhere in Florence!

And talk of the stake, of being burnt for a sorcerer, that was entirely possible. Not likely. But possible. It could happen very suddenly and spontaneously in a town like this, a mob gathering, denunciations by a local priest, people shouting and running to see what was up. This did now and then happen to people.

About this time, my meal was set out for me, a good meal with plenty of fresh fruit and well-cooked mutton and gravy, and as I started to dip my bread and eat, up came two men who asked to sit down with me and buy a cup of wine for me.

I realized one of them was a Franciscan, a very kindly-looking priest, poorer it seemed than the Dominicans, which was logical I suppose, and the other an elderly man with little twinkling eyes and long stiff white eyebrows, sticking up as if with glue, as if he were costumed as a cheerful elf to delight children.

"We saw you go in to the Dominicans," said the Franciscan quietly and politely and smiling at me. "You didn't look so happy when you came out." He winked. "Why don't you try us?" Then he laughed. It was no more than a good-natured joke and I knew it, about the rivalry of the two orders. "You're a fine-looking young man; you come from Florence?" he asked.

"Yes, Father, traveling," I said, "though where exactly, I don't know. I'm stopped here for a while, I think." I was talking with my mouth full, but I was too hungry to stop. "Sit down, please." I started to rise, but they sat down.

I bought another pitcher of red wine for the table.

"Well, you couldn't have found a finer place," said the little old man, who seemed to have his wits about him, "that is why I am so happy that God sent my own son, back here, to serve in our church, so that he could live out his days by his family."

"Ah, so you are father and son," I said.

"Yes, and I never thought I'd live so long," said the father, "to see such prosperity come to this town as has come. It's miraculous."

"It is, it is the blessing of God," said the priest innocently and sincerely. "It's a true wonder."

"Oh, really, instruct me in this, how so?" I asked. I pushed the plate of fruit to them. But they said they had eaten.

"Well, in my time," said the father, "you know we had more than our share of woes, or that's how it seemed to me. But now? It's utter bliss, this place. Nothing bad ever happens."

"It's true," said the priest. "You know, I remember the lepers we had in the old days, who lived outside the walls. They are all gone now. And then there were always a few really bad youths, young men causing trouble, you know, the really bad sort. You had them in every town. But now? You couldn't find one bad man in all of Santa Maddalana or in any of the villages around. It's as if people have returned to God with their whole hearts."

"Yes," said the old elfin man, shaking his head, "and God has been merciful in so many other ways."

I felt chills on my back again, as I had with Ursula, but it was not from pleasure.

"In what way is that, in particular?" I asked.

"Well, look around," said the old man. "Have you seen any cripples in our streets? Do you see any half-wits? When I was a child, why, when you, my son, were a child"—he said to the priest—"there were always a few unfortunate souls, born ill formed, or without good brains, you know, and one had to look out for them. I can remember a time when there were always beggars at the gates. We have no beggars, haven't had any for years."

"Amazing," I said.

"Yes, true," said the priest thoughtfully. "Everyone here is in good health. That's why the nuns left so long ago. Did you see the old hospital shut up? And the convent out of town, long abandoned. I think there are sheep in there now. The farmers use its old rooms."

"No one ever takes sick?" I asked.

"Well, they do," said the priest, taking a slow drink of his wine, as though he were a moderate man in this respect, "but they don't suffer, you know. It's not like the old days. It seems if a person is like to go, then he goes quickly."

"Yes, true, thanks be to God," said the elder.

"And the women," said the priest, "they are lucky here in birth. They are not burdened with so many children. Oh, we have many whom God calls home to himself in the first few weeks—you know, it's the curse of a mother—but in general, our families are blessedly small." He looked to his father. "My poor mother," he said, "she had twenty babies all told. Well, that never happens now, does it?"

The little old man stuck out his chest and smiled

proudly. "Aye, twenty children I reared myself; well, many have gone their way, and I don't even know what became of . . . but never mind. No, families are small here now."

The priest looked slightly troubled. "My brothers, maybe someday God will grant me some knowledge of what became of them."

"Oh, forget about them," said the old man.

"Were they a spirited bunch, might I ask?" I said under my breath, peering at both of them and trying to make it seem quite natural.

"Bad," muttered the priest, shaking his head. "But that's our blessing, see, bad people leave us."

"Is that so?" I asked.

The little old man scratched his pink scalp. His white hair was thin and long, sticking in all directions, rather like the hair of his eyebrows.

"You know, I was trying to remember," he said, "what did happen to those poor cripple boys, you remember, the ones born with such miserable legs, they were brothers . . ."

"Oh, Tomasso and Felix," said the priest.

"Yes."

"They were taken off to Bologna to be cured. Same as Bettina's boy, the one born without his hands, remember, poor little child."

"Yes, yes, of course. We have several doctors."

"Do you?" I said. "I wonder what they do," I murmured. "What about the town council, the *gonfalonier*?" I asked. *Gonfalonier* was the name for the governor in Florence, the man who nominally, at least, ran things.

"We have a *borsellino*," said the priest, "and we

pick a new six or eight names out of it now and then, but nothing much ever happens here. There's no quarreling. The merchants take care of the taxes. Everything runs smoothly."

The little elfin man went into laughter. "Oh, we have no taxes!" he declared.

His son, the priest, looked at the old fellow as though this was not something that ought to be said, but then he himself merely looked puzzled. "Well, no, Papa," he said, "it's only that the taxes are . . . small." He seemed perplexed.

"Well, then you are really blessed," I said agreeably, trying on the surface to make light of this utterly implausible picture of things.

"And that terrible Oviso, remember him?" the priest suddenly said to his father and then to me. "Now that was a diseased fellow. He nearly killed his son. He was out of his mind, roared like a bull. There was a traveling doctor who came through, said they would cure him at Padua. Or was it Assisi?"

"I'm glad he never came back," said the old man. "He used to drive the town crazy."

I studied them both. Were they serious? Were they talking double-talk to me? I could see nothing cunning in either one of them, but a melancholy was coming over the priest.

"God does work in the strangest ways," he said. "Oh, I know that's not quite the proverb."

"Don't tempt the Almighty!" said his father, downing the dregs of his cup.

I quickly poured out the wine for both of them.

"The little mute fellow," said a voice.

I looked up. It was the innkeeper, with his hands on his hips, his apron stretching over his potbelly, a tray in his hand. "The nuns took him with them, didn't they?"

"Came back for him, I think," said the priest. He was now fully preoccupied. Troubled, I would say.

The innkeeper took up my empty plate.

"The worst scare was the plague," he whispered in my ear. "Oh, it's gone now, believe you me, or I wouldn't utter the word. There's no word that will empty a town any faster."

"No, all those families, gone, just like that," said the old man, "thanks to our doctors, and the visiting monks. All taken to the hospital in Florence."

"Plague victims? Taken to Florence?" I asked, in obvious disbelief. "I wonder who was minding the city gates, and which gate it was by which they were admitted."

The Franciscan stared at me fixedly for a moment, as if something had disturbed him violently and deeply.

The innkeeper gave the priest's shoulder a squeeze. "These are happy times," he said. "I miss the processions to the monastery—it's gone too, of course—but we have never been better."

I let my eyes shift quite deliberately from the innkeeper to the priest and found that the priest was gazing directly at me. There seemed a tremor to the edge of his mouth. He was sloppily shaven and had a loose jaw, and his deeply creased face looked sad suddenly.

The very old man chimed in that there had been a whole family down with the plague out in the country not very long ago, but they had been taken to Lucca.

"It was the generosity of . . . who was it, my son, I don't . . ."

"Oh, what does it matter?" said the innkeeper. "Signore," he said to me, "some more wine."

"For my guests," I gestured. "I have to be off. Restless limbs," I said. "I must see what books are for sale."

"This is a fine place for you to stay," said the priest with sudden conviction, his voice soft as he continued to gaze at me, his eyebrows knitted. "A fine place indeed, and we could use another scholar. But—."

"Well, I'm rather young myself," I said. I made ready to rise, putting one leg over the bench. "There are no young men here of my age?"

"Well, they go off, you see," said the elfin one. "There are a few, but they are busy at the trades of their fathers. No, the rapscallions don't hang around here. No, young man, they do not!"

The priest studied me as if he didn't hear his father's voice.

"Yes, and you're a learned young man," said the priest, but he was clearly troubled. "I can see that, and hear it in your voice, and all about you is thoughtful and clever—." He broke off. "Well, I guess you'll be on your way very soon, won't you?"

"You think I should?" I asked. "Or stay, which is it?" I made my manner mild, not unkind.

He gave me a half-smile. "I don't know," he said. Then he looked dour again and almost tragic. "God be with you," he whispered.

I leant towards him. The innkeeper, seeing this confidential manner, turned away and busied himself somewhere else. The old elfin one was talking to his cup.

"What is it, Father?" I asked in a whisper. "Is the town too well-off, is that it?"

"Go on your way, son," he said almost wistfully. "I wish I could. But I'm bound by my vow of obedience and by the fact that this is my home, and here sits my father, and all the others have vanished into the wide world." He became suddenly hard. "Or so it seems," he said. And then, "If I were you, I wouldn't stay here."

I nodded.

"You look strange, son," he said to me in the same whisper. Our heads were right together. "You stand out too much. You're pretty and encased in velvet, and it's your age; you're not really a child, you know."

"Yes, I see, not very many young men in the town at all, not the sort who question things. Just the old and the complacent and those who accept and who don't see the tapestry for the one small monkey embroidered in the corner."

He didn't answer this overzealous streak of rhetoric, and I was sorry I'd said it. In that little lapse perhaps my anger and my pain had flashed through. Disgusting! I was angry with myself.

He bit his lip, anxious for me, or for himself, or for both of us.

"Why did you come here?" he asked sincerely, almost protectively. "By which way did you come? They said you came in the night. Don't leave by night." His voice had become such a whisper I could scarcely hear him.

"You don't need to worry about me, Father," I said. "Pray for me," I said. "That's all."

I saw in him a species of fear as real as that which I had seen in the young priest, but it was even more innocent, for all his age, and all his wrinkles, and the wetness of his lips with the wine. He looked fatigued by that which he couldn't comprehend.

I stepped free of the bench and was on my way when he grasped my hand. I bent my ear to his lips.

"My boy," he said, "there's something . . . something . . ."

"I know, Father," I said. I patted his hand.

"No, you don't. Listen. When you leave, take the main road south, even if it's out of your way. Don't go north; don't take the narrow road north."

"Why not?" I demanded.

Doubting, silent, utterly stricken, he let go of me.

"Why not?" I said in his ear.

He was no longer facing me. "Bandits," he said. "Toll bandits who control the road; they'll make you pay to go through. Go south." He turned sharply away from me and began to speak to his father in a soft gentle scolding manner as if I was already on my way.

I left.

I was stunned as I set foot in the hollow street. "Toll bandits?"

Many shops were shut now, as was definitely the custom after the heavy meal, but others were not.

My sword weighed a ton on my hip, and I felt

feverish from the wine and dizzy from all these people had revealed to me.

So, I thought, my face burning, we have a town here with no young men, no cripples, no half-wits, no diseased people and no unwanted children! And on the road north we have dangerous bandits.

I moved downhill, walking faster and faster, and went out the wide-open gates and into the open country. The breeze was at once magnificent and welcome.

All around me lay rich, well-tended fields, vineyards, patches of orchard and farmhouses—lush and fertile vistas which I couldn't see when I had come in by darkness. As for the road north, I could see nothing of it due to the immense size of the town, whose uppermost fortifications were northward.

I could see, below on a ridge, what must have been the ruins of the convent and, way down the mountain and far off to the west, what might have been the monastery.

I made my way to two farms within the hour, having a cup of cool water with both farmers.

It was all the same, talk of a paradise here, free of miscreants and the horror of executions, absolutely the most peaceful place in the world, and only well-formed children everywhere.

It had been years since any bandits had dared to linger in the woods. Of course you never knew who might pass through, but the town was strong and kept the peace.

"Oh, not even on the north road?" I asked.

Neither farmer knew anything about any north road.

When I asked what became of the unhealthy, the lame, the injured, it was the same. Some doctor or other, or priest, or order of friars or nuns, had taken them off to a university or city. The farmers sincerely couldn't remember.

I came back into the town well before twilight. I went poking around, in and out of every shop, in a near systematic manner, eyeing everyone as closely as I might without attracting undue attention.

Of course I couldn't hope to cover even one street of the place, but I was determined to discover what I could.

In the booksellers, I went through the old *Ars Grammatica* and *Ars Minor,* and the big beautiful Bibles that were for sale, which I could only see by asking that they be taken out of the cabinets.

"How do I go north from here?" I asked the bored man who leaned on his elbow and looked at me sleepily.

"North, nobody goes north," he said, and yawned in my face. He wore fine clothes without a sign of mending, and good new shoes of well-worked leather. "Look, I have much finer books than that," he said.

I pretended interest, then explained politely that all were more or less what I had and did not need, but thank you.

I went into a tavern where men were busy at dice and shouting over the game, lustily, as though they had nothing better to do. And then through the bakers' district, where the bread smelled wondrously delicious, even to me.

I had never felt so utterly alone in my life, as

I walked among these people listening to their pleasant talk and hearing the same tale of safety and blessings over and over again.

It froze my blood to think of nightfall. And what was this mystery of the road north? Nobody, nobody but the priest, even raised an eyebrow at the mention of that point of the compass.

About an hour before dark, I happened into one shop where the proprietor, a dealer in silks and lace from Venice and Florence, was not so patient with my idle presence, as others had been, in spite of the fact that I obviously had money.

"Why are you asking so many questions?" she said to me. She seemed tired and worn out. "You think it's easy to take care of a sick child? Look in there."

I stared at her as if she'd lost her mind. But then it dawned on me, clear and cold. I knew exactly what she meant. I poked my head through a curtained doorway and saw a child, feverish and sick, slumbering in a dirty narrow bed.

"You think it's easy? Year after year she doesn't get better," said the woman.

"I'm sorry," I said. "But what's to be done?"

The woman tore out her stitches and put down her needle. She seemed past all patience. "What's to be done? You mean to tell me you don't know!" she whispered. "You, a clever man like you!" She bit into her lip. "But my husband says, No, not yet, and so we go on with it."

She went back to her work, muttering to herself, and I, horrified and struggling to keep a straight face, made my way on. I went into a couple more shops. Nothing special happened. Then in the third on my way, I found an old man very out of his wits and his two daughters both trying to keep him from tearing his clothes off.

"Here, let me help you," I said at once.

We got him down in the chair, got his shirt over his head, and finally he stopped making incoherent noises. He was very wizened and drooling.

"Oh, thank God, this won't go on long," said one of the daughters, wiping her brow. "It's a mercy."

"Why won't it go on long?" I asked.

She glanced up at me, and away, and then back again. "Oh, you're a stranger here, Signore, forgive me, you are so young. I only saw a boy when I looked at you. I mean God will be merciful. He's very old."

"Hmmm, I see," I said.

She looked at me with cold cunning eyes, as if they were made of metal.

I bowed and went out. The old man had started to take off his shirt again, and the other sister, who had been silent all the time, slapped him.

I winced at it, and kept walking. I meant to see as much as I could right now.

Passing through rather peaceful little tailors' shops I came at last to the district of the porcelain dealers, where two men were having an argument about a fancy birthing tray.

Now, birthing trays, once used in practicality to receive the infant as it came from the womb, had become by my time fancy gifts given after the child was born. They were large platters painted with lovely domestic designs, and this shop had an impressive display of them.

I heard the argument before I was seen.

One man said to buy the damned tray, while the other said the infant wouldn't even live and the gift was premature, and a third man said the woman would welcome the beautiful gorgeously painted birthing tray anyway.

They stopped when I entered the shop proper to look at all the imported wares, but then when I turned my back, one of the men uttered under his breath, "If she has a brain in her head, she'll do it."

I was struck by the words, so struck that I turned at once to snatch a handsome plate from the shelf and pretend to be much impressed with it. "So lovely," I said, as if I hadn't heard them.

The merchant got up and started to extoll the contents on display. The others melted into the gathering evening outside. I stared at the man.

"Is the child sick?" I asked in the smallest most childish voice that I myself could muster.

"Oh, no, well, I don't think so, but you know how it is," said the man. "The child's smallish."

"Weak," I volunteered.

In a very clumsy way, he said, "Yes, weak." His smile was artificial, but he thought himself quite successful.

Then both of us turned to fussing over the wares. I bought a tiny porcelain cup, very beautifully painted, which he claimed to have bought from a Venetian.

I knew damned good and well I should leave without a word, but I couldn't stop myself from asking him as I paid, "Do you think the poor smallish weak child will live?"

He laughed a rather deep coarse laugh as he took my money. "No," he said, and then he glanced at me as though he'd been in his thoughts. "Don't worry about it, Signore," he said with a little smile. "Have you come to live here?"

"No, Sir, only passing through, going north," I said.

"North?" he asked, a little startled but sarcastic. He shut up the cashbox and turned the key. Then shaking his head as he put the box into the cabinet and closed the doors, he said, "North, eh? Well, good luck to you, my boy." He gave a sour chuckle. "That's an ancient road. You better ride as fast as you can from sunup."

"Thank you, Sir," I said.

Night was coming on.

I hurried into an alleyway and stood there, against the wall, catching my breath as though someone were chasing me. I let the little cup fall and it shattered loudly, the noise echoing up the towering buildings.

I was half out of my wits.

But instantly, and fully aware of my situation, and convinced of the horrors I had discovered, I made an inflexible decision.

I wasn't safe in the Inn, so what did this matter? I was going to do it my way and see for myself.

This is what I did.

Without going back to the Inn, without ever officially leaving my room in the Inn, I turned uphill when the shadows were thick enough to cover me, and I climbed the narrowing street towards the old ruined castle.

Now all day I had been looking at this imposing collection of rock and decay, and could see that it was indeed utterly ruined and empty of all save the birds of the air, except, as I have said, for the lower floors, which supposedly held offices.

But the castle had two standing towers remaining to it, one that faced over the town, and another, much fallen away, beyond and remote on the edge of a cliff, as I had seen from the lower farmland.

Well, I made for the tower that overlooked the town.

The government offices were shut up of course already, and the curfew soldiers would soon be out, and there was noise from only a couple of taverns that obviously stayed open no matter what the law was.

The piazza before the castle was empty, and because the three streets of the town took many a curve in their way downhill, I could see almost nothing now but a few dim torches.

The sky, however, was wondrously bright, clear of all but the most rounded and discreetly shaped clouds, very visible against the deeper blue of the night, and the stars seemed exquisitely numerous.

I found old winding stairs, too narrow almost for a human being, that curved around the useful part of the old citadel and led up to the first platform of stone, before an entrance to the tower.

Of course this architecture was no stranger to me whatsoever. The stones were of a rougher texture than those of my old home, and somewhat darker, but the tower was broad and square and timelessly solid.

I knew that the place was ancient enough that I would find stone stairways leading quite high, and I did, and soon came to the end of my trek in a high room which gave me a view of the entire town stretched out before me.

There were higher chambers, but they had been accessible in centuries past by wooden ladders that could be pulled up, to defeat an enemy and isolate him below, and I couldn't get to them. I could hear the birds up there, disturbed by my presence. And I could hear the breeze moving faintly.

However, this was fine, this height.

I had a view all around from the four narrow windows of this place, looking in all directions.

And most especially, and important to me, I could see the town itself, directly below me, shaped like a great eye—an oval with tapered ends—with random torches burning here and there, and an occasional dimly lighted window, and I could see a lantern moving slowly as someone walked in a leisurely pace down one of the thoroughfares.

No sooner had I seen this moving lantern than it went out. It seemed the streets were utterly deserted.

Then the windows too went dark, and very shortly there were not four torches that I could see anywhere.

This darkness had a calming effect on me. The open country sank into a deep dark tinge of blue beneath the pearly heavens, and I could see the forests encroaching on the tilled land, creeping higher here and there, as the hills folded over one another or sank steeply into valleys of pure blackness.

I could hear the total emptiness of the tower.

Nothing stirred now, not even the birds. I was quite alone. I could have heard the slightest footfall on the stairs down below. No one knew I was here. All slept.

I was safe here. And I could keep a vigil.

I was too full of misery to be frightened, and frankly I was prepared to take my stand against Ursula in this spot, preferred it, in fact, to the confines of the Inn, and I feared nothing as I said my prayers and laid my hand on my sword as usual.

What did I expect to see in this sleeping town? *Anything that happened in it.*

Now, what did I think that was to be? I couldn't have told anyone. But as I circled the room, as I glanced again and again down at the few scattered lights below and the hulk of the descending ramparts beneath the glowing summer sky, the place seemed loathsome, full of deceit, full of witchcraft, full of payment to the Devil.

"You think I don't know where your unwanted babies are taken?" I muttered in a rage. "You think that people who are down with the plague are welcomed right through the open gates of your neighboring cities?"

I was startled by the echoes of my own murmurings off the cold walls.

"But what do you do with them, Ursula? What would you have done with my brother and sister?"

My ruminations were madness perhaps, or might have seemed so to some. But I learnt this. Revenge takes one's mind from the pain. Revenge is a lure, a mighty molten lure, even if it is hopeless.

One blow from this sword and I can strike off her head, I thought, and heave it out that window, and then what will she be but a demon stripped of all worldly power?

Now and then I half-drew my sword, then put it back. I took out my longest dagger and slapped the palm of my left hand with its blade. I never stopped walking.

Suddenly, as I made one of my boring circumlocutions, I happened to spy far away, on a distant mountain, in which direction I really didn't know—but not the direction by which I had come—a great quantity of light playing behind the mesh of the sylvan darkness.

At first I thought this might be a fire, there was so much light, but as I narrowed my eyes and focused my mind, I saw that this was out of the question.

There was no riotous glare on the few visible clouds above, and the illumination, for all the breadth of it, was contained as if it emanated from a vast congregation gathered together with a fantastical quantity of candles. How steady yet pulsing was this orgy of fierce light!

I felt a chill in my bones as I looked at it. It was a dwelling! I leant over the window edge. I could see its complex and sprawling outline! It stood out from all the land, this one luxuriantly lighted castle, all by itself, and obviously visible from one entire side of this town, this spectacle of forest-shrouded house in which some celebration appeared to require that every torch and taper be lighted, that every window, battlement and coping be hung with lanterns.

North, yes, north, for the town dropped straight off behind me, and this castle lay north, and it was that direction of which I'd been warned, and who in this town could not have known of this place, yet there had not been one single solitary mention save for the whisper of the terrified Franciscan in the Inn at my table.

But what was I looking at? What could I see? Thick woods, yes; it was very high but surrounded by close and concealing woods, through which its light again and again palpitated like a great menace, but what was that coming from it, what was that wild, half-visible movement in the darkness, over the slopes that fell away from the mysterious promontory?

Were there things moving in the night? Moving from that very distant castle right towards this village? Amorphous black things, as if they were great soft shapeless birds following the alignment of the land but free of its gravity. Were they coming towards me? Had I been charmed?

No, I saw this. Or did I?

There were dozens of them!

They were coming closer and closer.

They were tiny shapes, not large at all, the largeness having been a delusion caused by the fact that they traveled in packs, these things, and now, as they came near to the town, the packs broke apart and I saw them springing up to the very walls beyond me on either side like so many giant moths.

I turned around and ran to the window.

They had descended in a swarm upon the town! I could see them dip down and vanish in the blackness. Below me on the piazza, there appeared two black shapes, men in streaming capes, who ran or rather leapt into the mouths of the streets, issuing from their lips an audible and audacious laughter.

I heard crying in the night, I heard sobs.

I heard a thin wail, and a muffled groan.

No lights appeared in the town.

Then out of the darkness, these evil things appeared again, on the tops of the walls, running right on the edge and then leaping free.

"God, I see you! Curse you!" I whispered.

There was a sudden loud noise in my ears, a great brush of soft cloth against me, and then the figure of a man reared up before my face.

"Do you see us, my boy?" It was a young man's voice, hearty, full of merriment. "My very curious little boy?"

He was too close for my sword. I could see nothing but rising garments.

With my elbow and shoulder and all my strength, I went for his groin.

His laughter filled the tower.

"Ah, but that does not hurt me, child, and if you're so curious, well then, we'll take you too with us to come and see what you long to see."

He caught me in a suffocating swaddle of fabric. And suddenly I felt myself lifted off the floor, encased in a sack, and I knew we had left the tower!

I was head down, sick to nausea. It seemed he flew, carrying me on his back, and his laughter was now half blown away by the wind, and I could not free my arms. I could feel my sword, but couldn't reach the handle.

Desperately I felt for my dagger, not the one which I must have dropped when I had been caught by him, but the other in my boot, and then having that, I twisted and turned towards the rough back on which I rode, bouncing and growling, and plunged the dagger through the cloth over and over again.

He gave a wild scream. I stabbed him again.

My whole body, inside the sack, was whipped up into the air, away from him.

"You little monster," he cried. "You wretched impudent child."

We descended sharply, and then I felt myself hit the ground, the rocky grassy ground, and I rolled over, tearing at the fabric of the blinding sack with my knife.

"You little bastard," he cursed.

"Are you bleeding, you filthy devil?" I called out. "Are you?" I ripped at the sack, lost in it, rolling over and over, then feeling the wet grass with my naked hand.

I saw the stars.

Then the cloth was torn free of my struggling limbs.

I lay at his feet, but only for a moment.

6

THE COURT OF THE RUBY GRAIL

NOTHING could have wrenched the dagger from my hand. I cut deep into his legs, bringing forth another riot of screams from him. He picked me up, indeed hurled me high in the air, and I fell, stunned, onto the dewy ground.

This gave me my first blurred but imperative glimpse of him. A great rush of red light illuminated him, a hooded and cloaked figure dressed as a knight, in long old-fashioned tunic and sleeves of shining mail. He twisted his torso, his golden hair tangling over his face, obviously in pain from the wounds inflicted on his back, and now stomped his wounded leg.

I rolled over twice, holding tight to the dagger, as I freed my sword sufficiently to draw it out of the scabbard. I was on my feet before he even so much as moved, and swung the sword with one hand, clumsily, but with all my force, hearing it smash into his side with a sickening moist slosh of a sound. The gush of blood in the bright light was horrific and monstrous.

There came his worst cry. He fell to his knees.

"Help me, you imbeciles; he's a devil!" he screamed. His hood fell back.

I scanned the immense fortifications rising to my right, the high crenelated towers with their fluttering flags in the unsteady glow of countless lights, just as I'd glimpsed from the distance of the town. It was a fantastical castle of pointed roofs, sharply broken arched windows, and high battlements crowded with dark figures moving in silhouette as they looked down on our struggle.

There came rushing down the wet grass the figure of Ursula in a red gown, cloakless, her hair in long braids with red ribbon, rushing towards me.

"Don't hurt him, I charge you," she screamed. "Don't touch him."

A group of male figures, all got up in the same old-fashioned knightly tunics, down to their knees, with somber pointed steel helmets, followed her. They had bearded faces all, and ghastly white skin.

My adversary pitched forward on the grass, spouting blood as if he were a hideous fountain.

"Look what he's done to me, look!" he shouted.

I stuck my dagger in my belt, grabbed the sword with two hands and went at his neck, letting a roar escape my teeth as I did, and saw the head roll over and over and down the hill. "Ah, now you're dead, you're bloody dead!" I cried out. "You murderous fiend, you're dead. Go get your head. Put that back on!"

Ursula flung her arms around me, her breasts sealed against my back. Her hand imprisoned mine once more and forced me to bow the tip of the sword to the ground.

"Don't touch him," she screamed again, with a threat in her voice. "Don't come near, I charge you."

One of the others had recovered the shaggy blond head of my foe and held it up as the others watched the body twitch and writhe.

"Oh, no, it's too late," said one of the men.

"No, put it back, put it on his neck," cried another.

"Let me go, Ursula," I said. "Let me die with honor, will you do me that courtesy!" I struggled. "Let me free, to die in my own way, will you do that much?"

"No," she said hotly into my ear. "I will not."

I was absolutely powerless against her strength, no matter how soft the cushion of her breasts or how cool and soft her fingers. She had complete mastery of me.

"Go to Godric," cried one of the men.

The other two had picked up the writhing, kicking, headless man. "Take him to Godric," said the one who carried the head. "Only Godric can pronounce on this."

Ursula let out a loud wail. "Godric!" It was like the howl of the wind or a beast, it was so shrill, so immense, echoing off the walls.

High up, against the wide gaping arched doorway of the citadel, his back to the light, there stood a slender elderly figure, limbs bent with age.

"Bring them both," he called out. "Ursula, quiet yourself, lest you frighten everyone."

I made a swift bid for freedom. She tightened her

grip. There came the pinprick of her teeth in my neck. "Oh, no, Ursula, let me see what's to happen!" I whispered. But I could feel the murky clouds rising about me, as though the air itself had thickened and was enfolding me with scent and sound and the sensuous force.

Oh, love you, want you, yes, I did and can't deny it. I felt myself holding her in the high moist grasses of the field, and she lay beneath me, but these were dreams and there were no wild red flowers, and I was being taken somewhere, and she had but weakened me, pulled on my heart with the force of her own.

I tried to curse her. All around us lay the flowers and the grasses, and she said, "Run," but this was quite impossible because it was not made of truth, but of fantasy and the sucking of her mouth on me and her limbs entwining me as if she were a serpent.

A French castle. It was as though I had been transported to the north.

I had opened my eyes.

All the accoutrements of a French court.

Even the dim sedate music which I could hear made me think of old-fashioned French songs sung at suppers in long-ago childhood.

I awoke, sitting cross-legged on a carpet, slumped over, and came to myself rubbing my neck and feeling about desperately for weapons which had all been taken from me. I nearly lost my balance and fell backward.

The music was repetitive and dull and pounding as it rose up from some faraway place below, with too many muffled drums and the thin nasal whine of horns. It had no melody.

I looked up. French, yes, the high narrow pointed archway that led to a long balcony outside, below which some great celebration was in noisy progress. Fancy French, the tapestries of the ladies with their tall cone-shaped hats, and their snow-white unicorns.

Quaint antique, like the illustrations in prayer books of courts in which poets sat reading aloud the boring and tedious *Roman de la Rose*, or the fables of Reynard the Fox.

The window was draped in blue satin covered in the fleurs-de-lys. There was old filigree crumbling about the high doorway and what I could see of the window frame. And cabinets were gilded and painted in the French style, decayed and stiff.

I turned around.

There stood the two men, their long tunics streaked with blood, and their mail sleeves coarse and thick. They had taken off their pointed helmets, and they stared at me with icy pale eyes, each a solemn bearded figure. The light positively glinted on their hard white skin.

And there stood Ursula, a silver-framed jewel upon the shadows, gazing down at me, her gown high-waisted and soft-falling and old-fashioned as their clothes, as though she too had come from some long-ago kingdom of the French, her snow-white breasts bare almost to her nipples, beneath a rich full little bodice of flowered red-and-gold velvet.

At a desk, on an X-shaped chair, there sat the

Elderly one, his age quite true to the posture I had glimpsed silhouetted against the castle light, and he was pale as they, of the same deadly white complexion, both beautiful yet awful and monstrous.

Turkish lamps hung on chains about the room, flames glittering deep inside them, giving off a hurtful light against my dazed eyes, and also a fragrance as of roses and summer fields, something alien to heat and burnt things.

The Elderly one had a bald head, as ugly as the unearthed bulb of an iris, upended and shaved of all root, and implanted with two gleaming gray eyes, and a long narrow solemn uncomplaining and unjudging mouth.

"Ah, so," he said to me in a soft voice, lifting one eyebrow, which was scarcely visible except for the sharp arching wrinkle of his perfect white flesh. He had thick slanting lines for cheeks. "You realize you've killed one of us, don't you?"

"I hope so," I said. I climbed to my feet. I nearly lost my balance. Ursula reached out, then stepped back, as though she had caught herself in a breach of decorum.

I righted myself, glaring at her quite ferociously and then at the bald Elderly one, who looked up at me with unbroken calm.

"Do you care to see what you've done?" he asked of me.

"Why should I?" I asked. But I did see.

On a great trestle-board table to my left lay the dead blond thief who had hefted me body and soul into his big cloth sack. Ah, the debt was paid in full.

He lay still, shrunken horridly, as if his limbs had

collapsed upon themselves, and his bloodless white head, lids open on dark clotted eyes, lay against his roughly torn neck. What a delight. I stared at one skeletal hand of the being, which hung over the edge of the table, white and like some shriveling creature of the sea beneath a merciless sun on sand by the oceanside.

"Ah, excellent," I said. "This man who dared to abduct me and bring me here by force, quite dead, thank you for the sight of it." I looked at the Elderly one. "Honor demands nothing less. We don't even have to talk of common sense, do we? And what others did you take from the village? The wild old man who tore at his shirt? The infant born small? The weak, the infirm, the sick, whatever they'd give you, and what do you give them in exchange?"

"Oh, do be quiet, young one," said the Elderly solemn male. "You are courageous beyond honor or common sense, that's plain enough."

"No, it isn't. Your sins against me demand I fight you with my last breath, you, all of you." I pivoted and stared at the open door. The plodding music in itself sickened me and threatened to make me dizzy from all the blows and falls I'd suffered. "Such noise from below. What are you, a bloody court?"

All three men broke into laughter.

"Well, you've very nearly got it right," said one of the bearded soldiers in a deep bass of a voice. "We are the Court of the Ruby Grail, that's our very name, only we prefer that you say it properly in Latin or in French, as we say it."

"The Court of the Ruby Grail!" I said. "Leeches,

parasites, blood drinkers, that's what you all are. What is the Ruby Grail? Blood?"

I struggled to remember the prick of her teeth against my throat without the spell which had always come with them, but there it was, threatening to swallow me, the drifting, fragrant memory of meadows and her tender breasts. I shook myself all over. "Blood drinkers. Ruby Grail! Is that what you do with all of them, the ones you take? Drink their blood?"

The Elderly one looked pointedly at Ursula. "What is it you're asking of me, Ursula?" he put the question to her. "How can I make such a choice?"

"Oh, but Godric, he's brave and fine and strong," said Ursula. "Godric, if you but say yes, no one will go against it. No one will question it. Please, I beg you, Godric. When have I ever asked—."

"Asked for what?" I demanded, looking from her solicitous and heartbroken face to the Elderly man. "For my life? Is that what you ask? You'd better kill me."

The old man knew that. I didn't have to tell him. There was no way I could be given mercy at this juncture. I would merely fling myself against them again, seeking to bring down another or another.

Suddenly, as if quite angry and impatient, the Elderly figure rose with surprising agility and grabbed me by the collar as he swept past me in a great graceful rustle of red robes, and dragged me with him, as if I weighed nothing, out through the archway and to the edge of the stone railing.

"Look down on the Court," he said.

The hall was immense. The overhang on which

we stood ran all around, and below there was scarcely a foot of bare stone, so rich were the hangings of gold and burgundy. The long table below hosted a string of Lords and Ladies, all in the requisite burgundy-red cloth, the color of blood, not wine, as I had believed, and before them glared the bare wood, with not a plate of food nor a cup of wine, but all were content and watching with cheerful eyes, as they chattered, the dancers who covered the great floor, dancing deftly on thick carpets as though they liked this padding beneath their slippered feet.

There were so many interlocking circles of figures moving to the throb and beat of the music that they made a series of arabesques. The costumes embraced a great nationality of styles, from the very French to the modern Florentine, and everywhere there were gay circles of red-dyed silk or the red field covered with flowers or some other design which looked very like stars or crescent moons, I could not quite see it.

It was a somber yet tantalizing picture, all of them in this same rich color which held sway somewhere between the putrid ghastliness of blood and the stunning splendor of scarlet.

I noted the sconces, candlesticks, torches galore. How easy it would be to set their tapestries afire. I wondered if they could burn, they themselves, like other witches and heretics.

I heard Ursula let out a little gasp. "Vittorio, be wise," she whispered.

At her whisper, the man at the center of the table below—he who held that very high-backed chair of honor, which my father would have held at home—looked up at me. He was blond-haired, blond as the shaggy one I'd slain, but his long locks were pampered and silky on his broad shoulders. His face was youthful, far more so than my father's yet plenty older than my own, and as inhumanly pale as all the rest, his searing blue eyes fixing upon me. He returned at once to his study of the dance.

The whole spectacle seemed to shiver with the hot smoking quaver of the flames, and as my eyes watered, I realized with a start that the figures worked into the tapestry were not the quiet ladies and unicorns of the small studious chamber from which we'd come, but devils dancing in Hell. Indeed, there were quite hideous gargoyles in the most violent and cruel style, carved beneath the porch all around, on which we stood, and I could see at the capitals of the branching columns that held up the ceiling above us more of the demonic and winged creatures carved into the stone.

Grimaces of evil were emblazoned on the walls behind me, across from me. In one tapestry below, the circles of Dante's Hell climbed one upon another ever higher and higher.

I stared at the shining bare table. I was dizzy. I was going to be sick, lose consciousness.

"Make you a member of the Court, that is what she asks," said the Elder, pushing me hard against the rail, not letting me free, not letting me turn away. His voice was unhurried and low and without the slightest opinion on the matter. "She wants us to bring you into our Court as a reward for the fact that you slew one of us, that is her logic."

His glance to me was thoughtful, cool. His hand on my collar was neither cruel nor rough, merely simple.

I was a tempest of half-uttered words and curses, when suddenly I realized I was falling.

In the Elderly one's grasp, I had fallen over the rail, and in a second descended to the thick layers of carpet below, where I was yanked to my feet, as the dancers made way for us on either side.

We stood before the Lord in the high-backed chair, and I saw that the wood figures of his regal throne were, of course, animalian, feline and diabolical.

All was black wood, polished so that one could smell the oil, and it mingled sweetly with the perfume of all the lamps, and there came a soft crackling from the torches.

The musicians had stopped. I couldn't even see them. And then when I did, saw the little band quite high up in their own little balcony or loft, I perceived that they too had the porcelain-white skin and the lethal cats' eyes, as they gazed down at me, all of them slender males, modestly clothed, and seemingly apprehensive.

I stared at the Lord. He had not moved or spoken. He was a fine, imperial figure of a man, his thick bulky blondish hair combed back from his face and falling, as I had seen before, in carefully combed locks on his shoulders.

His clothes too were of the old fashion, a great loose tunic of velvet, not a soldier's tunic, but almost a robe unto itself, trimmed in darkly dyed fur to match its lurid color, and beneath it he wore big beautiful full sleeves ballooning out loosely over his elbows and then tapering around his long narrow forearms and wrists. A huge chain of medallions hung about his neck, each heavily worked circle of gold set with a cabochon stone, a ruby, red as his clothing.

He held one slender naked hand curled on the table, simply. The other I could not see. He gazed at me with blue eyes. There was something puritanical and scholarly about his bare hand, and the refinement and cleanliness of it.

Across the thick overlapping carpets, Ursula came with a quick step, holding her skirts in two dainty hands. "Florian," she said, making a deep bow to the Lord behind the table. "Florian, I am begging you for this one, on account of character and strength, that you bring him into the Court for my sake, for my heart. It's as simple as that."

Her voice was tremulous but reasoning.

"Into the Court? Into this Court?" I demanded. I felt the heat rise in my face. I looked from right to left. I stared at their white cheeks, their dark mouths, which were all too often the color of fresh wounds. I stared at the blanched and colorless expressions with which they regarded me. Were their eyes full of demonic fire, or was it only that every other bit of humanity had been taken from their countenances?

I saw my own hands as I looked down, my own clenching fists, very ruddy and human, and quite suddenly, as if I were meant to smell it, I caught my own scent, the scent of my sweat and the dust from the road clinging to me and mingling with whatever in me was simply human.

"Yes, you are quite the morsel to us," said the Lord himself, speaking from the table. "You are indeed, and the hall is filled with your scent. And it is too early for us to feast. We feast when the bell rings twelve times, that is our infallible custom."

It was a beautiful voice, a voice of ringing clarity and charm, tinged with the accent of the French, which can in itself be so beguiling. It was with a French restraint and regality that he expressed himself.

He smiled at me, and his smile was gentle, as was Ursula's smile, but not pitying, and not at all cruel or sarcastic.

I had no eyes now for the other faces to the left and the right of him. I knew only that there were many, and some were men and some women, and the women wore the stately French headdresses of olden times, and somewhere in the corner of my eye, I thought I saw a man got up like a jester.

"Ursula, such a thing as this," the Lord said, "requires long consideration."

"Does it!" I cried out. "You mean to make me one of your Court? That takes no consideration."

"Oh, come now, my boy," the Lord said in his soft, calming voice. "We are not subject to death or decay or disease here. You squirm on the end of a hook, you're a doomed catch from the sea, and you do not even know that you are no longer in the life-sustaining water."

"My Lord, I do not wish to be part of your Court," I said. "Spare yourself your kindnesses and your advice." I looked about. "Don't talk to me of your Feast."

These creatures had adopted an abominable stillness, a frozen regard which was in itself utterly unnatural and menacing. A wave of revulsion came over me. Or was it panic, panic which I would not allow to form inside of me, no matter how completely and hopelessly I was surrounded by them, and how alone I stood.

The figures at the table might have been made of china, so fixed they were. Indeed it seemed that the very act of posing to perfection was inherently part of their attentiveness.

"Oh, if I had but a crucifix," I said in a soft voice, not even thinking about what I was saying.

"That would mean nothing to us," said the Lord matter-of-factly.

"Oh, how well I know; your lady here came into my very chapel to take my brother and sister prisoner! No, crosses mean nothing to you. But it would mean something to me just now. Tell me, do I have angels about me that protect me? Are you always visible? Or do you, now and then, melt with the night and vanish? And when that is so, can you see the angels that defend me?"

The Lord smiled.

The Elderly one, who had let go of my collar, for which I was very thankful, laughed softly under his breath. But there came no easy mirth from anyone else.

I glanced at Ursula. How loving and desperate she looked, how bold and steadfast as she glanced from me to this Lord, whom she had called Florian.

But she was no more human than any of them; she was the deathly semblance of a young woman, past all description in gifts and graces but long out of life, as they were. Some grail was this Ruby Grail.

"Hear his words, Sir, in spite of what he actually says," she begged. "It's been so very long since there was a new voice within these walls, one that would remain with us, be one of us."

"Yes, and he almost believes in his angels, and you think him wondrously clever," said the Lord understandingly. "Young Vittorio, let me assure you, there are no guardian angels that I can see about you. And we are always visible, as you know, for you have seen us at our best and at our worst. No, not really truly at our best, not at our finest."

"Oh," I said, "and for that I can't wait, my Lord, for I am so in love with you all, and your style of slaughtering, and there is of course the matter of what your corruption has done to the town below and how you've stolen the souls of the very priests themselves."

"Hush, you work yourself into a mortal fever," he said. "Your scent fills my nostrils as if the pot is boiling over. I might devour you, child, cut you up and give your pulsing parts up and down the table to be suckled while the blood is still very hot, and your eyes blink—."

On those words I thought I would go mad. I thought of my dead sister and brother. I thought of the hideous and hopeless tender expressions of their severed heads. I couldn't bear this. I shut my eyes tight. I sought for any image to banish these horrors. I raised from memory the spectacle of Fra

Filippo Lippi's Angel Gabriel on his knees before the Virgin, yes, angels, angels, fold your wings about me, now, oh, God, send me your angels!

"I curse your damned Court, you sweet-tongued devil!" I cried out. "How did you get your foot into this land! How did it happen?" I opened my eyes, but I saw only Fra Filippo's angels in a great tumbling, falling spectacle of remembered works, radiant beings filled with the warm carnal breath of earth mingled with Heaven. "Did he go to Hell?" I cried out louder. "The one whose head I cut off? Is he burning?"

If silence can swell and fall back upon itself, then so did the silence of this great hall or solar, and I heard nothing but my own anxious breath.

But still the Lord remained unperturbed.

"Ursula," he said. "This can be considered."

"No!" I cried out. "Never! Join you? Become one of you?"

The Elder's hand held me powerless with clamped fingers on my neck. I would only make myself foolish if I struggled. Were he to tighten his grip, I would be dead. And maybe that was best. Only I had more to say:

"I will never, I won't. What? How dare you think my soul so cheap you can have it for the asking!"

"Your soul?" asked the Lord. "What is your soul that it does not want to travel centuries under the inscrutable stars, rather than a few short years? What is your soul that it will not seek for truth forever, rather than for one paltry common lifetime?"

Very slowly, with the muted rustle of garments, he rose to his feet, displaying for the first time a long full mantle of red which fell down, making a great patch of blood-colored shadow behind him. He bent his head ever so slightly, and lamps gave his hair a rich gilded look, and his blue eyes softened.

"We were here before you and your kindred," he said. His voice never broke decorum. He remained civil, elegant. "We were here centuries before you came to your mountain. We were here when all these mountains round were ours. It is you who are the invader." He paused and drew himself up. "It is your species that draws ever closer with farm and village and fortress and castle, and encroaches upon us, upon the forests which are ours, so that we must be cunning where we would be swift, and visible where we would be as the Gospel 'thief in the night.' "

"Why did you kill my father and my family!" I demanded. I could keep silent no longer, I didn't care how beguiling his eloquence, his soft purring words, his charmed face.

"Your father and his father," he said, "and the Lord before him—they cut down the trees that crowded your castle. And so I must keep back the forest of humans from mine. And now and then I must range wide with my ax, and so I have, and so it was done. Your father could have given tribute and remained as he was. Your father could have sworn a secret oath that required all but nothing of him."

"You can't believe he would have surrendered to you our babes, for what, do you drink their blood or sacrifice them to Satan on some altar?"

"You shall see by and by," he said, "for I think you must be sacrificed."

"No, Florian," Ursula gasped. "I beg you."

"Let me put a question to you, gracious Lord," I said, "since justice and history weigh so heavily with you. If this is a Court, a true Court, why have I no benefit of human defense? Or human peers? Or any humans to defend me?"

He seemed troubled by the question. Then he spoke.

"We are the Court, my son," he said. "You are nothing, and you know it. We would have let your father live, as we let the stag live in the forest so that it may breed with the doe. It's no more than that."

"Are there any humans here?"

"None that can help you," he said simply.

"No human guards by day?" I asked.

"No guards by day," he said, and for the first time he smiled a little proudly. "You think we require them? You think our small pigeon coop is not content by day? You think we need human guards here?"

"I certainly do. And you're a fool if you think I'd ever join your Court! No human guards, when right below is an entire village which knows what you are and who you are and that you come by night and cannot by day?"

He smiled patiently. "They are vermin," he said quietly. "You waste my time with those who are beneath contempt."

"Hmm, you do yourself wrong with such a harsh judgment. I think you have more love of them, in some way or another, my Lord, than that!"

The Elder laughed. "Of their blood perhaps," he said under his breath.

There was a bit of uneasy laughter from somewhere else in the hall, but it fell away, like a fragment of something broken.

The Lord spoke again:

"Ursula, I will consider but I do not—."

"No, for I will not!" I said. "Even if I were damned, I wouldn't join you."

"Hold your tongue," cautioned the Lord calmly.

"You are fools if you do not think the townspeople below will rise up and take this citadel by the light of the day and open your hiding places!"

There was a rustling and noise throughout the great hall, but no words, none at least that I could hear, but it was as if these pale-faced monsters were communing with each other by thought or merely exchanging glances which made their ponderous and beautiful garments shift and move.

"You are numb with stupidity!" I declared. "You make yourselves known to the whole daylight world, and you think this Court of the Ruby Grail can endure forever?"

"You insult me," said the Lord. A bit of rosy color came divinely and beautifully into his cheeks. "I ask you with courtesy to be quiet."

"Do I insult you? My Lord, allow me to advise you. You are helpless by day; I know you are. You strike by night and only by night. All signs and words point to it. I remember your hordes fleeing my father's house. I remember the warning, 'Look at the sky.' My Lord, you have lived too long in your country forest. You should have followed my father's example and sent off a few pupils to the philosophers and priests of the city of Florence."

"Don't mock me anymore," he said imploringly with the same well-bred restraint. "You are causing anger in me, Vittorio, and I have no room for it."

"Your time is short, old Demon," I said. "So make merry in your antiquated castle while you can."

Ursula cried out under her breath, but I wouldn't be stopped.

"You may have bought off the old generation of idiots who run the town right now," I said, "but if you don't think the worlds of Florence and Venice and Milan are not moving in on you more fiercely than you can ever prevent, you are dreaming. It's not men such as my father who are a threat to you, my Lord. It's the scholar with his books; it's the university astrologers and alchemists who'll move in on you; it's the modern age of which you know nothing, and they will hunt you down, like some old beast of legend, and drag you out of this lair in the heat of the sun and cut off your heads, all of you—."

"Kill him!" There came a female voice from those who watched.

"Destroy him now," said a man.

"He isn't fit for the coop!" screamed another.

"He's unworthy to be kept in the coop for a moment, or even to be sacrificed."

Then a whole chorus let loose with demands for my death.

"No," cried Ursula, throwing out her arms to the Lord. "Florian, I beg you!"

"Torture, torture, torture," they began to chant, first two and three and then four.

"My Lord," said the Elder, but I could scarce hear his voice, "he's only a boy. Let us put him in the coop with the rest of the flock. In a night or two he won't remember his name. He'll be as tame and plump as the others."

"Kill him now," screamed one voice over all. And: "Be done with him," cried others, their demands rising ever louder in volume.

There came a piercing shout seconded at once:

"Tear him limb from limb. Now. Do it."

"Yes, yes, yes!" It was like the beat of battle drums.

7

THE COOP

ODRIC, the Elder, shouted loudly for silence, right at the moment that numerous rather glacial hands had tightened on my arms.

Now, once in Florence I had seen a man torn apart by a mob. I'd been far too close for my own desire to the spectacle, and had been nearly trampled in the efforts of those who, like me, wanted to get away.

So it was no fantasy to me that such could happen. I was as resigned to it as I was to any other form of death, believing, I think, as powerfully in my anger and my rectitude as I did in death.

But Godric ordered the blood drinkers back, and the entire pallid-faced company withdrew with a courtly grace that bordered upon the coy and the cloying, heads bowed or turned to one side, as if a moment before they had not been party to a rabble.

I kept my eyes fixed on the Lord, whose face now showed such a heat that it appeared near human, the blood pulsating in his thin cheeks, and his mouth as dark as a dried blood scar, for all its pleasing shape. His dark golden hair seemed almost brown, and his blue eyes were filled with pondering and concern.

"I say that he be put in with the others," said Godric, the bald Elder.

At once, Ursula's sobs broke forth, as though she could not restrain herself any longer. I looked over to see her, her head bowed, her hands struggling to completely shield her face, and, through the creases of her long fingers, droplets of blood falling as though her tears were made of it.

"Don't cry," I said, not even thinking about the wisdom of it. "Ursula, you have done all you can. I am impossible."

Godric turned and looked at me with one thickly creased raised eyebrow. This time I was close enough to see that his bald white head did have such hairs to it, scant eyebrows of gray as thick and ugly as old splinters.

Ursula brought up a rose-colored napkin from the fold of her long high-waisted French gown, a pale pink tissue of a thing stitched on the edges with green leaves and pink flowers, and on this she wiped her lovely red tears and looked at me, as if she were crushed with longing.

"My predicament is impossible," I said to her. "You've done all you can to save me. If I could, I would put my arms around you to protect you from this pain. But this beast here is holding me hostage."

There were outraged gasps and murmurs from the still dark-garbed company, and in a blur I allowed myself to see the thin, gaunt, bone-white faces that lined the long board on either side of the Lord, to glance at some of the Ladies who were so Frenchified in their old headdresses and wimples of rose red that they had not a single hair visible. There seemed both a Frankish absurdity and delicacy to them, and of course they were all demons.

The bald Elder, Godric, only chuckled.

"Demons," I said, "such a collection."

"The coop, my Lord," said Godric, the bald one. "With the others, and then I may make my suggestions to you in private, and with Ursula we shall talk. She grieves unduly."

"I do!" she cried. "Please, Florian, if only because I have never asked anything of this sort, and you know it."

"Yes, Ursula," said the Lord, in the softest voice which had issued from his lips yet. "I know that, my loveliest flower. But this boy is recalcitrant, and his family, when from time to time they had the advantage over those of us who wandered from here to hunt, destroyed those unfortunate members of our tribe. It happened more than once."

"Marvelous!" I cried out. "How brave, how wondrous, what a gift you give me."

The Lord was astonished and annoyed.

But Ursula hurried forward, in a flurry of dark shadowy velvet skirts, and leaned over the polished table to be close to him. I could see only her hair in its long thick braids, twined exquisitely with red velvet ribbons, and the shape of her gorgeous arms, so perfectly narrow and plump at the same time, enchanted me against my own will.

"To the coop, please, my Lord," she begged, "and let me have him at least for so many nights as I need to reconcile my heart to this. Let him be admitted tonight for the Midnight Mass, and let him wonder."

I made no answer to this. I merely memorized it.

Two of the company, clean-shaven men in court dress, suddenly appeared at my side, to assist Godric, it seemed, in having me taken off.

Before I knew what was to befall me, a soft binding of cloth was put over my eyes. I was sightless.

"No, let me see!" I cried out.

"The coop then, it is, very well," came the Lord's voice, and I felt myself being taken away from the room, fast, as if the feet of those who escorted me scarcely needed to touch the floor.

The music rose again, in an eerie throb, but I was mercifully being escorted away from it. Only Ursula's voice accompanied me as I was carried up staircases, my feet now and then bruised coarsely on the steps, and the fingers that held me carelessly hurting me.

"Be quiet, please, Vittorio, don't struggle, be my brave one now in silence."

"And why, my love?" I asked. "Why set your heart on me? Can you kiss me without your stinging teeth?"

"Yes, and yes, and yes," she said in my ear.

I was being dragged along a passage. I could hear a loud mingled chorus of voices, common ordinary speech, and the wind of the outdoors and a wholly different kind of music.

"What is this? Where do we go?" I asked.

Behind me, I heard doors shut, and then the blindfold was ripped from my eyes.

"This is the coop, Vittorio," she said, pressing her arm against mine and trying to whisper in my ear. "This is where victims are kept until needed."

We stood on a high barren stone landing, the stairs leading down and at a curve into the huge courtyard, which contained so much activity and of such bizarre sorts that I could not possibly comprehend all of it immediately.

We were high within the walls of the castle, that I knew. And the courtyard itself was enclosed on all four sides, and I could see as I looked up that the walls were faced in white marble and there were everywhere the narrow pointed twin-arched windows of the French style. And above, the heavens had a bright pulsing glow, fed no doubt by countless fluttering torches on the roofs and abutments of the castle.

This was all nothing much to my eyes, except that it meant escape was impossible, for the nearest windows were far too high, and the marble too smooth to be scaled in any physical way.

There were many tiny balconies overhanging above, and they too were impossibly high. I saw the pale red-clothed demons on those balconies looking down at me, as though my introduction were a spectacle. There were some very large porches, and these too had their idle gloating and merciless occupants.

Damn them all, I thought.

What stunned me and fascinated me was the great jumble of human beings and dwellings which I saw crowding the courtyard before me.

First of all, it was far more fiercely illuminated than the ghastly Court, where I had just stood trial, if it could be called such, and it was an entire world unto itself—a rectangular court planted with dozens of olive trees and other flowering trees, orange trees, lemon trees, and all of these strung with lanterns.

It was an entire little world full of what seemed to be drunken and confused persons. Bodies, some half-naked, others fully and even richly clothed, shuffled, stumbled or lay about with no purpose. Everyone was filthy, disheveled, degraded.

There were hovels all over, like old-fashioned peasant huts of mere straw, and open wooden shacks, and little stone enclaves, and trellised gardens and countless circuitous pathways.

It was a drunken labyrinth of a garden gone wild under the naked night.

The fruit trees grew thick in clusters and then broke open to reveal grassy places where people merely lay staring at the stars, as if they were dozing, though their eyes were open.

Myriad flowering vines covered wire enclosures that seemed to have no purpose but to create some alcove of privacy, and there were giant cages full of fat birds, aye, birds, and cooking fires scattered about—and big kettles simmering on beds of coals, from which a deeply spiced fragrance arose.

Kettles! Yes, full of broth.

I saw that a foursome of demons roamed about—there may have been more—scrawny-limbed and bleached as their Lords, and forced to the same blood-red dress, only they were in shapeless garments no better than rags—peasant garb.

Two tended a pot of the simmering broth or soup or whatever it was, whilst another swept with a big old broom, and yet another carried on his hip indifferently a small mewling human toddler, whose head rolled painfully on his weak neck.

It was more grotesque and disturbing than the hideous Court below, with its stately cadaverous mock aristocrats.

"It's stinging my eyes," I said. "I can feel the smoke rising from the kettles." It was a pungent delicious mingling of fragrances. I could identify many of the rich cooking spices, and the smell of mutton and beef, but there were other more exotic flavors intermingled with it.

Everywhere human beings were in this hopeless daze. Children, old women, the famed cripples who never appeared in the town below, hunchbacks, and little twisted bodies which had never grown to full size, and big hulking men as well, bearded and swart, and boys my age or older—all of them shuffling about or lying about, but dazed, and crazy, and looking up at us, and blinking and pausing as though our presence should mean something though they could not make out what.

I swayed on the landing, and Ursula held my arm. I felt ravenous as the heavy fumes filled my nostrils.

Hunger, hunger such as I'd never known. No, it was a pure thirst for the soup, as though there were no food that was not liquid.

Suddenly the two gaunt and aloof men who had not left us—they who had blindfolded me and dragged me here—turned and went down the steps, letting their heels make a sharp marching sound on the stones.

A few eager cries came up from the great mottled and scattered assemblage. Heads turned. Sluggish bodies tried to rouse themselves from the vaporous torpor.

The two Lords, with their long trailing sleeves and stiff backs, marched together as if they were kinsmen as they approached the first of the visible cauldrons.

I watched as drunken mortals gathered themselves up and stumbled towards the red-clad Lords. As for the red-clad Lords, they seemed to glory in mystifying all.

"What are they doing? What will they do?" I was sick. I was going to fall. Yet how sweet this soup smelled, and how much I wanted it. "Ursula," I said. But I didn't know what words to make to follow this prayer of her name.

"I'm holding you, my love, this is the coop. Look, do you see?"

Through a haze, I saw the Lords pass beneath the jagged thorny branches of the blooming orange trees, where fruit hung still, as though none of these swollen, lethargic souls needed such a fresh and bright thing as an orange.

The Lords took up a stance on either side of this

first kettle, and each, extending a right hand, slashed his right wrist with a knife which he held in his left hand, and let the blood flow copiously into the brew.

A weak happy cry rose from those humans gathering meekly around them.

"Oh, damnable, it's the blood, of course," I whispered. I would have fallen if Ursula had not taken hold of me. "The brew is spiced with blood."

One of the Lords turned away, as though the smoke and the fumes disgusted him, yet he allowed himself to bleed into the mix. Then turning swiftly, almost crossly, he reached out to snatch by the arm one of the thin, weak-looking white demons in peasant garb.

He caught the poor fellow and dragged him to the kettle. The thin paltry demon begged and whined to be allowed to be free, but his wrists were both slashed, and now, though he turned his bony face away, he was bled furiously into the soup.

"Ah, you are better than Dante with your circles of Hell, aren't you?" I said. But it hurt me that I had taken such a tone with her.

She supported me utterly.

"They are peasants, yes, they dream of being Lords, and if they obey, they might."

I recalled now that the demon soldiers who had brought me back to the castle had been rude huntsmen. How well it was all thought out, but this, my narrow-shouldered love, with her soft yielding arms and her shining tear-stained face, was a pure Lady, was she not?

"Vittorio, I want so badly for you not to die."

"Do you, dearest?" I said. I had my arms around her. I could no longer stand without this support.

My vision was fading.

Yet with my head against her shoulder, my eyes directed to the crowd below, I could see the human beings surrounding the kettles and dipping their cups into the brew, dipping their cups right where the blood had fallen, and then blowing on the hot liquid to cool it before they drank.

A soft, horrid laughter echoed up the walls. I think it came from those spectators above on the balconies.

There was a sudden swirl of red color, as if a giant unfurling flag had fallen.

But it was a Lady dropping down from the remote heights above, to land amid the worshipful hordes of the coop.

They bowed and saluted her, and backed away from her, and gave forth loud gasps of awe as she too approached the kettle and, with a loud rebellious laugh, cut her wrist and fed her blood into it.

"Yes, my darlings, my little chicks," she declared. She looked up at us.

"Come down, Ursula, have pity on our hungry little world; be generous tonight. So it is not your night to give; give in honor of our new acquisition."

Ursula seemed shamed by all of this, and held me gently with her long fingers. I looked into her eyes.

"I'm drunk, drunk merely from the fragrance."

"My blood is only for you now," she whispered.

"Give it to me then, I hunger for it, I'm weak to dying," I said. "Oh, God, you've brought me to this. No, no, I did it myself."

"Sshhh, my lover, my sweet," she said.

Her arm coiled about my waist, and there came just under my ear her tender lips sucking on the flesh, as if she meant to make a pucker there on my neck, warm it with her tongue, and then the prick of her teeth.

I felt ravaged, and with both hands in a fantasy I reached out for her figure as we ran together through the meadow which belonged only to us and to which these others could never be admitted.

"Oh, innocent love," she said even as she drank from me, "oh, innocent innocent love."

Then a sudden icy hot fire entered the wound in my neck, and I felt it as if it were a delicate parasite of long tendrils that once inside my body could find the most remote reaches of me.

The meadow spread out around us, vast and cool, and utterly given over to the blowing lilies. Was she with me? Beside me? It seemed in one radiant instant I stood alone and heard her cry out as if she were behind me.

I meant, within this ecstatic dream, this fluttering cooling dream of blue skies and tender breaking stems, to turn and go to her. But out of the corner of my eyes, I beheld something of such splendor and magnificence that my soul leapt.

"Look, yes, you see!"

My head fell back. The dream was gone. The high white marble walls of the prison castle rose above my hurting gaze. She held me and stared down at me, bewildered, her lips bloody.

She hoisted me in her arms. I was as helpless as a child. She carried me down the stairs, and there was nothing I could do to rouse my limbs.

It seemed all the world above was tiny figures ranging on balconies and battlements and laughing and pointing with their tiny outstretched hands, so dark against the torches all around them.

Blood red, smell it.

"But what was it; did you see it in the field?" I asked her.

"No!" she cried. She looked so frightened.

I lay on a heap of hay, a makeshift bed, and the poor underfed demon peasant boys stared stupidly down at me with bloodshot eyes, and she, she wept, her hands again to her face.

"I cannot leave him here," she said.

She was far, far away. I heard people crying. Was there a revolt among the drugged and the damned? I heard people weeping.

"But you will, and come to the kettle first and give your blood."

Who spoke those words?

I didn't know.

". . . time for the Mass."

"You won't take him tonight."

"Why are they crying?" I asked. "Listen, Ursula, they've all started crying."

One of the scrawny boys stared right into my eyes. He had a hand on the back of my neck and a warm cup of brew to my mouth. I didn't want it to slop down my chin. I drank and drank. It filled my mouth.

"Not tonight," came Ursula's voice. Kisses on my forehead, on my neck. Someone snatched her away. I felt her hand hold tight to mine, then I felt her pulled away.

"Come now, Ursula, leave him."

"Sleep, my darling," she cried in my ear. I felt her skirts brushing me. "Vittorio, sleep."

The cup was thrown aside. Stupidly, in utter intoxication I watched the contents spill and sink darkly into the mounded hay. She knelt before me, her mouth open and tender and luscious and red.

She took my face in her cool hands. The blood poured out of her mouth and into mine.

"Oh, love," I said. I wanted to see the field. It didn't come. "Let me see the field! Let me see it!"

But there was no meadow, only the shocking sight of her face again, and then a dimming light, a gathering embrace of darkness and sound. I could no longer fight. I could no longer speak. I could no longer remember . . . But someone had said that very thing.

And the crying. It was so sad. Such crying, such doleful, helpless weeping.

When next I opened my eyes, it was morning. The sun hurt me, and my head ached unbearably.

A man was on top of me, trying to get my clothes off me. Drunken fool. I turned over, dizzy and sick, sick to vomiting, and threw him off, and with a sound blow knocked him senseless.

I tried to get up but I couldn't. The nausea was

intolerable. All around me others slept. The sun hurt my eyes. It scalded my skin. I snuggled into the hay. The heat beat down on my head, and when I ran my own fingers through my hair, my hair felt hot. The pain in my head throbbed in my ears.

"Come into the shelter," a voice said. It was an old crone, and she beckoned to me from beneath a thatched roof. "Come in, where it's cool."

"Curse you all," I said. I slept. I drifted.

Sometime during the late afternoon I came to my senses.

I found myself on my knees near one of the kettles. I was drinking in a slovenly wretched manner from a bowl of brew. The old woman had given it to me.

"The demons," I said. "They are asleep. We can . . . we can . . ." but then the futility of it overcame me. I wanted to throw away the cup, but I drank the hot brew.

"It's not just blood, it's wine, it's good wine," said the old woman. "Drink it, my boy, and feel no pain. They'll kill you soon enough. It's not so terrible."

When it was dark again, I knew it.

I rolled over.

I could fully open my eyes, and they did not hurt as they had in the day.

I knew that I had lost the whole arc of the sun in this drugged and stupid and disastrous languor. I had fallen into their plans. I had been helpless when I should have been trying to rouse these useless ones around me to mutiny. Good God, how could I have let it happen! Oh, the sadness, the dim distant sadness . . . And the sweetness of slumber.

"Wake, boy."

A demon voice.

"They want you tonight."

"Oh, and who wants me for what?" I asked. I looked up. The torches were alight. All was twinkling and glowing, and there came the soft rustle of green leaves overhead—the sharp sweet smell of the orange trees. The world was woven of dancing flames above and the entrancing patterns of the black leaves. The world was hunger and thirst.

The brew simmered, and that scent blotted out all else. I opened my mouth for it, though there was none of it near me.

"I'll give it to you," said the demon voice. "But sit up. I must clean you up. You must look good for tonight."

"For what?" I said. "All of them are dead."

"Who?"

"My family."

"There is no family here. This is the Court of the Ruby Grail. You are the property of the Lord of the Court. Now, come, I have to prepare you."

"For what do you prepare me?"

"For the Mass, you're to go, get up," said the demon, who stood wearily over me, leaning on his broom, his shining hair an elfin mess around his face. "Get up, boy. They'll want you. It's almost midnight."

"No, no, not almost midnight, no!" I cried out. "No!"

"Don't be afraid," he said, coldly, wearily. "It's useless."

"But you don't understand, it's the loss of time, the loss of reason, the loss of hours during which my heart beat and my brain slept! I'm not afraid, you miserable demon!"

He held me flat to the hay. He washed my face.

"There, there, you are a handsome fine one. They always sacrifice those such as you right away. You're too strong, too fine of limb and face. Look at you, and the Lady Ursula dreaming of you and weeping for you. They took her away."

"Ah, but I was dreaming too . . ." I said. Was I talking to this monstrous attendant as though he and I were friends? Where was the great magnificent web of my dreams, the immense and luminous majesty?

"You can talk to me, why not?" he said. "You will die in rapture, my pretty young Lord," he said. "And you'll see the church all alight, and the Mass; you'll be the sacrifice."

"No, I dreamed of the meadow," I said. "I saw something in the meadow. No, it wasn't Ursula." I was talking to myself, to my own sick bedeviled mind, talking to my wits to make them listen. "I saw someone in the meadow, someone so . . . I can't . . ."

"You make things so painful for yourself," said the demon soothingly. "Here, I have all your buttons and buckles right. What a fine Lord you must have been."

Must have been, must have been, must have been . . .

"You hear that?" he asked.

"I hear nothing."

"It's the clock, striking the third quarter of the hour. It's almost time for the Mass. Don't pay attention to the noise. It's the others who'll be sacrificed. Don't let it unnerve you. Just so much common weeping."

8

REQUIEM, OR THE HOLY SACRIFICE OF THE MASS AS I HAD NEVER SEEN IT

HAD ever a chapel been more beautiful? Had ever white marble been used to such an advantage, and from which fount of eternal gold had come these glorious curlicues and serpentine adornments, these high-pointed windows, illuminated from without by fierce fires that brought into the perfection of jewels their tiny thick facets of tinted glass to form their solemn narrow and seemingly sacred pictures?

But they were not sacred pictures.

I stood in the choir loft, high above the vestibule, looking down over the great nave and at the altar at the far end. Once again I was flanked by ominous and regal Lords, who seemed now to be absolutely fervent in their duty as they held me firm and standing by the arms.

My mind had cleared, but only somewhat. The wet cloth was once again pressed to my eyes and forehead. The water was as if from a mountain stream of flowing melted snow.

In my sickness, in my fever, I saw everything.

I saw the demons fashioned in the glittering windows, as artfully put together of red and gold and blue glass as any angels or saints. I saw their leering faces as they peered down, these monsters with their webbed wings and clawlike hands, upon the congregation.

Below, allowing a broad central aisle, was gathered in its ruby dark finery the great Court on either side, standing to face the long heavily carved and broad Communion Rail and the high altar behind it.

Paintings covered the cove behind the altar. Demons dancing in Hell, graceful among the flames as though they bathed in a welcome radiance, and strung above them on loose and unfurling banners the golden letters from St. Augustine's words, so familiar to my study, that these flames were not the flames of real fire but only the absence from God, but the word "absence" had been replaced by the Latin word for "freedom."

"Freedom" was the word in Latin worked into the high white marble walls, in a frieze that ran beneath the balconies on either side of the church, on the same level as this, my place, in which more of the Court beheld the spectacle.

Light rose to flood the high-groined arches of the roof.

And what was this spectacle?

The high altar was draped in crimson trimmed in gilt fringe, its abundant cloths short enough to reveal the tableau in white carving of figures prancing in Hell, though from this great distance my eyes might have deceived me as to their levity.

What I did see with perfection were the thick candlesticks before not a crucifix but a huge carved stone replica of Lucifer, the fallen angel, long locks aflame, and garments too a torrent of rising fire, frozen in marble, and in his upraised hands the symbols of death—in the right the scythe of the grim reaper—and in the other the sword of the executioner.

I gasped when I beheld the image! Monstrous, it was positioned precisely where I wanted so to see my Crucified Christ, and yet in a moment of delirium and agitation, I felt my lips curl in a smile, and I heard my own mind tell me cunningly that there was nothing less grotesque about the Crucified God if He Himself had been there.

My guards held me firm. Had I tottered?

From the assemblage around me and behind me, from those whom I had not even regarded, there came suddenly the muted roll of drums, ominous and slow, mournful and beautiful in their own muffled simplicity.

At once there followed a deep-throated chorus of horns, in lovely weaving song and effortless sweet intermingling, playing not the repetitious chord music of the night before, but a strong plaintive and imploring polyphony of melodies so sad that they flooded my heart with sadness, stroked my heart and made the tears nearly spring to my eyes.

Oh, what is this? What is this blended and rich music, surrounding me and pouring forth into the nave to echo off the satiny marble and rebound gently and with perfect modulation to the place where I stood, staring, rapt at the distant figure of Lucifer?

At his feet, all flowers laid out in vessels of silver and gold were red, the red of roses and carnations, the red of the iris, the red of wildflowers I could not name, an altar alive and decked and crawling with all those things which were high color, his glorious tint, the one color left to him that might rise from his inevitable and unredeemable darkness.

I heard the dusty, sonorous songs of the reed shawm, the small oboe and the reed dulcian, and other small reed organs played by mouth, and then the more ringing tone of the brass sackbut horn, and perhaps even the light singing of the hammers striking the taut strings of the dulcimer.

This music alone might have engaged me, filled my soul, its threads of melody interweaving, overlapping, harmonizing and then drifting apart. It left me no breath to speak or eyes for other things. Yet I beheld the statues of the demons who ran from right to left—so like the Lords and Ladies of the Courtly table of last night—from the imposing figure of their Devil.

Were they blood drinkers all, these terrible gaunt saints of Hell, carved from hardwood with its own reddish mahogany glint, in their stark stylized garments, cleaving to thin bodies, their eyes half-lidded, their mouths open, and against each lower lip two white fangs, as if made from tiny bits of snow-white ivory to mark the purpose of each individual monster?

Oh, Cathedral of horrors. I tried to turn my head, to close my eyes, and yet the monstrosity of it enthralled me. Pathetic unformed thoughts never reached my lips.

The horns died around me, and the reedy woodland instruments died away. Oh, don't go, sweet music. Don't leave me here.

But what came was a chorus of the sweetest softest tenor voices; they called out the Latin words that I could not follow, an anthem for the dead, an anthem on the mutability of all things, and at once came a full lustrous harmonizing chorus of sopranos male and female, of basses and baritones, singing heartily in splendid polyphony in answer to these lone tenors:

"I go now to the Lord, for He has allowed these Creatures of Darkness to answer my supplications . . ."

What nightmarish words were these?

Once again there came the rich thick chorus of many voices to underscore the tenors:

"The instruments of death await me in their warm and devout kiss, and into their bodies, by the will of God, they shall take my life's blood, my rapture, my soul's ascent through their own, so as better to know both Heaven and Hell in their Dark Service."

The reed organ played its solemn song.

Into the Sanctuary of the church, there proceeded now, to the fullest most lustrous strength of the polyphony yet, a stream of priestly figures.

I saw the Lord Florian in a rich red chasuble as if he were the bishop of Florence himself, only this garment bore the Cross of Christ impudently upside down in honor of the Damned One, and on his untonsured head of dark blond hair he wore a gilded jeweled crown as if he were both Frankish monarch and servant of the Dark Lord.

The strong piercing notes of the horns dominated the song. A march had begun. The drums rumbled beneath, hushed and steady.

Florian had taken his place before the altar with his face to the congregation, and on one side of him stood the fragile Ursula, her hair full and loose and down on her shoulders, though shrouded like a Mary Magdalene in a scarlet veil which hung to the very edge of the hem of her tapering gown.

Her upturned face was directed to me, and I could see even from this great airy span that her hands, shaped as a steeple, with fingers pressed together, trembled.

On the other side of this high priest Florian stood his bald Elder, in his own chasuble and thick embroidered lace sleeves, another priestly assistant.

Acolytes came from either side, tallish young demons with faces of the usual chiseled ivory, and the simple surplices of those who attend the Mass. They took their positions ranked down the long marble Communion Rail.

Once again, there rose the magnificent chorus of voices around me, falsettos mingling with true sopranos and the throbbing basses of the males, as redolent of the woodlands as the wooden horns, and beneath it all the heavy driving brass declaration.

What did they mean to do? What was this hymn which now the tenors sang, and what was the answer that came from all the voices so close to me, the words in Latin unstrung and only incoherently enveloping me:

"Lord, I am come into the Valley of Death; Lord,

I am come to the end of my Sorrow; Lord, in thy deliverance I give life to those who would be idle in Hell were it not for thy divine plan."

My soul rebelled. I loathed it, and yet I could not look away from the spectacle below. My eyes swept the church. I saw for the first time the gaunt, demonic fanged demons on their pedestals rising between the narrow windows, and everywhere the glint of racks upon racks of tiny candles.

The music broke again for the solemn declaration of the tenors:

"Let the fount be brought forward, that those who are our sacrifices should be washed clean."

And it was done.

Ranks of young demons in their guise as Altar Boys came forward, carrying with them in their preternaturally strong hands a magnificent baptismal fount of deep-pink Carrara marble. This they set some ten feet before the Communion Rail.

"Oh, abominations, to make it so beautiful," I whispered.

"Quiet now, my young one," said the regal guard beside me. "Watch, for what you see here you will never see between Heaven and Earth again, and as you will go unconfessed to God, you will burn in darkness forever."

He sounded as if he believed it.

"You have no power to damn my soul," I whispered, trying in vain to clear my eyes, not to so love the weakness that still caused me to depend upon their clamping hands.

"Ursula, farewell," I whispered, making of my lips a kiss.

But in this miraculous and private little moment, seemingly unnoticed by the whole congregation, I saw her head shake in a small secretive negation.

No one saw because all eyes were now on another spectacle, far more tragic than any of the controlled and modulated ritual we had beheld.

Up the aisle, driven by acolyte demons in tunics of red and lace sleeves trimmed in red and gold, there came a poor wretched sampling of the lost ones of the coop, shuffling old women, drunken men and little boys, mere children, clinging to the very demons who escorted them to their deaths, like piteous victims of some horrid old trial where the offspring of the condemned are led to execution with their parents. Horror.

"I curse you all. I damn you. God, bring down your justice on this," I whispered. "God, bring down your tears. Weep for us, Christ, that this is happening."

My eyes turned up in my head. It seemed I dreamed, and once again came the bright green limitless meadow to my eyes, and once again, as Ursula ran from me, as her spirited young form rushed across the high breaking field of grass and lilies, there rose another figure, another familiar figure—.

"Yes, I see you!" I cried out to this vision in my half-rescued dream.

But no sooner had I recognized it, locked to it, than it vanished; it was gone, and with it was gone all comprehension of it, all memory of its exquisite face and form and its meaning, its pure and powerful meaning. Words fled from me.

From below I saw the Lord Florian look up, angered, silent. The hands beside me dug into my flesh.

"Silence," said the guards next to me, their commands overlapping one another.

The lovely music rose higher and higher, as though the climbing soprano voices and the throbbing, winding horns would hush me now and pay tribute only to the unholy baptism.

The baptism had begun. The first victim, an ancient woman of bent and bony back, had been stripped of her poor garments and washed with handfuls of water in the fount, and now was led to the Communion Rail, oh, so frail, so unprotected by her kith and kin and her guardian angels!

Oh, and now to see the children stripped, to see their tiny little legs and buttocks bare, to see their bony shoulders, those tiny parts where it seemed the winglets of baby angels once sprouted from their backs, to see them washed and then delivered to stand trembling along the stretch of marble balustrade.

It happened very fast.

"Cursed animals, for that is what you are, not airy demons, no!" I muttered, struggling in the grasp of the two loathsome minions. "Yes, cowardly minions, both of you, to be a party to this evil."

The music drowned out my prayers. "Dear God, send my angels to me," I said to my heart, my secret heart, "send my wrathful angels, send them with your fiery sword. God, this cannot be borne."

The Communion Rail now had its full complement of victims, naked and trembling all, and blazing with carnal human color against the luminous marble and the colorless priests.

The candles flickered on the giant Lucifer, with its great webbed wings, who presided over all.

The Lord Florian now stepped down to take the first Communicant in his hands, and lowered his lips to drink.

The drums beat fierce and sweet, and the voices twined and reached to Heaven. But there was no Heaven here beneath these branching white columns, these groined arches. There was nothing but death.

All the Court had begun to make two streams along the sides of the chapel marching silently up to come behind the Communion Rail, where each might take a victim from those who stood helpless and ready, and now Lord and Lady chose which they wanted, and some shared, and one victim was passed from one to another, and so on it went, this mockery, this lurid, predatory Communion.

Only Ursula did not move.

The Communicants were dying. Some were already dead. None struck the floor. Their pliant dried-up limbs were captured silently and deftly by the attendant demons, and bodies were whisked away.

More victims were still being bathed. Others were taken to the Rail. On it went.

The Lord Florian drank again and again, one child after another put before him, his slender fingers capturing the small neck and holding it as he bent his lips.

I wonder what Latin words he dared to speak.

Slowly the members of the Court slipped out of the Sanctuary, moving down the side aisles again to pivot and take their old stance. They had had their fill.

All through the room the color of blood infused once pallid faces, and it seemed to my misted vision, to my head so full of the loveliness of song, that they all were human now, human for this little while.

"Yes," said Florian, his voice arching out soft and sure to my ears over the length of the nave. "Human now for this one instant, with the blood of the living, incarnated again, we are, young prince. You have understood it."

"Ah, but Lord," I said, in my exhausted whisper, "I do not forgive it."

An interval of silence fell. Then the tenors declared:

"It is time, and the midnight hour is not finished."

The sure and tight hands in which I was held focused me now to the side. I was spirited out of the choir loft and down the winding screw stairs of white marble.

As I came to myself, still supported, staring up the center aisle, I saw that only the baptistry fount remained. All victims were gone.

But a great cross had been brought into the hall. It had been positioned *upside down*, to one side of the altar, and forward, at the Communion Rail.

The Lord Florian held up for me to see five huge iron nails in his hand, and beckoned for me to come.

The cross was anchored into place, as though it had often been brought to this spot. It was made of rich hardwood, thick, heavy and polished smooth, though it bore the marks of other nails, and no doubt the stains of other blood.

The very bottom of it fitted right at the Railing itself against the marble banister, so that he who was to be crucified would be three feet above the floor and visible to all the worshippers.

"The worshippers, you filthy lot!" I laughed. Thank God and all his angels that the eyes of my father and mother were filled with celestial light and could see nothing of this crude degradation.

The Elder revealed to me in his outstretched hands two golden goblets.

I knew the meaning. With these, to catch my blood as it gushed from the wounds made by the nails.

He bowed his head.

I was forced up the aisle. The statue of Lucifer grew immense behind the glittering pontifical figure of Florian. My feet did not touch the marble. All around me the members of the Court turned to attend my progress, but never so much that their eyes were not upon their Lord.

Before the baptismal fount my face was washed.

I tossed my head, twisting my neck, throwing the water impudently on those who tried to bathe me. The acolytes were in fear of me. They approached and reached hesitantly for my buckles.

"Strip him," said the Lord, and once again he held up the nails for me to see.

"I see well enough, my cowardly Lord," I said. "It is nothing to crucify a boy such as me. Save your soul, Lord, do that! And all your Court will wonder."

The music swelled from the loft above. The chorus came again, answering and underscoring the anthem of the tenors.

There were no words for me now; there was only candlelight and the knowledge that my clothes were about to be taken from me, and that this horror would take place, this evil inverted crucifixion, never sanctified by St. Peter himself, for the inverted cross not now to be a symbol of the Evil One.

Suddenly the trembling hands of the acolytes withdrew.

Above, the horns played their most beautiful poignant melody.

The tenors hurled out their question, in flawless voices, from the loft above:

"Can this one not be saved? Can this one not be delivered?"

The chorus rose, in unison:

"Can this one not be released from the power of Satan?"

Ursula stepped forward and drew from her head the immense long red veil that hung to her feet, and threw it out so that it descended like a cloud of red around her. Beside her, an acolyte appeared with my very sword in his hand, and my daggers.

Once again the tenor voices implored:

"One soul released to go forth into the world, mad, and bearing witness only to the most patient ears to the power of Satan."

The chorus sang, a riot of melody erupting from them, and it seemed a swift affirmation had overtaken their song.

"What, not to die!" I said. I strained to see the

face of the Lord in whose hands all of this rested. But he was blocked from my view.

Godric the Elder had come between. Opening the gate of the marble Communion Rail with his knee, he moved down the aisle towards me. He thrust one of his golden cups to my lips.

"Drink and forget, Vittorio, else we lose her heart and her soul."

"Oh, but then you must lose it!"

"No!" she screamed. "No." Over his shoulder, I could see her snatch three of the nails from Florian's left hand and fling them out on the marble. The singing rose high and rich under the arches. I couldn't hear the nails strike the stone.

The sound of the choir was jubilant, celebratory. The mournful tones of requiem were gone.

"No, God, if you would save her soul, then take me to the cross, take me!"

But the golden cup was forced to my lips. My jaws were opened by Ursula's hand, and the liquid poured down my throat. I saw my sword lifted before my closing eyes as if it were a cross, the long hilt, the handles.

Soft mocking laughter rose and blended with the magical and indescribable beauty of the choir.

Her red veil swirled about me. I saw the red fabric rise up in front of me. I felt it come down around me like a spellbinding shower, full of her perfume, soft with her tenderness.

"Ursula, come with me . . ." I whispered.

Those were my last words.

"Cast out," cried the swelling voices above. "Cast out . . ." cried the huge choir, and it seemed the Court sang with the chorus, "Cast out," and my eyes closed as the red fabric covered my face, as it came down like a witch's web over my struggling fingers and sealed itself over my open mouth.

The horns blared forth the truth. "Forgiven! Cast out!" sang the voices.

"Cast out to madness," whispered Godric in my ear. "To madness all of your days, and you, you might have been one of us."

"Yes, one of us," came Florian's smooth unperturbed whisper.

"Fool that you were," said Godric. "You might have been immortal."

"One of us forever, immortal, imperishable, to reign here in glory," said Florian.

"Immortality or death," said Godric, "and these were choices royal, but you shall wander witless and scorned through the world."

"Yes, witless and scorned," came a childish voice at my ear. And then another, "Witless and scorned."

"Witless and scorned," said Florian.

But the choir sang on, obliterating all sting from their words, its delirious hymn growing ever more tremendous in my half-slumber.

"A fool to wander the world in contempt," said Godric.

Blinded, sealed in the softness of the veil, intoxicated by the drink, I could not answer them. I think I smiled. Their words were too senselessly mingled with the sumptuous soothing voices of the choir. And fools that they were, they had never known that what they said simply had not mattered.

"And you could have been our young prince."

Was it Florian at my side? Cool, dauntless Florian. "We could have loved you as she loves you."

"A young prince," said Godric, "to rule here with us forever."

"Become the jester of alchemists and old wives," said Florian sadly, solemnly.

"Yes," said a childish voice, "fool to leave us."

How wondrous were the anthems that made their words mere sweet and contrapuntal syllables.

I think I felt her kiss through the silk. I think I felt it. I think. It seemed in the tiniest of feminine whispers, she said simply, without ceremony:

"My love." It had her triumph and her farewell within it.

Down, down, down into the richest, kindest sleep that God can give, I sank. The music gave a shape to my limbs, gave air to my lungs, when all other senses had been abandoned.

9

ANGELS WE HAVE HEARD ON HIGH

IT was pouring down rain. No, the rain had stopped. They still couldn't understand me.

I was surrounded by these men. We were right near Fra Filippo's workshop. I knew this street. I'd just been here with my father a year ago.

"Speak more slowly. Corrr . . . blub, it doesn't make sense!"

"Look," said the other one. "We want to help you. Tell me your father's name. Speak it slowly."

They shook their heads. I thought I was making perfect sense, I could hear it, Lorenzo di Raniari, why couldn't they hear it, and I was his son, Vittorio di Raniari. But I could feel my lips, how swollen they were. I knew I was filthy from the rain.

"Look, take me to Fra Filippo's shop. I know them there," I said. My great painter, my passionate and tormented painter, his apprentices would know me. He would not, but the helpers who had seen me weep that day at his work. And then, then, these men would take me to the house of Cosimo in the Via del Largo.

"Fee, fee?" they said. They repeated my clumsy attempts at speech. I had failed again.

I started towards the workshop. I staggered and almost fell. These were honest men. I had the heavy bags over my right shoulder, and my sword was clanking against me, practically throwing me off balance. The high walls of Florence were closing in on me. I almost hit the stones.

"Cosimo!" I shouted at the top of my voice.

"We can't take you to Cosimo like this! Cosimo won't see you."

"Ah, you understand; you heard me."

But the man now cocked his ear. An honest merchant, drenched to the skin in his somber green robes, and all because of me no doubt. I wouldn't come in out of the rain. No sense. They'd found me lying in the rain right in the middle of the Piazza della Signoria.

"It's coming back, it's coming clear."

I saw the entrance to Fra Filippo's workshop up ahead. The shutters were being taken down. They were opening it up now that the thunderous storm had ceased, and the water was drying up on the stone streets. People were coming out.

"Those men in there," I shouted.

"What, what are you saying?"

Shrugs all around, but they aided me. An old man held my elbow.

"We should take him to San Marco, let the monks care for him."

"No, no, no, I need to talk to Cosimo!" I shouted.

Again, they shrugged and shook their heads.

Suddenly I stopped. I rocked and steadied myself by rudely grabbing hold of the younger man's shoulder.

I stared at the distant workshop.

The street was no more than an alleyway here, barely sufficient for horses to pass and for the pedestrians not to be injured, and the stone facades all but closed out the slate-gray sky above. Windows were opened, and it seemed that a woman could reach across upstairs and touch the house opposite her.

But look what was there, right before the shop.

I saw them. I saw the two of them! "Look," I said again. "Do you see them?"

The men couldn't see. Lord, the two figures before the shop were bright as if illuminated from within their flushed skin and loosely girdled robes.

I held the shoulder bags over my left shoulder and put my hand on my sword. I could stand, but my eyes must have been wide as plates staring blindly at what I beheld.

The two angels were arguing. The two angels, with their wings moving ever so slightly in time with their words and their gestures, were arguing with each other where they stood, right before the shop.

They stood oblivious to all humans who passed them and couldn't see them, and they argued one with another, both angels blond, both angels I knew, I knew these angels, I knew them from the paintings of Fra Filippo, and I could hear their voices.

I knew the rolled curls of the one, whose head was crowned with a wreath of small perfectly matched flowerlets, his loose mantle crimson, his undergarment a bright clear sky blue trimmed in gold.

And the other, I knew him as well, knew his bare head and soft shorter hair, and his golden collar, and the insignia on his mantle, and the thick bands of ornament on his wrists.

But above all I knew their faces, their innocent pink-tinged faces, their serene full yet narrow eyes.

The light melted down, somber and stormy still, though the sun was burning up there behind the gray sky. My eyes began to water.

"Look at their wings," I whispered.

The men couldn't see.

"I know the wings. I know them both, look, the angel with the blond hair, the ringlets in rows coming down his head, it's from the *Annunciation,* and the wings, his wings are made like the peacock, brilliantly blue, and the other, his feathers are tipped in the purest dust of gold."

The angel with the crown of flowers gestured excitedly to the other; from a mortal man, the gestures, the posture, would have evinced anger, but it was nothing so heated as that. The angel was only seeking to be understood.

I moved slowly, pulling loose of my helpful companions, who couldn't see what I saw!

What did they think I stared at? The gaping shop, the apprentices in the deep shadows within, the meager half-tinted flashes of canvases and panels, the yawning mouth beyond which the work was carried out.

The other angel shook his head somberly. "I don't go along with it," he said in the most serene and lilting voice. "We can't go that far. Do you think this doesn't make me weep?"

"What?" I cried out. "What makes you weep?"

Both angels turned. They stared at me. In unison, they collected their dark, multicolored and spectacled wings close to themselves, as though they meant to shrink thereby into invisibility, but they were no less visible to me, shining, both so fair, so recognizable. Their eyes were full of wonder as they gazed at me. Wonder at the sight of me?

"Gabriel!" I cried out. I pointed, "I know you, I know you from the *Annunciation*. You are both Gabriel, I know the paintings, I have seen you, Gabriel and Gabriel, how can it be?"

"He can see us," said the angel who had been gesturing so pointedly. His voice was subdued but seemed to reach my ears effortlessly and gently. "He can hear us," he said, and the wonder in his face increased, and he looked above all innocent and patient, and ever so gently concerned.

"What in the name of God are you saying, boy?" asked the old man beside me. "Now, collect your wits. You're carrying a fortune in your bags. Your hands are covered in rings. Now speak sensibly. I'll take you to your family, if you'll only tell me who they are."

I smiled. I nodded, but I kept my eyes fixed on the two startled and amazed angels. Their clothes appeared light, near translucent, as though the fabric were not of a natural weave any more than their incandescent skin was natural. All of their makeup was more rarefied, and fine-woven with light.

Beings of air, of purpose, made up of presence

and of what they do—were these the words of Aquinas coming back to me, the *Summa Theologica* on which I had learnt my Latin?

Oh, how miraculously beautiful they were, and so safely apart from all around them, standing transfixed in the street in their quiet wide-eyed simplicity, pondering as they gazed with compassion and interest at me.

One of them, the one crowned with flowers, the one who wore the sky-blue sleeves, the one who had so caught my heart when I had seen him in the *Annunciation* with my father, the one with whom I had fallen in love, moved towards me.

He became larger as he drew closer, taller, slightly larger all over than an ordinary being, and so full of love in the soundless shuffle of his loose and gracefully spilling clothes that he seemed more immaterial and monumentally solid, more perhaps the very expression of God's creation, than anything of flesh and blood might be.

He shook his head and smiled. "No, for you are yourself the very finest of God's creation," he said in a low voice that stole its way through the chatter that surrounded me.

He walked as if he were a mortal being, with clean naked feet over the wet dirty stones of the Florentine street, oblivious to the men who could not see him as he stood now so close to me, letting his wings spread out and then folding them again tight, so that I only saw the high feathered bones of them above his shoulders, which were sloped like those of a young boy.

His face was brilliantly clean and flushed with all

the radiant color Fra Filippo had painted. When he smiled, I felt my entire body tremble violently with unadulterated joy.

"Is this my madness, Archangel?" I asked. "Is this their curse come true, that I shall see this as I gibber and incur the scorn of learned men?" I laughed out loud.

I startled the gentlemen who had been trying so much to help me. They were thoroughly flustered. "What? Speak again?"

But in a shimmering instant, a memory descended upon me, illuminating my heart and soul and mind all in one stroke, as though the sun itself had flooded a dark and hopeless cell.

"It was you I saw in the meadow, you I saw when she drank my blood."

Into my eyes he looked, this cool collected angel, with the rows and rows of immaculate blond curls and the smooth placid cheeks.

"Gabriel, the Archangel," I said in reverence. The tears flooded to my eyes, and it felt like singing to cry.

"My boy, my poor wretched boy," said the old merchant. "There is no angel standing in front of you. Pay attention, now, please."

"They can't see us," said the angel to me simply. Again came his smooth easy smile. His eyes caught the light falling from the brightening sky as he peered into me, as if he would see deeper with every moment of his study.

"I know," I answered. "They don't know!"

"But I am not Gabriel, you must not call me that," he said very courteously and soothingly. "My young one, I am very far from being the Archangel Gabriel. I am Setheus, and I'm a guardian angel only."

He was so patient with me, so patient with my crying and with the collection of blind and concerned mortals around us.

He stood close enough for me to touch, but I didn't dare.

"My guardian angel?" I asked. "Is it true?"

"No," said the angel. "I am not your guardian angel. Those you must somehow find for yourself. You've seen the guardian angels of another, though why and how I don't know."

"Don't pray now," said the old man crankily. "Tell us who you are, boy. You said a name before, your father, tell us."

The other angel, who stood as if too shocked to move, suddenly broke his reserve and he too came forward in the same silent barefooted style, as though the roughened stones and the wet and dirt could not mar him or harm him.

"Can this be good, Setheus?" he asked. But his pale iridescent eyes were focused on me with the same loving attention, the same rapt and forgiving interest.

"And you, you are in the other painting, I know you too, I love you with my whole heart," I said.

"Son, to whom are you speaking?" demanded the younger man. "Whom do you love with your whole heart?"

"Ah, you can hear me?" I turned to the man. "You can understand me."

"Yes, now tell me your name."

"Vittorio di Raniari," I said, "friend and ally of

the Medici, son of Lorenzo di Raniari, Castello Raniari in the north of Tuscany, and my father is dead, and all my kinsmen. But—."

The two angels stood right before me, together, one head inclined towards the other as they regarded me, and it seemed that the mortals, for all their blindness, could not block the path of the angels' vision or come between me and them. If only I had the courage. I so wanted to touch them.

The wings of the one who'd spoken first were rising, and it seemed a soft shimmer of gold dust fell from the awakening feathers, the quivering, sparkling feathers, but nothing rivaled the angel's meditative and wondering face.

"Let them take you to San Marco," said this angel, the one named Setheus, "let them take you. These men mean well, and you will be put in a cell and cared for by the monks. You cannot be in a finer place, for this is a house under Cosimo's patronage, and you know that Fra Giovanni has decorated the very cell in which you'll stay."

"Setheus, he knows these things," said the other angel.

"Yes, but I am reassuring him," said the first angel with the simplest shrug, looking wonderingly at his companion. Nothing characterized their faces so much as subdued wonder.

"But you," I said, "Setheus, may I call you by name, you'll let them take me away from you? You can't. Please don't leave me. I beg you. Don't leave me."

"We have to leave you," said the other angel. "We are not your guardians. Why can't you see your own angels?"

"Wait, I know your name. I can hear it."

"No," said this more disapproving angel, waving his finger at me as if correcting a child.

But I would not be stopped. "I know your name. I heard it when you were arguing, and I hear it now when I look at your face. Ramiel, that's your name. And both of you are Fra Filippo's guardians."

"This is a disaster," whispered Ramiel, with the most touching look of distress. "How did this occur?"

Setheus merely shook his head, and smiled again generously. "It has to be for the good, it must be. We have to go with him. Of course we do."

"Now? Leave now?" demanded Ramiel, and again, for all the urgency, there was no anger. It was as though the thoughts were purified of all lower emotions, and of course it was so, it was perfectly so.

Setheus leaned close to the old man, who couldn't of course either see him or hear him, and he said in the old man's ear:

"Take the boy to San Marco; have him put in a goodly cell, for which he has plenty of money, and have him nursed to health."

Then he looked at me. "We'll go with you."

"We can't do that," said Ramiel. "We can't leave our charge; how can we do such a thing without permission?"

"It's meant to be. This is permission. I know that it is," said Setheus. "Don't you see what's happened? He's seen us and he's heard us and he's caught your name, and he would have caught mine if I hadn't revealed it. Poor Vittorio, we are with you."

I nodded, almost ready to weep at the sound of myself addressed. The whole street had gone drab and hushed and indistinct around their large, quiet and flushed figures, the finespun light of their garments stirring about them as if the celestial fabric were subject to the invisible currents of the air which men cannot feel.

"Those are not our real names!" said Ramiel scoldingly to me, but gently, as one would scold an infant.

Setheus smiled. "They are good enough names by which to call us, Vittorio," he said.

"Yes, take him to San Marco," said the man beside me. "Let's go. Let the monks handle all this."

The men rushed me towards the mouth of the street.

"You'll be very well cared for at San Marco," said Ramiel, as though he were bidding me farewell, but the two angels were moving beside us, and only falling a little behind.

"Don't you leave me, either of you, you can't!" I said to the angels.

They seemed perplexed, their lovely folded gossamer robes unstained by rain, the hems clean and shining as if they had not touched the street, and their bare feet looking so exquisitely tender as they followed at our pace.

"All right," said Setheus. "Don't worry so, Vittorio. We're coming."

"We can't simply leave our charge like this for another man, we can't do it," Ramiel continued to protest.

"It's God's will; how can it be otherwise?"

"And Mastema? We don't have to ask Mastema?" asked Ramiel.

"Why should we ask Mastema? Why bring care to Mastema? Mastema must know."

And there they were, arguing again, behind us, as I was hurried through the street.

The steel sky gleamed, then grew pale and gave way above to blue as we came to an open piazza. The sun shocked me, and made me sicken, yet how I wanted it, how I longed for it, and yet it rebuked me and seemed to scourge me as if it were a whip.

We were only a little ways from San Marco. My legs would soon give out. I kept looking over my shoulder.

The two lustrous, gilded figures came on, silently, with Setheus gesturing for me to go along.

"We're here, we're with you," said Setheus.

"I don't know about this, I don't know!" said Ramiel. "Filippo has never been in such trouble, he has never been subjected to such temptation, such indignity—."

"Which is why we have been drawn off now, so that we do not interfere with what must take place with Filippo. We know we were on the very verge of getting into trouble on account of Filippo and what Filippo has done now. Oh, Filippo, I see this, I see the grand design."

"What are they talking about?" I demanded of the men. "They're saying something about Fra Filippo."

"And who would that be, who is talking, may I ask?" said the old man, shaking his head as he escorted me along, the young madman in his charge with the clanking sword.

"My boy, be quiet now," said the other man, who took the larger burden of supporting me. "We can understand you only too well now, and you are making less sense than ever, talking to people that no one can see and hear."

"Fra Filippo, the painter, what's happening with him?" I demanded. "There's some trouble."

"Oh, it is unbearable," said the angel Ramiel behind me. "It is unthinkable that this should happen. And if you ask me, which no one has and no one will, I believe that if Florence were not at war with Venice, Cosimo de' Medici would protect his painter from this."

"But protect him from what?" I demanded. I looked into the eyes of the old man.

"Son, obey me," said the old man. "Walk straight, and stop banging me with that sword. You are a great Signore, I can see this, and the name of the Raniari rings loud in my ears from the distant mountains of Tuscany, and the gold on your right hand alone weighs more than the dowry of both of my daughters put together, not to mention the gems, but don't shout in my face."

"I'm sorry. I didn't mean to. It's only, the angels won't say precisely."

The other man who led me so kindly, who helped me honestly with the saddlebags in which was my fortune, and did not even seek to steal anything from me, began to speak:

"If you're asking about Fra Filippo, he's deep

into trouble again. He's being put to the torture. He's on the rack."

"No, that can't happen, not to Filippo Lippi!" I stopped dead and shouted. "Who would do such a thing to the great painter?"

I turned, and the two angels suddenly covered their faces, as tenderly as ever Ursula had covered hers, and they started weeping. Only their tears were marvelously crystalline and clear. They merely looked at me. Oh, Ursula, I thought with excruciating pain suddenly, how beautiful are these creatures, and in what grave do you sleep beneath the Court of the Ruby Grail that you cannot see them, cannot see their silent secret progress through the city streets?

"It's true," said Ramiel. "It's all too terribly true. What have we been, what sort of guardians, that Filippo has gotten himself into this trouble, that he is so contentious and deceiving, and why have we been so helpless?"

"We are only angels," said Setheus. "Ramiel, we do not have to accuse Filippo. We are not accusers, we are guardians, and for the sake of the boy who loves him, don't say such things."

"They can't torture Fra Filippo Lippi," I cried out. "Who did he deceive?"

"He did it to himself," said the old man. "He's into fraud this time. He sold off a commission, and everybody knows that one of his apprentices painted too much of the work. He's been put on the rack, but he didn't really get hurt."

"Didn't really hurt him! He's only magnificent!" I said. "You tell me they tortured him. Why was he tortured, how can anyone justify such a stupidity, such an insult, it's an insult to the Medici."

"Silence, child; he confessed," said the younger of the two mortal men. "It's almost over. Some monk if you ask me, Fra Filippo Lippi; if he isn't chasing women, he's in a brawl."

We had come to San Marco. We stood in the Piazza San Marco right before the doors of the monastery, which were flush with the street, as was the case with all such buildings in Florence, as if the Arno never overflowed its banks, which it did. And I was glad, oh, so glad to see this haven.

But my mind was rampant. All memories of demons and horrid murder had been swept clean from me in an instant by the horror that the artist whom I cherished most in all the world had been put on the rack like a common criminal.

"He sometimes . . . well," said Ramiel, "behaves like a common . . . criminal."

"He'll get out of it, he'll pay a fine," said the old man. He rang the bell for the monks. He patted me with a long, tired, dry hand. "Now stop crying, child, stop. Filippo is a nuisance, everybody knows it. If only there were a little of the saintliness of Fra Giovanni in him, only a little!"

Fra Giovanni. Of course, by this man, Fra Giovanni, they meant the great Fra Angelico, the painter who in centuries to come would bring the awestruck to all but kneel before his paintings, and it was in this monastery that Fra Giovanni worked and lived, it was here that, for Cosimo, he painted the very cells of the monks.

What could I say? "Yes, yes, Fra Giovanni, but I

don't . . . I don't . . . love him." Of course I loved him; I honored him and his wondrous work, but it was not like my love for Filippo, the painter I had glimpsed only once—. How explain these strange things?

A surge of nausea caused me to bend double. I backed away from my kindly helpers. I heaved up the contents of my stomach into the street, a bloody stream of filth from the demons who had fed me. I saw it drip and flow into the street. I smelled the putrid stench of it, and I saw it spill from me into the cracks between the cobblestones, this mess of half-digested wine and blood.

The whole horror of the Court of the Ruby Grail seemed manifest in this moment. Hopelessness seized me, and I heard the whisper of demons in my ear, *witless and scorned,* and I doubted all that I'd seen, all that I was, all that had transpired only moments before. In a dreamy woodland, my father and I rode together and we talked of Filippo's paintings, and I was a student and a young lord and had all the world before me, and the strong good smell of the horses filled my nostrils with the smell of the woods.

Witless and scorned. Mad when you might have been immortal.

As I rose up again, I leant back against the wall of the monastery. The light of the blue sky was bright enough to shut my eyes, but I bathed in its warmth. Slowly, as my stomach settled, I tried to gaze steadily before me, to fight the pain of the light and love it and trust in it.

My vision was filled with the face of the angel

Setheus right in front of me, only a foot from me, peering at me with the deepest concern.

"Dear God, you *are* here," I whispered.

"Yes," he said. "I promised you."

"You aren't leaving me, are you?" I asked.

"No," he said.

Over his shoulder, Ramiel peered at me closely, as if studying me at leisure and with commitment for the first time. His shorter looser hair made him seem younger, though such distinctions made no difference.

"No, none at all," he whispered, and for the first time, he too smiled.

"Do as these gentle people tell you," said Ramiel. "Let them take you inside, and then you must sleep a natural sleep, and when you wake we'll be with you."

"Oh, but it's a horror, a story of horrors," I whispered. "Filippo never painted such horrors."

"We are not painted things," said Setheus. "What God has in store for us we will discover together, you and Ramiel and I. Now you must go inside. The monks are here. Into their care we give you, and when you wake we will be at your side."

"Like the prayer," I whispered.

"Oh, yes, truly," Ramiel said. He raised his hand. I saw the shadow of his five fingers and then felt the silken touch of his fingers as he closed my eyes.

10

IN WHICH I CONVERSE WITH THE INNOCENT AND POWERFUL SONS OF GOD

WOULD sleep and deeply, yes, but not until much later. What came was a hazy, dreamlike wonderland of protective images. I was carried by a burly monk and his assistants into the monastery of San Marco.

There could be no place better for me in all of Florence—other than Cosimo's own house perhaps—than the Dominican Monastery of San Marco.

Now, in all of Florence, I know of many exquisite buildings and so much magnificence that even then, as a boy, I could not catalogue in my mind all the riches that lay before me.

But nowhere is there any cloister more serene, I think, than that of San Marco, which had only recently been renovated by the most humble and decent Michelozzo at the behest of Cosimo the Elder. It had a long and venerable history in Florence, but only in recent times had it been given over to the Dominicans, and it was endowed in certain sublime ways in which no other monastery was.

As all Florence knew, Cosimo had lavished a fortune on San Marco, maybe to make up for all the money he made by usury, for as a banker he was a taker of interest and therefore a usurer, but then so were we who had put money in his bank.

Whatever the case, Cosimo, our capo, our true leader, had loved this place and given to it many many treasures, but most of all perhaps its marvelously proportioned new buildings.

His detractors, the whiners, the ones who do nothing great, and suspect all that isn't in a state of perpetual disintegration, they said of him, "He even puts his coat of arms in the privies of the monks."

His coat of arms, by the way, is a shield with five protuberant balls on it, the meaning of which has been variously explained, but what these enemies actually said was: Cosimo had hung his balls over the monks' privies. Eh! That his enemies would be so lucky to have such privies, or such balls.

How much more clever it might have been for those men to point out that Cosimo often spent days at this monastery himself in meditation and prayer, and that the former Prior here, who was Cosimo's great friend and advisor, Fra Antonino, was now the Archbishop of Florence.

Ah, so much for the ignorant, who still to the day five hundred years from then tell lies about Cosimo.

As I passed under the door, I thought, What in the name of God shall I say to these people in this House of God?

No sooner had that thought popped out of my sleepy head and, I fear, my drugged and sleepy mouth, than I heard Ramiel's laugh in my ear.

I tried to see if he was at my side. But I was blubbering and sick again, and dizzy, and could make out only that we had entered the most tranquil and pleasing cloister.

The sun so burnt my eyes that I couldn't thank God yet for the beauty of the square green garden in the center of this place, but I could see very starkly and sweetly the low rounded arches created by Michelozzo, arches which created gentle colorless and humble vaults over my head.

And the tranquillity achieved by the pure columns, with their small rolled Ionic capitals, all of this added to my sense of safety and peace. Proportions were always the gift of Michelozzo. He opened up things when he built them. And these wide spacious loggias were his stamp.

Nothing would erase the memory for me of the soaring dagger-tipped Gothic arches of the French castle in the North, of the filigreed stone peaks everywhere there that seemed to point in animosity at the Almighty. And though I knew I misjudged this architecture and its intent—for surely, before Florian and his Court of the Ruby Grail had taken hold of it, it had been born from the devotions of the French and the Germans—I still could not get the hated vision of it out of my head.

Trying desperately not to heave up my guts again, I relaxed all my limbs as I saw this Florentine enclosure.

Down around the cloister, down around the burning hot garden, the large monk, a bear of a man, beaming down at me in habitual and inveterate kindness, carried me in his burly arms, while there came others in their flowing black and white robes, with thin radiant faces seeming to encircle us even in our rapid progress. I couldn't see my angels.

But these men were the nearest to angels that the world provides.

I soon realized—due to my former visits to this great place—that I was not being taken to the hospice, where drugs were dispensed to the sick of Florence, or to the pilgrims' refuge, which was always swarming with those who come to offer and pray, but up the stairs into the very hall of the monks' cells.

In a glaze of sickness in which beauty brought a catch in my throat, I saw at the head of the stairway, spread out on the wall, the fresco of Fra Giovanni's *Annunciation*.

My painting, the *Annunciation*! My chosen favorite, the painting which meant more to me than any other religious motif.

And no, it wasn't the genius of my turbulent Filippo Lippi, no, but it was my painting, and surely this was an omen that no demon can damn a soul through the poison of forced blood.

Was Ursula's blood forced on you too? Horrid thought. Try not to remember her soft fingers being pulled loose from you, you fool, you drunken fool, try not to remember her lips and the long thick kisslet of blood slipping into your own open mouth.

"Look at it!" I cried out. I pointed one flopping arm towards the painting.

"Yes, yes, we have so many," said the big smiling bear of a monk.

Fra Giovanni was of course the painter. Who could have not seen it in one glance? Besides, I knew it. And Fra Giovanni—let me remind you one more time that this is Fra Angelico of the ages—had made a severe, soothing, tender but utterly simple Angel and Virgin, steeped in humility and devoid of embellishments, the visitation itself taking place between low rounded arches such as made up the very cloister from which we had just come.

As the big monk swung me around to take me down the broad corridor—and broad it was, and so polished and austere and beautiful to me—I tried to form words as I carried the image of the angel in my mind.

I wanted to tell Ramiel and Setheus, if they were still with me, that look, Gabriel's wings had only simple stripes of color, and look, how his gown fell in symmetrical and disciplined folds. All of this I understood, as I understood the rampant grandeur of Ramiel and Setheus, but I was blubbering nonsense again.

"The halos," I said. "You two, where are you? Your halos hover over your heads. I saw them. I saw them in the street and in the paintings. But you see in the painting by Fra Giovanni, the halo is flat and surrounds the painted face, a disk hard and golden right on the field of the painting . . ."

The monks laughed. "To whom are you speaking, young Signore Vittorio di Raniari?" one of them asked me.

"Be quiet, child," said the big monk, his booming bass voice pushing against me through his barrel of a chest. "You're in our tender care. And you must hush now, see, there, that's the library, you see our monks at work?"

They were proud of it, weren't they? Even in our progress when I might have vomited all over the immaculate floor, the monk turned to let me see through the open door the long room crowded with books and monks at work, but what I saw too was Michelozzo's vaulted ceiling, again, not soaring to leave us, but bending gently over the heads of the monks and letting a volume of light and air rise above them.

It seemed I saw visions. I saw multiple and triple figures where there should only be one, and even in a flash a misty confusion of angelic wings, and oval faces turned, peering at me through the veil of supernatural secrecy.

"Do you see?" was all I could say. I had to get to that library, I had to find texts in it that defined the demons. Yes, I had not given up! Oh, no, I was no babbling idiot. I had God's very own angels at my assistance. I'd take Ramiel and Setheus in there and show them the texts.

We know, Vittorio, wipe the pictures from your mind, for we see them.

"Where are you?" I cried out.

"Quiet," said the monks.

"But will you help me go back there and kill them?"

"You're babbling," said the monks.

Cosimo was the guardian patron of that library. When old Niccolo de' Niccoli died, a marvelous collector of books with whom I had many times spoken at Vaspasiano's bookshop, all of his religious books, and maybe more, had been donated by Cosimo to this monastery.

I would find them in there, in that library, and find proof in St. Augustine or Aquinas of the devils with which I'd fought.

No. I was not mad. I had not given up. I was no gibbering idiot. If only the sun coming in the high little windows of this airy place would stop baking my eyeballs and burning my hands.

"Quiet, quiet," said the big monk, smiling still. "You are making noises like an infant. Hhhhh. Burgle, gurgle. Hear? Now, look, the library's busy. It's open to the public today. Everybody is busy today."

He turned only a few steps past the library to take me into a cell. "Down there . . ." he went on, as if cajoling an unruly baby. "Only a few steps away is the Prior's cell, and guess who is there this very minute? It's the Archbishop."

"Antonino," I whispered.

"Yes, yes, you said it right. Once our own Antonino. Well, he's here, and guess why?"

I was too groggy to respond. The other monks surrounded me. They wiped me with cool cloths. They smoothed back my hair.

This was a clean large cell. Oh, if the sun would only stop. What had those demons done to me, made me into a half-demon? Dare I ask for a mirror?

Set down on a thick soft bed, in this warm, clean place, I lost all control of my limbs. I was sick again.

The monks attended me with a silver basin. The sunlight pierced brilliantly upon a fresco, but I couldn't bear to look at the gleaming figures, not in this hurtful illumination. It seemed the cell was filled with other figures. Were they angels? I saw transparent beings, drifting, stirring, but I could catch hold of no clear outline. Only the fresco burned into the wall in its colors seemed solid, valid, true.

"Have they done this to my eyes forever?" I asked. I thought I caught a glimpse of an angelic form in the doorway of the cell, but it was not the figure of either Setheus or Ramiel. Did it have webbed wings? Demon wings? I started in terror.

But it was gone. Rustling, whispering. *We know.*

"Where are my angels?" I asked. I cried. I told out the names of my father and his father, and of all the di Raniari whom I could remember.

"Shhhhh," said the young monk. "Cosimo has been told that you are here. But this is a terrible day. We remember your father. Now let us remove these filthy clothes."

My head swam. The room was gone.

Sodden sleep, a glimpse of her, my savior Ursula. She ran through the blowing meadow. Who was this pursuing her, driving her out of the nodding, weaving flowers? Purple irises surrounded her, were crushed under her feet. She turned. Don't, Ursula! Don't turn. Don't you see the flaming sword?

I woke in a warm bath. Was it the cursed baptismal fount? No. I saw the fresco, the holy figures, dimly, and more immediately the real live monks who surrounded me on their knees on the stone, their big sleeves rolled back as they washed me in the warm, sweet-scented water.

"Ah, that Francesco Sforza . . ." they spoke in Latin to one another. "To charge into Milan and take possession of the Dukedom! As if Cosimo did not have enough trouble, without Sforza having done such a thing."

"He did it? He has taken Milan?" I asked.

"What did you say? Yes, son, he has. He broke the peace. And your family, all your poor family murdered by the freebooters; don't think they'll go unpunished, rampaging through that country, those damned Venetians . . ."

"No, you mustn't, you must tell Cosimo. It was not an act of war, what happened to my family, not by human beings . . ."

"Hush, child."

Chaste hands sponged the water over my shoulders. I sat slumped against the warm metal back of the tub.

". . . di Raniari, always loyal," said one of them to me. "And your brother was to come to study with us, your sweet brother, Matteo . . ."

I let out a terrible cry. A soft hand sealed my lips.

"Sforza himself will punish them. He'll clean out that country."

I cried and cried. No one could understand me. They wouldn't listen to me.

The monks lifted me to my feet. I was dressed in a long comfortable soft linen robe. It came to me that I was being dressed for execution, but the hour of such danger had passed.

"I am not mad!" I said clearly.

"No, not at all, only grief-stricken."

"You understand me!"

"You are tired."

"The bed is soft for you, brought specially for you, hush, don't rave anymore."

"Demons did it," I whispered. "They weren't soldiers."

"I know, son, I know. War is terrible. War is the Devil's work."

No, but it wasn't war. Will you listen to me?

Hush, this is Ramiel at your ear; didn't I tell you to sleep? Will you listen to us? We have heard your thoughts as well as your words!

I lay down on the bed flat on my chest. The monks brushed and dried my hair. My hair was so long now. Unkempt, country Lord hair. But this was an immense comfort to be bathed and gentlemanly clean.

"Those are candles?" I asked. "The sun has gone down?"

"Yes," said the monk beside me. "You have slept."

"May I have more candles?"

"Yes, I'll bring them to you."

I lay in the darkness. I blinked and tried to shape the words of the *Ave*.

Many lights appeared in the door, some six or seven in a cluster, each a sweet small perfectly shaped flame. Then they fluttered as the monk's feet came softly towards me. I saw him clearly as he knelt to place the candelabra beside my bed.

He was thin and tall, a sapling in hollow willowy robes. His hands were so clean. "You are in a special cell. Cosimo has sent men to bury your dead."

"Thanks be to God," I said.

"Yes."

So now I could speak!

"They are still talking down there, and it's late,"

said the monk. "Cosimo is troubled. He'll stay the night here. The whole city is filled with Venetian agitators stirring up the populace against Cosimo."

"Now hush," said another monk who appeared suddenly. He bent down and lifted my head to place another thick pillow beneath it.

What bliss this was. I thought of the damned ones imprisoned in the coop. "Oh, horrors! It's night, and they're waiting for the horrible Communion."

"Who, child? What Communion?"

Once again, I glimpsed figures moving, drifting, as it were, in the shadows. But they were too soon gone.

I had to vomit. I needed the basin. They held my hair for me. Did they see the blood in the candlelight? The pure streak of blood? It smelled so rotten.

"How can one survive such poison?" one monk whispered to the other in Latin. "Do we dare purge him?"

"You'll frighten him. Be quiet. He has no fever."

"Well, you're damned wrong if you think you took my wits," I declared suddenly. I shouted it to Florian and to Godric and to all of them.

The monks looked at me in urgent astonishment.

I laughed. "I only was talking to those who tried to hurt me," I said, again letting each word have a clear distinct shape.

The thin monk with the remarkably scrubbed hands knelt by me. He smoothed my forehead. "And the beautiful sister, the sister who was to be married, is she too . . . ?"

"Bartola! She was to be married? I didn't know.

Well, he can have her head for a maidenhead." I wept. "The worms are at work in the dark. And the demons dance on the hill, and the town does nothing."

"What town?"

"You're raving again," said a monk who stood beyond the candles. How distinct he looked, though he was beyond the light, a round-shouldered individual with a hooked nose and thick somber heavy eyelids. "Don't rave anymore, poor child."

I wanted to protest, but I saw suddenly a giant soft wing, each feather tinged with gold, come down over me, enfolding me. I was tickled all over by the softness of the feathers. Ramiel said:

What must we do to make you shut up? Filippo needs us now; will you give us some peace and quiet for Filippo, whom God sent us to guard? Don't answer me. Obey me.

The wing crushed out all vision, all woe.

Shadowy pale darkness. Even and complete. The candles were behind me, set up high.

I woke. I rose up on my elbows. My head was clear. A lovely even illumination gave just the smallest tremble as it filled the cell. From the high window came the moon. The shaft of the moon struck the fresco on the wall, the fresco obviously painted by Fra Giovanni.

My eyes could see it with amazing clarity. Was this my demonic blood?

A strange thought came to me. It rang in my consciousness with the clarity of a golden bell. I myself possessed no guardian angels! My angels had left me; they had departed, because my soul was damned.

I had no angels. I had seen Filippo's because of the power the demons had given me, and because of something else. Filippo's angels argued so much with each other! That's how I had seen them. Some words came to me.

They came back to me from Aquinas, or was it Augustine? I'd read so much of both to learn my Latin, and their endless excursuses had so delighted me. The demons are full of passion. But angels are not.

But those two angels had such spirit. That's why they'd cut through the veil.

I pushed back the covers and set my bare feet on the stone floor. It was cool, and pleasing, because the room, having received the sun all day, was still warm.

No drafts swept the polished and immaculate floor.

I stood before the wall painting. I wasn't dizzy or sick, or like to fall. I was myself again.

What an innocent and untroubled soul Fra Giovanni must have been. All his figures were devoid of malice. I could see the figure of Christ seated before a mountain, round gold halo decorated with the red arms and top of a cross. Beside him stood ministering angels. One held bread for him, and the other, whose figure was cut off by the door that was cut into the wall, this other angel, whose wingtips were barely visible, carried wine and meat.

Above, on the mountain, I saw Christ also. It was a painting of different incidents, in sequence, and above, Christ was standing in His same smooth and multiwrinkled pink robes, but here He was agitated, as agitated as Fra Giovanni could make Him, and Christ had lifted His left hand, as if in wrath.

The figure who fled from Him was the Devil! It was a horrid creature with the webbed wings I thought I'd glimpsed earlier, and it had hideous webbed feet. It had dewclaws on its webbed feet. Sour-faced and in a dirty gray robe, it fled from Christ, who stood firm in the Desert, refusing to be tempted, and, only after this confrontation, then had the ministering angels come, and had Christ taken His place with His hands clasped.

I sucked in my breath in terror as I beheld this image of the demon. But a great rush of comfort passed through me, causing my hair to tingle at its roots, causing my feet to tingle against the polished floor. I had routed the demons, I had refused their gift of immortality. I had refused it. Even faced with the cross!

I retched. The pain caught me as if I'd been kicked in the stomach. I turned. The basin was there, clean and polished, sitting on the floor. I dropped to my knees and heaved up more of their syrupy filth. Was there no water?

I looked around. There stood the pitcher and the cup. The cup was full and I spilt some of it as I put it to my lips, but it tasted thin and rancid and awful. I threw down the cup.

"You've poisoned me for natural things, you monsters. You will not win!"

My hands trembling, I picked up the cup, filled it once more and tried again to drink. But it tasted unnatural. To what can I compare it? It was not foul like urine; it was like water that is full of minerals and metal and will leave a chalk on you and choke you. It was bad!

I put it aside. Very well then. Time to study. Time to take up the candles, which I now did.

I went out of the cell. The hall was empty and glowing in the pale light that came from tiny windows over the low-ceilinged cells.

I turned to my right and approached the doors of the library. They were unlocked.

I entered with my candelabra. Once again, the tranquillity of Michelozzo's design brought a warmth to me, a faith in all things, a trust. Two rows of arches and Ionic columns moved down the center of the room to make a broad aisle to the far distant door, and on either side were the study tables, and all along the far walls were racks and racks of codices and scrolls.

Across the herringbone stones of the floor I walked barefoot, lifting the candle higher so that the light would fill up the vaulted ceiling, so happy to be here alone.

Windows on either side let in shafts of pale illumination through the overwhelming clutter of shelves, but how divine and restful were the high ceilings. How boldly he had done it, made a basilica of a library.

How could I have known, child that I was then, that this style would be imitated all over my beloved Italy? Oh, there were so many wondrous things then for the living and for all time.

And I? What am I? Do I live? Or am I walking always in death, forever in love with time?

I stood still with my candles. How my eyes loved the moonlighted splendor. How I craved to stand here forever, dreaming, near to things of the mind, and things of the soul, and far away in memory from the wretched enchained town on its cursed mountain and the castle nearby, which at this very moment probably gave forth its ghastly, ugly light.

Could I discern the order of this wealth of books?

The very cataloger of this library, the very monk who had done the work here, the very scholar, was now the Pope of all Christendom, Nicholas V.

I moved along the shelves to my right, holding high my candles. Would it be alphabetical? I thought of Aquinas, for I knew him more freely, but it was St. Augustine whom I found. And I had always loved Augustine, loved his colorful style and his eccentricities, and the dramatic manner in which he wrote.

"Oh, you wrote more about demons, you are better!" I said.

The City of God! I saw it, copy after copy. There were a score of codices of this very masterpiece, not to mention all of the other work of this great saint, his *Confessions*, which had gripped me as much as a Roman drama, and so much more. Some of these books were ancient, made of big sloppy parchment, others were extravagantly bound, some almost simple and very new.

In charity and consideration, I must take the most sturdy of these, even though there might be errors, and God only knew how hard monks worked to avoid errors. I knew which volume I wanted. I knew the volume on demons, because I had thought it so very fascinating and funny and so much poppycock. Oh, what a fool I'd been.

I took down the hefty fat volume, number nine of the text, slipping it into the crook of my arm, moved to the first desk and then carefully placed the candelabra in front of me, where it would light me but throw no shadows under my fingers, and I opened the book.

"It's all here!" I whispered. "Tell me, St. Augustine, what were they so that I may convince Ramiel and Setheus that they must help me, or give me the means to convince these modern Florentines, who care about nothing right now but making war with paid soldiers on the Serene Republic of Venice up north. Help me, Saint. I'm telling you."

Ah, Chapter Ten, of Volume Nine, I knew this . . .

Augustine was quoting Plotinus, or explaining him:

> *. . . that the very fact of man's corporal mortality is due to the compassion of God, who would not have us kept for ever in the misery of this life. The wickedness of demons was not judged worthy of this compassion, and in the misery of their condition, with a soul subject to passions, they have not been granted the mortal body, which man had received, but an eternal body.*

"Ah, yes!" I said. "And this is what Florian offered me, bragging that they did not age or decay and were not subject to disease, that I could have lived there with them forever. Evil, evil. Well, this is proof, and I have it here, and I can show it to the monks!"

I read on, skimming to find the kernels that would make my case grow. Down to Chapter Eleven:

Apuleius says also that the souls of men are demons. On leaving human bodies they become lares if they have shown themselves good, if evil, lemures or larvae.

"Yes, lemures. I know this word. Lemures or larvae, and Ursula, she said to me that she had been young, young as me; they were all human and now they are lemures."

According to Apuleius, larvae are malignant demons created out of men.

I was overcome with excitement. I needed parchment and pens. I had to note the place. I had to mark down what I had discovered and go on. For the next point was obviously to convince Ramiel and Setheus that they had gotten into the biggest—.

My thoughts were brought to an abrupt halt.

Behind me, a personage had come into the library. I heard a heavy footfall, but there was a muffled quality to it, and a great darkening occurred behind me, as though all the slim, sly beams of the moon that fell through the passage beyond had been cut off.

I turned slowly and looked over my shoulder.

"And why do you choose the left?" asked this personage.

He rose up before me, immense and winged, peering down at me, his face luminous in the flicker of the candles, his eyebrows gently raised but straight so that there was no arch to them to make them anything but severe. He had the riotous golden hair of Fra Filippo's brush, curling beneath a huge red battle helmet, and behind him his wings were heavily sheathed in gold.

He wore a suit of armor, with the breast-plates decorated and the shoulders covered with immense buckles, and around his waist was a blue sash of silk. His sword was sheathed, and on one lax arm he wore his shield, with its red cross.

I had never seen his like.

"I need you!" I declared. I stood up, knocking the bench back. I reached out so that it would not clatter to the floor. I faced him.

"You need me!" he said in muted outrage. "You do! You who would lead off Ramiel and Setheus from Fra Filippo Lippi. You need me? Do you know who I am?"

It was a gorgeous voice, rich, silken, violent and piercing though deep.

"You have a sword," I said.

"Oh, and for what?"

"Killing them, all of them!" I said. "Going there with me by day to their castle. Do you know what I am speaking of?"

He nodded. "I know what you dreamt and what you babbled and what Ramiel and Setheus have gleaned from your feverish mind. Of course I know. You need me, you say, and Fra Filippo Lippi lies in bed with a whore who licks his aching joints, and one in particular that aches for her!"

"Such talk from an angel," I said.

"Don't mock me, I'll slap you," he said. His wings rose and fell as if he were sighing with them, or gasping rather, at me in umbrage.

"So do it!" I said. My eyes were feasting fiendishly on his glistering beauty, on the red silk cloak that was clasped just below the bit of tunic that showed above his armor, at the solemn smoothness of his cheeks. "But come with me to the mountains and kill them," I implored him.

"Why don't you go yourself and do it?"

"Do you think I can?" I demanded.

His face went serene. His lower lip gave the smallest most thoughtful pout. His jaw and neck were powerful, more powerful by far than the anatomy of Ramiel or Setheus, who seemed more youths, and this their splendid elder brother.

"You are not the Fallen One, are you?" I asked.

"How dare you!" he whispered, waking from his slumber. A terrible frown broke over him.

"Mastema, then, that's who you are. They said your name. Mastema."

He nodded and sneered. "They would, of course, say my name."

"Which means what, great angel? That I can call on you, that I have the power to command you?" I turned and reached for the book of St. Augustine.

"Put down that book!" he said impatiently yet

coolly. "There is an angel standing before you, boy; look at me when I speak to you!"

"Ah, you speak like Florian, the demon in that far castle. You have the same control, the same modulation. What do you want of me, angel? Why did you come?"

He was silent, as if he couldn't produce an answer. Then, quietly, he put a question to me. "Why do you think?"

"Because I prayed?"

"Yes," he said coldly. "Yes! And because they have come to me on your account."

My eyes widened. I felt light fill them up. But the light didn't hurt them. A soft cluster of sweet noises filled my ears.

On either side of him there appeared Ramiel and Setheus, their milder, gentler faces focused on me.

Mastema raised his eyebrows again as he looked down at me.

"Fra Filippo Lippi is drunk," he said. "When he wakes up, he'll get drunk again until the pain stops."

"Fools to rack a great painter," I said, "but then you know my thoughts on that."

"Ah, and the thoughts of all the women in Florence," said Mastema. "And the thoughts of the great ones who pay for his paintings, if their minds were not on war."

"Yes," said Ramiel, glancing imploringly to Mastema. They were of the same height, but Mastema didn't turn, and Ramiel came forward some, as if to catch his eye. "If they weren't all so carried away with war."

"War is the world," said Mastema. "I asked you before, Vittorio di Raniari, do you know who I am?"

I was shaken, not by the question, but that the three had now come together, and that I stood before them, the only mortal being, and all the mortal world around us seemed to sleep.

Why had no monk come down the passage to see who whispered in the library? Why had no Watchman of the night come to see why the candles floated along the passage? Why the boy murmured and raved?

Was I mad?

It seemed to me quite suddenly and ludicrously that if I answered Mastema correctly, I would not be mad.

This thought brought from him a small laugh, neither harsh nor sweet.

Setheus stared at me with his obvious sympathy. Ramiel said nothing but looked again to Mastema.

"You are the angel," I said, "whom the Lord gives permission to wield that sword." There came no response from him. I went on. "You are the angel who slew the firstborn of Egypt," I said. No response. "You are the angel, the angel who can avenge."

He nodded, but only really with his eyes. They closed and then opened.

Setheus drew close to him, lips to his ears.

"Help him, Mastema, let us all go help him. Filippo cannot use our counsel now."

"And why?" demanded Mastema of the angel beside him. He looked at me.

"God has given me no leave to punish these demons of yours. Never has God said to me, 'Mastema, slay the vampires, the lemures, the larvae, the blood drinkers.' Never has God spoken to me and said, 'Lift your mighty sword to cleanse the world of these.' "

"I beg you," I said. "I, a mortal boy, beg you. Kill these, wipe out this nest with your sword."

"I can't do it."

"Mastema, you can!" declared Setheus.

Ramiel spoke up. "If he says he cannot, he cannot! Why do you never listen to him?"

"Because I know that he can be moved," said Setheus without hesitation to his compatriot. "I know that he can, as God can be moved."

Setheus stepped boldly in front of Mastema.

"Pick up the book, Vittorio," he said. He stepped forward. At once the large vellum pages, heavy as they were, began to flutter. He put it in my hand, and marked the place with his pale finger, barely touching the thick black crowded writing.

I read aloud:

> *And therefore God who made the visible marvels of Heaven and Earth does not disdain to work visible miracles in Heaven and Earth, by which He arouses the soul, hitherto preoccupied with visible things, to the worship of Himself.*

His finger moved, and my eyes moved with it. I read of God:

To Him, there is no difference between seeing us about to pray and listening to our prayers, for even when His angels listen, it is He Himself who listens in them.

I stopped, my eyes full of tears. He took the book from me to guard it from my tears.

A noise had penetrated our small circle. Monks had come. I heard them whispering in the corridor, and then the door swung open. Into the library they came.

I cried, and when I looked up I saw them staring at me, two monks whom I didn't know or didn't remember, had never known.

"What is it, young man? Why are you here alone crying?" the first spoke.

"Here, let us take you back to bed. We'll bring you something to eat."

"No, I can't eat it," I said.

"No, he can't eat it," said the first monk to the other. "It still makes him sick. But he can rest." He looked at me.

I turned. The three radiant angels stood silently staring at the monks who could not see them, who had no clue that the angels were there!

"Dear God in Heaven, please tell me," I said. "Have I gone mad? Have the demons won out, have they so polluted me with their blood and their potions that I see things which are delusions, or am I come like Mary to the tomb to see an angel there?"

"Come to bed," said the monks.

"No," said Mastema, quietly addressing the monk

who didn't even see him or hear him. "Let him stay. Let him read to quiet his mind. He is a boy of education."

"No, no," said the monk, shaking his head. He glanced to the other. "We should let him stay. He's a boy of education. He can read quietly. Cosimo said that he must have anything he desired."

"Go on, leave him now," said Setheus softly.

"Hush," said Ramiel. "Let Mastema tell them."

I was too flooded with sorrow and happiness to respond. I covered my face, and when I did so I thought of my poor Ursula, forever with her demon Court, and how she had wept for me. "How could that be?" I whispered into my own fingers.

"Because she was human once, and has a human heart," said Mastema to me in the silence.

The two monks were hurrying out. For one moment the collection of angels was as sheer as light, and I saw through them to the two retreating figures of the monks who closed up the doors as they left.

Mastema looked at me with his still, powerful gaze.

"One could read anything into your face," I said.

"So it is with almost all angels all of the time," he answered.

"I beg you," I said. "Come with me. Help me. Guide me. Do what you just did with those monks! That you can do, can't you?"

He nodded.

"But we can't do more than that, you see," said Setheus.

"Let Mastema say," said Ramiel.

"Go back to Heaven!" said Setheus.

"Please, the both of you, be quiet," said Mastema. "Vittorio, I cannot slay them. I have no leave. That you can do, and with your own sword."

"But you'll come."

"I'll take you," he said. "When the sun rises, when they sleep under their stones. But you must slay them, you must open them to the light, and you must set free those awful wretched prisoners, and you must stand before the townsmen, or let loose that crippled flock and flee."

"I understand."

"We can move the stones away from their sleeping places, can't we?" asked Setheus. He put up his hand to hush Ramiel before Ramiel could protest. "We'll have to do it."

"We can do that," said Mastema. "As we can stop a beam from falling on Filippo's head. We can do that. But we cannot slay them. And you, Vittorio, we cannot make you go through with it, either, if your nerve or your will fails."

"You don't think the miracle of my having seen you will uphold me?"

"Will it?" Mastema asked.

"You speak of her, don't you?"

"Do I?" he asked.

"I will go through with it, but you must tell me . . ."

"What must I tell you?" Mastema asked.

"Her soul, will it go to Hell?"

"That I cannot tell you," said Mastema.

"You have to."

"No, I have to do nothing but what the Lord God

has created me to do, and that I do, but to solve the mysteries over which Augustine pondered for a lifetime, no, that is not what I have to do or should do or will do."

Mastema picked up the book.

Once again the pages moved with his will. I felt the breeze rising from them.

He read:

There is something to be gained from the inspired discourses of Scripture.

"Don't read those words to me; they don't help me!" I said. "Can she be saved? Can she save her soul? Does she possess it still? Is she as powerful as you are? Can you Fall? Can the Devil come back to God?"

He put down the book with a swift, airy movement that I could scarcely follow.

"Are you ready for this battle?" he asked.

"They'll lie helpless in the light of day," said Setheus to me. "Including her. She too will lie helpless. You must open the stones that cover them, and you know what you must do."

Mastema shook his head. He turned and gestured for them to get out of his way.

"No, please, I beg you!" said Ramiel. "Do it for him. Do it, please. Filippo is beyond our help for days."

"You know no such thing," said Mastema.

"Can my angels go to him?" I asked. "Have I none that can be sent?"

I had no sooner spoken these words than I

realized that two more entities had taken form directly beside me, one on either side, and when I looked from left to right I saw them, only they were pale and remote from me, and they hadn't the flame of Filippo's guardians, only a quiet and quasi-visible and undeniable presence and will.

I looked at one for a long time and then the other, and could draw no descriptive words from my mind from them. Their faces seemed blank and patient and quiet. They were winged beings, tall, yes, I can say that much, but what more could I say, because I couldn't endow them with color or splendor or individuality, and they had no garments or motion to them or anything that I could love.

"What is it? Why won't they speak to me? Why do they look at me that way?"

"They know you," said Ramiel.

"You're full of vengeance, and desire," said Setheus. "They know it; they have been at your side. They have measured your pain and your anger."

"Good God, these demons killed my family!" I declared. "Do you know the future of my soul, any of you?"

"Of course not," said Mastema. "Why would we be here if we did? Why would any of us be here if it were ordained?"

"Don't they know that I faced death rather than take the demon blood? Would not a vendetta have required of me that I drink it and then destroy my enemies when I had powers such as theirs?"

My angels drew closer to me.

"Oh, where were you when I was about to die!" I declared.

"Don't taunt them. You have never really believed in them." It was Ramiel's voice. "You loved us when you saw our images, and when the demon blood was full inside you, you saw what you could love. That is the danger now. Can you kill what you love?"

"I will destroy all of them," I said. "One way or another, I swear it on my soul." I looked at my pale unyielding yet unjudging guardians, and then to the others who burnt so brightly against the shadows of the vast library, against the dark colors of the shelves and the crowded books.

"I will destroy them all," I vowed. I closed my eyes. I imagined her, lying helpless by day, and I saw myself bend and kiss her cold white forehead. My sobs were muffled and my body shook. I nodded again and again that I would do it, yes, I would do it, I would do it.

"At dawn," said Mastema, "the monks will have fresh clothes laid out for you, a suit of red velvet, and your weapons freshly polished, and your boots cleaned. All will be finished by then. Don't try to eat. It's too soon, and the demon blood is still churning in you. Prepare yourself, and we will take you north to do what has to be done in the light of day."

11

And the light shineth in darkness, and the darkness did not comprehend it.

—THE GOSPEL ACCORDING TO ST. JOHN 1:5

ONASTERIES wake early, if they ever sleep at all.

My eyes opened quite suddenly, and only then, as I saw the morning light cover the fresco, as if the veil of darkness had been drawn from it, only then did I know how deeply I had slept.

Monks moved in my cell. They had brought in the red velvet tunic, the clothes as Mastema described, and were just laying them out. I had fine red wool hose to wear with them, and a shirt of gold silk, and to go over that, another of white silk, and then a thick new belt for the tunic. My weapons were polished, as I had been told they would be—my heavy jeweled sword gleaming as though my father himself had been toying with it all of a peaceful evening long by the fire. My daggers were ready.

I climbed out of the bed and dropped down to my knees in prayer. I made the Sign of the Cross. "God, give me the strength to send in your hands those who feed on death."

It was a whisper in Latin.

One of the monks touched me on the shoulder and smiled. Had the Great Silence not yet ended? I had no idea. He pointed to a table where there was food laid out for me—bread and milk. The milk had foam on the top of it.

I nodded and smiled at him, and then he and his companion made me a little bow and went out.

I turned around and around.

"All of you are here, I know it," I said, but I gave no more time to it. If they didn't come, then I had recovered my wits, but no such thing was true, any more than it was true that my father was alive.

On the table, not far from the food, and held in place beneath the weight of the candelabra, was a series of documents, freshly written and signed in ornate script.

I read them hastily.

They were receipts for all my money and jewels, those things which had been with me in my saddlebags when I came in. All these documents bore the seal of the Medici.

There was a purse of money there, to be tied to my belt. All my rings were there, cleaned and polished, so that the cabochon rubies were brilliant and the emeralds had a flawless depth. The gold gleamed as it had not in months perhaps, for my own negligence.

I brushed out my hair, annoyed at its thickness and length, but having no time to ask for a barber to cut it shorter than my shoulders. At least it was long enough, and had been for a while, to stay back over my shoulders and off my forehead. It was luxurious to have it so clean.

I dressed quickly. My boots were a little snug because they had been dried by a fire after the rain. But they felt good over the thin hose. I made right all my fastenings and positioned my sword.

The red velvet tunic was plaited along the edges with gold and silver thread, and the front of it was richly decorated with the silver fleurs-de-lys, which is the most ancient symbol of Florence. Once my belt was tightly fastened, the tunic didn't come to halfway down my thigh. That was for handsome legs.

The whole raiment was more than fancy for battle, but what battle was this? It was a massacre. I put on the short flaring cloak they had given me, fastening its gold buckles, though it would be warm for the city. It was lined in soft thin dark-brown squirrel fur.

I ignored the hat. I tied on the purse. I put on my rings one by one until my hands were weapons on account of their weight. I put on the soft fur-lined gloves. I found a dark-amber-beaded rosary that I had not noticed before. It had a gold crucifix, which I kissed, and this I put in my pocket under my tunic.

I realized that I was staring at the floor, and that I was surrounded by pairs of bare feet. Slowly I lifted my gaze.

My angels stood before me, my very own guardians, in long flowing robes of dark blue, which appeared to be made of something lighter yet more opaque than silk. Their faces were ivory white and shimmering faintly, and their eyes were large and like opals. They had dark hair, or hair that seemed to shift as if it were made of shadows.

They stood facing me, their heads together, so that their heads touched. It was as though they were communing silently with one another.

They overwhelmed me. It seemed a terrifying intimacy that I should see them so vividly and so close to me, and know them as the two who had been with me always, or so I was to believe. They were slightly larger than human beings, as were the other angels I had seen, and they were not tempered by the sweet faces I had seen on the others, but had altogether smoother and broader countenances and larger though exquisitely shaped mouths.

"And you don't believe in us now?" one of them asked in a whisper.

"Will you tell me your names?" I asked.

Both shook their heads in a simple negation at once.

"Do you love me?" I asked.

"Where is it written that we should?" answered the one who had not yet spoken. His voice was as toneless and soft as a whisper, but more distinct. It might have been the same voice as the other angel.

"Do you love us?" asked the other.

"Why do you guard me?" I asked.

"Because we are sent to do it, and will be with you until you die."

"Lovelessly?" I asked.

They shook their heads again in negation.

Gradually the light brightened in the room. I turned sharply to look up at the window. I thought it was the sun. The sun couldn't hurt me, I thought.

But it wasn't. It was Mastema, who had risen up

behind me as if he were a cloud of gold, and on either side of him were my arguers, my advancers of the cause, my champions, Ramiel and Setheus.

The room shimmered and seemed to vibrate without a sound. My angels appeared to glisten, and to grow brilliantly white and deep blue in their robes.

All looked to the helmeted figure of Mastema.

An immense and musical rustling filled the air, a singing sound, as if a great flock of tiny golden-throated birds had awakened and rushed upwards from the branches of their sun-filled trees.

I must have closed my eyes. I lost my balance, and the air became cooler, and it seemed my vision was clouded with dust.

I shook my head. I looked around me.

We stood within the castle itself.

The place was damp and very dark. Light crept in around the seams of the immense drawbridge, which was of course pulled up and locked into place. On either side were rustic stone walls, hung here and there with great rusted hooks and chains that had not been used in many a year.

I turned and entered a dim courtyard, my breath suddenly taken from me by the height of the walls that surrounded me, climbing to the distinct cube of the bright blue sky.

Surely this was only one courtyard, the one at the entrance, for before us there loomed another immense pair of gates, quite large enough to admit the greatest haywagons imaginable or some newfangled engine of war.

The ground was soiled. High above on all sides

were windows, rows upon rows of the double-arched windows, and all were covered over with bars.

"I need you now, Mastema," I said. I made the Sign of the Cross again. I took out the rosary and kissed the crucifix, looking down for a moment at the tiny twisted body of Our Tortured Christ.

The huge doors before me broke open. There was a loud creaking sound, then the crumpling of metal bolts, and the gates groaned back on their hinges, revealing a distant and sun-filled inner court of far greater size.

The walls through which we walked were some thirty to forty feet in depth. There were doors on either side of us, heavily arched in worked stone and showing the first signs of care that I had glimpsed since we entered.

"These creatures do not go and come as others do," I said. I hurried my pace so as to reach the full sun of the courtyard. The mountain air was too cool and too damp in the foul thickness of the passage.

Here, as I stood up, I saw windows such as I remembered, hung with rich banners and strung with lanterns that would be lighted by night. Here I saw tapestries carelessly thrown over window ledges as if rain were nothing. And very high up I saw the jagged battlements and finer white marble copings.

But even this was not the great courtyard that lay beyond. These walls too were rustic. The stones were soiled and untrodden in many a year. Water was pooled here and there. Rank weeds sprang from crevices, but, ah, there were sweet wildflowers, and

I looked at them tenderly and reached out to touch them, and marveled at them, existing here.

More gates awaited us, these two—huge, wooden, banded in iron and severely pointed at the top in their deep marble archway—gave way and sprang back to let us pass through yet another wall.

Oh, such a garden greeted us!

As we made our way through another forty feet of darkness, I saw the great groves of orange trees ahead of us, and heard the cry of the birds. I wondered if they were not caught down here, prisoners, or could they soar all the way up to the top and escape?

Yes, they could. It was a great enough space. And here was the fine white marble facing I remembered, all the way to the summit, so high above.

As I made my way into the garden, as I walked on the first marble path that traversed the beds of violets and roses, I saw the birds coming and going, circling broadly in this wide place, so that they could clear the towers that rose so distantly and majestically against the sky.

Everywhere the scent of flowers overcame me. Lilies and irises were mingled in patches, and the oranges were ripe and almost red as they hung from the trees. The lemons were hard still and touched with green.

Shrubbery and vines hugged the walls.

The angels gathered around me. I realized that all along it was I who had led the way, I who had initiated any movement, and it was I who held us all still now, within the garden, and that they waited as I bowed my head.

"I am listening for the prisoners," I said. "But I can't hear them."

I looked up at more of the luxuriously decorated balconies and windows, the twin arches, and here and there a long loggia, but made of their style of filigree, not ours.

I saw flags fluttering, and all were in that dark blood-red color, stained with death. I looked down for the first time at my own brilliant crimson clothes.

"Like fresh blood?" I whispered.

"Tend to what you must do first," Mastema said. "Twilight can cover you when you go to the prisoners, but you must take your quarry now."

"Where are they? Will you tell me?"

"In deliberate sacrilege, and in old-fashioned rigor, they lie beneath the stones of the church."

There was a loud, searing noise. He had pulled out his sword. He pointed with it, his head turned, his red helmet on fire with the glint of the sun reflected off the marble-faced walls.

"The door there, and the stairs beyond it. The church lies on the third floor, up to our left."

I made for the door without further delay. I rushed up the steps, taking turn after turn, my boots clattering on the stone, not even looking to see if they followed me, not wondering how they did it, knowing only that they were with me, feeling their presence as if I could feel their breath on me when no breath came.

At last we entered the corridor, broad and open on our right to the courtyard below. There was an endless strip of rich carpet before us, full of Persian flowers deeply embedded within a field of midnight blue. Unfaded, untrammeled. On and on it went until it turned, ahead of us. And at the end of the corridor was the perfectly framed sky and the jagged speck of green mountain beyond.

"Why have you stopped?" Mastema asked.

They had materialized around me, in their settling garments and their never-still wings.

"This is the door to the church here, you know it."

"Only looking at the sky, Mastema," I said. "Only looking at the blue sky."

"And thinking of what?" asked one of my guardians in his toneless, clear whisper. He clung to me suddenly, and I saw his parchment-colored fingers, weightless, settled on my shoulder. "Thinking of a meadow that never existed and a young woman who is dead?"

"Are you merciless?" I asked him. I pressed close to him, so my forehead touched him, and I marveled to feel it against me and see his opalescent eyes so distinct.

"No, not merciless. Only one who reminds, and reminds, and reminds."

I turned to the doors of the chapel. I pulled on both giant hooks until I heard the clasp give, and then I opened wide one side and then the other, though why I made such a vast and broad escape for myself I do not know. Maybe it was a passage for my mighty band of helpers.

The great empty nave lay before me, which last night no doubt had been crowded with the gaudy blood-drenched Court, and above my head was their choir loft from which the most ethereal dirge had come.

Sun violently pierced the demonic windows.

I gasped in shock to see the webbed spirits emblazoned so immensely in the fractured and welded fragments of glittering glass. How thick was this glass, how heavily faceted, and how ominous the expressions of those webbed-winged monsters who leered at us as if they would come alive in the blazing light of day and stop our progress.

There was nothing to be done but to rip my eyes off them, to look down and away and along the great sprawling marble floor. I saw the hook, I saw it as it had been in the floor of my father's chapel, lying flat in a circle cut in the stone, a hook of gold, polished and smoothed so it did not rise above the floor and would not catch a toe or a heel. It had no cover.

It merely marked decisively the position of the one long main entrance to the crypt. One narrow marble rectangle cut into the center of the church floor.

I strode forward, heels echoing throughout the whole empty church, and went to pull the hook.

What stopped me? I saw the altar. At that very instant the sun had struck the figure of Lucifer, the giant red angel above his masses and masses of red flowers, which were fresh as they had been the night when I had been brought to this place.

I saw him and saw his fierce burning yellow eyes, fine gems set into the red marble, and saw the white ivory fangs that hung from his snarling upper lip. I saw all the fanged demons who lined the walls to the right and the left of him, and all their jeweled eyes seemed greedy and glorying in the light.

"The crypt," said Mastema.

I pulled with all my might. I couldn't budge the marble slab. No human could have done it. It would have taken teams of horses to do it. I locked both hands more tightly around the hook, yanking it harder, and still I couldn't budge it. It was like trying to move the walls themselves.

"Do it for him!" Ramiel pleaded. "Let us do it."

"It's nothing, Mastema; it's only like opening the gates."

Mastema reached out and pushed me gently aside, so that I was caught on my own feet for a moment and then righted myself. The long narrow trapdoor of marble was raised slowly.

I was astonished at its weight. It was more than two feet in thickness. Only its facing was marble, the rest being a heavier, darker, denser stone. No, no human could have lifted it.

And now, from the mouth below, there came a spear as if from a hidden spring.

I leapt back, though I had never been near enough to be in danger.

Mastema let the trapdoor fall on its back. The hinges were broken at once by its own weight. The light filled the space below. More spears awaited me, glinting in the sun, pointed at an angle, as if affixed in parallel to the angle of the stairs.

Mastema moved to the top of the stairs.

"Try to move them, Vittorio," he said.

"He can't. And if he trips and falls, he falls down

into a pit of them," said Ramiel. "Mastema, move them."

"Let me move them," said Setheus.

I drew my sword. I hacked at the first of the spears and knocked off its metal point, but the jagged wooden shaft remained.

I stepped down into the crypt, at once feeling a coldness rise and touch my legs. I hacked again at the wood, and broke off more of it. Then I stepped beside it, only to find with my left hand that I felt a pair of spears awaiting me in the uneven light. Again I lifted my sword, the weight of it making my arm ache.

But I broke these two with swift blows until their metal heads had gone clattering from their wooden stems as well.

I stepped down, holding tight with my right hand so as not to slip on the steps, and suddenly, with a loud cry, I swung out and off the edge of nothing, for the stairway broke there and was no more.

With my right hand I grabbed at the shaft of the broken spear, which I already held in my left. My sword went clattering down below me.

"Enough, Mastema," said Setheus. "No human can do it."

I was hanging, both hands locked around this splintery wood, staring up at them as they rimmed the mouth of the crypt. If I fell, I would no doubt die, for the fall was that far. If I did not die, I would never get out to live.

I waited, and I said nothing, though my arms ached excruciatingly.

Suddenly, they descended, as soundlessly as they

did all things, in a rush of silk and wings, slipping into the crypt at once, all of them, and surrounding me, embracing me and carrying me down in a soft plummet to the floor of the chamber.

I was at once let go. And I scrambled around in the dimness until I found my sword. I had it now.

I stood up, panting, holding it firmly, and then I looked up at the sharp distinct rectangle of brightness above. I shut my eyes, and bowed my head, and opened my eyes slowly so as to become accustomed to this deep damp dusk.

Here the castle had no doubt let the mountain rise up under it, for the chamber, though vast, seemed made of only the earth. At least this is what I saw before me, in the rude wall, and then turning around I saw my quarry, as Mastema had called them.

The vampires, the larvae—they lay sleeping, coffinless, cryptless, open in long rows, each exquisitely dressed body covered in a thin shroud of spun gold. They ringed three walls of the crypt. At the far end hung the broken stairs over nothingness.

I blinked and narrowed my eyes, and the light seemed to filter more fully upon them. I drew near to the first figure until I could see the dark-burgundy slippers, and the deep-russet hose and all of this beneath the webbing as if each night fine silkworms wove this shroud for the being, so thick and perfect and fine was it. Alas, it was no such magic; it was only the finest of what God's creatures can make. And it had been spun of the looms of men and women, and it had a fine-stitched hem.

I ripped off the veil.

I drew near the creature's folded arms, and then saw to my sudden horror that his sleeping face was quickened. His eyes opened, and one arm moved violently towards me.

I was yanked back out of the clutch of his fingers only just in time. I turned to see Ramiel holding me, and then he closed his eyes and bowed his forehead into my shoulder.

"Now you know their tricks. Watch it. You see. It folds its arm back now. It thinks it's safe. It closes its eyes."

"What do I do! Ah, I'll kill it!" I said.

Snatching up the veil in my left hand, I raised my sword in my right. I advanced on the sleeping monster, and this time, when the hand rose, I snared it with the veil, swirling the fabric around it, while, with my sword, I came down like the executioner on the block.

At once the head rolled off onto the floor. A wretched sound came, more from the neck perhaps than from the throat. The arm flopped. By light of day, it could not struggle as it might have in the dark of night in my early battle, when I had decapitated my first assailant. Ah, I had won.

I snatched up the head, watching the blood spill out of the mouth. The eyes, if they had ever opened, were now shut. I hurled the head into the middle of the floor beneath the light. At once the light began to burn the flesh.

"Look at it, the head's burning!" I said. But I myself didn't stop.

I went to the next, snatching the transparent silken shroud from a woman with great long braids, taken to this eerie death in the prime of her life, and snaring her rising arm, severed her head with the same fury and caught it up by one braid and hurled it to land by its mate.

The other head was shriveling and turning black in the light that poured down from the high opening above.

"Lucifer, you see that?" I called out. The echo came back to taunt me, "See that? See that? See that?"

I rushed to the next. "Florian!" I cried out, as I grabbed the veil.

Terrible error.

When he heard his name, his eyes snapped open even before I had drawn abreast of him, and like a puppet yanked on a chain he would have risen if I had not struck him hard with my sword and gashed open his chest. Expressionless, he fell back. I brought the sword down on his tender gentlemanly neck. His blond hair was caked with blood, and his eyes went half-mast and empty and died before my sight.

I snatched him up by his long hair, this bodiless one, this leader of them all, this silver-tongued fiend, and I hurled his head into the smoking, stinking pile.

On and on I went, down the line to the left, why to the left I do not know, except it was my path, and each time I pulled back the veil, I leapt forward with ferocious speed, snaring the arm if it should rise, but sometimes gaining such momentum on it that it had no time to rise, and chopping off the head so fast that I became sloppy and my blows ugly, and I smashed the jawbones of my foes, and even their shoulder bones, but I killed them.

I killed them.

I ripped off their heads and fed them to the mountain, which had gained such smoke now that it seemed a simmering fire of autumn leaves. Ashes rose from it, tiny thin ashes, but in the main, the heads languished, greasy and blackening, and the mass thickened and the ashes were only a few.

Did they suffer? Did they know? Where had their souls fled on invisible feet in this harsh and terrible moment when their Court was dissolved, when I roared in my work and stomped my feet and threw back my head and cried and cried until I couldn't see through my tears?

I had done with some twenty of them, twenty, and my sword was so thick with blood and gore that I had to wipe it clean. On their bodies, making my way back to go down the other side of the crypt, I wiped it, on one doublet after another, marveling at how their white hands had shriveled and dried up on their chests, at how the black blood flowed so sluggishly by day from their torn necks.

"Dead, you are all dead, and yet where did you go, where did the living soul in you go!"

The light was dimming. I stood breathing heavily. I looked up at Mastema.

"The sun is high overhead," he said gently. He was untouched, though he stood so near to them, the charred and reeking heads.

It seemed the smoke issued more truly from their eyes than anywhere else, as if the jelly melted into smoke more surely.

"The church is dim now, but it is only midday. Be quick. You have twenty more this side, and you know it. Work."

The other angels stood stock-still, clustered together, the magnificent Ramiel and Setheus in their rich robes, and the two simpler, plainer, more somber souls—all of them looking at me in utter suspense. I saw Setheus look at the pile of smoldering heads, and then again at me.

"Go on, poor Vittorio," he whispered. "Hurry on."

"Could you do it?" I asked.

"I cannot."

"No, I know that you are not permitted," I said, my chest aching from the exertion and now the talk I forced from myself. "I mean could you do it? Could you bring yourself to do it!"

"I am not a creature of flesh and blood, Vittorio," Setheus answered helplessly. "But I could do what God told me to do."

I went on past them. I looked back at them in their glorious radiance, the cluster of them, and the masterly one, Mastema, his armor gleaming in the falling light, and his sword so brilliant against his flank.

He said nothing.

I turned. I ripped off the first veil. It was Ursula.

"No." I stood back.

I let the veil drop. I was far enough away from her that she didn't appear to wake; she didn't move. Her lovely arms lay folded still in the same pose of graceful death which all of them had borne, only with her it was sweet, as if in her most innocent girlhood a gentle bane had taken her, not mussing so much as a single hair of long rippling unbraided locks. They made a nest of gold for her head and her shoulders, her swan neck.

I could hear my heaving breaths. I let the edge of my sword drag, singing on the stones. I licked at my parched lips. I didn't dare to look at them, though I knew they were collected only a few yards from me, staring at me. And in the thick stillness, I heard the crisping and sizzling of the burning heads of the damned.

I thrust my hand inside my pocket, and I drew out the rosary of amber beads. My hand shook shamefully as I held it, and then I lifted it, letting the crucifix dangle, and I hurled it at her, so that it struck her, just above her small hands, right on the white swell of her half-bared breasts. It lay there, the crucifix nestled in the curve of her pale skin, and she didn't so much as stir.

The light clung to her eyelashes as if it were dust.

Without excuse or explanation, I turned to the next one, ripping off the veil and assaulting him or her, I knew not which, with a loud raucous cry. I grabbed up the severed head by its thick brown locks and threw it crashing past the angels into the mass of slop that lay at their feet.

Then to the next. Godric. Oh, God, this will be sweet.

I saw his bald head before I ever touched the veil, and now, tearing the veil loose, hearing it rip on account of my carelessness, I waited for him to open his eyes, waited for him to rise up halfway from the slab and glare at me.

"Know me, monster? Know me?" I roared. The sword sliced through his neck. The white head hit the floor, and with my sword I speared it through its dripping stump of a neck. "Know me, monster?" I cried again to the fluttering eyes, the gaping, drooling red mouth. "Know me?"

I walked with him to the pile of the other heads and laid him like a trophy on top of it. "Know me?" I wailed again.

And then in a fury I went back to my work.

Two more, then three, then five, then seven and then nine, and then some six more, and the Court was finished, and all its dancers and Lords and Ladies were dead.

And then, reeling to the other side, I made swift work of those poor peasant servants, who had no veils to cover their simple bodies, and whose feeble half-starved white limbs could scarce rise in defense.

"The huntsmen, where are they?"

"At the far end. It is almost dark in here. Take great care."

"I see them," I said. I drew myself up and caught my breath. They lay in a row of six, heads to the wall like all the others, but they were perilously close together. It would be a hard approach.

I laughed suddenly at the simplicity of it. I laughed. I snatched off the first veil and chopped at the feet. The corpse rose and then my blade could easily see the place to strike, while the blood had already begun to gush.

The second, I cut to stumps at once and then sliced across the middle, and only descended on the head before his hand had caught my blade. I ripped back my sword and chopped the hand off him. "Die, bastard, you who stole me with your fellow; I remember you."

And at last I came to the final one and had his bearded head hanging from my hand.

Slowly I walked back with this one, kicking others before me, others I had not had the strength to hurl very far, and I kicked them like so much refuse until the light fell on all of them.

It was bright now. The afternoon sun was coming in the west side of the church. And the opening above gave forth a terrific and fatal heat.

Slowly I wiped my face with the back of my left hand. I laid down my sword, and I felt for the napkins the monks had put in my pockets, and I took these and cleaned my face and cleaned my hands.

Then I picked up my sword, and I went to the foot of her bier again. She lay as before. The light was nowhere near her. It could not have touched any of them where they lay.

She was safe on her bed of stone, her hands as still as before, fingers beautifully folded, the right hand over the left, and on her mound of white breast there rested the Crucified Christ in gold. Her hair was stirring in a faint draft that seemed to come from the narrow opening above. But this was a mere halo of tendrils about her otherwise lifeless face.

Her hair, in its loose ripples, without its ribbons or pearls, had fallen a little over the edges of the bier, so narrow was it, and so had the folds of her long gold-embroidered dress. It was not the same that she'd worn when I'd seen her. Only the deep rich blood red was the same, but all the rest was splendid and ornate and new, as if she were a regal princess, always prepared for the kiss of her prince.

"Could Hell receive this?" I whispered. I drew as close as I dared. I could not bear the thought of her arm rising in that mechanical fashion, the sudden clutch of her fingers on the empty air or her eyes opening. I couldn't bear it.

The points of her slippers were small beneath her hem. How daintily she must have lain down to her rest at sunrise. Who had pulled closed the trapdoor, whose chains had fallen? Who had set the trap of the spears, whose engines I had never inspected or compassed with my thoughts?

For the first time in the dimness, I saw a tiny golden circlet on her head, lying just around the crown and fixed by the tiniest pins into the waves so that its single pearl rested on her forehead. Such a small thing.

Was her soul so small? Would Hell take it, like the fire would take any tender part of her anatomy, like the sun would burn to horror her immaculate face?

In some mother's womb she had once slept and dreamt, and into some father's arms been placed.

What had been her tragedy to bring her to this foul and reeking grave, where the heads of her slain companions lay burning slowly in the sun's ever patient, ever indifferent light?

I turned on them. I held my sword down at my side.

"One, let one only live. One!" I declared.

Ramiel covered his face and turned his back on me. Setheus continued to stare but shook his head. My guardians only gazed at me with their level coldness, as they always had. Mastema stared at me, soundlessly, concealing whatever thought he possessed behind his serene mask of a face.

"No, Vittorio," he said. "Do you think a bevy of God's angels has helped you past these barriers to leave one such as these to live?"

"Mastema, she loved me. And I love her. Mastema, she gave me my life. Mastema, I ask in the name of love. I beg in the name of love. All else here has been justice. But what can I say to God if I slay this one, who has loved and whom I love?"

Nothing in his countenance changed. He only regarded me with his eternal calm. I heard a terrible sound. It was the weeping of Ramiel and Setheus. My guardians turned to look at them, as though surprised, but only mildly so, and then their dreamy soft eyes fixed again, unchanging, on me.

"Merciless angels," I said. "Oh, but such is not fair, and I know it. I lie. I lie. Forgive me."

"We forgive you," said Mastema. "But you must do what you have promised me you would do."

"Mastema, can she be saved? If she herself renounces . . . can she . . . is her soul still human?"

No answer came from him. No answer.

"Mastema, please, tell me. Don't you see? If she can be saved, I can stay here with her, I can wring it out of her, I know I can because her heart is good. It's young and good. Mastema, tell me. Can such a creature as she is be saved?"

No answer. Ramiel had lain his head against Setheus's shoulder.

"Oh, please, Setheus," I said. "Tell me. Can she be saved? Must she die by my hand? What if I stay here with her, and wring it out of her, her confession, her final disavowal of all that she has ever done? Is there no priest who can give her absolution? Oh, God . . ."

"Vittorio," came the whisper from Ramiel. "Are your ears stopped with wax? Can you hear those prisoners starving, crying? You have not even set them free yet. Will you do it by night?"

"I can do it. I can yet do it. But can I not stay here with her, and when she finds she is all alone, that all the others have perished, that all the promises of Godric and Florian were tyranny, is there no way that she can render her soul to God?"

Mastema, without ever a change in his soft cold eyes, slowly turned his back.

"No! Don't do it, don't turn away!" I shouted. I caught hold of his powerful silk-clad arm. I felt his unsurmountable strength beneath the fabric, the strange, unnatural fabric. He gazed down at me.

"Why can't you tell me!"

"For the love of God, Vittorio!" he roared suddenly, his voice filling the entire crypt. "Don't you realize? We don't know!"

He shook me loose, the better to glare down at me, his brows furrowed, his hand closing on the hilt of his sword.

"We don't come from a species that has ever known forgiveness!" he shouted. "We are not flesh and blood, and in our realm things are Light or they are the Darkness, and that is all we know!"

In a fury, he turned and marched towards her. I rushed after him, pulling at him, but unable to deter him a fraction from his purpose.

He plunged his hand down, past her groping hands, and clutched her tiny neck. Her eyes stared up at him in that terrible, terrible blindness.

"She has a human soul in her," he said in a whisper. And then he drew back as if he did not want to touch her, couldn't bear to touch her, and he backed away from her, shoving me away, forcing me back as he did.

I broke into weeping. The sun shifted, and the shadows began to thicken in the crypt. I turned finally. The patch of light above was now pale. It was a rich radiant gold, but it was pale.

My angels stood there, all gathered, watching me and waiting.

"I'm staying with her here," I said. "She'll wake soon. And I'll put it to her, that she pray for God's grace."

I knew it only as I said it. I understood it only as I made it plain.

"I'll stay with her. If she renounces all her sins for the love of God, then she can remain with me, and death will come, and we will not lift a hand to hasten it, and God will accept us both."

"You think you have the strength to do that?" Mastema asked. "And you think it of her?"

"I owe her this," I said. "I am bound. I never lied to you, not to any of you. I never lied to myself. She slew my brother and sister. I saw her. No doubt she killed many of them, my own. But she saved me. She saved me twice. And to kill is simple, but to save is not!"

"Ah," said Mastema as though I'd struck him. "That's true."

"So I'll stay. I expect nothing from you now. I know I cannot get out of here. Perhaps even she cannot."

"Of course she can," said Mastema.

"Don't leave him," said Setheus. "Take him against his will."

"None of us can do that, and you know it," said Mastema.

"Only out of the crypt," pleaded Ramiel, "as if from a canyon into which he's fallen."

"But it is not such a thing, and I cannot."

"Then let us stay with him," said Ramiel.

"Yes, let us stay," said my two guardians, more or less at the same time and in similar muted expressions.

"Let her see us."

"How do we know that she can?" asked Mastema. "How do we know that she will? How many times does it happen that a human being can see us?"

For the first time I saw anger in him. He looked at me.

"God has played such a game with you, Vittorio!" he said. "Given you such enemies and such allies!"

"Yes, I know this, and I will beg Him with all my strength and the weight of all my suffering for her soul."

I didn't mean to close my eyes.

I know that I did not.

But the entire scene was altered utterly. The pile of heads lay as before, and some at random, shriveling, drying up, the acrid smoke still rising from them, and the light above had darkened, yet it was still golden, golden beyond the broken stair, and the jagged broken spears, golden with the last burnt dregs of the late afternoon.

And my angels had gone.

12

DELIVER ME NOT INTO TEMPTATION

OR all my youth, my body could take no more. Yet how could I remain in this crypt, waiting for her to awake, without attempting some form of exit?

I gave no thought to the dismissal by my angels. I deserved it, but I was convinced of the rectitude of the chance I meant to give her, that she throw herself on the mercy of God, and that we leave this crypt and, if necessary, find the priest who could absolve her human soul of all her sins. For if she could not make a perfect confession for the love of God alone, well, then, the absolution would surely save her.

I poked around the crypt, stepping among the drying-up corpses. What light there was gleamed on dried founts of blood that ran down the sides of the stone biers.

At last I found what I had hoped to find, a great ladder that could be lifted and thrown up to the ceiling above. Only, how could I wield such a thing?

I dragged it towards the center of the crypt, kicking out of my path the heads which were now damaged beyond reprieve, and I laid down the ladder, and stepped at midpoint, between two of the rungs, and tried from there to lift it.

Impossible. I simply did not possess the leverage. It weighed too much, slight as it was, because it was so long. Three or four strong men might have hoisted it sufficiently to make its topmost rungs catch on the broken spears, but I alone could not do it.

Alas, there was another possibility. A chain, or a rope, that could be tossed to the spears above. In the gloam, I made a search for such but found none.

No chains anywhere here? No coil of rope?

Had even the young larvae been able to leap the gap between the floor and the broken stairway?

At last I moved along the walls, searching for any bump or hook or excrescence which might indicate a storeroom or, God forbid, another crypt of these fiends.

But I could find nothing.

Finally, I staggered towards the center of the room again. I gathered all the heads, even the loathsome bald head of Godric, which was now black like leather with its yellowed slits of eyes, and I piled these heads where the light could not fail to continue its work on them.

Then, stumbling over the ladder, I fell on my knees at the foot of Ursula's bier.

I sank down. I would sleep this little while. No, not sleep, rest.

Not willing it, indeed, fearing it and regretting it, I felt my limbs go limp and I lay on the stone floor, and my eyes closed in a blessed restorative sleep.

How curious it was.

I had thought her scream would awaken me, that like a frightened child she would have risen up in the darkness on the bier, finding herself alone with so many dead ones.

I had thought the sight of the heads in the pile would have terrified her.

But no such had happened.

Twilight filled the space above, violet-colored, like the flowers of the meadow, and she stood over me. She had put the rosary around her neck, which is not common, and she wore it as a beautiful ornament with the gold crucifix turning and twisting in the light, a glinting speck of gold that matched the specks of light in her eyes.

She was smiling.

"My brave one, my hero, come, let's escape this place of death. You've done it, you have avenged them."

"Did you move your lips?"

"Need I do that with you?"

I felt a thrill pass through me as she lifted me to my feet. She stood looking up into my face, her hands firmly on my shoulders.

"Blessed Vittorio," she said. Then clasping me about the waist, she rose upwards and we passed the broken spears, without so much as touching their splintered tips, and found ourselves in the chapel in the dusk, the windows darkened and the shadows playing gracefully but mercifully around the distant altar.

"Oh, my darling, my darling," I said. "Do you

know what the angels did? Do you know what they said?"

"Come, let's free the prisoners as you wish," she told me.

I felt so refreshed, so full of vigor. It was as if I'd suffered no exhausting labor at all, as if war hadn't worn down my limbs and broken me, as though battle and struggle hadn't been my portion for days.

I rushed with her through the castle. We threw open the doors, one pair after another, on the miserable occupants of the coop. It was she who scurried on her light, feline feet through the pathways beneath the orange trees and the bird aviaries, overturning the kettles of soup, crying out to the poor and the lame and the hopeless that they were free, that no one imprisoned them now.

In a twinkling we stood on a high balcony. I saw far below their miserable procession in the half-light, the long winding line of them progressing down the mountain under the purple sky and the rising evening star. The weak helped the strong; the old carried the young.

"Where will they go, back to that evil town? Back to the monsters who gave them up in sacrifice?" I was in a fury suddenly. "Punished, that's what they must be."

"In time, Vittorio; there is time. Your poor sad victims are free now. This is our time, yours and mine, come."

Her skirts went out in a great dark circle as down we flew, down and down, down past the windows, and down past the walls, until my feet were allowed to touch the soft ground.

"Oh, Lord God, it's the meadow, look, the meadow," I said. "I can see it as clearly under the rising moon as ever I saw it in my dreams."

A sudden softness filled me completely. I twined her in my arms, my fingers digging deep into her rippling hair. All the world seemed to sway about me, and yet I was anchored in dance with her, and the soft airy movement of the trees sang to us as we were bound together.

"Nothing can ever part us, Vittorio," she said. She tore loose. She ran ahead of me.

"No, wait, Ursula, wait!" I cried. I ran after her, but the grass and the irises were tall and thick. It wasn't so like the dream, but then again it was, because these things were alive and full of the verdant smell of the wild, and the sylvan woods were gently heaving their limbs on the scented wind.

I fell down exhausted and let the flowers climb up on either side of me. I let the red irises peer down upon my upturned face.

She knelt above me. "He will forgive me, Vittorio," she said. "He will forgive all in his infinite mercy."

"Oh, yes, my love, my blessed, beautiful love, my savior, He will."

The tiny crucifix dangled down against my neck.

"But you must do this for me, you who let me live below, you who spared me and fell asleep in my trust at the feet of my grave, you must do this . . ."

"What, blessed one?" I asked. "Tell me and I'll do it."

"Pray first for strength, and then into your human body, into your wholesome and baptized body, you must take all the demon blood out of me which you can, you must draw it from me, and thereby free my soul from its spell; it will be vomited forth out of you like the potions we gave you, which cannot hurt you. Will you do it for me? Will you take the poison out of me?"

I thought of the sickness, of the vomit that had streamed from my mouth in the monastery. I thought of it all, the terrible gibbering and madness.

"Do this for me," she said.

She lay against me and I felt her heart trapped in her chest, and I felt my own, and it seemed I had never known such dreamy languor. I could feel my fingers curl. For an instant it seemed they rested on hard rocks in this meadow, as if the backs of my hands had found harsh pebbles, but once again I felt the broken stems, the bed of purple and red and white irises.

She raised her head.

"In the Name of God," I said, "for your salvation, I will take whatever poison I must from you; I will draw off the blood as if from a cankerous wound, as if it were the corruption of a leper. Give it to me, give me the blood."

Her face was motionless above mine, so small, so dainty, so white.

"Be brave, my love, be brave, for I must make room for it first."

She nestled in against my neck, and into my flesh there came her teeth. "Be brave, only a little more to make room."

"A little more?" I whispered. "A little more. Ah, Ursula, look up, look up at Heaven and Hell in the sky, for the stars are balls of fire suspended there by the angels."

But the language was stretched and meaningless and became an echo in my ears. A darkness shrouded me, and when I lifted my hand it seemed a golden net covered it and I could see far, far away, my fingers shrouded in the net.

The meadow was suddenly flooded with sunlight. I wanted to break away, to sit up, to tell her, Look, the sun has come, and you're not hurt, my precious girl. But on and on there came these waves of divine and luscious pleasure passing through me, pulled from me, pulled up from my loins, this coaxing and magnificent pleasure.

When her teeth slipped from my flesh, it was as if she had tightened the grip of her soul on my organs, on all parts of me that were man and babe once, and human now.

"Oh, my love, my darling, don't stop." The sun made a bewildering dance in the branches of the chestnut trees.

She opened her mouth, and from her came the stream of blood, the deep dark kiss of blood. "Take it from me, Vittorio."

"All your sins into me, my divine child," I said. "Oh, God help me. God have mercy on me. Mastema—."

But the word was broken. My mouth was filled with the blood, and it was no rank potion mixed of parts, but that searing thrilling sweetness that she had first given me in her most secretive and perplexing kisses. Only this time it came in an overwhelming gush.

Her arms were tucked beneath me. They lifted me. The blood seemed to know no veins within but to fill my limbs themselves, to fill my shoulders and my chest, to drown and invigorate my very heart. I stared up at the twinkling playing sun, I felt her blinding and soft hair across my eyes but peered through its golden strands. My breath came in gasps.

The blood flowed down into my legs and filled them to my very toes. My body surged with strength. My organ pumped against her, and once more I felt her subtle feline weight, her sinuous limbs hugging me, holding me, binding me, her arms crossed beneath me, her lips sealed to mine.

My eyes struggled, grew wide. The sunlight filled them, and then contracted. It contracted, and my sighs seemed to grow immense, and the beating of my heart to echo, as though we were not in a wild meadow, and the sounds that came from my empowered body, my transformed body, my body so full of her blood, echoed off stone walls!

The meadow was gone or never was. The twilight was a rectangle high above. I lay in the crypt.

I rose up, throwing her off, back away from me as she screamed in pain. I sprang to my feet and stared at my white hands outstretched before me.

A horrid hunger reared up in me, a fierce strength, a howl!

I stared up at the dark-purple light above and screamed.

"You've done it to me! You've made me one of you!"

She sobbed. I turned on her. She backed up, bent

over, her hand over her mouth, crying and fleeing from me. I ran after her. Like a rat she ran, round and round the crypt, screaming.

"Vittorio, no, Vittorio, no, Vittorio, no, don't hurt me. Vittorio, I did this for us; Vittorio, we are free. Ah, God help me!"

And then upwards she flew, just missing my outstretched arms. She had fled to the chapel above.

"Witchlet, monster, larva, you tricked me with your illusions, with your visions, you made me one of you, you did it to me!" My roars echoed one upon the other as I scrambled about in the dark till I found my sword, and then dancing back to gain my momentum, I too made the leap and cleared the spears and found myself high up on the floor of the church, and she hovering with glittering tears before the altar.

She backed up into the bank of red flowers that barely showed in the starlight that passed through the darkened windows.

"No, Vittorio, don't kill me, don't do it. Don't," she sobbed and wailed. "I am a child, like you, please, don't."

I tore at her, and she scrambled to the end of the sanctuary. In a rage, I swung at the statue of Lucifer with my sword. It tottered and then crashed down, breaking on the marble floor of the cursed sanctuary.

She hovered at the far end. She dropped down on her knees and threw out her hands. She shook her head, her hair flying wildly from side to side.

"Don't kill me, don't kill me, don't kill me. You send me to Hell if you do; don't do it."

"Wretch!" I moaned. "Wretch!" My tears fell as freely as hers. "I thirst, you wretch. I thirst, and I can smell them, the slaves in the coop. I can smell them, their blood, damn you!"

I too had gone down on my knees. I lay down on the marble, and kicked aside the broken fragments of the hideous statue. With my sword I snagged the lace of the altar cloth and brought it down with all its many red flowers tumbling on me, so that I could roll over into them and crush my face into their softness.

A silence fell, a terrible silence full of my own wailing. I could feel my strength, feel it even in the timbre of my voice, and the arm that held the sword without exhaustion or restraint, and feel it in the painless calm with which I lay on what should have been cold and was not cold, or only goodly cold.

Oh, she had made me mighty.

A scent overcame me. I looked up. She stood just above me, tender, loving thing that she was, with her eyes so full of the starlight now, so glinting and quiet and unjudging. In her arms she held a young human, a feeble-minded one, who did not know his danger.

How pink and succulent he was, how like the roasted pig ready for my lips, how full of naturally cooking and bubbling mortal blood and ready for me. She set him down before me.

He was naked, thin buttocks on his heels, his trembling chest very pink and his hair black and long and soft around his guileless face. He appeared to be dreaming or searching the darkness, perhaps for angels?

"Drink, my darling, drink from him," she said, "and then you'll have the strength to take us both to the Good Father for Confession."

I smiled. The desire for the feeble-minded boy before me was almost more than I could endure. But it was a whole new book now, was it not, what I might endure, and I took my time, rising up on my elbow as I looked at her.

"To the Good Father? You think that's where we'll go? Right away, just like that, the two of us?"

She began to cry again. "Not right away, no, not right away," she cried. She shook her head. Beaten.

I took him. I broke his neck when I drained him dry. He made not a sound. There was no time for fear or pain or crying.

Do we ever forget the first kill? Do we ever?

Through the coop I went all that night, devouring, feasting, gorging on their throats, taking what I wanted from each, sending each to God or to Hell, how could I ever know, bound now to this earth with her, and she feasting with me in her dainty way, ever watching for my howls and wails, and ever catching hold of me to kiss me and ply me with her sobs when I shook with rage.

"Come out of here," I said.

It was just before sunrise. I told her I would spend no day beneath these pointed towers, in this house of horrors, in this place of evil and filthy birth.

"I know of a cave," she said. "Far down the mountains, past the farmlands."

"Yes, somewhere on the edge of a true meadow?"

"There are meadows in this fair land without

count, my love," she said. "And under the moon their flowers shine as prettily for our magical eyes as ever they do for humans by the light of God's sun. Remember His moon is ours.

"And tomorrow night . . . before you think of the priest . . . you must take your time to think of the priest—."

"Don't make me laugh again. Show me how to fly. Wrap your arm around my waist and show me how to drop from the high walls to safety in a descent that would shatter a man's limbs. Don't talk of priests anymore. Don't mock me!"

". . . before you think of the priest, of Confession," she went on, undeterred in her dainty sweet small voice, her eyes brimming with tears of love, "we'll go back to the town of Santa Maddalana while it's fast asleep, and we'll burn it all down around them."

13

CHILD BRIDE

WE didn't put the torch to Santa Maddalana. It was too much of a pleasure to hunt the town.

By the third night, I had stopped weeping at sunrise, when we retired together, locked in each other's arms inside our concealed and unreachable cave.

And by the third night, the townspeople knew what had befallen them—how their clever bargain with the Devil had rebounded upon them—and they were in a panic, and it was a great game to outsmart them, to hide in the multitude of shadows that made up their twisted streets, and to tear open their most extravagant and clever locks.

In the early hours, when no one dared to stir, and the good Franciscan priest knelt awake in his cell, saying his rosary, and begging God for understanding of what was happening—this priest, you remember, who had befriended me at the inn, who had dined with me and warned me, not in anger like his Dominican brother, but in kindness—while this priest prayed, I crept into the Franciscan church and I too prayed.

But each night I told myself what a man says to himself under his breath when he couches with his adulterous whore: "One more night, God, and then I'll go to Confession. One more night of bliss, Lord, and then I'll go home to my wife."

The townspeople had no chance against us.

What skills I did not acquire naturally and through experimentation, my beloved Ursula taught to me with patience and grace. I could scan a mind, find a sin and eat it with a flick of my tongue as I sucked the blood from a lazy, lying merchant who had put out his own tender children once for the mysterious Lord Florian, who had kept the peace.

One night we found that the townsmen had been by day to the abandoned castle. There was evidence of hasty entry, with little stolen or disturbed. How it must have frightened them, the horrid saints still flanking the pedestal of the Fallen Lucifer in the church. They had not taken the golden candlesticks or the old tabernacle in which I discovered, with my groping hand, a shriveled human heart.

On our last visit to the Court of the Ruby Grail, I took the burned leathery heads of the vampires from the deep cellar and I hurled them like so many stones through the stained-glass windows. The last of the brilliant art of the castle was gone.

Together, Ursula and I roamed the bedchambers of the castle, which I had never glimpsed or even imagined, and she showed me those rooms in which the members of the Court had gathered for dice or chess or to listen to small ensembles of music. Here and there we saw evidence of something stolen—a coverlet ripped from a bed and a pillow fallen to the floor.

But obviously the townspeople were more afraid than greedy. They took little from the castle.

And as we continued to prey upon them, artfully defeating them, they began to desert Santa Maddalana. Shops lay open when we came into the empty streets at midnight; windows were unbolted, cradles empty. The Dominican church had been deconsecrated and abandoned, its altar stone removed. The cowardly priests, whom I had not granted the mercy of a quick death, had abandoned their flock.

The game became ever more invigorating to me. For now, those who remained were quarrelsome and avaricious and refusing to give up without a fight. It was simple to sort the innocent, who believed in the faith of the vigil light or the saints to protect them, from those who had played with the Devil and now kept an uneasy watch in the dark with sword in hand.

I liked to talk to them, spar with them verbally, as I killed them. "Did you think your game would go on forever? Did you think the thing you fed would never feed on you?"

As for my Ursula, she had no stomach for such sport. She could not endure the spectacle of suffering. The old Communion of Blood in the castle had for her been tolerable only because of the music, the incense and the supreme authority of Florian and Godric, who had led her in it with every step.

Night after night, as the town was slowly emptied, as the farms were deserted, as Santa Maddalana, my school town, became ever more ruined,

Ursula took to playing with orphaned children. She sat sometimes on the church steps cradling a human infant and cooing to it, and telling it stories in French.

She sang old songs in Latin from the courts of her time, which had been two hundred years ago, she told me, and she talked of battles in France and in Germany whose names meant nothing to me.

"Don't play with the children," I said. "They'll remember it. They'll remember us."

A fortnight went by before the community was irreparably destroyed. Only the orphans remained and a few of the very old, and the Franciscan father, and his father, the elfin little man who sat in his lighted room at night, playing a game of cards with himself, as if he did not even now guess what was going on.

On the fifteenth night, it must have been, when we arrived in the town, we knew at once that only two persons were left. We could hear the little old man singing to himself in the empty Inn with the doors open. He was very drunk, and his wet pink head gleamed in the light of the candle. He slapped the cards down on the table in a circle, playing a game of solitaire called "clock."

The Franciscan priest sat beside him. He looked up at us, fearlessly and calmly, as we came into the Inn.

I was overcome with hunger, ravening hunger, for the blood in them both.

"I never told you my name, did I?" he asked me.

"No, you never did, Father," I said.

"Joshua," he said. "That's my name, Fra Joshua.

All the rest of the community has gone back to Assisi, and they took with them the last of the children. It's a long journey south."

"I know, Father," I said. "I've been to Assisi, I've prayed at the shrine of St. Francis. Tell me, Father, when you look at me, do you see angels around me?"

"Why would I see angels?" he asked quietly. He looked from me to Ursula. "I see beauty, I see youth fixed in polished ivory. But I don't see angels. I never have."

"I saw them once," I said. "May I sit down?"

"Do as you like," he said to me. He watched us, drawing himself up in his hard simple wooden chair, as I seated myself opposite him, much as I had been on that day in the village, only now we were not in the fragrant arbor under the sun but inside, in the Inn itself, where the candlelight gave more volume and more warmth.

Ursula looked at me in confusion. She didn't know what was in my mind. I had never witnessed her speaking to any human being except for me myself and for the children with whom she'd played—in other words, only with those for whom her heart had quickened and whom she did not mean to destroy.

What she thought of the little man and his son, the Franciscan priest, I couldn't guess.

The old man was winning the card game. "There, you see, I told you. Our luck!" he said. He gathered up his greasy loose cards to shuffle them and to play again.

The priest looked at him with glazed eyes, as

though he could not gather his own wits even to fool or reassure his old father, and then he looked at me.

"I saw these angels in Florence," I said, "and I disappointed them, broke my vow to them, lost my soul."

He turned from his father to me sharply.

"Why do you prolong this?" he asked.

"I will not hurt you. Neither will my companion," I said. I sighed. It would have been that moment in a conversation when I would have reached for the cup or the tankard and taken a drink. My hunger hurt me. I wondered if the thirst hurt Ursula. I stared at the priest's wine, which was nothing to me now, nothing, and I looked at his face, sweating in the light of the candle, and I went on:

"I want you to know that I saw them, that I talked to them, these angels. They tried to help me to destroy those monsters who held sway over this town, and over the souls of those here. I want you to know, Father."

"Why, son, why tell me?"

"Because they were beautiful, and they were as real as we are, and you have seen us. You have seen hellish things; you have seen sloth and treachery, cowardice and deceit. You see devils now, vampires. Well, I want you to know that with my own eyes I saw angels, true angels, magnificent angels, and that they were more glorious than I can ever tell you in words."

He regarded me thoughtfully for a long time, and then he looked at Ursula, who sat troubled and looking up at me, rather afraid that I would unduly suffer, and then he said:

"Why did you fail them? Why did they come with you in the first place, and if you had the aid of angels, why did you fail?"

I shrugged my shoulders. I smiled. "For love."

He didn't answer.

Ursula leaned her head against my arm. I felt her free hair brushing my back as she let me feel her weight.

"For love!" the priest repeated.

"Yes, and for honor as well."

"Honor."

"No one will ever understand it. God will not accept it, but it's true, and now, what is there, Father, that divides us, you and I, and the woman who sits with me? What is between us—the two parties—the honest priest and the two demons?"

The little man chuckled suddenly. He had slapped down a marvelous run of cards. "Look at that!" he said. He looked up at me with his clever little eyes. "Oh, your question, forgive me. I know the answer."

"You do?" asked the priest, turning to the little old man. "You know the answer?"

"Of course, I do," said his father. He dealt out another card. "What separates them now from a good Confession is weakness and the fear of Hell if they must give up their lives."

The priest stared at his father in amazement.

So did I.

Ursula said nothing. Then she kissed me on the

cheek. "Let's leave them now," she whispered. "There is no more Santa Maddalana. Let's go."

I looked up, around the darkened room of the Inn. I looked at the old barrels. I looked in haunted perplexity and appalling sorrow at all things that humans used and touched. I looked at the heavy hands of the priest, folded on the table before me. I looked at the hair on his hands, and then up at his thick lips and his large watering and sorrowful eyes.

"Will you accept this from me?" I whispered. "This secret, of angels? That I saw them! I! And you, you see what I am, and you know therefore that I know whereof I speak. I saw their wings, I saw their halos, I saw their white faces, and I saw the sword of Mastema the powerful, and it was they who helped me sack the castle and lay waste to all the demons save for this one, this child bride, who is mine."

"Child bride," she whispered. It filled her with delight. She looked at me, musingly, and hummed a soft, old-fashioned air, one of those threads of songs from her times.

She spoke to me in an urgent persuasive whisper, squeezing my arm as she did:

"Come, Vittorio, leave these men in peace, and come with me, and I'll tell you how indeed I was a child bride." She looked at the priest with renewed animation. "I was, you know. They came to my father's castle and purchased me as such, they said that I must be a virgin, and the midwives came and brought their basin of warm water, and they examined me and they said I was a virgin, and only then did Florian take me. I was his bride."

The priest stared fixedly at her, as if he could not move if he wanted to move, and the old man merely glanced up again and again, cheerfully, nodding as he listened to her, and went on playing with his cards.

"Can you imagine my horror?" she asked them. She looked at me, tossing her hair back over her shoulder. It was in its ripples again from the plaits in which she'd had it bound earlier. "Can you imagine when I climbed onto the couch and I saw who was my bridegroom, this white thing, this dead thing, such as we look to you?"

The priest made no answer. His eyes filled slowly with tears. Tears!

It seemed a lovely human spectacle, bloodless, crystalline, and such an adornment for his old soft face, with its jowls and fleshy mouth.

"And then to be taken to a ruined chapel," she said, "a ruined place, full of spiders and vermin, and there before a desecrated altar, to be stripped and laid down and taken by him and made his bride."

She let go of my arm, her arms forming a loose embracing gesture. "Oh, I had a veil, a great long beautiful veil, and a dress of such fine flowered silk, and all this he tore from me, and took me first with his lifeless, seedless stone-hard organ and then with his fang teeth, like these very teeth which I have now. Oh, such a wedding, and my father had given me over for this."

The tears coursed down the priest's cheeks.

I stared at her, transfixed with sorrow and rage, rage against a demon I had already slaughtered, a rage that I hoped could reach down through the smoldering coals of Hell and find him with fingers like hot tongs.

I said nothing.

She raised her eyebrow; she cocked her head.

"He tired of me," she said. "But he never stopped loving me. He was new to the Court of the Ruby Grail, a young Lord and seeking at every turn to increase his might and his romance! And later, when I asked for Vittorio's life, he couldn't refuse me on account of our vows exchanged on that stone altar so long ago. After he let Vittorio leave us, after he had him cast down in Florence, certain of Vittorio's madness and ruin, Florian sang songs to me, songs for a bride. He sang the old poems as though our love could be revived."

I covered my brow with my right hand. I couldn't bear to weep the blood tears that flow from us. I couldn't bear to see before me, as if painted by Fra Filippo, the very romance she described.

It was the priest who spoke.

"You are children," he said. His lip trembled. "Mere children."

"Yes," she said in her exquisite voice, with certainty and a small accepting smile. She clasped my left hand in hers and rubbed it hard and tenderly. "Children forever. But he was only a young man, Florian, just a young man himself."

"I saw him once," said the priest, his voice thick with his crying but soft. "Only once."

"And you knew?" I asked.

"I knew I was powerless and my faith was desperate, and that around me were bonds that I could not loose or break."

"Let's go now, Vittorio, don't make him cry anymore," said Ursula. "Come on, Vittorio. Let's leave here. We need no blood tonight and cannot think of harming them, cannot even . . ."

"No, beloved, never," I said to her. "But take my gift, Father, please, the only clean thing which I can give, my testimony that I saw the angels, and that they upheld me when I was weak."

"And won't you take absolution from me, Vittorio!" he said. His voice rose, and his chest seemed to increase in size. "Vittorio and Ursula, take my absolution."

"No, Father," I said. "We cannot take it. We don't want it."

"But why?"

"Because, Father," said Ursula kindly, "we plan to sin again as soon as we possibly can."

14

THROUGH A GLASS DARKLY

SHE didn't lie.

We journeyed that night to my father's house. It was nothing for us to make that journey, but it was many miles for a mortal, and word had not reached that forlorn farmland that the threat of the night demons, the vampires of Florian, was gone. Indeed, it is most likely that my farms were still deserted because ghastly tales were given out by those who had fled Santa Maddalana, traveling over hill and valley, mouth to mouth.

It didn't take me long to realize, however, that the great castle of my family was occupied. A horde of soldiers and clerks had been hard at work.

As we crept over the giant wall after midnight, we found that all the dead of my family had been properly buried, or placed in their proper stone coffins beneath the chapel, and that the goods of the household, all of its abundant wealth, had been taken away. Only a few wagons remained of those which must have already started their progress south.

The few who slept in the offices of my father's

steward were keepers of the accounts of the Medici bank, and on tiptoe, in the dim light of a star-studded sky, I inspected the few papers they had left out to dry.

All of the inheritance of Vittorio di Raniari had been collected and catalogued, and was being taken on to Florence for him, to be placed in safety with Cosimo until such time as Vittorio di Raniari was twenty-four years of age and could thereby assume responsibility for himself as a man.

Only a few soldiers slept in the barracks. Only a few horses were quartered in the stables. Only a few squires and attendants slept in proximity to their Lords.

Obviously the great castle, being of no strategic use to Milanese or German or French or Papal authority, or to Florence, was not being restored or repaired, merely shut down.

Well before dawn, we left my home, but before going, I took leave of my father's grave.

I knew that I would come back. I knew that soon the trees would climb the mountain to the walls. I knew that the grass would grow high through the crevices and cracks of the cobblestones. I knew that things human would lose all love of this place, as they had lost their love of so many ruins in the country round.

I would return then. I would come back.

That night, Ursula and I hunted the vicinity for the few brigands we could find in the woods, laughing gaily when we caught them and dragged them from their horses. It was a riotous old feast.

"And where now, my Lord?" my bride asked me

towards morning. We had again found a cave for shelter, a deep and hidden place, full of thorny vines that barely scratched our resilient skin, behind a veil of wild blueberries that would hide us from all eyes, including that of the great rising sun.

"To Florence, my love. I have to go there. And in its streets, we'll never suffer hunger, or discovery, and there are things which I must see with my own eyes."

"But what are those things, Vittorio?" she asked.

"Paintings, my love, paintings. I have to see the angels in the paintings. I have to . . . face them, as it were."

She was content. She had never seen the great city of Florence. She had, all her wretched eternity of ritual and courtly discipline, been contained in the mountains, and she lay down beside me to dream of freedom, of brilliant colors of blue and green and gold, so contrary to the dark red that she still wore. She lay down beside me, trusting me, and, as for me, I trusted nothing.

I only licked the human blood on my lips and wondered how long I might have on this earth before someone struck off my head with a swift and certain sword.

[illegible] mountains. We had [illegible] had [illegible] [illegible] [illegible] [illegible] [illegible] [illegible] [illegible] that has scattered our [illegible] [illegible] beyond a [illegible] wild [illegible] that would hate us [illegible] all eyes, unfolding [illegible] the great [illegible].

[illegible] Loved [illegible] I have [illegible] [illegible] [illegible] [illegible] [illegible] and there are things which I must see with my own eyes."

"What are these things, Vittoria?" she asked.

"Paintings, [illegible] I have to see [illegible] [illegible] [illegible] [illegible] [illegible]."

She was [illegible] she had ever seen the great [illegible] of Florence. [illegible] [illegible] [illegible] [illegible] [illegible] [illegible] [illegible] [illegible] [illegible] [illegible] [illegible] [illegible] [illegible] of brilliant [illegible] and [illegible] [illegible] [illegible] that she [illegible] She lay down beside me [illegible] and, as [illegible] [illegible] [illegible].

I [illegible] [illegible] on my [illegible] and wondered how [illegible] [illegible] [illegible] [illegible] [illegible] with a [illegible] and [illegible].

15

THE IMMACULATE CONCEPTION

THE city of Florence was in an uproar.

"Why?" I asked.

It was well past curfew, to which no one was paying much attention, and there was a huge crowd of students congregated in Santa Maria Maggiori—the Duomo—listening to a lecture by a humanist who pleaded that Fra Filippo Lippi was not such a pig.

No one took much note of us. We had fed early, in the countryside, and wore heavy mantles, and what could they see of us but a little pale flesh?

I went into the church. The crowd came out almost to the doors.

"What's the matter? What's happened to the great painter?"

"Oh, he's done it now," said the man who answered me, not even bothering to look at me or at the slender figure of Ursula clinging to me.

The man was too intent on looking at the lecturer, who stood up ahead, his voice echoing sharply in the overwhelming large nave.

"Done what?"

Getting no answer, I pushed my way a little

deeper into the thick, odiferous human crowd, pulling Ursula with me. She was still shy of such an immense city, and she had not seen a Cathedral on this scale in the more than two hundred years of her life.

Once again I put my question to two young students, who turned at once to answer me, fashionable boys both, about eighteen, or what they called then in Florence *giovani*, being the most difficult of youths, too old to be a child, such as I was, and too young to be a man.

"Well, he asked for the fairest of the nuns to pose for the altarpiece that he was painting of the blessed Virgin, that's what he did," said the first student, black-haired and deep-eyed, staring at me with a cunning smile. "He asked for her as a model, asked that the convent choose her for him, so that the Virgin he painted would be most perfect, and then . . ."

The other student took it up.

". . . he ran off with her! Stole the nun right out of the convent, ran off with her and her sister, mind you, her blood-kindred sister, and has set up his household right over his shop, he and his nun and her sister, the three of them, the monk and the two nuns . . . and lives in sin with her, Lucrezia Buti, and paints the Virgin on the altarpiece and does not give a damn what anyone thinks."

There was jostling and pushing in the crowd about us. Men told us to be quiet. The students were choking on their laughter.

"If he didn't have Cosimo," said the first student, lowering his voice in an obedient but mischievous whisper, "they'd string him up, I mean her family, the Buti, would at least, if not the priests of the Carmelite Order, if not the whole damned town."

The other student shook his head and covered his mouth not to laugh out loud.

The speaker, far ahead, advised all to remain calm and let this scandal and outrage be handled by the proper authorities, for everyone knew that nowhere in all of Florence was there a painter any greater than Fra Filippo, and that Cosimo would tend to this in his own time.

"He's always been tormented," said the student beside me.

"Tormented," I whispered. "Tormented." His face came back to me, the monk glimpsed years ago in Cosimo's house in the Via Larga, the man arguing so fiercely to be free, only to be with a woman for a little while. I felt the strangest conflict within, the strangest darkest fear. "Oh, that they don't hurt him again."

"One might wonder," came a soft voice in my ear. I turned, but I saw no one who could have spoken to me. Ursula looked about.

"What is it, Vittorio?"

But I knew the whisper, and it came again, bodiless and intimate, "One might wonder, where were his guardian angels on the day that Fra Filippo did such a mad thing?"

I turned in a mad frantic circle, searching for the origin of the voice. Men backed away from me and made little gestures of annoyance. I snatched up Ursula's hand and made for the doors.

Only when I was outside in the piazza did my

heart stop pounding. I had not known that with this new blood I could feel such anxiety and misery and fear.

"Oh, run off with a nun to paint the Virgin!" I cried out under my breath.

"Don't cry, Vittorio," she said.

"Don't speak to me as if I were your little brother!" I said to her, and then was full of shame. She was stricken by my words, as if I'd slapped her. I took her fingers and kissed them. "I'm sorry, Ursula, I am sorry."

I pulled her along beside me.

"But where are we going?"

"To the house of Fra Filippo, to his workshop. Don't question me now."

Within moments we had found our way, echoing and clattering down the narrow street, and we stood before the doors that were shut up and I could see no light, save in the third-story windows, as though he had had to flee to that height with his bride.

No mob was gathered here.

But out of the darkness there came suddenly a handful of filth heaved at the bolted doors, and then another and then a volley of stones. I stepped back, shielding Ursula, and watched as one passerby after another slunk forward and hurled his insults at the shop.

Finally, I lay against the wall opposite, staring dully in the darkness, and I heard the deep-throated bell of the church ring the hour of eleven, which meant surely that all men must vacate the streets.

Ursula only waited on me and said nothing, and

she noted it quietly when I looked up and saw the last of Fra Filippo's lights go out.

"It's my doing," I said. "I took his angels from him, and he fell into this folly, and for what did I do it, for what, that I might possess you as surely now as he possesses his nun?"

"I don't know your meaning, Vittorio," she said. "What are nuns and priests to me? I have never said a word to wound you, never, but I say such words now. Don't stand here weeping over these mortals you loved. We are wedded now, and no convent vow or priestly anointment divides us. Let's go away from here, and when by light of lamps you want to show me the wonders of this painter, then bring me, bring me to see the angels of which you spoke rendered in pigment and oil."

I was chastened by her firmness. I kissed her hand again. I told her I was sorry. I held her to my heart.

How long I might have stood with her there, I don't know. Moments passed. I heard the sound of running water and distant footsteps, but nothing of consequence, nothing which mattered in the thick night of crowded Florence, with its four- and five-story palaces, with its old half-broken towers, and its churches, and its thousands upon thousands of sleeping souls.

A light startled me. It fell down upon me in bright yellow seams. I saw the first, a thin line of brilliance. It cut across her figure, and then there came another, illuminating the alley-like street beyond us, and I realized that the lamps had been lighted within Fra Filippo's shop.

I turned just as the bolts inside were made to slide

back with a low, grating noise. The noise echoed up the dark walls. No light shone above, behind the barred windows.

Suddenly the doors were opened and slapped back softly, soundlessly almost, against the wall, and I saw the deep rectangle of the interior, a wide shallow room filled with brilliant canvases all blazing above candles enough to light a Bishop's Mass.

My breath left me. I clutched her tightly, my hand on the back of her head as I pointed.

"There they are, both of them, the *Annunciations*!" I whispered. "Do you see the angels, the angels who kneel, there, and there, the angels who kneel before the Virgins!"

"I see them," she said reverently. "Ah, they are more lovely even than I supposed." She shook my arm. "Don't cry, Vittorio, unless it's for beauty's sake, only for that."

"Is that a command, Ursula?" I asked. My eyes were so clouded I could scarce see the poised flat kneeling figures of Ramiel and Setheus.

But as I tried to clear my vision, as I tried to gather my wits and swallow the ache in my throat, the miracle I feared more than anything in this world, yet craved, yet hungered for—that miracle commenced.

Out of the very fabric of the canvas, they appeared simultaneously, my silk-clad blond-haired angels, my haloed angels, to unravel from the tight weave itself. They turned, gazing at me first and then moving so that they were no longer flat profiles but full robust figures, and then they stepped out and onto the stones of the shop.

I knew by Ursula's gasp that she had seen the same vivid series of miraculous gestures. Her hand went to her lips.

Their faces bore no wrath, no sadness. They merely looked at me, and in their sweet soft looks was all the condemnation I have ever understood.

"Punish me," I whispered. "Punish me by taking away my eyes that I can never see your beauty again."

Very slowly, Ramiel shook his head to answer no. And Setheus followed with the same negation. They stood side by side in their bare feet, as always, their abundant garments too light for movement on the heavy air, as they merely continued to gaze.

"What then?" I said. "What do I deserve from you? How is it that I can see you and see your glory even still?" I was a wreck of childish tears again, no matter how Ursula stared at me, no matter how she tried with her silent reproach to make the man of me.

I couldn't stop myself.

"What then? How can I see you still?"

"You'll always see us," Ramiel said softly, tonelessly.

"Every time you ever look at one of his paintings, you will see us," said Setheus, "or you will see our like."

There was no judgment in it. There was merely the same lovely serenity and kindness that they had always bestowed on me.

But it was not finished. I saw behind them, taking dark shape, my own guardians, that solemn ivory pair, draped in their robes of shadowy blue.

How hard were their eyes, how knowing, how disdainful yet without the edge which men lend to such passions. How glacial and remote.

My lips parted. A cry was there. A terrible cry. But I dared not rouse the night around me, the infinite night that moved out over the thousands of slanted red-tile rooftops, out over the hills and the country, out under the numberless stars.

Suddenly the entire building began to move. It trembled, and the canvases, brilliant and shimmering in their bath of burning light, were glittering as if shaken by a tremor of the very earth itself.

Mastema appeared suddenly before me, and the room was swept backward, broadened, deepened, and all those lesser angels were swept back from him as if by a soundless wind that cannot be defied.

The flood of light ignited his immense gold wings as they spread out, crowding the very corners of the vastness and pushing it even to greater breadth, and the red of his helmet glared as if it were molten, and out of his sheath, he drew his sword.

I backed up. I forced Ursula behind me. I pushed her back against the damp cold wall and imprisoned her there, behind me, as safe as I could make her on the face of the earth, with my arms stretched back to hold her so that she could not, must not, be taken away.

"Ah," said Mastema, nodding, smiling. The sword was uplifted. "So even now you would go into Hell rather than see her die!"

"I would!" I cried. "I have no choice."

"Oh, yes, you have a choice."

"No, not her, don't kill her. Kill me, and send me there, yes, but give her one more chance . . ."

Ursula cried against my shoulders, her hands clinging to my hair, catching hold of it, as if by means of it she'd be safe.

"Send me now," I said. "Go ahead, strike off my head and send me to my judgment before the Lord that I may beg for her! Please, Mastema, do it, but do not strike her. She does not know how to ask to be forgiven. Not yet!"

Holding the sword aloft, he reached out and grabbed my collar and jerked me towards him. I felt her fly against me. He held me beneath his face, and glowered down at me with his beaming eyes.

"And when will she learn, and when will you?"

What could I say? What could I do?

"I will teach you, Vittorio," said Mastema in a low, seething whisper. "I will teach you so that you know how to beg forgiveness every night of your life. I will teach you."

I felt myself lifted, I felt my garments blown by the wind, I felt her tiny hands clinging to me, and the weight of her head on my back.

Through the streets we were being dragged, and suddenly there appeared before us a great crowd of idle mortals issuing from a wine shop, drunken and laughing, a great jumble of swollen, natural faces and dark breeze-tossed clothes.

"Do you see them, Vittorio? Do you see those upon whom you feed?" Mastema demanded.

"I see them, Mastema!" I said. I groped for her hand, trying to find her, hold her, shield her. "I do see them, I do."

"In each and every one of them, Vittorio, there is what I see in you, and in her—a human soul. Do you know what that is, Vittorio? Can you imagine?"

I didn't dare to answer.

The crowd spread out over the moonlighted piazza, and drew closer to us, even as it loosened.

"A spark of the power that made all of us is within each of them," cried Mastema, "a spark of the invisible, of the subtle, of the sacred, of the mystery—a spark of that which created all things."

"Ah, God!" I cried out. "Look at them, Ursula, look!"

For each and every one of them, man, woman, it did not matter old or young, had taken on a powerful hazy golden glow. A light emanated from and surrounded and embraced each figure, a subtle body of light shaped to the very form of the human being who walked in it, unheeding of it, and the entire square was full of such golden light.

I looked down at my own hands, and they too were surrounded by this subtle, etheric body, this lovely gleaming and numinous presence, this precious and unquenchable fire.

I pivoted, my garments snagging around me, and I saw this flame envelop Ursula. I saw her living and breathing within it, and, turning back to the crowd, I saw again that each and every one of them lived and breathed in it, and I knew suddenly, understood perfectly—I would always see it. I would never see living human beings, be they monstrous or righteous, without this expanding, blinding, fire of the soul.

"Yes," Mastema whispered in my ear. "Yes. Forever, and every time you feed, every time you raise one of their tender throats to your cursed fangs, every time you drink from them the lurid blood you would have, like the worst of God's beasts, you will see that light flicker and struggle, and when the heart stops at the will of your hunger, you will see that light go out!"

I broke away from him. He let me go.

With her hand only, I ran. I ran and ran towards the Arno, towards the bridge, towards the taverns that might still be open, but long before I saw the blazing flames of the souls there, I saw the glow of the souls from hundreds of windows, I saw the glow of souls from beneath the bottoms of bolted doors.

I saw it, and I knew that he spoke the truth. I would always see it. I would see the spark of the Creator in every human life I ever encountered, and in every human life I took.

Reaching the river, I leant over the stone railing. I cried out and cried out and let my cries echo over the water and up the walls on either side. I was mad with grief, and then through the darkness there came a toddling child towards me, a beggar, already versed in words to speak for bread or coins or any bit of charity that any man would vouchsafe him, and he glowed and sputtered and glittered and danced with brilliant and priceless light.

16

AND THE DARKNESS GRASPED IT NOT

VER the years, every time I saw one of Fra Filippo's magnificent creations, the angels came alive for me. It was only for an instant, only enough to prick the heart and draw the blood, as if with a needle, to the core.

Mastema himself did not appear in Fra Filippo's work until some years later, when Fra Filippo, struggling and arguing as always, was working for Piero, the son of Cosimo, who had gone to his grave.

Fra Filippo never did give up his precious nun, Lucrezia Buti, and it was said of Filippo that every Virgin he ever painted—and there were many—bore Lucrezia's beautiful face. Lucrezia gave Fra Filippo a son, and that painter took the name Filippino, and his work too was rich in magnificence and rich in angels, and those angels too have always for one instant met my eyes when I came to worship before those canvases, sad and brokenhearted and full of love and afraid.

In 1469, Filippo died in the town of Spoleto, and there ended the life of one of the greatest painters the world has ever known. This was the man who was put on the rack for fraud, and who had debauched a convent; this was a man who painted Mary as the frightened Virgin, as the Madonna of Christmas Night, as the Queen of Heaven, as the Queen of All Saints.

And I, five hundred years after, have never strayed too far from that city which gave birth to Filippo and to that time we call the Age of Gold.

Gold. That is what I see when I look at you.

That is what I see when I look at any man, woman, child.

I see the flaming celestial gold that Mastema revealed to me. I see it surrounding you, and holding you, encasing you and dancing with you, though you yourself may not behold it, or even care.

From this tower tonight in Tuscany, I look out over the land, and far away, deep in the valleys, I see the gold of human beings, I see the glowing vitality of beating souls.

So you have my story.

What do you think?

Do you not see a strange conflict here? Do you see a dilemma?

Let me put it to you this way.

Think back to when I told you about how my father and I rode through the woods together and we spoke of Fra Filippo, and my father asked me what it was that drew me to this monk. I said that it was struggle and a divided nature in Filippo which so attracted me to him, and that from this divided nature, this conflict, there came a torment to the faces which Filippo rendered in paint.

Filippo was a storm unto himself. So am I.

My father, a man of calm spirits and simpler thoughts, smiled at this.

But what does it mean in relationship to this tale?

Yes, I am a vampire, as I told you; I am a thing that feeds on mortal life. I exist quietly, contentedly in my homeland, in the dark shadows of my home castle, and Ursula is with me as always, and five hundred years is not so long for a love as strong as ours.

We are demons. We are damned. But have we not seen and understood things, have I not written things here that are of value to you? Have I not rendered a conflict so full of torment that something looms here which is full of brilliance and color, not unlike Filippo's work? Have I not embroidered, interwoven and gilded, have I not bled?

Look at my story and tell me that it gives you nothing. I don't believe you if you say that.

And when I think back on Filippo, and his rape of Lucrezia, and all his other tempestuous sins, how can I separate them from the magnificence of his paintings? How can I separate the violation of his vows, and his deceits and his quarrels, from the splendor which Filippo gave to the world?

I am not saying I am a great painter. I am not such a fool. But I say that out of my pain, out of my folly, out of my passion there comes a vision—a vision which I carry with me eternally and which I offer to you.

It is a vision of every human being, bursting with fire and with mystery, a vision I cannot deny, nor blot out, nor ever turn away from, nor ever belittle nor ever escape.

Others write of doubt and darkness.

Others write of meaninglessness and quiet.

I write of indefinable and celestial gold that will forever burn bright.

I write of blood thirst that is never satisfied. I write of knowledge and its price.

Behold, I tell you, the light is there in you. I see it. I see it in each and every one of us, and will always. I see it when I hunger, when I struggle, when I slaughter. I see it sputter and die in my arms when I drink.

Can you imagine what it would be like for me to kill you?

Pray it never takes a slaughter or a rape for you to see this light in those around you. God forbid it that it should demand such a price. Let me pay the price for you instead.

THE END

SELECTED AND ANNOTATED BIBLIOGRAPHY

I went to Florence to receive this manuscript directly from Vittorio di Raniari. It was my fourth visit to the city, and it was with Vittorio that I decided to list here a few books for those of you who might want to know more about the Age of Gold in Florence and about Florence itself.

Let me recommend first and foremost, and above all others, the brilliant *Public Life in Renaissance Florence* by Richard C. Trexler, published today by Cornell University Press.

Professor Trexler has also written other wonderful books on Italy, but this book is a particularly rich and inspiring one, especially for me, because Professor Trexler's analyses and insights regarding Florence have helped me to understand my own city of New Orleans, Louisiana, better than anything directly written by anyone about New Orleans itself.

New Orleans, like Florence, is a city of public spectacles, rituals and feast days, of demonstrations of communal celebration and belief. It is almost impossible to realistically explain New Orleans, and its Mardi Gras, its St. Patrick's Day and its annual

Jazz Fest, to those who have not been here. Professor Trexler's brilliant scholarship gave me tools to gather thoughts about and observations pertaining to those things I most love.

Other works by Professor Trexler include his *Journey of the Magi: Meanings in History of a Christian Story*, a work only recently discovered by me. Readers familiar with my previous novels might remember the intense and blasphemously fervent relationship between my character the vampire Armand and the Florentine painting *The Procession of the Magi*, created for Piero de' Medici by Benozzo Gozzoli, which can be seen in all its glory in Florence today.

On the subject of the great painter Fra Filippo Lippi, let me first recommend his biography by the painter Vasari for its rich though unauthenticated details.

Also, there is the bright and shiny book *Filippo Lippi*, published by Scala, text by Gloria Fossi, which is for sale in numerous translations in Florence and other places in Italy as well. The only other book of which I know that is exclusively devoted to Filippo is the immense *Fra Filippo Lippi* by Jeffrey Ruda, subtitled *Life and Work, with a Complete Catalogue*. It is published by Phaidon Press in England and distributed in America by Harry N. Abrams.

The most enjoyable books for the general reader that I have read on Florence and on the Medici have been by Christopher Hibbert, including his *Florence: The Biography of a City*, published by Norton, and *The House of Medici: Its Rise and Fall*, published by Morrow.

There is also *The Medici of Florence: A Family Portrait*, by Emma Micheletti, published by Becocci Editore. *The Medici* by James Cleugh, published originally in 1975, is available now through Barnes & Noble.

Popular books on Florence and Tuscany—travelers' observations, loving memoirs and tributes—abound. Primary sources in translation—that is, letters and diaries and histories written during the Renaissance in Florence—are everywhere on library and bookstore shelves.

In trying to render correctly Vittorio's quotations from Aquinas, I used the translation of the *Summa Theologica* by Fathers of the English Dominican Province. In dealing with St. Augustine, I have used Henry Bettenson's translation of *The City of God*, published by Penguin Books.

I caution readers to avoid abridged versions of Augustine's works. Augustine lived in a pagan world where the most theologically scrupulous Christians still believed in the demonic existence of fallen pagan gods. To understand Florence and her fifteenth-century romance with the joys and freedoms of a classical heritage, one must read Augustine and Aquinas in their full context.

For those who would read more about the marvelous museum of San Marco, there are countless works on Fra Angelico, the monastery's most famous painter, which include descriptions and details regarding the building, and there are many books available on the architecture of Florence entire. I owe a debt of gratitude not only to the museum of San Marco for having so beautifully preserved the architectural work of Michelozzo, so praised in this novel, but for the publications readily available in the shop there on the monastery's architecture and art.

In closing, let me add this: if Vittorio were asked to name a recording of Renaissance music which best captures the mood of the High Mass and Communion which he witnessed at the Court of the Ruby Grail, it would inevitably be the *All Souls' Vespers*, requiem music from Córdoba Cathedral, performed by the Orchestra of the Renaissance led by Richard Cheetham—though I must confess, this music is described as circa 1570—some years after Vittorio's fearful ordeal. The recording is available on the Veritas label, through Virgin Classics London and New York.

In closing these notes, allow me one final quote from St. Augustine's *The City of God*.

> *For God would never have created a man, let alone an angel, in the foreknowledge of his future evil state, if he had not known at the same time how he would put such creatures to good use, and thus enrich the course of the world history by the kind of antithesis which gives beauty to a poem.*

I personally do not know whether or not Augustine is right.

But I do believe this: it is worthwhile to try to make a painting, or a novel . . . or a poem.

Anne

Anne Rice

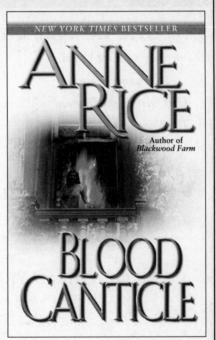

PHOTO: JOYCE RAVID

ANNE RICE is the author of more than twenty-five books. She lives in New Orleans.